SUN
MOUNTAIN

By Richard S. Wheeler
from Tom Doherty Associates

SAM FLINT

Flint's Gift

Flint's Truth

*Flint's Honor**

SKYE'S WEST

Sun River

Bannack

The Far Tribes

Yellowstone

Bitterroot

Sundance

Wind River

Santa Fe

Rendezvous

Dark Passage

Aftershocks

Badlands

The Buffalo Commons

Cashbox

Fool's Coach

Goldfield

*Masterson**

Montana Hitch

Second Lives

Sierra

Sun Mountain

Where the River Runs

*forthcoming

SUN MOUNTAIN

A Comstock Memoir

Richard S. Wheeler

A TOM DOHERTY ASSOCIATES BOOK

NEW YORK

SUN MOUNTAIN: A COMSTOCK MEMOIR

Copyright © 1999 by Richard S. Wheeler

This book is printed on acid-free paper.

A Forge Book
Published by Tom Doherty Associates, Inc.
175 Fifth Avenue
New York, NY 10010

Forge® is a registered trademark of Tom Doherty Associates, Inc.

Library of Congress Cataloging-in-Publication Data

Wheeler, Richard S.
    Sun Mountain : a Comstock memoir / Richard S. Wheeler.—1st ed.
      p.   cm.
    "A Tom Doherty Associates book."
    ISBN 0-312-86725-5
    1. Mineral industries—Nevada—Virginia City Region—History
Fiction. 2. Virginia City Region (Nev.)—History Fiction. 3. Journalists—
Nevada—Virginia City Fiction. 4. Comstock Lode (Nev.)—History
Fiction. I. Title.
PS3573.H4345S8   1999
813'.54—dc21   99-21741
                                                  CIP

First Edition: May 1999

Printed in the United States of America

0 9 8 7 6 5 4 3 2 1

SUN
MOUNTAIN

CHAPTER 1

. . . .

January 1, 1900

 supposed I would not live to see this day or enter this new century. Not many men reach the age of sixty-one, especially those in my profession, who commonly drink themselves to death.

I will celebrate this passage to the twentieth century by writing about my life in the nineteenth. I have thought long about this: Most men's lives aren't worth writing about, and I have wondered whether mine is. Has it been so extraordinary, or filled with achievement, or unusual that I should presume upon the patience of a reader and unburden myself of a thousand memories, some of them painful?

I think so. And now, on this virgin day of a virgin century, I am quite sure of it. It is not only that I have lived an amazing life but also that I have witnessed amazing events and met amazing men and women. With the sun of a new era shining on me, I wish to make account of all this before my own sun sets and all these matters are lost in the eternal darkness. So bear with me, reader. I must needs pen a few words about who I am in order to lay the foundations, so to speak, of this memoir.

I was christened Henry Jackson Stoddard, having been born in 1838 in Zanesville, Ohio. But I have no recollection of that place, because my parents soon removed to Platteville, Wisconsin, which is where I grew up. Platteville was a good place to mature. It nestled serenely in upland country dominated by great forested ridges, well-watered and verdant valleys dotted with farmsteads, and a number of lead mines worked largely by Cornishmen. Those lead mines were important to me and did much to settle my fate, though as a happy and comfortable child I was scarcely aware of them or that I lived in a mining district, one of very few in the Badger State.

I wanted for nothing. My father, William Squires Stoddard, was a circuit court judge and an eminent citizen of the new town. My mother, Mary Jackson Stoddard, was healthy, beautiful, and a worthy consort of my father. I had an older sister and two younger brothers, so was lost in the middle of the deck. I well remember the spacious white clapboard home, guarded by towering elms, where I grew up. On three sides a great veranda shaded its downstairs windows from the sun. It seemed a large place to a boy, larger than it would look to an old man. Judge Stoddard was neither rich nor poor. He owned two mercantile buildings and three homes, and two farms, which he rented. Before he became a judge, he practiced law, drawing much of his business from those lead-mining companies in that area.

I was a perfectly ordinary youth, lost in the middle, neither ambitious nor lacking industry. Life went by comfortably, and apart from a bout with scarlet fever and another with measles, and the death of my youngest brother, James, from diphtheria, I scarcely remarked my passages from child to adolescent and from adolescent to awkward youth and maturity. At that point, my life was totally unremarkable. The firm and amiable hand of my father steered me from trouble, and that sufficed, except for the time I got into a little difficulty one Halloween and another time when I was sparking Lizette—well, there are things, reader, that I will not delve into even though I intend this to be an honest and unsparing account of an unusual life.

We were Methodists, garden variety in every respect, and I inhaled piety just as easily as I had absorbed iambic pentameter and the tragedies of Shakespeare. There was nothing remarkable about my religion, just as there was nothing else remarkable about Judge Stoddard's second-born.

If I was troubled by anything as my body filled into manhood, it was simply that I hadn't the foggiest idea of what to do with my life. Worse, I didn't know what life was about, why I had been set upon the earth, what I should do for a living or vocation. I was approaching the time when I was expected to acquire a vocation, support myself, cleave from my parents, and begin my own household, and yet I hung back, not from fear, but from bewilderment. To select one vocation, such as law or accounting, was to foreclose the others. To select one sweetheart was to abandon all hope of finding someone better.

This estate governed my adolescence, and as I approached the conclusion of my normal schooling it grew acute. It was compounded by the myriad self-doubts and agonies that are the normal lot of adolescents, and every pimple was proof positive that I was doomed to a life of misery and rejection.

In those benign days in the sheltered valleys of the young state of Wisconsin, I was scarcely aware of the storm clouds gathering over the nation. Up in Ripon, northeast of our home, some radical young men had grown weary of Whigs and Democrats and formed a new party they called Republican—an apt name in a nation organized as a republic. But what these fellows wanted first and foremost was the abolition of slavery, and apparently a lot of other decent folk thought the same way, because the new party swept the North and the talk of conflict grew hotter and hotter.

I was aware of all this—Judge Stoddard had become a stalwart of the new party—but somehow it failed to touch me. I remained a young man desultorily searching for a life, for meaning, for anything that might make my passage on earth momentous. But it never came.

"Henry," my father said one day, "it is time for you to lay your foundations. I haven't heard a word from you about what lies ahead. May I suggest college?"

I had always known I would go to college; my father was well able to send me. I acceded at once, the paternal will still operating upon me, and selected Beloit rather than the state school in Madison. They were equidistant, but I rather thought that Beloit had the prouder credentials and was renowned for its commodious and gracious campus.

Reader, I must hasten this story along. I matriculated at Beloit and spent a year without majoring in anything, although I did gravitate toward English courses, having an easy way with words. But that was laziness. Words came readily to mind, so words became my study. Even so, I was far from the head of the class and just as far from its straggling rear guard. Once again, Henry Jackson Stoddard was caught in the middle. And so the term passed and I knew no more about what I should do with my life than I had before I started it. Beloit was a civilized place, only a two-day stagecoach ride from Platteville, and life there demanded nothing of me.

The year passed, and another, and part of a third, and that coarse fellow Lincoln was elected president, and suddenly war loomed. I had become an upperclassman with no more notion of what to do with my life than when I had started. Maybe less, because education was introducing me to possibilities and the genial faculty was introducing me to society, as was the custom in those days, and the more options that opened up to me, the less certain I became about what to do with myself.

I won't belabor this narrative with all that happened in Washington City, Mr. Lincoln's efforts to hold the Union together, South Carolina's secession, followed by the rest. Better heads than mine have recorded it all. Suffice it to say that during my third year of wandering through academe the nation went to war. There, around Platteville, shot towers arose, and the North looked upon the Wisconsin lead mines as a principal source of its ammunition.

Now from this perspective, early in a new century, I am inclined to look sternly upon that youth, Henry Jackson Stoddard, and tax him with the accusation that he calculated a way to evade the war. But on reflection, I've concluded that would be neither kind nor true. Yes, the young man was well aware that all that exploding powder and flying lead could puncture his fragile flesh and he, in turn, might inflict mortal wounds upon the flesh of other young men he really had no quarrel with—which repelled him. And it could be argued that young Stoddard was a coward escaping his duty to his country, saving his precious hide, and all that.

But I won't say it. I do remember that college had become unbearable and a lust for excitement, for meaning, for purpose, was percolating through me. Of course, the war itself might have served to stir life's juices, but my mind was drifting in other directions, namely, what lay beyond the Great American Desert, and, in particular, an arid mountain slope a little east of the Sierras where any man with wits could get rich. In short, I had been absorbing the sensational news of the Comstock Lode, its incalculable mountains of gold and silver ore, the wildness of its inhabitants, its excitements and daily disasters, its madness and joy. Virginia City and its neighbor, Gold Hill, were seducing that young man. I refer to him in the third person because truly he was not the same as the present writer, nothing more than a chrysalis of the man to come.

I had learned about all this from the Cornish miners in my district, who spun tales of incredible bonanzas, opportunity, and the one-chance-in-a-lifetime trip west. Over two hundred of them abandoned the Wisconsin lead mines and headed west, and many of them I knew by name.

"She's a place ought like any on airth, boyo," said my friend Tim Penrose. "Me and t'others, we're packing her up. They pay four dollars a day to a good man. Four dollars!"

I resolved to go. Maybe life in the Far West would give me some clue about why I was set upon the earth, why I was alive, what I might do, and what I might wish to become. Up until that hour, I had no notion at all of the destiny of Henry Stoddard and not even a dream or a hope. I think if my father had insisted I study law, I would now be a barrister. Or if my mother had told me to become a schoolmaster, I might now be conjugating verbs upon a slate board.

I knew that persuading the judge would not be easy. I did not wish to earn or work my way west, but to ride in an overland stagecoach to the fabled bonanza. And that took money. I make no apology for this. I had grown up in comfort, and transporting myself by the easiest means was simply the expected thing. And yet if my sole recourse was to walk or work my way out there, I would have done that. Once the idea took hold in my skull, it rooted there. It was, really, the first time in my tender life that I had seriously wanted anything.

And this I conveyed to the judge one June evening shortly after I had returned from Beloit, bearing yet another modest report card, consisting largely of Cs and one B. He listened sharply, his rheumy eyes boring into me the way they burned into witnesses before his court, and I knew I was on trial.

I expected rebuke. The judge would tell me it would be a fool's mission, folly, madness, and, in any case, my duty belonged with the Union in its grave crisis.

But he didn't. Instead, he stood, walked to the mullioned window, peered out across the valley to the verdant wooded slopes in spring dress, stared upon that tree-girt haven of comfort and peace and abundance, that land of milk and honey, of shrewd yeomen farmers, devoutly Methodist Cornish miners, settled village life—and said yes.

"You need to find yourself," he said. "I've been watching you. I've been waiting for you to make a move."

There was a proviso. He would give me the exact amount required to put me through my last year at Beloit—tuition, room, and board—and that would be the end of his largesse. If I wished to finish college, I could do so. If I wished to go west, I could do that. From that moment on, I would be on my own.

I calculated swiftly. The benefaction would get me to Virginia City with some to spare.

"I will go," I told him.

He nodded, and I detected a skeptical glint in his eye.

My mother cried. My sister and brother looked solemn.

I took the cash in a mixture intended to assure its safety: some in greenbacks sewn into my greatcoat, some in gold, which I intended to hide upon my person, some in a letter of credit upon the State Bank of Platteville.

Within a fortnight I was ready, and bidding my mother and father good-bye, and promising to write regularly, I boarded a mud wagon for Dubuque, Iowa, there to catch a Mississippi paddle wheeler to Saint Louis, there to transfer to another that would take me to Council Bluffs, and there to board a coach that would, eventually, deposit me not far from the foot of Sun Mountain and the Comstock. For the first time in my life, unbearable excitement coursed through my young body and soul.

I doubted that I would ever see my family again—and that proved to be the case.

CHAPTER 2

n older man might have viewed the Comstock in a more sober light, but I was intoxicated with youth and dreams and thought only of putting the parental nest behind me and becoming a man of substance in my own right. A more experienced man, upon entering the district for the first time, would have discovered two jerry-built towns, Gold Hill and Virginia City, perched upon the bleak eastern slopes of Sun Mountain, which was also called Mount Davidson, both of that pair of deuces looking ready to blow away with the next Washoe zephyr, as the denizens quaintly called the local gale. Many of the structures were nothing but canvas nailed to wooden frames. There was scarcely a brick or quarried stone in sight to give the place some semblance of permanence.

But I saw none of that. I had endured a bone-jarring, wearisome stagecoach ride across the continent with scarcely a complaint, because my mind was piling up fortunes. When the Wells, Fargo stage that had carried me the last leg, from Dayton on the Carson River, reached A Street in Virginia City, I stepped into a wonderland, for here were fortunes made daily; here was life lived twenty-four hours a day in a city that never shut its eyes. Here was Golconda, the future, adventure, and an undertow of excitement. I emerged from the Concord without experiencing the slightest weariness even after a dozen sleepless days, after choking on alkali dust and wolfing wretched food at stage stops—prairie dog du jour, as one fellow traveler put it. None of that affected me at that moment. I peered about me on C Street impressed by the fine business houses everywhere, the crowds of men patrolling the street, the vitality, energy, spirit, excitement that swiftly permeated my flesh to my soul and wrought joy within.

So my very youth blinded me to the dreary realities of the Comstock and turned it into a Potemkin Village. I had traveled light, intending to save freight charges, and carried the whole of my belongings in a single portmanteau, which the jehu unloaded from the boot and laid before me. The evening air, at that altitude, seemed crisp and clean.

An older man would have seen at once that these ragged rows of insubstantial buildings signaled distrust of the lode, the future, the dreams that brought men to the Comstock from all the corners of the world, and that the whole city might blow away in a week. No sane merchant would build a brick edifice in a burg that might vanish in six months. But that was not important to young Henry Stoddard. I had arrived with a nest egg of $253, and I intended to invest it wisely in producing mines that paid dividends and had proven reserves. Had I not grown up in a lead-mining district and absorbed mine talk and mine technology all my young life? I knew all about assays and leads and drifts and winzes and shafts and Cornish pumps and ores, and that would give me the advantage over the horde of ignorant speculators trying to squeeze a fortune out of barren rock. I intended to get rich. After that, I would travel, find a sweetheart, and ultimately live comfortably upon rents.

It happened to be dusk when the stage rolled to a stop at the Wells, Fargo office on A Street. Beyond the black outline of Mount Davidson, the lingering blue light of a dying day cast its glow over the city. Yellow lamplight spilled from every street window, shooting gentle light into the dusty street. I was enchanted.

But my first step, of course, was to engage a room in some boarding establishment or other. So I braced the mustachioed Wells, Fargo clerk, and he eyed me sourly.

"Mister," he said with exaggerated patience of the sort reserved for greenhorns, "this is a boomtown. You don't arrive here and rent a room—not for any price."

That set me back. "Well, what do I do, then?" I asked.

"Most of the saloons have a rear room they rent to any that want to lay down there. The boardinghouses are all double- or triple-rented." He stared, wondering if I grasped what that meant, and decided rightly that I didn't. "Double-rented rooms mean you share with someone else. You get twelve hours. It works well for miners on the day shift and night shift, but they have trouble on Sundays. Triple-rented—and that's the most common around here—means you get a bed for eight hours."

"You mean I would have to sleep in a bed used by others?"

The man was growing impatient. "You're learning," he said, and turned to help another customer.

That was a shock. I did not wish to lie on the floor of a saloon or some tent erected for the purpose of housing a floating population of rough-looking males. My cash wouldn't be safe, not even the greenbacks sewn into my greatcoat, which crackled under the caress of a hand.

I checked my portmanteau and returned to the street, enjoying the scent of sagebrush on the breeze and the lingering lavender light. Now, suddenly, I grasped the reason why the streets were so crowded and every saloon seemed to burst with people—no one had anywhere else to go. The saloons were the parlors, the dining rooms, and the bedrooms of Virginia City.

My first step would be to tour the burg and perhaps arrange for some sort of lodging. After that I would dine. The heady scent of roasting beef eddied through the air. In spite of all the crowds of men, Virginia City was not large. The streets upslope from the business district were lined with the better class of homes, while the crowded neighborhoods below C Street contained humbler buildings, rooming houses, darker and meaner saloons, and neighborhood groceries. I began to look for quarters in that district, studying the plain two-story shotgun buildings that announced themselves as rooming houses. On North D Street I made my first mistake, drawn to the door of a gaily lit establishment from which the mellow sound of a parlor organ reached the street, suggesting happy times within.

I entered.

I saw at once how things were in that establishment. The gent at the parlor organ wore garters on his sleeves, and gathered about were several demimondaines in diaphanous gowns that hinted of the pleasures that lay beneath. I had heard of such establishments and resisted that sort of life, though I would be a false witness if I were to say that temptation did not immediately undermine my morals and upbringing and ideals. It did, with the force of a Niagara. Before I could retreat, a bejeweled woman with brassy hair swooped down on me.

"Welcome, dear; come right in and make yourself at home."

"I, ah, I'm just looking for a rooming house. I thought—"

"Well, you're welcome to stay right here. We'll just make you right at home."

She had me in hand, tugging me into the room, and I was hard put to resist. But I hadn't lost all of my senses and squirmed free. "This was a mistake. Thank you. I shall leave now," I said, thinking myself a bit priggish. The lovelies around the organ caught my eye, and I blush to think of the things that passed through my mind. But I retreated, determined to begin my new life in proper style.

The mistress of this establishment showed me to the door. "You try Mrs. Flowers on South D, at Taylor," she said.

I thanked the lady and fled into the night, my thoughts tugging in various directions. I confess a part of me wished to stay right there.

I found Mrs. Flowers's boardinghouse readily enough and soon was negotiating a twelve-hour room while she dried battered dishes. I was in luck. She was about to evict a tenant for nonpayment of rent and would accept me—providing that I gave her the week's room and board, eighteen dollars, then and there. I attempted to pay her with greenbacks, but she refused the tender, saying that no one accepted paper there, only silver or gold. That seemed strange, but understandable in a town that produced both precious metals.

"Oh, and your roommate, Streeter, has the night from six in the evening to six in the morning, so you come back tomorrow. We serve two meals, breakfast and supper. Come for breakfast at six."

That rattled me. I would have to turn my life on its ear and live by night. Where on earth would I while away the small hours, and what on earth would I do? I was tempted to try elsewhere but decided to hang onto what I had, given the acute shortage of quarters. A room of any sort was a treasure on the Comstock.

I wouldn't let a small setback like that discourage me. Had I not just weathered day after sleepless day imprisoned in a jolting Concord stage? The night loomed long, but I purposed to put it to good use mastering the city. For one thing, most saloons stayed open, and many businesses as well. I had already learned a deal about the Comstock and was prepared for the long night.

The better saloons charged two bits for a drink, the poorer ones charged one bit for a beer, but a dime would do. The town lacked small change, and the prices expressed that. I had learned that nothing was sold by the penny or nickel or dime; all prices were astronomical because of the cost of wagoning goods from California, and each winter shortages plagued the new city, with flour and potatoes rocketing to a dollar a pound until relief supplies arrived. Hay and grain for horses were impossible to come by at any price, and the dray horses in the area were simply starving to death.

Much of this I had gotten from worldly passengers on the various stagecoaches, especially the Wells, Fargo coach that toiled up the long final grade. Between Dayton and Virginia I had turned myself into an expert simply by asking questions. The obvious source of information would be the foremost local rag, the *Territorial Enterprise,* so I determined to find a copy.

Hunger and weariness overtook me at the same time, so I toiled upslope to C Street and began examining the saloons abounding there, hoping to find food and succor and maybe a copy of the paper. I scarcely knew which of them was best: the Delta, the Silver Palace, El Dorado, the Palace, the Capitol, the Sawdust Corner, Spiro's, Dan O'Connell's–

There was no lack of these establishments; indeed, they populated C Street in such numbers that one could justly presume that spirits were the principal commerce of the principal street of Virginia City. I chose one at random, the Silver Palace, and it turned out to suit my needs admirably. Beyond the elaborate rosewood bar and mirrored back bar were faro and keno tables, and beyond that a restaurant with pretty serving girls. I repaired to the rear of the establishment, ordered a beer and the four-bit plate du jour, which was all the choice they offered, and discovered a stack of local papers, from which I extracted a recent copy to peruse the advertisements.

It was then, with my nose in the columns of the *Territorial Enterprise,* that I made a fateful discovery. Most of the half-dozen stock brokerage firms were open twenty-four hours a day, no doubt to accommodate the miners who worked the night shifts. Their four-dollar-a-day pay sufficed to make them speculators, just the same as more moneyed men.

Well, that would be a grand way to begin my sojourn on the Comstock: after eating whatever the saloon girl laid before me, I would venture south on C Street and sit down with a broker. I would question him closely; no jackanape could flummox a young man who had grown up around mines and miners. I would sort out the information and invest in a solid, proven, producing mine that was paying dividends and not assessing its shareholders. Maybe, just maybe, I would strike bonanza ore within hours of landing on the Comstock Lode.

CHAPTER 3

ater that evening, scarcely five hours after arriving on the Comstock, I wandered into the lamplit office of Driscoll and Tritle, mining stock brokers. In spite of a tiresome overland journey and lack of sleep, I felt not the slightest weariness and was keen to test my wits. Body and soul were infused with strange vitality, a young man's exuberance at arriving in the storied city.

In that brief sojourn I had walked the town from end to end, located a room, eaten, and surveyed an issue of the local paper, concentrating on the numerous ads. This securities house promised prompt trades, low commissions, margin purchases for those who qualified, and expert knowledge of the mines. I intended to probe that point, knowing that I could trip up anyone who couldn't tell a drift from a crosscut.

My entry activated a bell upon the flimsy door, and presently a bald, raptor-beaked gentlemen in shirtsleeves emerged from what I took to be a private office at the rear. No one else was present. The office seemed tiny by Wisconsin standards, and the red-flocked wallpaper had been pasted over plank walls that bulged and dimpled. If the place had been decorated to convey an aura of substance, it failed. But I suspected that most structures on the frontier were no better.

"I am newly arrived on the Comstock and am thinking of investing a bit," I said.

"Muggeridge here. And who are you?"

"Stoddard. I arrived on the eight o'clock stage and have spent my time acquainting myself with Virginia City."

"Well, I can help you. Just what are you looking for?"

"Shares of an established ore-producing, dividend-paying mine with proven reserves. The ones I'm considering include the Imperial, the Yellow Jacket, the Chollar, the Potosi, the Eldorado, the Gould & Curry, and the Ophir."

He smiled, baring brown teeth. "You certainly know the producers," he said. "Most admirable. Some people come here and squander their money on wildcats, which I don't recommend. There are some promising companies adjacent to those producing mines, which are showing good assays but not yet yielding ore. If you really want to make money, get in on the ground floor and buy low in order to sell high—"

"No. I am interested only in producing, dividend-paying mines actually raising milling ore and shipping bullion out. I prefer ones that yield both gold and silver, so that each is an insurance against a slack demand for the other. I also want shares in a mine that has not levied an assessment recently and does not intend to do so, because it is financing operations out of profits."

Muggeridge smiled again, taking stock of me. I noticed his gaze assessing the fullness and texture of my suit, my shoes, and the condition of my hands. "Yes, I congratulate you. Most of the fellows who come in here have simply heard a name and a price—always low, sometimes less than a dollar—and buy shares in a high-risk enterprise. Now, of course some of them do pay off—we've some overnight fortunes here. Why, just a few days ago a fellow came in and bought fifty feet of the Bullion mine—"

"Fifty feet?" The phrase was entirely new to me.

"Feet, yes. We do trade in shares, at least the shares of those companies organized into joint-stock corporations. But more commonly we trade in feet."

I had never heard of trading in feet. The term was unknown in the lead-mining district where I had grown up. But I hated to confess that to Muggeridge. Much depended on his belief that I was a seasoned trader and knew mining. But the uncertainty on my face must have clued the man. He smiled faintly and waved me to a lamplit desk, where we sat down.

"The mines on the Comstock," he explained, "are based on the original location claims of various discoverers, some alone and some in combination. One mine might have a narrow piece of the lode—which runs generally north and south—say a hundred feet, while another claim, the joint claim of several men, might run five hundred feet. There's a lively trade in the feet. You might, if you were a Midas, have fifty feet in one mine, twenty feet of another, a hundred feet of another.

"But it's not the same as shares. If a mine that occupies a hundred feet of the lode were to issue a hundred thousand shares, and those shares were worth, say, five dollars apiece on the market, then one foot of that mine would be worth a thousand shares times five dollars, or five thousand dollars. The mine itself would be valued at half a million dollars." He paused. "Unfortunately, Mr. Stoddard, I can't think of any mine on the Comstock that fits your expectations and sells for anything like five dollars a share. Eighty or a hundred would be more typical."

I absorbed that dismally.

"Ah, how much do you wish to invest?"

I wasn't sure I should confess that, but the man seemed honorable enough. "Two hundred dollars," I murmured.

"I see. Well, we all have to start somewhere. I must caution you that you could buy no more than two or three shares of the proven and producing mines for that amount, and that the instant the mine hits borrasca, or even declining ore values, your stock would tumble. There's more risk buying such shares at astronomical prices than buying shares of an upcoming and promising mine that is not yet yielding." He shrugged. "Buy high and hope to go higher, or buy low . . . and make a killing."

"But buying low means assessments."

"Oh, yes, they all assess now and then, even the proven mines, because they wish to expand or upgrade machinery or build their own mill—whatever, you know."

So far, at least, Muggeridge seemed on the level. I thought to test him a little: "How about wildcats?" I asked.

"I'll sell you wildcats if you want, but I don't recommend them. Anything that's not located right on the lode, as far as we know where it runs, is risky—you're likely to throw your money away."

"Well, for a person without much money like me, what do you suggest?"

Muggeridge stared at the flame within the glass chimney of the coal oil lamp. "Buying shares, or feet, of mines next to the bonanza mines, especially feet of mines between two bonanza mines. Often these go for pennies a share, although every time a neighboring property hits bonanza ore they all go up."

"Where I come from, the best ore is near the surface."

"Where's that, Mr. Stoddard?"

"Platteville, Wisconsin. Lots of lead mines there. Lots of Cornishmen who came here. I expect I'll run into them soon, and they'll tell me true."

"Tell you true?"

"They're the best miners in the world. They're friends. They'll keep me posted on what they see in the mines."

"That's good information. I'll tell you one thing, though, Mr. Stoddard: most expert opinion here is that the best ore lies deeper and is yet to be discovered. I know that's unusual in mining."

I smiled. "Hope springs eternal," I said.

Muggeridge smiled, or maybe it was a grimace. "Well, what I'm suggesting is some shares in any of several properties that lie next to producing mines. These include, starting at the south end, at Gold Hill, the Belcher, Crown Point, Kentucky, Yellow Jacket, Bullion, Crossus Fairview, Milton, Julia, Combination, Hale & Norcross, Savage, Best & Belcher, Sides, Andes, and Mount Blanc."

"A lot of mines—if they're mines at all."

He read my skepticism. "I would recommend three because they are smack against successful ones: the Julia, the Mount Blanc, and the Savage."

He wanted me to buy. I wasn't going to satisfy his wish. "I'll want share prices on these, recent assessments, prospects, recent assays, and any other information that would be helpful."

He looked disappointed. "Once you miss an opportunity, you may never see it again. He who hesitates—"

"Is safe," I said, a small curl of smile on my face.

"And without profit," he retorted. "But I like your caution. You remind me of a San Francisco man, George Hearst, came here when this was just a tent town, quietly looked it over, bought a piece of the Ophir, the one proven and producing mine, waited for the rise, and just as quietly sold for a good gain and left town. He never did speculate. He had a certain touch, I'll say that."

"Well, think of me as the same sort. You put that information together and I'll stop tomorrow."

He nodded. "You're an intelligent young man. I think you'll enjoy working with us."

I shook hands with him. His grip was firm, and I thought he had been pretty square with me. But I wasn't about to pour my small nest egg into mines I scarcely knew, and I didn't intend to invest until I had talked with some of my Cornish friends, who would have better knowledge than anyone sitting in a brokerage office.

I stepped into a sharp chill, even though it was midsummer. An icy breeze eddied down from Sun Mountain and harried me toward the saloons. It wasn't much after midnight, and at last the long and sleepless day of travel was taking its toll. I scarcely knew how I would survive until breakfast and bed.

The Silver Palace invited me; I had found its crowded confines inviting and its food tolerable. No such establishment existed in the lead-mining district of Wisconsin. Such saloons as existed there served family men, weary miners whetting their parched throats after a day in the pits.

I meandered through the gaudy place, which seemed as crowded at one in the morning by my turnip watch as it had been at dusk, and simply watched. Its male denizens quaffed beer and traded jokes with the serving girls, who wore short ankle-length skirts and filmy blouses. And they gambled.

That fascinated me. I was particularly absorbed with the faro tables, where two cadaverous dealers—I suspected that they were consumptives—dealt cards out of a wooden faro box onto a green-oilcloth-covered table with the spade suit painted on it. Miners laid chips on cards, sometimes adding a copper token, and awaited their fate. Some of them were getting well ahead, judging from the growing stack of chips before them. I didn't quite know how the game worked, but I decided to learn, and maybe risk a few dollars to while away the evening. If I was careful, there would be no harm in it. *Who knows?* I thought. Maybe if I bucked the tiger, as they were calling it, I might increase my stake to invest in the mines.

. . . .

CHAPTER 4

I am sure you are expecting young Henry Stoddard to lose his small stake playing faro his first night on the Comstock. But you should know better than that. I imagine you have read too many of those romantic novels that soften the brains of young people these days. In those trashy affairs, a hero or heroine does something stupid and then pays the consequences. But a stupid protagonist doesn't win the sympathies of a reader, who would prefer to see a worthy and intelligent hero encounter difficulties not of his making. That is the very difference between a serious novel and a trashy one. No, young Henry Stoddard was not that sort of protagonist.

I did not lose all of my stake that night in the Silver Palace saloon. I understood perfectly well that I was a greenhorn in tempting circumstances and it behooved me to be careful. So I stood at the faro table and watched the action until I had fairly well mastered the way of it. The tinhorn, a man with a slightly cast eye and greased-back hair, conducted the game in a brisk fashion, often referring to players by their first names. Nearby was a man called the casekeeper, who operated a contraption made of wires and beads, the purpose of which was to inform the players which cards had been played.

I swiftly learned how it went: the tinhorn shuffled a deck with a picture of an Egyptian on the back—the pharaoh, from which the game derived its name—and then turned over the first and last cards, which he called the soda and hock. These he placed face up on the bottom, and inserted the deck in the wooden box, the bank, which had a tiger painted on its lid. Then he extracted two cards at a time from a slot in the box; the first card was the loser, the second was the winner, and these were duly recorded by the casekeeper with the flip of beads on wires.

The player could bet any card to win or lose by placing a coin or chip on the layout. If he was betting the card would lose, he placed a token, or Chinese copper on top of his bet, and this was called coppering the bet. The odds in all cases were even—except when the two cards were the same denomination, in which case the house won. Thus, if the player bet the seven to win and it was the second card drawn in that turn, he would be paid an amount equal to his bet. If it was the first card drawn in that turn, he lost. If no seven appeared that turn, his bet would ride. If the draw yielded two sevens, the house won all bets on sevens. Of course, the more cards played, the better the players understood what ones were left in the deck, so the latter portions of the game became more fevered.

That seemed easy enough. After watching for half an hour and seeing not a single instance in which the dealer drew two cards of the same denomination, I became quite certain the odds were just about even and faro was a pretty square game. I could not see how the tinhorn could cheat since he was drawing cards from a slot in a box rather than shuffling the deck. But I reserved judgment on that, knowing that a young man from Platteville, Wisconsin, would be the soul of naïveté in a place like the Silver Palace.

The gambler must have sensed that I was ready for the plunge, because he braced me while he was shuffling the deck for another round.

"You want to buy in, fella?"

I hated to confess that I had never played before for fear that he would take advantage of me, but he seemed to know that anyway. "I guess I'll give it a whirl," I said. "Do I have to buy dollar chips?"

"No, you can make them two bits, a dollar, ten dollars, or any amount you want."

I pulled an eagle from my pocket and laid it on the oilcloth. "I'll try some two-bit chips," I said. He examined the eagle swiftly, running a fingernail across it, and then handed me forty white chips in two stacks.

Even though it was two or three in the morning, a half a dozen players hovered about the layout, and I edged in among them. One looked drunk. But two others were obviously miners just off shift or about to begin. Back in Platteville, people would be deep in slumber now and nary a lamp would have lit the town.

I played desultorily through the wee small hours, finding the game absorbing and not taxing. My exhaustion was taking its toll, and I looked forward to the bed in Mrs. Flowers's rooming house as one looks forward to the Pearly Gates of heaven. Players came and went, gaudy, hirsute men, some sinister, some just weary denizens of the dark, and I marveled that here was a city that never shut its eye.

My stack of chips grew and shrank. Several times I lost to the house when the dealer drew identical cards. I grew canny enough to bet winners as the deck dwindled and one could see that, say, three jacks remained in the stack, or four deuces, or two treys. Still, at three-thirty, my original stack dwindled down to one and I bet the last chip on an eight, to lose. It won. I was still some hours from bedrest, so I purchased another five dollars of white chips and watched those slowly vanish into the dealer's own hoard.

I consoled myself that at least I had found a means to while away the long, wearisome night in peace. Still, I should not be true to my readers if I neglect to say I ached to win and hoped to finance the purchase of some sound shares in a good mine. Toward four I ventured a breathtaking five chips on the queen. Two remained in the box with three deals left to play. The first draw yielded no queen, which meant that the remaining two draws would perforce display one or two. I coppered the bet—and lost.

That left me with only a handful of chips, but about then a gaggle of miners wandered in, ordered beers, and drifted to the table. Joyously I found myself peering into the work-wearied face of Tim Polgarth, a classmate of mine at the Platteville Academy.

"Tim!"

"Is it you?" he asked. " 'enry Stoddard in Virginny?"

"It is, and I want to talk!" I cried.

I turned my chips in and we repaired to the brass rail of the bar, where I bought him a mug of a local draft beer. Swiftly I apprised him of my arrival only hours before and my hope to find some of the Wisconsin Cornishmen, or Cousin Jacks, not only to renew friendships but also to get some expert opinion on mines and ores and prospects.

"And how's the judge and she, your ma?"

"Same as ever."

"I heard Beloit, that's where you went."

"Tim, I'm a truant."

He laughed and sipped. "Has the tinhorn cleaned ye out?"

"No, but I'm down a little."

"You're a caution, 'enry. Most greenhorns would be flat broke by now."

"I've held back a little to invest, and nothing offered by the Silver Palace, or any other of these places, is going to tempt me to spend it."

Polgarth laughed, perhaps a bit cynically. "Always a caution," he said.

I soon learned which mine employed him—the Mexican—and where various others from Wisconsin toiled. They were so valuable in Virginia that the least of them commanded a handsome four dollars a day and some of them had become supervisors, foremen, or shift bosses, at six or eight dollars a day, and were waxing fat.

"Tim," I said, "a bed and breakfast await me soon, but I want to sound you out about shares. If you were in my shoes, what would you buy with two hundred dollars?"

"I think I'd start a grocery and I'd eat the wages of the miners."

"Seriously, Tim. I'm trusting you. All you miners hear what's looking good and what isn't."

Polgarth sighed. "That's a weight you're putting on me, 'enry."

"Well, let's start with your mine, the Mexican."

"You can't afford that, 'enry."

"I know, but how does the lode look?"

"We're down four 'undred and she looks good to some, but to my eye, she's starting to pinch. However, they're drifting south into fine ores at that level. That's the Chollar that direction, and she's beyond ye, too, 'enry."

"What's to the north?"

"The Hale & Norcross, and she's not yielded a nickel or shown her investors a bit of color."

"How deep is their shaft?"

"She's three hundred down and the drifts show nothing."

"You think when they get down another hundred they'll find the same ore body as the others?"

Polgarth shrugged. " 'enry, I'm not a diviner, and if I was, I'd be dressed in a suit and bib shirt, not mucking silver ore."

"Do you think the Hale & Norcross would be a good bet?"

"It's selling for pennies a share, 'enry. But they're assessing every few months."

"Tell me about the others—you keep in touch?"

"Of course we do. Michael Pengallen, he's at the Savage; Tom Tremble, he's with the Bullion. Ah, she's a one that has yet to yield a nickel, over on the Divide. But they have 'igh hopes."

"Is the Bullion worth a shot?"

"She's worth two cents. You're a caution, 'enry."

"Is there any other good gamble, Tim?"

He eyed me dourly. "Am I a soothsayer? Well, I hear a good bit about the Best & Belcher, good assays but not yet pay dirt. And next to the Gould & Curry, too. Trouble is, she don't come cheap. Now that's all the words of wisdom I got stuffed in my head, and she's all you'll get, 'enry. Next thing I know, you'll be losing your two 'undred and blaming old Tim."

I didn't press him further. We downed two mugs of beer, and he hiked off to his rooming house. I watched dawn etch the barren mountains to the east and illumine the whole flank of Sun Mountain with an eerie light. It hadn't been such a bad night. I'd lost a dozen dollars, but I'd gotten a whole sheaf of information from Tim Polgarth.

It was time to head for Mrs. Flowers's place, eat some of her johnny-cakes, and then collapse in my twelve-hour sanctuary. In the afternoon, after I awakened, I would seek out Muggeridge and buy some speculative shares in three mines: Hale & Norcross, the Bullion, and Best & Belcher. And I wouldn't copper my bets, either.

C H A P T E R   5

he next afternoon, feeling much refreshed in spite of several bedbug bites, I purchased my first shares of the Comstock: fifty of the Bullion mine, twenty Hale & Norcross, and twenty Savage. I had high hopes for them all, especially the Bullion, whose name I liked. It was located squarely on the known lode and was neighbored by producers. The total, including the commission, came to $179, which I paid with my letter of credit, some currency, and gold. Muggeridge wasn't happy about those financial instruments except for the gold eagles, but he accepted them.

I was a small-time owner of the new bonanza. Or at least I would be if even one of those three mines bored into bonanza ore. How could I lose? I still had a few dollars in spite of paying for a week's room and board, losing almost fifteen dollars at the faro layout, and squandering a bit for beer and food.

That seemed a good start. The next step was to find employment while my investments ripened. I had no intention of being a mere speculator, living by cunning and wit, and intended to do something more substantial and valuable with my life. I supposed that the best way to find employment was to examine, once again, the help-wanted ads in the lively *Territorial Enterprise* to see what openings there might be. I did not intend to enter the pits or mine if I could help it. I was better suited for other occupations, and had something of a college education toward such employment.

As I look back upon young Henry Stoddard, from the dawn of a new century and advanced age, I see a certain solidity, a certain character, in the youth that brought me to where I am today. But of course he was yet a fledgling and Virginia City would test his mettle over and over and transform that fellow into the man who pens these words now, four decades later.

Now, reader, I imagine you envision the lay of this story; it's about a fellow growing up in one of the wildest towns of the West, riding the tiger and succeeding. It is that, to a degree, but it is more. I am not the sole protagonist in this story. More important is Virginia City itself, the rowdy, raucous, brilliant, restless, audacious City on the Hill. Now I know, when I use that metaphor, that people think of a City on a Hill in biblical terms, a beacon of light and wholesome living and spiritual riches. No, I don't mean it that way, nor do I mean it in any literal sense, even though Virginia City did indeed perch on the slope of a hill.

Rather, in its brief, epic, fabulous heyday Virginia City was the most significant place in America, and—I imagine this will shock people now reading the augurs to see what the twentieth century will bring—the city that most perfectly expressed the future of America, both its good and evil natures. So there is more than just Henry Stoddard to all this, which I will make plain as, one by one, I fill sheets of foolscap with my memories.

I well remember repairing once again to the Crystal Palace that next evening, which I had made a sort of home, knowing that henceforth I would live in its confines from six o'clock in the evening to the same hour of the morning, when my quarters belonged to a fellow whose name, I discovered, was Miles Streeter. I might have supper and breakfast at the board of Mrs. Flowers, but any midnight snack would be out of my pocket. Possessing a room for just half a day was bad enough; I could scarcely imagine how those who triple-rented managed. One thing was plain, though: swarms of carpenters were erecting lodging from dawn to dusk, using green lumber cut in the Sierra Nevada and hauled by ox team to the burgeoning city. Someday the builders would catch up to demand—unless the bonanza multiplied itself over and again.

Mrs. Flowers's beef and biscuits were rather bland but filling, and I left her table content, having made the acquaintance of the others in her establishment—miners all, whose insights into events underground I intended to plumb. I knew that no information was equal to that given by the men working the stopes and mucking the ore. But I did not raise such matters that first night, and listened closely to talk about aches and pains, a narrowly avoided accident when an ore car rolled into the shaft, almost dragging a man with it, and sundry other things that were well worth my attention.

Streeter vanished up the rough plank stairs, and I repaired to the streets, promenading down D, then C, then B, and then A before I slipped and slid down to C Street and the Crystal Palace. I intended to explore some of the other establishments, especially the Delta and the Sawdust Corner, but that would wait. I found a copy of the newspaper—there usually were a few lying on tables—and settled down for another tour of the fabled city, with advertising being my chariot of choice.

I was taken at once by a prominent advertisement for one Maxfield, a funeral director. His wares, advertised in gaudy display typefaces of various levels of ferocity, included mahogany and metallic coffins, lead coffins, shrouds, collars, cravats, silver coffin plates, gravestones, hearses and coaches, and every variety of funeral equipment. Maxfield announced himself a specialist in disinterring bodies and shipping them east. He also did a trade in iron and wood grave enclosures and marble tombstones.

Now, I thought, a man so lavishly equipped in the funerary arts and equipments must mean that there was a lot of dying in Virginia City—a surmise that, it turned out, was something of an understatement. Virginia City excelled at dying and did record amounts of it, in every novel and horrifying and bizarre fashion. One could well call Virginia the dying capital of the entire republic, and it was so practiced at the business that most every death was celebrated with a parade, bands, and ninety-nine-gun salutes, which left celebrants half-deaf before they put the late lamented under the turf.

But I am getting ahead of myself. My perusal of the local sheets was not encouraging. There wasn't much in the way of help-wanted advertising. But plainly, it was a boomtown, and such places can use every functioning body they can employ. I would probably have no trouble signing on as a carpenter or a construction man in spite of my lack of experience. The mines required an endless supply of timbers, and I supposed I could work as a woodcutter somewhere.

But I was going to have to hunt for a job, and even though it was the shank of the evening, I set out on a tour of C Street to see if I might discover HELP WANTED posters in the windows of the various enterprises there, many of which were still open. I pushed through the crowded street—single men everywhere, in amazing numbers, some of them carrying side arms—and examined windows. I found not one HELP WANTED sign and knew suddenly that keeping myself fed wasn't going to be quite as easy as I had imagined, boom or not.

That turned out to be a bad night. I wanted to go to bed. My body was not accustomed to sleeping by day; neither had I recovered from the transcontinental journey. I drifted into one saloon after another—the Delta, the Sawdust Corner, Spiro's—and found a differing clientele in each. The one-bit saloons catered to miners and tradesmen, the two-bit saloons to merchants and speculators. I sipped beer, watched the clock, and wondered how I could possibly endure the night. I gravely considered flopping in one of the saloon dormitories—a dollar to lie on the floor with a roof overhead—but decided to make the best of my time.

Only when I drifted back to the Crystal Palace and began perusing the *Territorial Enterprise* once again did it dawn on me that maybe I had found my métier. I was reading a column of humorous animadversions about the people of Virginia City by a man named Denis McCarthy when it dawned on me that I wasn't half-bad with words myself. I would inquire in the morning. But then I realized that the rag was a morning paper and the staff would probably be wide awake, lively, and busily putting the new edition to bed right now.

It was a fateful insight. I drank up, making sure to swallow all the foam in the mug to get my money's worth, and departed into a soft night with chill air eddying down from Sun Mountain. In those days the *Territorial Enterprise* was up on A Street and well north of the saloon district on C. So I labored upslope, keeping a sharp eye out for yeggs and footpads, and eventually stumbled upon a long frame building stuck into the slope, with a sign heralding the paper and its publisher, J. T. Goodman & Co., barely visible in the subdued light. At that time, no gas lamps illumined the city streets.

Young Stoddard, peering through a grimy window, beheld a perfect furor of activity. Compositors were laying type in their sticks, a Chinaman was running about doing errands, and serious-looking fellows were standing at slanted desks, scribbling on foolscap for all they were worth. I stood outside the window for some while, absorbing this remarkable lamplit tableau. Off toward the rear stood an inky flatbed press surrounded by acolytes and high priests who were performing high-church ritual. They plainly were approaching deadline, and I feared that it was an inopportune time to ask for a job.

While I was thus gazing through the sooty window, a gent braced me: "You looking to rob the place or are you relieving yourself against our edifice?"

I whirled, embarrassed.

"Neither," I said. "I . . . Well, I was nerving myself to ask for a job, but you're obviously about to print, and I—"

He laughed. I examined him in the window light. He seemed an urbane young fellow, with muttonchops and a mustache, and was in his shirtsleeves. He carried a brown quart bottle of beer.

"And what is your trade?" he asked.

I hadn't really had time to measure that bolt of cloth, so I confessed. "I am a good hand with words but not with type."

"A reporter. Where have you been?"

"Ah, in college, sir. Beloit—"

"In college. In college! College is the ruination of reporters. There's where you learn to use six words to replace one, and similar vices. Meet me in half an hour over there. . . ." He nodded toward a darkly lit saloon I had scarcely noticed.

"The saloon?"

"The Express Bar. Under the Wells, Fargo office. That's my office."

"And who are you?"

"Joe Goodman, editor and proprietor. I've a mind to try you out."

I gawked. "You do?"

"Only after we put this issue to bed. Dull night. No murders, one suicide among the frails, and only two brawls. I was reduced to writing about the water supply. We drink arsenic lemonade that flows out of the mountainside, and that's always good for a word when all else fails. See you in a bit—ah, what was your handle?"

"Henry Stoddard, sir."

"All right, Stoddard. Drink a few beers. Tell Charlie Sturm to put them on my tab. I will not have a reporter, even a cub, who can't hold his beer. If you write better cold sober, don't apply."

"Yes, sir," I responded dubiously.

He wandered into the building.

Any port in a storm, I thought. I might learn the trade at this disreputable rag, but I didn't intend to stay long—if I got the job.

CHAPTER 6

ooking back now, from the dawn of the new century, I can see what I didn't see back then: that the job interview between young Henry Stoddard and Joe Goodman would have fateful consequences and forever shape my life. From then on I was a reporter covering the most fabulous city on earth. Had I not ended up on the *Territorial Enterprise,* I never would have met Sam Clemens or gotten that stock tip from John Mackay or given a lollipop to Jim Fair's daughter, who ended up marrying a Vanderbilt, or watched them pull bodies out of the Yellow Jacket after the great fire—or married the most delightful woman on earth. I never would have known William Sharon or Senator Jones or watched the coolies, building the Virginia & Truckee Railroad, snake the track right up the mountainside.

I never would have won and lost several modest fortunes or known that genius Adolph Sutro or hobnobbed with Adah Isaacs Menken or bellied up to the bar at the Washoe Club, which some men said was the finest gents' club in the world, or seen the machinery that advanced science and technology fifty years in one leap, so that the rest of the world is just now catching up to what was accomplished in two heady decades in Virginia.

But I have a habit of getting ahead of myself.

I didn't have to wait long for Goodman at the Express Bar. It squatted under the Wells, Fargo office across A Street and Sutton from the *Territorial Enterprise* and was, it turned out, its editorial annex. Goodman walked in soon after I had ordered a mug of draft beer and settled beside me. I took him for a man of means and a cosmopolitan and learned later that I was not wrong. He was an urbane San Franciscan, a Bohemian, and had been an editor of that city's literary magazine, *Golden Era,* before acquiring the *Territorial Enterprise* in partnership with others. I soon discerned he could tell vintage claret from its imitators and knew all about the epicurean arts.

"I dodged the proofing. That's what I've got cubs for. They'll end up here in a bit, and so will the compositors, and after that the pressmen, so this is my only chance to shake your pockets and see what falls out."

"Not very much," I confessed.

"But you had the notion to become a newsman."

"Yes. I'd be good at it. I can fling words. Tonight, over at the Crystal Palace, I got to reading the *Enterprise*, and enjoying a piece by that fellow De Quille, and I thought, *That's what I like. Maybe I could do that. I'd sure like to give it a whirl.*"

"De Quille, eh? I buy his stuff when I can. He mostly works for the opposition and has literary aspirations. I'd hire him if I could."

That nonplussed me. "I, ah, have no person opinion about him, Mr. Goodman. I've been here two nights now and read one of his pieces and just took a liking to him."

"Well, he certainly can write," said Goodman. "What makes you think you can handle the news?"

"Uh, I did well in college—"

"Yes, you mentioned that."

"Ah, I lasted three years and couldn't stand it anymore."

"Well, now we're getting somewhere," Goodman said expansively. "That's the first sensible thing to emerge from your mouth."

. . . .

I saw how this was going and supposed I'd be out in the street in two minutes, so I simply blurted out my meager story and told him I wanted a chance.

He ordered two glasses of claret from Sturm, whom he called Charlie, and stared into space for a while. "Fact is, this town's growing so fast I could use another reporter. You seem to have a passing acquaintance with nouns and verbs, and you've even met some adjectives. We've got the advertising. I can handle it. I'd have to unlearn you of everything you got in college. Don't you be starting some story saying, 'It is to be presumed that,' or stuff like that. Now tell me something: you think you can get stories? The problem is, we have dull days sometimes, and we got to dig stories where there's no ore. That's what I want. I want some young fella who can conjure up a good story out of a cat in a tree."

It was dawning on me that I was virtually hired. At least, that was how Goodman's mind was running.

"I think so, sir."

"I've got regulars, but not a one can manufacture news. They come back skunked and want to fill the news hole—that's what's left over after the advertising—with filler. That's Greek quotations, Bible verses, and anything that passes for humor. I don't want that kind of paper. I want a writer with imagination. I want a cub who'll write about a tiger running loose on Taylor Street—even if there was no tiger."

That shocked me.

"Oh, don't take me so seriously, kid. What you have to do is corral some drunk before the constable gets to him and ask him how it goes and get him to tell you he saw the tiger on Taylor just before he passed out. And if you can't find a drunk, find someone who says he talked to the drunk who saw the tiger on Taylor." He cocked a formidable brow. "You following me?"

"I think so."

"You get me a tiger on Taylor every night, and you're hired."

"I'll do it, sir. I'll have a tiger on Taylor every night."

He glared and sipped and glared. "Now, you wouldn't be planning to manufacture news, would you?"

That confused me and I thought I had just been snookered. "Sir," I stammered, "I value truth. When I am working on a story, I want it to be as honest and complete and fair as I know how to make it. But I noticed that your paper does some stories that, well, they're fun; they're entertainment; they're sport."

"How about twenty a week?"

"Ah . . ." That was thin. In fact, with prices what they were in the boomtown, I didn't see how I could survive. "Ah . . . I'd better keep on looking."

"Stoddard, lissen," he said. "You get a bunk in the back room. We've got most of our men there, all the compositors and pressmen and some reporters. And you get fed. The Celestial conjures up frycakes in the morning and cooks up a stew at night. That's all part of it. The salary is beer money, speculation money, faro money."

I gaped at him. "You mean you bunk your employees? And feed them?"

"Yes, those that can stand snoring in a dormitory and pied type in the stew."

"Try me, Mr. Goodman," I said.

He didn't ask to see any of my writing; neither did he put me to the test, and I wondered about that. Maybe it was because Judge Stoddard spoke elegantly or because my mother's tongue was poetic and I had picked up some of that. In any case, Goodman simply told me to start in at noon the next day; my shift would run until the paper was put to bed.

That's how I became a newsman. That interview turned out to be the most fateful of my life. It cost me a few dollars to get out of Mrs. Flowers's boardinghouse—she wouldn't return any part of my week's room and board—but I was soon ensconced in an upper bunk at the *Territorial Enterprise*. I swiftly learned that the arrangement had its advantages for Joe Goodman: he could roust out a reporter any time, day or night, having a supply of them at hand, stacked like cordwood and ready to toss into the stove.

I swiftly discovered the pickings were plenty slim for a newcomer and a cub reporter. The senior men, Goodman, Denis McCarthy, Steve Gillis, and George Birdsall, blanketed the boomtown, especially the sheriff, the constables, the mines, and the saloons. I produced so little those first days that Goodman began staring at me and I could see the clock ticking in his head. Another week, another fortnight . . . I'd be out.

I learned my trade, though. I was taught not to wait until the end of the day to turn in my story, but to scribble it early so the compositors—vagabonds with names like Dirty Shirt Smith, Thin Space Jones, and Kid Glove Willie—could set it ahead of the deadline rush. Goodman merely grunted when he read my stuff, neither commending nor condemning me, and rarely changing a word. I knew I was losing ground.

Then one day, while resting my sore feet on a brass rail, I invented Caspar the Barkeep, who had a contrary opinion about everything. Let the citizens rejoice in a golden day, and Caspar would assail the weather.

Let the miners celebrate the discovering of a new seam or lead, and Caspar would opine that it would peter out in a month. Let the strongly pro-Union citizens assure themselves that the Confederates would be whipped in weeks, and Caspar would counter that they would last five years.

All I had to do, really, was tour the saloons, afternoons and evenings, and listen, and sooner or later I would have a story. So I wrote a few. I didn't know how long that would last, but at least Goodman stopped staring at me and now and then my hungry ears heard a word or two of praise.

Meanwhile, I was mastering the real art of reporting, of winning the confidence of businessmen, workers, wives, madams, and tramps. They all had stories if only I could extract them. And with Caspar always on hand, I could balloon the most modest stuff into ten or fifteen column inches.

I did break a few stories that had eluded my betters at the *Territorial Enterprise*. I surveyed the boardinghouses about town, printed their prices, and collected opinions about their board, its quantity, tastiness, and reliability. That put not a few landladies in a pet, including Mrs. Flowers, whose meals were soundly criticized, but at least it pleased my editor and stirred the juices of Virginia City. Not a few miners ripped out the story and filed it in a pocket against the day they would shift to new quarters.

But after some weeks it became clear that I never would be on the same footing as the fellows who had spent years at the trade. Somehow, they came up with gory murders, stabbings, saloon brawls, suicides, company wars among the Celestials, tunnel collapses, bizarre mine accidents, the price of cigars, the shortage of flour and potatoes, new arrivals, stock and bond prices, rumored bonanzas, consolidations, lawsuits, and mining claims extracted from the Storey County Courthouse.

Gillis, who specialized in crime, was in clover for a while when it was bruited about town that the sheriff was empaneling unusual juries. One consisted entirely of midgets, another of cross-eyed veniremen, and another was composed of Paul Bunyans, none of whom was under six and a half feet. The town had its special brand of justice. Well, that was Virginia City for you; no place like it on earth.

About then, my speculations expired. The Bullion assessed its stockholders two dollars a share, which I couldn't pay, so the stock was sold out from under me. Hale & Norcross took a dive, down to pennies a share, and the Savage slowly sank into obscurity. My investment had shrunk to about ten dollars, even though the news from the mines was good and getting better.

That was a cold dash of reality. The last of my patrimony had all but vanished, and now my fate lay entirely with the *Territorial Enterprise*. I celebrated my demise from the ranks of the moneyed by buying my colleagues a mug of beer at Charlie Sturm's, but beneath my bravado I felt desolate.

CHAPTER 7

eader, I know what you are waiting for: my first encounter with Sam Clemens, and maybe a few tidbits about the man. But that was well in the future. Sam Clemens and I rode the overland trail to Nevada within a few weeks of each other in 1861, but he squandered months as an argonaut in a feckless pursuit of silver, and months more trying to harvest timber for the mines, and still more time in Carson City, hobnobbing and swapping lies with the new territory's political potentates, before finally wending his way up the slope to Virginia City and the *Enterprise,* which he joined in September 1862. By that time I had been there over a year.

During that year I was learning my trade. About me was a city changing its face each day, turning itself from a camp ready to blow away in the next Washoe zephyr into a rock-solid metropolis perched on a desolate slope in a yellow clay wilderness. I focused on the mines, since that was what this odd municipality was all about. I found out soon enough that mine owners and speculators all had designs on me; a newspaper reporter was just the ticket to leak a rumor, float a lie, preach doom and gloom to drive down the price of shares, or announce a bonanza, real or imagined.

I had only to show up in some superintendent's cubbyhole—the mines avoided fancy quarters, at least in those days—and I was welcomed with open arms. I could fairly hear the clockwork in the skulls of the mine's owners when I braced them for a story. And not a few offered me "feet"—real estate in a claim—ten of this, fifty of that, just for printing a little story or two.

If I had kept all the feet heaped on me I would now have twenty or thirty thousand shares of obscure holes in the ground, of which maybe one in a hundred ever yielded an ounce of ore. Most of my colleagues began accumulating portfolios of Comstock feet—and counted themselves millionaires, at least until the ephemeral disintegrated into the mythical. No reporter on the Comstock lacked for funds. If ever he was short, he simply sold some feet he had acquired for writing a fawning story or two.

I had a stock reply. "Thanks for the feet," I'd say. "But it won't affect my story any."

"Just wanted you to have a piece of the property. A little goodwill," they'd respond blandly.

Not for nothing was I Judge Stoddard's son. Perhaps it was my natural skepticism. Let a manager announce a bonanza, and I insisted on going down to the works and seeing it, plain and unsalted, and having some independent assays run by an assayer of my choosing, before I would publish a word. What's more, I relied heavily on my Cousin Jack friends from Wisconsin to steer me true. Theirs was always the final word when it came to bonanza or borrasca. Sometimes I voiced my skepticism in one of my Caspar the Bartender columns. That way I could be contrary whenever I felt like it.

Because of my caution I was often scooped, much to Joe Goodman's annoyance.

"Secondhand goods!" he bellowed at me. "Stoddard, just once, beat out Clement Rice over at the *Union.*"

The opposition sheet was bedeviling us at every step, largely because it was less couth and more reckless, which is the highroad to sensationalism. But Goodman knew that when I finally weighed in with a story, it usually embarrassed the opposition. Mostly I pricked bubbles. So Goodman grumbled but held his grumbling to a dull roar, because the *Territorial Enterprise* was becoming the *authority* on the Comstock mines— and the ads were rolling in; the circulation was catapulting.

I paid attention to the new machinery going into the mines and mills. Most of the mines on the Comstock were running into water problems as their shafts pierced deeper. The old Cornish pumps weren't adequate, and mining engineers and tinkerers in California were rigging up new machines that could lift water from lower depths than ever before, while other tinkerers were fiddling with gigantic grinding and pounding devices that would crush ore more efficiently than ever before. All these were painfully hauled by ox team over the Sierras and into the Comstock for trial.

Down in the drifts and on the faces, the miners were beginning to run into warmth, though it was nothing like the heat they had to deal with later when the shafts were fifteen hundred feet deeper. Still, even in 1861 and 1862, the mining companies were pumping air into their works and lifting water out, and consuming amazing amounts or cordwood in the process.

All this I covered in detail and with some technical precision, including prices and capacities. Once in a while an innovation caught my eye. The mines started to use flat woven steel cable instead of the old, round variety. The new cable was safer, less likely to snap, and rolled over the hoisting drums more evenly, making it possible for the engineers to stop the cage precisely at one mine level or another. They no longer had to jockey the cage up or down an inch or two so the miners could roll the ore cars on or off.

I was never very comfortable underground, even though I tried to arrange for my Cornish friends from the old days to guide me. No sooner did the cage begin its dizzy descent, sunlight vanish, and those rock walls loom over me than claustrophobia overtook me. I felt certain that the shaft above me would tumble in upon itself and choke all of us to death. Even the largest drifts and crosscuts were tiny affairs, and the log timbering that propped the rock over our heads seemed puny compared to the massive weight of the rock above us.

It was only because of the Cornishmen that I was able to swallow my terror and get to the task at hand, which was usually to examine a new seam or take samples for my own independent assay. But I was never so glad as when the cage popped into sunlight and I was on grass again. I marveled that sane men would risk their hours, their days, their months and years and lives toiling in such menacing and gloomy conditions.

The year sailed by uneventfully, and I will not belabor the reader with my young life. I spent my free time carousing with my newsroom colleagues, Steve Gillis, Denis McCarthy, and Joe Goodman, watching the largely male population of the Comstock hunt for an angle. It was, after all, a city whose bedrock was greed. Miners and Cyprians and hausfraus, as well as snake oil salesmen, speculators, brokers, and young Henry Stoddard, were hunting for the edge, the bonanza, the shares and feet of mines that would put them on Easy Street the rest of their lives. All that was well worth covering, and we dotted the pages with mountebanks who made a killing, magnates who went broke, miners who had inside information and got rich, and whiskey peddlers who got bilked by little old ladies with a few feet of wildcat to sell.

Virginia City was the Bilking Capital of the World. There were bilkers on every street corner and bilkees in abundance, and sometimes they were one and the same. The burg somehow got the reputation for being violent, but that was shamelessly exaggerated by its denizens. The truth of it was that we had a good murder to report only once or twice a week, although saloon brawls were ordinary sport and assorted muggings, burglaries, stagecoach robberies, bloody accidents, runaway horses, bullion theft, and stabbings in the disreputable quarter were daily fare. Our problem was to find something unique or comic to separate one from another, and this we managed to do.

So the days and months flew; seasons rolled by; the Washoe zephyrs blew away everything that wasn't nailed down (somehow in the direction of the Celestials, or so we thought until we learned better).

My days sailed by happily, and I fancied that I had mastered my trade. I managed to spend my entire twenty a week and then some, so had nothing to invest, but at least I wasn't thereby flummoxed out of hard-won earnings by the nearest reprobate stock diddler. I always had a bunk and meals; the cash went for mugs of draft beer, an occasional item of fancy clothing, some seegars, a therapeutic Turkish bath, and now and then a melodeon show.

As tempting as the restricted quarter was, I had sense enough to steer clear of it, although my youthful hungers in that respect didn't make my young life any easier. But I had set my sights on something larger—a mistress wearing my ring—and so I hunted futilely, quixotically, in a town that was about 90 percent male.

I had no notions of change, or growth, or rising to the top of my trade, or anything like that; I was a middling sort, with middling dreams and ambitions, and middling skills. But I should have known that nothing lasts and change always arrives.

Change arrived at the *Territorial Enterprise* in June of 1862, in the form of a fragile, cadaverous, hollow-eyed young Quaker named William Wright. He wore a halfhearted black beard that looked as if it had given up growing about a third of the way toward honest whiskerdom. Joe Goodman signed him on as city editor—thus placing him over me in spite of my seniority, which I resented. Wright was placed over Gillis and the other reporters, too, but I neglected to notice that. Goodman started Wright at twenty-five a week, which made him my senior in that respect. I was sure the stranger would lord it over us like some potentate.

He came with a fancy reputation, which was why Goodman had hired him. Wright had established himself as a litterateur, a man of letters, and therefore a man to grace the escutcheon of the premiere paper of the Territory of Nevada. He wrote under the curious nom de plume of Dan De Quille, and I knew him more by his fruits—if I may use the phrase—than as a mortal. He had come west in 1857, poked about the goldfields of California without wresting any wealth out of them, and then begun working his way toward the Comstock, entranced by the legends that tickled his ears. During this period he began writing comic, colorful pieces for San Francisco's *Golden Era*, then edited by Joe Goodman, and also shipping wildly exaggerated stories back to the Cedar Falls *Gazette*. Cedar Falls was sufficiently distant from his largely abandoned wife and children, who were rooted down in West Liberty, Iowa, to keep them in the dark. Dan De Quille's comic sketches did not alight in West Liberty, where his poor family awaited the wayward husband and father for the next several decades.

Wright earned enough on the side, churning out his humorous masterpieces, so that he chose not to bunk at the paper with the hoi polloi, which affronted me further. The new city editor was putting on airs. I must have oozed the sullenness I felt, for he largely ignored me at first while making himself entirely at home in the boozy precincts of the *Enterprise* and hobnobbing with Goodman and his partner, Denis McCarthy. Unlike the rest of us, Wright had a solemn mien, and he dressed far more formally than we, sometimes in a black cloak that made him look like a mortician. I told myself he didn't fit. Later I imagined it was penitential clothing—sackcloth and ashes—for a riotous life. Wright, it turned out, was a master of the debauch.

My nose was so out of joint that I didn't then realize I was in the presence of genius, or that he would win a reputation better deserved than Sam Clemens's. In fact, although I'm getting ahead of myself again, Clemens embezzled most of Dan De Quille's thunder, and if it had been De Quille roaming far and abroad and Clemens who hung on in Virginia City the nation would now be celebrating quite another man.

I stayed, not having any prospects, although I was tempted to leap to the *Virginia Daily Union*. But the *Union* wasn't half the paper ours was and was barely holding its own while the *Enterprise* was growing daily. So I settled into a new routine, loathing Wright, doing my daily stint in a mood of sour cynicism, and taking a new and jaundiced view of the Comstock.

I take no pride in my youthful attitude, but there's some silver lining this Comstock cloud. In my new frame of mind, I began to see the groveling, greedy, gouging denizens and life of the Comstock in a darker light. And that, oddly enough, was what healed my distemper, gave me judgment, and made a man of me—as you shall see.

. . . .

CHAPTER 8

That was an eventful summer. As I look back upon it now I can see what had been wrought in me during 1862. The war was raging, the Union was taking a whipping, but I paid little heed. I was busy nursing my resentment toward William Wright, and it had not yet occurred to me that I was and am a man of modest talents and the man set over me was much my superior and would become a legend. Maybe it is a virtue of the young not to know their limits, but it is a distinct virtue in an old man. I learned mine by bloodying my nose enough so that the lesson was hammered home the hard way.

It was clear that Wright enjoyed people. He hobnobbed with the rest of the staff, often in a boozy haze, and was soon on a first-name basis with everyone—except me. I maintained a sullen distance from the interloper and was a bit surly about completing my assignments. Wright wasn't a desk-bound editor. He was out as much as the rest of us, often snaring the best stories, which we missed entirely.

Then one day he approached my desk. I thought I was about to be cashiered and braced myself for the blow. I hadn't saved a dime, and exile from the *Enterprise* spelled trouble.

"Stoddard," he began. "Let's go have a beer."

That was a bad omen. I jabbed my steel-nibbed pen down and followed him through a blistering August morning to the cool confines of the annex. He bought. That was a worse omen.

He sipped, stared in that squinty way of his, and scraped some words out of his throat. He was almost a whisperer. "Stoddard, you know something? The reason we're the leading sheet in town is because of your mining coverage. People don't believe a word about mining if it appears in the other rags, but they believe us—they believe you. You seem impervious to the temptations. You don't let yourself get manipulated by every swindler in every superintendent's office."

He paused, sipped, and stared at the fly crawling up the back bar.

I nodded.

"I think we can make our strong suit even stronger," he ventured. "I think the *Enterprise* can become so trusted that it becomes the last word on the Comstock mines. It happens that I like mining; did a heap of it in California and learned the whole shebang, even if I have nothing to show for it. Now, there are dozens of mines to cover on the lode and scores more everywhere in the district, most of them barren gloryholes, but all of them touting themselves as bonanza prospects. We need another man, because you can't do it alone."

He paused, eyed me dolefully, and smiled faintly. "Would it offend you if I did some of it?"

I stared, warily, not liking that at all.

"You talk about how you dread the pits. Now I don't mind them a bit. I'm at home down there. What I'm thinking is that we need one man to work belowground, take samples and have them assayed, and talk to the miners down there. And we need another to keep an unblinking eye on the brokers and speculators, the woodcutters, teamsters, mine superintendents, the gamblers, swashbucklers, swindlers, manipulators, and all the rest of the greedy bunch. How'd you like to do that while I rummage around five hundred feet under grass?"

I nodded warily, relieved that I would not longer be descending in those alarming cages into the bowels of the earth, thinking only of the millions of tons of rock ready to squash me into the thickness of a bug. But I saw a problem:

"Mr. Wright, I rely on a score of Cornishmen, old friends from the Wisconsin lead mines where I grew up. They're the ones who really put me straight."

"That's a problem. Suppose you introduce me to them. Would they talk?"

"I think, if I asked them to. But they are honorable men, unbribable, proud to be the finest and most skilled men on the Comstock. I'll ask them, but they'll take their time getting the measure of you."

"I'll try to measure up," he said.

I sipped. This had all been a left-handed compliment. He didn't praise my writing; he just said that what I was doing gave our paper the edge over our rivals. I decided that would do for a compliment, and smiled.

He ordered a refill.

And so the pact was sealed. I would cover the mines from above grass; Wright would descend to hell. By the time we retreated to the composing room, two mugs later, I was thinking old Wright was a fine fellow and didn't deserve all the rancid notions I had been bottling in my skull.

That, too, was a fateful moment. During my first year in Virginia City I rarely questioned the things I witnessed and gazed upon the place with an uncritical eye. The City on the Hill seemed to be a place brimming with entrepreneurial genius, of men who refused to say no or accept defeat and thus pioneered and innovated the means to mine ore in conditions never before experienced. I saw Virginia City as a place of boundless optimism and good cheer. People refused to let bad luck or disaster demolish them; they laughed off defeat, practiced audacity as a way of life, helped one another, papered over the pain of living with practical jokes, bonhomie, and hope. Tomorrow would bring a bonanza, and never mind today's borrasca.

If the town was a bit wild, well, that was the unique American spirit making the most of life. If it drank too much, well, that was the natural exuberance of a rich city celebrating its good fortune. Everything about the magical city appealed to me, even its ornate funerals and pass-the-hat collections given to widows and orphans of fallen miners. Virginia City was the place that made the wounded whole, took care of its sick and injured, chased away the blues, and rewarded anyone brilliant enough to find new ways of bringing ore to the surface and refining it more efficiently than ever before.

But that was the rosy side. I would call it a young cub's view of the world he was reporting. I had always known about the seamy underside, the violence, the labor struggles, the greed-driven madness, the schemes and machinations of crooks, but they hadn't mattered. Then, suddenly, Wright assigned me to cover the countinghouses and law courts, and when I did my perception of the City on the Hill split in two. The place had a dark underbelly.

The ways by which men devoid of conscience found means to manipulate wealth, bilk the unsuspecting, or rob the successful are beyond recounting here. But I'll mention one or two. Whenever a working crew down in the pits uncovered a bonanza seam of ore, it became routine to lock them down there for two or three days—politely forbidding them to come to grass—while the insiders scurried about in the mining exchanges in the city and San Francisco buying feet. What was two or three days of involuntary imprisonment for a few oafs compared to the riches to be gotten from scooping up every share in sight at a bargain?

The reverse was true as well. When a mine's managers learned that a seam was pinching out, they hid the news from their own shareholders and the world until they could quietly sell out their own holdings at a better price than they would get after the bad news broke. I had expected more from people in responsible positions and found all this to be disillusioning.

Managers played endless games to fill their pockets. One was to levy an assessment on shares just when a promising new lead had been discovered. An assessment usually dropped the price of the stock and shook loose a number of shares that would be forfeited by those who couldn't pay the levy, and these were promptly snatched by the insiders who knew their value was about to rocket. Thus did the conscienceless men in the countinghouses bilk widows and orphans, people attempting to put by something for their old age, hapless clerks, miners, teamsters, mill men, and others who hoped to parlay a few shares into a bit of security and comfort. It really didn't matter to managers and financiers whether their cash came from rich veins of ore or from assessments on shares. Both sources of boodle ended up in their pockets.

Meanwhile, men with grievances awaited the formation of the first territorial court, which opened in February 1862, Judge Gordon Mott presiding. At once the court was clogged with lawsuits largely filed by schemers and dreamers, by mine owners eager to steal the bonanza next door and willing to use any implausible argument so long as it led to a fat settlement. The lawyers abounded, got rich, and walked away with a large share of the Comstock's bonanza. The dean of them all, William Stewart, made a fortune litigating mining suits. I spent so much time sitting on that hard spectator bench I contoured my tailbones to fit it. That's where you would find Stoddard day after day, listening to the drone.

The practice of selling feet in a mine soon gave way to selling shares, which was a far more practical and fluid way of negotiating ownership, especially in faraway places like San Francisco. The purchase of feet in a mine was, theoretically, the purchase of real estate and required recording and notarizing. Often a foot in a mine was owned by dozens of people, which further complicated the transactions. Ten feet of a mine might be owned by fifty people, and five other feet might be held by one person. The transition to shares resolved all that.

Almost every week we received news of a new mine, full of promise, located right next to such and such a producing mine and now being offered to the public for just a dollar a share. One could walk into the brokerage and study the promising assay reports, look at a location map, see the handsome, engraved stock certificates—and invest in a sucker's trap. We, in turn, tried to have a spy on every level of every mine— some miner or another who'd tip us to anything unusual in exchange for an eagle or some similar inducement. I always thought the whole situation was comic.

More than ever before, the brokers and managers tried to use me and the *Territorial Enterprise*, and I dutifully reported each attempt to Wright. They offered me shares and feet galore, and my standard response was that I was going to report what I saw and they could expect nothing from their offers. I stuck to that even while collecting scores of worthless certificates, which I tucked away in my trunk. Maybe someday one in a hundred would be worth a few dollars—but that notion proved to be optimistic.

Wright and I began coordinating what we learned, he from his tours underground and I from what the managers and brokers were saying. We ran some stories in which we contrasted the news from the pits with the news from management, which usually evoked horselaughs among the town's savvy citizens. Gradually, our daily became the most trusted on the Comstock, and those who trusted it were the very speculators and owners who tried to manipulate us.

I remember one case where the crafty Wright defeated the operators of a certain Gold Hill mine. The managers had suddenly excluded all visitors, and for weeks no one but staff went underground, and no news leaked in spite of generous inducements offered the miners. The loyal miners were unbribable because they were being well paid for their silence in cash and stocks. Something big was going on, but Wright was stymied at every hand. He hung around the headframe, waiting for a break, but it eluded him—until one day he spotted the manager himself emerging from the cage, begrimed with clay and dirt.

The manager went to the changing room, left his dirty duds there, and headed for his office. Wright saw that was his chance. He slipped into the changing room and with his jackknife scraped away the muck and rock from the manager's duds, rolled it into a ball, and had the stuff assayed. It was loaded with silver. So the *Enterprise* broke the story of a major strike there, long before the operators had bought up the shares they wanted.

Maybe it was all a game. Broken men laughed, bought a round of beers, and began scheming again. But somehow, the city began to acquire a new face. Maybe I was becoming more sophisticated, or maybe just growing up. But after a month or two on my new beat, I found myself still admiring the genius that built the city—and also the genius of the mountebanks and crooks whose business was to milk the bonanzas by litigation, fraud, falsifying information, or bilking the poor.

Then, in September, Joe Goodman hired still another man, this one compact, skinny, cynical, hot-tempered, and somehow not quite grown-up. He introduced himself as Sam Clemens.

CHAPTER 9

. . . .

From the perspective of this new century, I look back upon Samuel Langhorne Clemens as an unhappy young man. I didn't see it at first. He struck me as a man with an edge, a volatile temper, that could and did get him into jams. Now, with perspective, I fathom him as a man who was disappointed in himself and for that reason disappointed with the whole human race. He arrived at the *Territorial Enterprise* at the age of twenty-six, having spent his earlier life as a compositor in various newspapers, usually in the company of his brother Orion, a riverboat pilot, and, more recently, a failed argonaut and woodcutter.

My first audit revealed a slender man of five feet, eight inches, small-boned, with delicate hands. I noticed at once that he was not a toucher. He kept his paws to himself, unlike the typical Washoe denizen, who slapped backs, threw arms about shoulders, and poked and patted. He seemed gentle and sensitive and also very private. He seemed to come from nowhere, so little did he talk of his origins and family. A distinct Southern languor of tongue revealed his origins, but I knew little else about him until he became a celebrity. We shook hands—he had a good firm grip—and I sensed he was eyeing me as a rival.

I learned later that his father had been a lawyer and judge and a fine linguist but had plunged the family into chronic poverty because he was a poor businessman whose farm and store failed and whose land speculations were disasters. Nonetheless, Judge Clemens had been counted among the first citizens of Hannibal. Sam inherited his father's gift of language and also his father's weakness in business.

Sam now lives in England, having manfully assumed the wretched task of paying off heavy debts not entirely of his own making, much honored as a man of American letters. He need fear nothing of this memoir if he should chance to read it. I have nothing dark to say of him. He is not well, I understand, but who of us is at our advanced age? Although I was his senior at the paper, he is my senior in years.

Sam Clemens was an obvious asset for Joe Goodman. Clemens had already proven himself as a comic writer, and during his short sojourn in Virginia City he perfected the art of the literary hoax, advanced his skill in writing sketches, and generally raised a laugh or two among the readers of our rag. He was good at everything except reporting. His mind was too quick and his cynicism too deep to gather stories from reluctant people.

I speak of cynicism because that was a corrosive, acid aspect of his nature. And like most cynics, he subscribed to an impossible idealism. In fact, one could well say that lofty ideals are the reverse side of any cynic's coinage and the very reason they turn so bitter. I myself think that this lofty idealism is rooted in despair. I've never met a cynic who was not, at bottom, deeply disappointed in himself because he could not live up to impossible ideals.

Whatever the case, Clemens took quarters in the same rooming house as William Wright—eventually sharing a room with Wright after he returned from a visit to the East to see his neglected family—and disdained the grubby bunks where those of us less privileged or affluent boarded. Clemens proved to be a quick study and was soon imitating the wry columns of Dan De Quille. He was signing himself as "Josh," but I gather he had used a variety of absurd and presumably comic noms de plume before his arrival in our precincts. He wasn't with us long enough for me to form a lasting impression, which is why I'll dwell upon him only briefly.

Virginia City shaped and matured Clemens. The world well knows that he first used the name Mark Twain there, but I don't consider that important. Far more portentous was his discovery that he could get up before a crowd and entertain them with a mix of self-deprecating humor, barbs, tall tales, absurd yarns, and exaggerations. He did this at first in the saloons. Mark Twain was a man who could turn anything into a quiet laugh simply by stretching it beyond recognition. He loved to do it; his auditors in the saloons he frequented loved it; the miners loved it. Mark Twain the monologuist was born there, although it wasn't until he whiled away some time in San Francisco that he made a commercial success of the declamatory skills he had perfected in a rude mining camp.

He began to run soberly written sketches, such as "The Petrified Man" and "The Empire City Massacre," which seemed so realistic that readers scarcely knew he was pulling their leg, even when the exaggerations reached a clattering, clanging climax that should have startled all but the buffalo-witted out of their credulity. I'm persuaded that he got all that from studying Wright, but Clemens soon equaled his mentor at the game.

I don't mean to dwell on things that literary critics have long since set down in dry textbooks. Clemens was sociable—and yet apart. He would hoist mugs of beer along with the rest of us, drinking democratically with reporters, editors, compositors, or anyone else. And yet, in all those carousing hours, I don't think any of us got to know him. I didn't. In later years, as I began reading his many books, I fathomed much more of him than I did when we were elbow to elbow in Virginia's oases. He liked practical jokes, but his usually had an edge to them and evoked pain in the victim. And he disliked being the butt of one. That told me much about the man.

Sam Clemens was a loner and made no close friends there—or anywhere else—all his early life. I know now that he was starved for attention, ached to make a name for himself, and kept to himself because he thought he was no match for those of us who were senior to him. He even fathomed friendship as a type of competition for status among us.

I once asked him whether he planned to stick with the *Enterprise*.

"Sure, until something better grabs me by the arm," he replied.

So he wasn't putting down roots.

He was more at home with a type stick and casebox than any of our compositors, but he usually distanced himself from the mechanical aspects of publishing a daily. Compositors were the princes of the skilled trades and were paid on a piecework basis, sixty-five cents per thousand ems of type—which a good man could set in an hour. A fast compositor could earn a handsome income, and some did. Clemens would no doubt have earned more setting type than he earned as a reporter, but he had found his calling and a type stick wasn't a part of it. Not that he reported much. One does not find much ordinary news in the *Enterprise* that can be ascribed to the young man.

He gadded about Virginia until eighteen and sixty-four, then departed for San Francisco and the California mining camps, as restless when he left as when he came. He was still a young man in search of a calling—and, more important, a mission. I always thought he was more a preacher than a reporter and just beneath the constantly shored-up levity lay a black sorrow. We spent amazing amounts of time together, but we really weren't friends. He had none, not even his roommate, De Quille. He did have a raft of acquaintances and was well liked even if no one became a confidant.

During his sojourn in our fair city I never saw him court a woman. It wasn't that he didn't care about them but that he could not bring himself to believe that a woman might return his affection. He was so proper that if male conversation took a bawdy turn he would vanish. I often wondered if he would ever marry, or even court a woman or enjoy a sweetheart. Eventually he did, but not during the fleeting weeks when he alighted at our paper like a bird of passage on a spar of a ship, ready to sail off as soon as he got his wind and a compass heading.

I can only report what I know of a young man in his twenty-sixth and -seventh years, blotting up the tragedy of a town built of dreams. And I'll tell you something: Clemens may be the best-known facet of Virginia's life and heyday, but he was little more important than a fly on a wall. Great things happened there, things more exciting than the emergence of a comic writer and lecturer, things that set the tone of the new century. Things that will affect this twentieth century in ways I will not live to see. These mechanical marvels weren't glamorous things and wouldn't stir the interest of a shop girl craving romance, but these things would affect her life all the more.

During that period, Virginia City boomed. Every day brought more good news as one after another of the mines perched directly on the lode found good ore pockets. I had plenty to cover. During that period there were magnificent bonanzas at the Yellow Jacket, Imperial, Alpha, and Belcher over in Gold Hill and in the Savage, Gould & Curry, Combination, and California. Several lesser mines were producing good ore as well.

None of this would have been possible but for the genius of a young mining engineer named Philipp Deidesheimer. Beginning in 1860, the Ophir mine, in particular, began to find itself enjoying an embarrassment of riches. The ore seams, consisting of black sulphurets, had enlarged to the point where their excavation was creating gigantic galleries underground, and these were subject to constant caving and settling because none of the known means of supporting the ceilings of these caverns was adequate. Those chambers extended several stories high, and the rickety upright timbering employed by the mines was not effective or safe. Men were being endangered and killed by cave-ins.

Deidesheimer solved the problem by designing a new system of timbering called square sets. These were mining timbers fashioned into cubes and stacked atop one another story after story to build a solid framework in a gallery that, on the surface of the earth, would have been as high as a multistoried building. These sets, consisting of four uprights and a cap of timbers to form the hollow cube, proved to be the answer, and when floored, provided easy and comfortable access to the stopes and faces where the miners worked. This was one of the earliest of many innovations that transformed mining worldwide. The Ophir, thus transformed from a company sitting on a bonanza it couldn't mine into a company fully capable of taking every last pound of ore from the earth, soared in value. And so did all the mines on the Comstock.

I wrote about all this and also the innovations in milling ore, day after day, in sober stories that won little acclaim from Joe Goodman or Denis McCarthy. I took pride in my reportage—for such it was—and whatever it lacked in entertainment it more than compensated for in coverage that added to the paper's popularity. Wright knew it, and commended me now and then, and I knew my perch on the paper was secure.

My careful reporting didn't win me a raise, though. I have come to believe that newspaper publishers haven't the foggiest idea of the true value of a good reporter. They see the value of a good advertising salesman or an entertaining columnist, of course, but scarcely realize that the reporter who makes the paper unique and valuable to readers makes the ad man's job possible—and not the other way around.

I covered the fevered efforts to make the mills more efficient in extracting the precious metals from their ores by improving the efficiency of pans and mullers. Because of progress in that field, the mines were able to find a profit in lower-grade ores that they had previously thrown away or stockpiled. Thus their reserves expanded. By the end of 1861 there were an incredible seventy-six mills operating within sixteen miles of the Comstock. These mills had a total of 1,153 stamps and a crushing capacity of twelve hundred tons of ore daily.

Still more mills were opening regularly, and it was my task to report them all, and also the results of their trial runs. Thus my reportage was filled with such information as this: An eight-ton sample of Yellow Jacket "back lode" ore yielded $69.88 in gold and $18.84 in silver, for a total of $11.80 a ton. And a twenty-ton Crown Point sample yielded $398.65 in gold and $61.36 in silver, or $20 a ton.

I kept track of the costs of salt and mercury, cordwood, and other materials essential to reducing the ores and reported them regularly. I spent my days walking from one mill to another to get a brief story from a manager half-deaf from the constant roar, and all of this usually appeared on page 3, somewhere under the obituaries.

There were breathtaking breakthroughs in the realm of milling, but these were even less exciting to most readers than such things as Deidesheimer's square-set timbering, and no one noticed my reportage—except those who counted. My editor, Wright, knew what I was adding to the paper, and sometimes he even played a mining or milling story on page 1.

I turned my attention to the other major crisis besetting the Comstock mines: litigation. Each day things were happening in the Storey County Courthouse, where Judge Mott was presiding in the First District Court of the new territory. These spelled bonanza or doom, busts or fortunes, for those present. Not a mine hit bonanza but that it wasn't immediately besieged by lawsuits, most of them of the noxious variety rising from the calculated greed of those who wanted a slice of the pie without earning it.

But there were many legitimate suits as well, occasioned by the careless way that the first prospectors had recorded their claims and the loose manner in which the rules of the mining district had been drafted. But no matter whether the suits had some legitimacy or were the legal teeth of sharks, they cost money, and in the end much of the fabulous wealth of the Comstock slipped into the pockets of attorneys such as William Stewart, who not only coined a fortune in the courts but also went on to become one of Nevada's first senators. And all that courtroom coverage appeared each day, several column feet of it, under the name of Henry Stoddard. I really had nothing to complain about except my twenty-a-week wage.

CHAPTER 10

he longer I covered events in Virginia City, the more of a mystery the town became to me. Was it greed that brought thousands of pilgrims to an arid slope of western Nevada where the winters were vicious, the water poisonous, the whole of it so inhospitable that men dreamed of trees and lawns and gardens and graces?

Greed was the easy, facile—and shallow—answer. And it didn't make sense. Did the miners who flocked there really imagine they would get rich? Did the boardinghouse widows who bought a few shares of mining stock really imagine they would retire with a fortune? Even now, at the beginning of a new century, the mystery remains unsettled in my mind, but I like to think that what brought people there was simply hope. We are each entitled to that, and there is no evil in it. In my advanced age I take a kinder view of human nature than I did as a choleric and judgmental young man.

For that matter, what had brought *me* to the city? Looking back, I can't quite say what was in the head of Henry Stoddard when he abandoned the land of milk and honey and set off for the West. I suppose a lot of things drew people to Virginia City. By the midseventies the town had grown to twenty thousand and Gold Hill had grown to ten thousand, making them major metropolises in the virgin West. Other than hope,

what had all those people in mind? I sometimes think that what pro-
pelled them to that arid slope were such ephemeral things as adventure,
whimsy, curiosity, and the promise of wild times in an unsettled and
lawless land. Maybe nothing more than having fun, enjoying some excitement in an otherwise drab world.

Whatever the case, I spent more and more time perched on the
spectator benches in Judge Mott's courtroom, where I watched the daily
dance of the mongoose and cobra. These lawsuits were usually won by
neither party, because the juries would hang. On some days, the proceedings were the best entertainment in town, better than anything in
the opera houses, as they called theaters in those days.

I do not wish to burden the reader with all the technical and legal
details of these complex cases, but I have chosen one to illustrate the
tangled affairs of the mines of the Comstock. As it happens, this one
came to trial in the Twelfth District Court in California, and Joe Goodman deemed the case so important that he opened his purse and sent
me packing over the Sierras—a grim ride in a Pioneer Stage Company
Concord coach—to keep an eye on matters in Sacramento. It was my
first escape from the City on the Hill since I had arrived, but Virginia
was never far from mind during those contentious days.

The newly organized Grosche Gold and Silver Mining Company
brought suit against the Gould & Curry, Mexican, and Ophir mining
companies, claiming that its ownership of 3,750 feet on the Comstock
Lode had been usurped by the defendants. The Grosche company was
supposedly first capitalized at $5 million and later at $10 million, presumably to develop its alleged claim comprising nearly four thousand
feet of the best ground on the Comstock!

This California company had been formed by wealthy and prominent Californians who served as its trustees and directors and based its
dubious claim on practically nothing. Among the earliest prospectors on
Sun Mountain were the Grosch brothers, in 1859. The brothers had
found an outcrop of silver in a ledge at some location unknown because
they never staked it or laid claim to it. The brothers both died untimely
deaths, leaving their claims in limbo, unknown and unrecorded. As fragile as was this preposterous claim, it formed the basis of the Grosche
(who knows where that extra *e* came from?) Gold and Silver Mining
Company's lawsuit.

In short, California's bluebloods were embarked upon grand larceny
and it did not matter to them that they were engaged in ordinary theft,
employing lawyers rather than six-guns, or that they made themselves
no better—actually worse—than the desperadoes who robbed stages or

mugged citizens in the dark. It mattered little to them whether by harassment and litigation they acquired the whole disputed ledge or merely a piece of the pie as a settlement of the dispute. The point of their enterprise was to gang up on the three most productive mines on the Comstock and steal them from their rightful owners. Now, that was entertainment, and my dispatches captivated the denizens of our fair metropolis.

It even inspired doggerel:

The Ophir on the Comstock
Was rich as bread and honey,
The Gould & Curry further south
Was raking out the money.

The Savage and the others
Had machinery all complete
When in came the Grosches
And nipped all our feet.

By then I was largely inured to the criminality of our species, but that one shocked me, perhaps because the thievery had been initiated by a privileged class of citizens who should have known better and scarcely needed a second or third million. I wondered if these pirates served as deacons or vestrymen on Sundays, adhering to the forms of their faith one day a week and flouting them for six. I wondered what sort of barristers would prosecute a suit like that, line up assorted "witnesses" who were doubtless well paid and would invent what they knew to be lies and soberly present them to the magistrates. Who among them could even wash his dirty hands?

The suit dragged on for years but was eventually thrown out, which I suppose says something in favor of California jurisprudence and maybe even something about the credulity of judges. But it had cost the Gould & Curry mine thousands of dollars in legal fees and costs, and the burden fell heavily on the other defendants as well. I sometimes think that it was tawdry spectacles of this sort that led young Sam Clemens to his corrosive and despairing view of human nature. The suit wasn't settled until long after his departure, but he was present during much of it and was living in California when it was settled.

That was but one of hundreds of such lawsuits. I covered many of them for the *Territorial Enterprise,* and they left their fangs in me and sometimes haunted me, afflicted my sleep, and lowered my esteem for the genus *Americanus.* I would almost have preferred to stay in Platteville, where life was sweeter and more honorable. But that was not what I preferred, and maybe that was a clue to the mysterious city.

Virginia City was not an unhappy place, in spite of the skullduggery in the courts, in brokerage offices, and in the countinghouses at the mines. We Americans are, as a people, remarkable risk takers. The swashbucklers who rode into town on every stagecoach won, lost, won and lost, but never questioned the wisdom of speculating. If anything, losing entertained them as much as winning, and many a time, when elbowed down on the bar, I heard a fellow imbiber brag about how much he had lost that day. That puzzled me.

I worked steadily those months, watching Wright transform himself into the celebrated Dan De Quille and Clemens imitate him and add a twist of his own—public monologues—to begin his path toward celebrity. I toiled on, lacking the gaudy nature of a Clemens and the stylistic humor of a De Quille. No doubt I was too much the sober young man. Substance meant everything to me, and I scarcely paid attention to style or passion. What counted for me was truth or falsity, wisdom or folly, goodness or evil, and thus I wrote. I would rather deliver truth in a monotone than falsehood with verve.

Clemens and Wright became celebrities; young Stoddard slid deeper into the background, one of those nameless men who, day upon day, put out news. The *Territorial Enterprise* swiftly outstripped its rivals, boasting a circulation three or four times that of the *Virginia Daily Union* and dominating the other rivals even more. By 1865, our circulation ran 745, while the *Union*'s was 190 and the *Gold Hill News*'s was 150. The several California papers weren't even in the running. It was my private conceit that my sober reportage, more than Twain's and De Quille's gaudy contributions, had given my paper its formidable edge.

During that period rivals came and vanished with such regularity that I can barely remember them now. We at the *Enterprise* competed with the *Trespass, Daily Safeguard, Virginia Evening Bulletin, Daily Democratic Standard, Occidental, Nevada Pioneer,* and *Daily Old Piute.*

That particular paper provoked a celebrated incident one evening at the Sazarac Bar, where Joe Goodman had repaired for some Bordeaux. A gent reading the *Old Piute* spotted Goodman beside him and informed our publisher and editor that he used the *Territorial Enterprise* to wipe his behind.

"Keep right on, friend," Goodman replied unflappably, "and in a short time your behind will know more than your head will."

I believed then that one reason the *Enterprise* trounced its rivals was its cheerful reportage—we focused through a comic lens. The other reason, I confess, is that it was unexcelled in covering crime in the fair city. It carefully ran a lurid daily diet of shootings, stabbings, suicides—especially the self-poisonings of the girls on the Line—along with assaults, embezzlements, and flamboyant infidelities. We did handsomely one issue when we reported a billiard parlor stabbing that occurred one night when the coroner was away. The deceased had fallen under the table, and there he remained until the following noon, when the coroner at last arrived, greatly inconveniencing the players, who had to crouch and contort themselves to make a proper shot.

Now, as I plunge into a new century, I am not so certain about whether serious reportage helped the paper maintain its domination of the field, because I have discovered that readers of newspapers don't really want news; they want entertainment. And that was what Mark Twain, as he had renamed himself, was providing. He had become something of a local character and had reached the elegant status in life where strangers bought him drinks. A bibulous newsman could go far on something like that, and Twain always fared well as he patrolled Barnum's Restaurant, the Café de Paris, the Smokery, Gentry & Crittenden's, the Howling Wilderness, the International Hotel's bar, and other oases. He and Wright began to review the troupes coming to Maguire's Opera House on D Street, a gaudy red plush and crystal chandelier and Turkish carpet affair with a curtain depicting Lake Tahoe at sunset, occupying front-center seats and dawdling in the greenroom with assorted hoydens—as I will describe later.

It was the custom of the time for traveling troupes to draw their extras and bit players from among the locals, especially newspaper people who might publicize the show. The result was that Virginia was occasionally treated to a scribbler all got up as a knight in armor or Roman gladiator, and if these were gents employed by the opposing papers they did not escape the attention of the ruthless Twain and De Quille—who wisely never performed as spear-carriers themselves.

The boards were often occupied not by thespians, but by lecturers, magicians, reformers, and assorted mountebanks, all of which were fodder for our famous scribes, and also a source of champagne, spirits, viands, and loose female company.

I was a little envious, and perhaps still am. Here, at the dawn of the century, is Stoddard, still unknown and a man of modest means. No one has celebrated me as a great humorist or called me an American original. And yet I would have it no other way, for I console myself with the belief that my mining reportage was really what put cash in the pockets of Joe Goodman and Denis McCarthy. I think I was born to be anonymous, and maybe one of those astrologists whose conjuring I don't credit would tell me it was fated.

The truth of it is that Henry Stoddard was coming to know his worth. He was living in the shadow of literary lights, but he had come to understand his own value. He liked himself, his work, and his life in Virginia City.

That's why I stayed.

CHAPTER 11

y the time 1863 rolled around, the Union army was finally showing its muscle, and those of us on the Comstock—solidly in favor of the North—began to take heart. Our silver and gold were an important reason that Abe Lincoln's army was winning victories. We knew it and followed the war closely, though news was scarce. Up until October 1861, war news came to Virginia City by the Pony Express, run by Russell, Majors, and Waddell, but the transcontinental telegraph soon replaced it and we received our news from the East almost instantaneously. There were Southern sympathizers on the Comstock, and those were watched carefully to make sure that the treasure dug from our ground reached the right side.

I had, by 1863, grown hungry for female company. I bunked in a rude and noisome dormitory annexed to the *Territorial Enterprise,* along with other lesser reporters and assorted printers and compositors and that wretch of a printer's devil, few of them ever sober. Its roof leaked and heat was a scarce item in winter. I had to put up with that sinister printer's devil, named Noyes perhaps because he was noisome, and an equally sinister Chinaman named Old Joe, who served up what passed for meals, which he served on the imposing stones upon which pages in various stages of composition rested. I was sick of male company. That was all one could find in the saloons, on the streets, in the gaudy orchestra seats at Maguire's Opera House, and in the mercantiles on C Street. The few females in town were almost all married or else widows of advanced years who ran boardinghouses or sewed or were in service to the rich. For a young man like Henry Stoddard, a youth without means or reputation, the prospects of female companionship were nil.

I began to think I should pack up and move to San Francisco, where prospects for female company—indeed, starting the family I dreamed of—would be brighter. But I didn't. The Comstock had its hammerlock on me for reasons I don't fathom even now, decades later. I do remember sliding into melancholy, especially Saturday evenings when the work of the week was done and I was footloose. I knew the life histories of all my associates, even the reticent Clemens, who, when properly lubricated with some mellow Kentuck, would be good for an hour on piloting riverboats or the art of setting brevier or agate type.

My Saturday solace was to ramble through the hundred or so saloons that made Virginia the drinkingest place on earth. I would bravely begin at, say, the Greyhound, retire to Pat Bell's, wander into the Delta, stop at Adolph Kuhnhaeser's German Coffee Saloon on North B Street, retreat to the Old Corner Saloon, go for a nightcap at Haynes and Berry's Saloon, and drop into my scabrous bunk at the paper. I knew all sorts of people, and none of them were female. I concluded that I didn't have much of a life and wondered why the Washoe continued to spellbind me.

A district on South C Street came to be called the Barbary Coast because its grog shops imitated the more famous quarter in San Francisco. The dives, such as Nellie Sayer's and Peter Larkin's, never seriously tempted me. Everything was for sale there. But I refused even to carouse in that quarter, priding myself that I had at least a residue of good sense. More tempting was the restricted district on North D Street where public ladies practiced their easy ways. Several bordellos, typically two-story frame buildings, occupied the ground around D and Union Street. In addition, there were a dozen or so identical cabins, or cribs, occupied by window-framed ladies who chose to ply their profession without the security of a madam. One of these was Julia Bulette, who was neither French nor a New Orleans courtesan, though she professed to be. But more about that celebrated demimondaine later.

I resisted such folly, though I don't quite know why. I was in my twenties, as randy as all the rest my age, and in a city without women I suffered. If I managed to avoid the vices it was not because of superior virtue or strength of character but because syphilis and the clap terrified me. Most of those in my bunkhouse suffered one or the other; the loathsome diseases scythed through the Comstock, ruining lives, curdling brains, and devastating spouses and innocents.

The *Enterprise* was loaded with small, discreet ads touting cures, none of which were known to be effective. From any pharmacy one could obtain Red Drops or Unfortunate's Friend or Pine Knot Bitters, and one local doctor named Price touted his "infallible remedies." He proclaimed that his drugs were "surest and quickest known for all private diseases of both sexes, young and old. Chronic venereal disease quickly relieved. No mercury used."

That appealed to some, because mercury had a way of ulcerating flesh and addling brains, if not outright killing the patient. But even that may have been better than the alternative. Alf Doten, editor of the *Gold Hill News,* once described to me in lurid detail an operation he had witnessed in a house on Summit Hill where his friend Dr. Hiller surgically removed two inches or so of an Irishman's private part, the suppurating head being rotten with pox, as we all called syphilitic chancre. I believe that Doten's lurid tale, spun over a mug of pilsner at the Delta, rescued me from the sporting districts. It lifted the hair on my scalp. Little did I then know that the teller of that tale was a legendary customer of most of the bordellos on the Comstock and kept a private diary recording every one of his encounters. The risks he took didn't faze him in the slightest.

So, a fleshly terror held me in check—more or less. I valued my health and life more than did the restless thousands of miners, mill men, clerks, and laborers who made regular pilgrimages to the houses of ill repute. I did on one occasion visit such a house in a moment of boozy frivolity. An Irish widow in her early thirties named Caroline Thompson, or Cad as she called herself, had just opened a new resort on D Street near Sutton, which swiftly won a reputation as a classy place, with elegant furnishings, Turkish carpets, a pleasant parlor with a pianoforte, and gracious young ladies. That combination all but undid my stern resolve, and properly fortified with several drams of claret one Saturday after we had put the paper to bed I braved a chill night and sallied into the unknown.

I entered a well-lit parlor and was smitten with incense and warmth. A dozen or so sports were lounging about, and I surveyed them nervously, hoping not to be recognized. But Virginia had ballooned to ten thousand and I had remained an obscure reporter. All the gents in the parlor were strangers. Some had gathered about an upright piano where a musicale, of sorts, was proceeding, an Irish ballad being sung by assorted gents and two kimono-clad ladies.

At that point, Cad Thompson descended on me and drew me into the parlor with a ready smile.

"Welcome, friend," she said. "Come join us."

I liked her smile as much as I liked her throaty voice. She was a small woman of great vivacity and warmth, though not pretty. I nodded and allowed myself to be tugged to the piano. A Chinaman materialized and handed me a goblet of ruby claret.

Cad patted me on the arm. "You want anything, dear, you just talk to me. That's what I'm here for."

I thanked her and surveyed the Cyprians with unbounded curiosity. One was a weary blonde, the other almost dusky, with jet hair, perhaps an octoroon, though I had scarcely encountered such as she in Platteville. Neither interested me, but both stirred my juices as I beheld the thin and multihued kimonos and what lay beneath.

I took the measure of the establishment, only half-listening to the ballad. These gents had smooth hands, an excess of avoirdupois, and reminded me of drummers and patent medicine purveyors. Maybe they were. I fathomed that Cad's house was too expensive for miners and mill men—and probably me, though I had ten dollars in my pocket, all of it in silver. I told myself that I would down the claret and then retreat; I was drifting toward shoals I wished to avoid. So I sipped, avoided the forced heartiness of the crowd around the piano, and wondered whether the fellow who massaged the ivories was Cad's employee or a customer. Something was different about this place: everyone present had assessing eyes, a gaze that sized up the others—for money, for beauty, for seductiveness, for violence or danger. The ballad may have been friendly, but the gazes weren't.

Then a new girl wandered in from the hallway leading to the stairs, looking heated and disheveled and weary. She glanced at us all, and my gaze met hers and locked. She made my pulse lift. What was there about her that appealed to me? Maybe it was her cascading brown hair—or was it chestnut?—or the slenderness of her figure, which was faintly visible under her gauzy wrapper. Whatever it was, we drifted toward each other.

"I'm Annie," she said. "You want to sit and talk a minute?"

"Uh, yes," I replied.

"You're a shy one."

We settled on a red plush divan, and I examined her closely, drawn by some magnetism that defies description. She reminded me of the brown-haired girls of Platteville, the girls of middling beauty and form, with a middling tint, neither blond nor dark-haired, soft-eyed and prim rather than brazen. Had she not been there, at Cad's place, I would have taken her for a lady.

"Well, what do you do?"

"I don't do anything," I said. I didn't want her to know what I did or who I was.

I saw fever in her bright brown eyes, and it startled me. Her flesh was waxen and colorless. I knew at once she was sick, and when she coughed delicately it came to me in an instant: she was consumptive, and the fevered brightness of her face was that of a gravely ill woman.

"Well, then you're lucky. Most people have to get a living."

"I don't earn much," I said ungallantly.

My answer must have seemed abrupt to her, because she grimaced slightly and came to the point. "Would you like to join me upstairs?" she asked. She smiled and slipped a hand over mine, and I liked her touch. How many nights had I lain in my bunk at the paper yearning just to hold the hand of a sweetheart?

"Uh," I said stupidly.

"Perhaps you'd like to sing."

I knew that was her delicate way of suggesting that I might be more interested in someone else.

"Uh, no, I sound like a bullfrog."

She patted me gently. "Is this your first time in a parlor house?"

"Oh, no, uh, yes."

"Well, sweetheart, I would enjoy showing you how it is. I think you're special. You come with me, and we'll just close the door and it'll just be the two of us, all alone and very happy together."

"Uh," I replied, feeling idiotic.

"Are you worried about money? We can talk to Cad."

"Yes!"

"Let me go talk to her. I'd love to have you stay. I know I can make you very happy."

She smiled, patted me again, and drifted into the back somewhere.

I bolted up, set down the claret on a side table, recovered my coat, and fled into the bracing night. I trudged back to the paper in a blackening mood, angry at the Comstock for beguiling me and determined to flee as fast as I could resign.

CHAPTER 12

h, that year, 1863, when the *Territorial Enterprise* was the only place on earth for a young newsman to be and Virginia City had become the Athens of the Far West. Although my yearnings for a more stable life tugged at me, I stayed on, and now, as I look back across the years, I'm glad I did. Nothing in American journalism has ever come close to those wild times.

That was Mark Twain's year. I wasn't a part of his immediate circle, which consisted of Dan De Quille and Joe Goodman and, later, Steve Gillis. But neither was I distant from all the light and heat radiating from Clemens's direction, and many a time I hoisted a glass of claret beside him at one of Virginia's hundred saloons.

I wish I could tell you I was present during some of the most celebrated moments of his sojourn among us, but I wasn't. I heard about them later in exquisite and hungover detail, and I think that will suffice for me to present them to you as if I were a fly on the wall, watching it all.

In February of that eventful year Sam Clemens grew weary of signing his contributions "Josh," for reasons he has never disclosèd. One day he signed himself Mark Twain, and an American legend was born. Years later he explained that he had not invented that name. It had first been employed by a late friend from his riverboating days, Capt. Isaiah Sellers, who used it to sign his shipping news contributions to the *New Orleans Picayune*. Clemens explained that he "had laid violent hands on it without asking permission of the proprietor's remains."

During that same period Clemens had mastered the art of the literary hoax from Dan De Quille, the past master in that esoteric realm of letters. Perhaps the most famous of Mark's contributions was "The Empire City Massacre." This purported to be an account, appropriately bloody, of a mass murder committed in dense woods near a station on the Carson River called Dutch Nick's, where Empire now stands. The alleged murderer, Pete Hopkins, supposedly killed his wife and seven children, injured two others, severed his wife's head, and then fled to Carson City, where he cut his throat and fell dead before the Magnolia Saloon, which he owned. Twain cited Abe Curry, Carson's most eminent citizen, as his source and concluded that Hopkins's madness was the result of losses in mining speculation.

Most of the town's cognoscenti spotted the hoax instantly. Hopkins was a veteran bachelor, and most of the yarn's geography didn't make sense. There wasn't a tree within miles of Dutch Nick's. But that didn't stop the *Gold Hill News* from reprinting the story, or much of credulous California from believing it. The press on the west side of the Sierras solemnly declared it was the most shocking crime ever witnessed upon the Pacific coast.

We published a retraction promptly, but that only improved the uproar, and Clemens's exploit became the toast of Virginia City. Our rivals proclaimed that the hoax was particularly heinous, which enhanced the soiree. But Joe Goodman decided enough was enough, and hoaxes swiftly disappeared from our famous columns.

Sam was all aglow over the notoriety he had won. One evening at the Sazarac I asked him why he had done it.

"Well, I thought the place needed livening up," he replied.

"Liveliest town I've ever been in. I think maybe you did it to win a vile reputation."

He smiled. I knew I was not far off. Sam Clemens ached to become known and would keep on taunting fate until he succeeded.

Those were our salad days. Later the *Enterprise* became more sober and less entertaining. Clemens was sent downhill to cover the Territorial Legislature and proceeded to make enemies and trade insults, which he did in fine fettle. Never before had Joe Goodman's sheet glowed with such pyrotechnics. There were moments when I envied Twain and De Quille—and moments when I was glad to write from the obscurity of my beat.

I confess I was at my most envious of Mark Twain when Maguire opened his posh opera house on D Street and began to draw some of the best theatrical troupes in the country. In fact, Virginia swiftly acquired the reputation of being the best theater town between Chicago and San Francisco, a reputation that lasted for two decades. The opening event was Bulwer-Lytton's *Money,* starring Julia Dean Hayne and Walter Lehman, straight from London.

But just about curtain time, two tinhorns who were not exactly friends discovered that they were seated across from each other in opposing boxes. They did what tinhorns do: extracted their pieces and had at each other. Nothing was hurt save for some wood and plaster, and these students of Thespis were expelled from school for the duration of the class.

Mark Twain, Dan De Quille, Joe Goodman, and assorted other luminaries of the *Territorial Enterprise,* and myself on occasion, had aisle seats for each of the performances. And so we were present and watching when the celebrities trod the boards. As the curtain fell, we would repair to an accommodating bar rail, usually that of the International Hotel, there to debate the merits of the performance over claret and assign one of our number to write the lubricious review. Since these were usually fawning, if not lickspittle worshipful, we had no trouble maintaining our row of privileged seats at Maguire's.

Then Artemus Ward arrived at the behest of Maguire, who was always on the lookout for ways to keep his footlights lit. The legend had it that Maguire asked the New Yorker what he would take for one hundred nights and Ward replied, "Brandy and soda."

Ward, whose real name was Charles Farrar Browne, had started as a printer's apprentice and then become a compositor for the *Carpet-Bag,* a Boston humor magazine. He became an editor for the Toledo *Commercial* and then the Cleveland *Plain Dealer.* At that paper he invented Artemus Ward, the humorous commentator on the ways of the world. Eventually he decamped to New York to be a staff writer for *Vanity Fair,* but his skills as a humorist soon took him out upon the lecture circuit.

Whatever the case, Maguire reeled him in and the country's most eminent humorist and proprietor of the Great Moral Show was an instant sensation among the miners, mill men, card sharks, and speculators of Washoe. His stock in trade was a long, pained, solemn, deadpan silence that somehow always tickled observers into cascades of laughter. Not least among Ward's admirers were Mark Twain and Dan De Quille. The threesome became fast friends, while Twain blotted up everything that Ward could teach him about monologues.

Ward, actually an urbane and well-schooled man, had developed the stage persona of a rural rube and laced his lecture, called "Babes in the Woods," with homely anecdotes and country humor delivered deadpan, which caught the fancy of the miners and mill men, who returned to the opera house over and over to hear him. Maguire had signed him for three performances—but Ward promptly fell in love with the Comstock and stayed.

The result was a lengthy debauch for Mark Twain, Dan De Quille, Joe Goodman, and, alas, the young Henry Stoddard. Each night after the final curtain it became the bounden duty of the editorial staff of the *Territorial Enterprise* to introduce Artemus Ward to the allures of the Washoe. Thus did I enjoy champagne and claret, oysters and clams, antelope and venison, Turkish baths and nightcaps, night after night. And ran up debt. Twain and De Quille were famous moochers and largely floated through the debauch on Ward's generosity, but I had a perverse streak of principle.

In time I came to my senses and was no longer present in the reserved seats at Maguire's. The Comstock boomed that year, and I had more than enough to report from the countinghouses, brokerages, and mine shafts. In fact, with De Quille not entirely present—the compositors were telling me that his hand was becoming indecipherable, even to those of them who could translate the Rosetta Stone—it had befallen the steady Stoddard to write up the mines.

There was plenty to cover. Even as the ore bodies were proving to be bountiful the lawsuits were multiplying and making the profession of law uncommonly fruitful. It was later calculated that just one lengthy contest, between the Chollar and Potosi mining companies, eventually cost the litigants over two million dollars and left them so exhausted that they fell into each other's arms and became one. That suit caused the resignation of the whole corrupt territorial bench and was without parallel in the history of mining litigation. By 1866 the Comstock mines had spent ten million dollars on litigation—which amounted to a lot of silver and gold. So I was in the courts day after day, now reporting the Burning Moscow case, now the Grass Valley case, and, again, the Gould & Curry litigation.

The mines were booming. I have some data compiled by Eliot Lord of the United States Geological Survey, who spent years in the Washoe district minutely examining the greatest mining boom in the history of the world. In 1860 the Comstock mines extracted, in all, about 12,500 tons of ore, which yielded a million dollars in gold and silver bullion. In 1861 the mines produced 30,336 tons of ore, which yielded $2,275,256 in bullion. In 1862, the mines produced 93,031 tons or ore, which yielded $6,247,047 in bullion. And then came 1863: 249,724 tons of ore, which yielded $12,486,238. The next three years were even better, but I am getting ahead of my story.

Mark Twain's sojourn among us coincided with the arrival of good times, fat purses, innumerable miners employed at a minimum of four dollars a day, a princely sum then and now. And the skilled mill men, supervisors, and shift bosses corralled even more. Of course mining camp prices were high; the district was scores of miles from anywhere, and subsistence for ten thousand people in Virginia and another five thousand in Gold Hill was freighted in by ox team and wagons, the muscle power of thousands of mules, horses, and oxen dragging all that, plus mining timbers, cordwood, and heavy equipment up the long hard slopes to the City on the Hill. The rough roads to Sacramento were so jammed that the traffic formed an endless procession from spring melt to autumn storm.

I reported all that. And the more I learned about the precarious economy of the Comstock, the more I wondered what its fate would be. A few of the mines were in bonanza; most were in borrasca and busily assessing shareholders for all they were worth. Seen from Eliot Lord's perspective in 1880, the Comstock was a bust. Of the 103 mining companies in the district, only 6 showed an excess of dividends over assessments, only 14 paid dividends, and 102 levied assessments. Even in 1863, while I was covering the mines, it was becoming plain to me that some of the great ones that everyone in town set store by were pretty poor pickings.

Take the Gould & Curry, for instance. That was the mine that everyone wanted a piece of. It paid dividends of $3,826,800, while assessing its shareholders $3,152,000. More typical was the great Ophir, one of the original mines on the Comstock and the one that had treated George Hearst so well. In the end, it paid out $1,595,800 in dividends and assessed its shareholders $2,689,400. No one was getting very rich—except the lawyers, the supervisors, and the handful who knew how to milk a corporation for personal profit. Some of those nabobs were getting plenty rich—at the cost of constantly assessed shareholders—and my understanding of how things worked in the countinghouses deepened my cynicism. I loved the Comstock—and despised it. My reportage took on a certain cynical cast that I can easily see as I look back through my yellowed clippings, now pasted into several scrapbooks.

These were not matters that dampened the enthusiasms of Mark Twain, Dan De Quille, or the celebrated Artemus Ward, as they rollicked through the fall of 1863. But then, as the year waned, Ward finally grew weary of our neighborhood and decided to hie himself to the City on the Bay. Twain tried to keep the Great Man around Nevada by arranging some tours, but Ward begged off. Some of those towns Twain was touting for a tour had a habit of executing theatrical personages who didn't quite measure up. In Bodie, for example, a phrenologist who read bumps on the noggin and recited Byron had gotten himself shot in the middle of a stanza of "Childe Harold."

Ward's announced departure was good news for Joe Goodman, whose two celebrity newsmen had all but abandoned their livelihood. The compositors told me that Twain's scribblings had become indecipherable as a result of all this festivity, while De Quille's hand had deteriorated into chicken tracks.

Ward booked stagecoach passage for New Year's Day, 1864, and as December waned Ward and Twain and De Quille, not to mention Joe Goodman and the whole *Enterprise* staff, set their sights on New Year's Eve and a last hurrah. The great event was to occur in a private room at Barnum's Restaurant, and nothing was to be spared.

Now that was a party, and after all these busy years the thing I most remember about it was shattered glass. I must confess that certain of the events are hazy in my mind, especially the latter portion of the evening. I vividly remember Gov. James Nye presenting Artemus Ward with a gold watch chain so heavy that Ward staggered under it. Along with it came a gaudy citation got up by Joe Goodman and our compositors naming the great monologist "Speaker of Pieces to the People of Washoe for the Term of His Natural Life."

I don't remember a whole lot after that. Only that Mumm's and similar intoxicants flowed; one corner of the room became the graveyard of bottles, champagne glasses, tumblers, jeroboams, plates, bowls, and other dubious items, including dead fowl; and I was still present in that chamber New Year's Day, too addled to retreat to my own bunk.

Artemus Ward caught the stage, and little did we imagine that his natural life would last only three more years and he would die in 1867, a few weeks shy of his thirty-third birthday.

CHAPTER 13

ighteen and sixty-four opened upon grief for the young reporter Henry Stoddard. A telegram from Judge Stoddard wended its way over the uncertain transcontinental telegraph to the offices of the *Territorial Enterprise,* and it contained hard news. My mother had died January 7 of double pneumonia, which had come on suddenly after a windy period in which the spacious old Platteville house had bled heat. It had started as catarrh and progressed swiftly. She was forty-six.

I read the somber message again and again, not really absorbing the bitter truth—that she was gone and I would never see her again. She had lived about as long as most people do, but somehow she seemed much younger in my mind. I had been away from her nearly four years.

I had no further news and knew nothing of the funeral arrangements. I wired my father acknowledging the message and asking whether he needed me. A trip overland in the dead of winter, careening from one rude station to another on the Overland Trail, would be a lengthy ordeal, but I was ready and willing to go if called. I would have to borrow money from Goodman because, truth to tell, I had squandered everything I possessed during the endless debauch of recent months. Goodman offered me time off, but I declined. I wanted to keep my mind occupied and avoid brooding about the loss of a good and generous and even-spirited woman who had nurtured a middling sort of son. There was another reason as well: the news staff of the *Enterprise* had sunk into stupefaction. Both De Quille and Twain were out of commission and spent their days staring at walls or valiantly trying to taper off by limiting themselves to one claret an hour.

I was the only functional reporter at Goodman's disposal, and I was well aware of what a sacrifice he was making when he offered me some time. I did take a day and wandered the city restlessly, finding only blankness and very little consolation in anything perched upon the flank of Sun Mountain.

Apart from the torpor of his best reporters, Goodman was enjoying the best of times. The boom had wrought page after page of advertising—and some ready cash. He and McCarthy sold a small chunk of the paper to a printer named Driscoll, a madman for mechanical improvements, and Driscoll would have none other than a new brick building down on C Street, properly surrounded by saloons and dry-goods stores, with the latest in printing equipment, including a steam press and a new job press. So change was afoot, but all of that little affected young Henry Stoddard, who filled in for the boozy Dan De Quille on the mining front and somehow kept the paper in news that wasn't days old. But the *Union*—in the person of Rice, its wiliest reporter, whom Twain dubbed "the Unreliable"—was getting the best of us day after day while Twain and De Quille practiced hair-of-the-dog.

I buried myself in work, but it did little good. I mourned, awaited news by post from my father, which never came, and kept a wary eye on the mines.

And then Adah Isaacs Menken rolled into town with a troupe playing *Mazeppa,* one of the more bizarre offerings to be illuminated by the footlights of Maguire's Opera House. The thing abounded in excess, ranging from melodramatic posturing to garish sets. But none of that prevented flocks of miners and mill men and voyeurs from laying out hard silver to watch the Menken, as she was called, perform her final and most notorious scene, in which she, feigning nudity in flesh-colored tights, was hauled to her fate on a snorting charger—no doubt rented from the livery stable.

Her illusion was altogether successful. In those dim footlights, before the days of electricity, she managed to look perfectly naked and thus enthralled those male audiences, which clapped thunderously as she vanished and the final curtain rolled down—and then reappeared in a flimsy little thing for the curtain calls, looking all the more nude as she soaked up applause.

It scandalized a few, and the proper ladies of Virginia City wouldn't be caught dead at Maguire's. It even scandalized a few gents who huffed and puffed about closing the show down—after, of course, seeing the show to make sure that what was said about it was the honest truth.

The arrival of the Menken perked up the floundering staff of the *Enterprise* right smartly. We marched into our accustomed aisle at Maguire's in full peacock feather, swooned over the lady, thumped our hands and feet during the dozen curtain calls, and repaired to the International Hotel to discuss matters over a few gallons of claret. It was no coincidence that the Menken was quartered there in a lavish suite, accompanied by retainers, her miserable husband, and assorted poodles and mutts.

Nothing like Adah Isaacs Menken had ever graced the Washoe district before, and there was no help for it but to write one review apiece rather than delegate this pleasant task to one of our number. Even our bookkeeper wrote a review. Properly lubricated and still aglow with memories of the most memorable theater we had ever witnessed, we descended on the compositors and began to scratch out our paeans to the great lady. I think Joe Goodman was pleased to see, at last, some signs of life among his knights-errant.

All of this had the effect of making our compositors grouchy and envious, and we knew there would be some delinquencies in the ranks of our printing staff about the hour of the next performance.

Our multiple reviews occupied an infamous portion of the next day's paper, and as it turned out, we all said about the same thing. We were in the presence of thespian genius. And to a man, we neglected to say a word about anyone else in the cast or the play itself. The result should have been anticipated, but we were too far gone in sentimentality to see it. The envious cast was in a pet. During the next performances they sabotaged the show, forgot lines, lost props, missed cues, and spread mayhem through the acts like printer's ink across a floor.

This, in turn, enraged Maguire, who focused on the news staff as the source of his misfortune and forthwith canceled the free row of front-center seats that we had come to believe was our birthright. That did not please Joe Goodman, who vowed, in riposte, never to review another production at Maguire's Opera House until we got our rightful fiefdom back.

The other effect of all this adulation was to turn Adah Menken into the boon companion of her journalistic admirers. We were invited to her hotel suite after her performances, and she would greet us lounging upon a tiger skin in a little robe of yellow satin, nibbling bonbons and sipping exotic spirits. On these occasions the Menken managed to banish her current husband, Orpheus Kerr, to the streets, where he wandered about in a quilted smoking jacket and something resembling a fez. The queen preferred to hold court sans the king—if that was the word for the little mouse. Often present at these affairs of state was an ingenue named Ada Clare, whose opinions on free love had been known to awaken the auditory senses in stone-deaf males.

Miss Menken became the toast not only of the entire reporting staff of the *Enterprise* but also of the whole Washoe district. She was serenaded by brass bands, presented with honorary memberships in assorted fraternal societies, and made much of by the hotel staff, which delighted in satisfying her every whim. And she did not lack whims. The gentlemen of Virginia City even named a street after her. And mysteriously, a frank portrait of the Menken—"naked to the pitiless storm"—appeared in the Sazarac Bar. Nor was that the ultimate of Washoe's fealty to the lady. A new mining company christened itself Menken Shaft & Tunnel, a name that won wicked acclaim.

The result was plain to Joe Goodman. Just as he was pulling his editorial staff into fighting trim, the Menken arrived and wrought new havoc. He himself was one of Menken's acolytes, so he could scarcely blame the rest of us for neglecting our duties and turning in slapdash and largely fictitious stories. There wasn't much he could do about it. Even I, his rock, had abandoned my duties wherever possible to spend a lustful moment in the presence of female divinity. And as for Twain and De Quille, they had both sunk into uselessness. But the paper staggered on, in part because of the ingenuity of the compositors, who knew how to stretch stories, invent news, and stuff holes with filler.

For Sam Clemens, the puritanical youth from Hannibal, the Menken was an education. She was obviously his first contact with worldly women, and his instinctive reaction was to deny what he was witnessing and focus on the Menken's great spiritual beauty.

"She's divinity. She's the soul of pure womanhood. She's the spirit of a hundred mothers," he would opine over his claret. Sam, it seemed, had not yet figured out some aspects of life, and we waited for him to express an earthier view—which he never did. But he grew moody whenever the topic came up, which was constantly.

The end came suddenly, and can be ascribed to Sam Clemens's bad aim. The Menken decided to throw a dinner to end all dinners, and engaged the International's fine chef to prepare the viands, which included quail in aspic, foie gras on toast, fillets of antelope, and oysters, along with gallons of claret. All this was to take place in the celebrated lady's suite, surrounded by every sort of diversion except her husband. Orpheus Kerr had been banished.

Henry Stoddard was not invited, lacking the celebrity of Mark Twain and Dan De Quille, and so this account is secondhand, but I believe it is a faithful one because I got the details from both men. The Toast of Two Continents had hoped for an evening of elevated conversation about the arts but instead got an evening of mining news and eventually a stanza of "The Old Gray Mare," repeatedly sung by Sam Clemens in a voice that set the dogs to howling. Virginia City was not quite the Athens of the West Coast that it pretended to be. The Menken felt that her beloved pooches ought to share in the general levity and began feeding them cognac-soaked lump sugar. In no time the mutts were in the same general condition as the mortals gathered about the Menken's commodious table—and that was a fatal defect in the evening. One of those mutts got it into his canine brain that Sam Clemens's leg was a fire hydrant, even though that particular leg was swathed in elegant cashmere trousers. Sam kicked. The Menken howled. Moments later she was rolling on the Turkish carpet, holding her bruised shin and shedding copious tears.

There were proper and profuse apologies, I'm told, but the party had stopped cold and the celebrated Mark Twain and Dan De Quille retreated to William Tell House to ponder their misfortune.

Mazeppa pulled out. The Washoe district quieted.

Twain and De Quille actually settled down to do some serious writing, and for the briefest time the *Enterprise* started looking like a competitive newspaper again. I thought maybe the troubles lay behind us, and rejoiced.

But I was wrong.

CHAPTER 14

 look back upon Sam Clemens's sojourn in Virginia City as a brief diversion. He was present less than two years, early in the city's two-decade flight to glory and oblivion. Late in 1864 he hastily decamped for San Francisco, having gotten himself into various jams, and from the metropolis on the bay he continued to send us dispatches, acting as our stringer down there in Gomorrah. And when he finally was chased out of San Francisco a year or two later he paused briefly in our town to deliver one of his monologues at Maguire's—and got himself into more trouble, or perhaps I should say his bosom companions on the *Enterprise* got him into trouble. But more of that later.

Joe Goodman, taking a long, hard look at Dan De Quille, who had sunk into chronic delirium tremens, decided that the *Territorial Enterprise*

could best use Sam's services as city editor. So Dan was deposed and Clemens given the post and a raise to forty dollars a week. I was again passed over, but by then I knew who I was—a solid reporter without the flair of the mercurial talents Goodman had collected. I minded it but consoled myself that I was contributing the substantial stuff that makes a paper prosper.

Sam seemed almost driven, as if he had to test the limits of Goodman's tolerance. Or maybe he was simply competitive: he wanted to write the best hoax of all, and he kept on trying, even though there was less space in the paper for that sort of thing now that the boom was yielding its own harvest of stories. Sam had started to drink with Steve Gillis, a man with a two-foot-wide wild streak running through him. But somehow, at least for a few weeks, the *Territorial Enterprise* ran smoothly.

The quaint quietness emboldened Joe Goodman to take a couple of weeks off and go fishing in the Sierras. Problems abounded—the construction of the new building down on C Street was causing headaches—but Goodman felt that Sam Clemens could iron them out.

But Sam couldn't. The sum total of Sam's business sense could fit in a thimble, and as the pressures built he began sending urgent missives to Goodman, imploring the fisherman to return—all of which Goodman ignored. Sam, meanwhile, had sunk into acute distemper, editing the paper on one hand and engaging in alien pursuits associated with publishing on the other. Day after day, he fired off urgent dispatches, hand-carried by the jehus of Allman and Company's stagecoaches. But no response was forthcoming from the truant floating the cold waters of Lake Tahoe.

Then, driven to extreme measures, no doubt with the connivance of Steve Gillis, Sam prepared a special edition of the paper—in fact, a single copy—and fired it off to Goodman. The edition intended only for Goodman contained a page that casually libeled nearly every prominent and powerful personage in Virginia City. It sullied the reputation of the city's most virtuous women, charged assorted gents with larceny and debauchery, and left no one of consequence unoffended. The compositors swiftly broke down the heinous stories while the regular edition hit the streets.

That did it. Goodman avalanched down the mountain, found Clemens and Gillis and me peacefully sipping lager at the Delta, and began howling.

"By God, Sam, what got into you? Are you mad?" he bawled.

"What are you talking about, Joe?" Clemens replied blandly.

"Libeling half the city. This is no hoax! We're likely to run out of town! I'm ruined!"

I watched with a certain delight as Goodman unfolded the offending sheet and popped it in front of Sam's face while waving a hysterical finger. "There! There!" he bellowed.

"I guess it got you back," the young editor said. "A few things here require your earnest concentration."

I will always remember the look on Goodman's face when he discovered he'd been had. He didn't laugh that time. He didn't take it at all kindly. He sulked back to the A Street building and irritably began being a publisher again, while Sam, Steve, and I continued to nurse our beers, steeped in smug silence.

But it was the beginning of the end for Sam. The prank emboldened him to resume his hoaxes. Soon thereafter, Goodman took off for San Francisco, recklessly leaving the paper to Clemens, though he should have known better.

During those Civil War years, an organization called the United States Sanitary Commission had been formed to nurse the sick, wounded, and disabled Union soldiers harmed by war. In some ways it was a forerunner of Clara Barton's Red Cross. It was funded by volunteer efforts across the North and actually did a great deal of good.

The prominent matrons in Carson City, the territorial capital, held a fund-raising charity ball for the Sanitary Commission and managed to raise a hefty three thousand dollars for the cause. But for some reason unknown to us they delayed sending the cash east. That was too much for our editor, and he penned a little item asserting that the cash had been diverted to "a miscegenation society somewhere in the East."

Oh, that did it. The matrons voiced their displeasure at the dastardly reportage.

Sam thought it was a pretty good jape, one that would eventually sort itself out. But it didn't.

Our rival in those days was the *Virginia Daily Union,* edited by James Laird, a man who entertained the notion he was an orator and leader of men. He took umbrage at our editor's volatile humor and retorted that the author of the insult upon Carson womanhood was, ah, untruthful.

In fact, he delivered himself of a stemwinder:

Never before in a long period of newspaper intercourse, never in any contact with a contemporary, however unprincipled he might have been, have we found an opponent, in statement or in discussion, who had no gentlemanly sense of professional propriety, who conveyed in every purpose of all his words such a

grovelling disregard for truth, decency, and courtesy as to seem
to court the distinction of being understood as a vulgar liar.

Sam felt flattered. He was in the limelight at last. The whole Washoe
district perked up.

Sales of both papers leapfrogged to new heights.

Steve Gillis informed our young editor that now he would have to
fight a duel for the sake of his honor. Of course I seconded that. We
promised Sam a fine obit if worse came to worst and told him we'd take
up a collection to plant him in the best coffin money could buy.

"I'm a writer, not a perforator," he replied. "And even less do I wish
to be perforated."

"Well, it's your reputation," I replied.

"You'll be done for here," Gillis added. "A bad joke. You'll blush
every time you enter a saloon."

Clemens listened dutifully and finally consented after we had poured
an appropriate amount of pilsner down his gullet.

He and Laird exchanged further insults, none of which were particularly poetic, original, or memorable. Honor beckoned and both editors
decided that it was in their interest not to be labeled craven cowards or
live in ignominy the rest of their lives.

Thus it came about that Sam Clemens reluctantly met Laird on the
field of honor, which was an abandoned woodlot far from town. I was
not present, not having been selected as a second, and I beg the reader
to bear with me as I report the story secondhand. Our unhappy editor,
accompanied by Gillis and Rollin Daggett of our staff, appeared at the
appointed hour. Gillis supplied the Colt's Navy revolver, standard dueling weaponry.

Gillis was a crack shot and master of small arms, and upon the
arrival of the *Union* party he casually popped a sage hen, which flopped
and died in sight of the opposing forces. Swiftly he jammed the revolver
in Sam's hand.

"Good shooting, Sam!" he cried. "Very good indeed, winging a bird
at thirty paces." He thumped our man on the back.

Laird's seconds retreated to consult with their man, informing him
that it would be certain death to go up against the crack shot from the
Territorial Enterprise. Laird decided he would prefer cowardice to certain
doom, and retreated.

All this I learned from Daggett and Gillis, in boozy detail, a few
hours later.

But it wasn't quite over. Dueling was illegal, and soon a warrant for the arrest of our youthful editor issued forth. But our friend and political ally Governor Nye let it be known that service of that dread document would be delayed for various reasons, for exactly twenty-four hours.

"I think San Francisco is wooing me," Sam said.

So that evening the *Territorial Enterprise* lost an editor who hastily boarded a California-bound stagecoach. He left Virginia City, but we were not done with him. He returned later, and I will recount all that in due course.

Looking back upon all this from the perspective of most of a lifetime, I am tempted to say that Sam Clemens's departure left a hole in our ranks and hearts. But that was not the case. We gave him a cheery send-off in the paper and returned to our business of imbibing news and spirits and dispensing news. He was, at that time, half Sam, half Mark, and responded to both. None of us dreamed that he would swiftly become this nation's foremost humorist, novelist, and slayer of dragons.

Duels were not new to the *Enterprise*. A while earlier Joe Goodman himself had gotten into one with the formidable Tom Fitch, then editor of the *Union*. Politics was at the root of it. At the constitutional convention of 1863, Fitch bolted his party, and that was all that Goodman and his *Enterprise* needed to have some fun.

Fitch, in turn, retorted that the opinions of the *Territorial Enterprise* were similar to the love of God. Goodman connected the nose of that biblical verse to the tail—"the love of God passeth all understanding"—and the duel was certain. On September 27 of that fateful year, Goodman and Fitch and their seconds drove to Ingraham's Ranch, accompanied by about half of Virginia City, most notably the sports and demimonde. And there, using a Dragoon Colt, Goodman put a .44 caliber ball into Fitch's kneecap, much to the ecstasy of the crowd. Honor had been satisfied, and the *Enterprise* cackled about it in print.

We moved over to C Street in the summer of 1864, and the Old Magnolia Bar became our editorial annex, along with a dozen other annexes within spitting distance. But as I look back I see more than a shift of address; I see a change in the paper, a pilgrimage. We were moving into a solid brick building and out of a flammable shack, and that seems a pretty good metaphor for what was happening. We were becoming respectable.

But, fortunately, not entirely.

. . . .

CHAPTER 15

I look back upon eighteen and sixty-four as the year of my first bonanza. I also remember less cheerful things about it—such as the discovery that I was as much a fool as all the speculators I had laughed at for years.

It happened in this wise. I had a drawer full of stock certificates and some deeds to feet in assorted gloryholes. These had been pressed upon me—and most every other reporter in Virginia City—by mine owners, speculators, proprietors of assorted holes in rock far from the heart of the lode, and not a few mountebanks. They wanted me to slip an item or two into the paper to the effect that they had come upon "good color" or some "promising quartz" or "a new assay was exciting its owners" or—on rare occasions—quite the opposite: the mine was in borrasca. I rarely did.

I had acquired a whole portfolio of the certificates, some of them gorgeously engraved with heroic miners, American flags, crossed pick-axes, and other voluptuary devices intended to supply a fig leaf of re-spectability to the crassest of human lusts. The usual attempt to bribe a newsman was ten shares, or a foot or two. Periodically I had examined my remarkable portfolio, choosing to pay the inevitable assessments only on producing mines. Thus all that gloryhole paper in my portfolio was suited only for starting bonfires, but it had sentimental value, and for amusement I sometimes added up the shares and feet and pro-nounced myself a millionaire.

It is also true that some of these stocks actually had value even though the mine had yet to produce a nickel's worth of ore. Hope springs eternal, and never more than among the shop girls, clerks, drum-mers, barkeeps, greengrocers, rag pickers, confidence men, and board-inghouse cooks who persuaded themselves that one or another wildcat would bear a litter. On occasion, when I had overspent my weekly twenty dollars in the watering holes of Virginia, I would extract one or another of these documents, hie myself to the nearest broker, and unload it for five or seven dollars in silver.

All in all, these tenders of stock failed to divert me from my purpose, which was to cover the mining industry just as honestly as I knew how. Which is what I told them. I swear, those who tendered these securities must have thought I was winking my eye, or perhaps they thought I was repeating some pro forma incantation required by the newsman's occult trade. But I meant it, much to the consternation of some of these entrepreneurs, who didn't get the sort of story that they thought they would.

Daily I compared notes with De Quille, whose skill at sniffing out what was going on underground was unsurpassed. Sometimes our researches would supply us with entertaining diversions, and then we would jointly pen a story. I remember on one occasion that De Quille had tracked down a bonanza in the Savage Mine while its managers were publicly groaning—to me—about declining ore reserves, seams pinching out, and all the rest of the folderol sharpers use to drive down the price of a security.

De Quille's first indication was simple enough: management wouldn't let him into the mine. That almost always meant bonanza, and he took the rebuff as a challenge. The miners remained closemouthed, but in time he did learn that four men working a face on level seven had been kept underground for two days and had not yet returned to grass.

Of course we published everything: the bonanza and the efforts of speculators and management to grab every share at the lowest possible price. The mine's managers fumed at us, roundly denounced us as a pack of liars, and threatened to bar the *Territorial Enterprise* from its portals evermore. But these threats always came to no account for the simple reason that we had become the paper of record for Comstock mining news.

My good fortune arrived with De Quille's news that the Crown Point mine had hit a major body of excellent ore, the extent of which was unknown but believed formidable because they were drifting into a broad seam—no country rock—and had pushed fifty feet or so into the massive ore body.

I hastily repaired to my portfolio and hunted up my shares—bestowed upon me during one of the Crown Point's borrasca years with the implied desire that I would pump up the prospects in print—and found that, yes, I owned exactly ten shares; I had paid the assessments, and now I was rich and getting richer by the hour.

In the space of a week, my shares had gone from a few dollars each to well over five hundred and were climbing at a dizzy pace. My net worth exceeded five thousand dollars, or about five times my annual salary. I began to inflate like a rooster and walked about the newsroom on stilts.

We were, at that time, close to our move down to the new red brick plant on C Street. A much more comfortable dormitory awaited us there, but I knew at once that my good fortune had bought me a ticket to a rooming house and privacy.

The only question was whether to sell all ten shares or just one and let the other nine ride to the crest of the boom. I haunted the brokerages, gimlet-eyed, learning of every trade within moments. There was sudden thirst for any Crown Point share, and its owner could literally negotiate a price, often doing better privately than a broker could do by posting the shares on his chalk board and accepting bids.

I decided to wait. In fact, I concluded that it was the better part of wisdom not to sell at all, but to let my ten-share bonanza double and redouble and then sell as soon as Dan De Quille ascertained the assay values and extent of the new bonanza. There were, indeed, some heart-stopping pauses en route upward, when I wished I had unloaded the previous day. But those passed, and the weather at the Crown Point continued to be sunny and warm.

The stock did double, and by late eighteen and sixty-four I was worth about ten thousand dollars and could almost consider retiring. I hunted down the best quarters, there being no sense in depriving myself of creature comforts. I did stop short of renting a suite in the International Hotel but settled on a rear apartment in a fine private home on South B Street, up in the hoity-toity district populated by superintendents, brokers, lawyers, speculators, ice merchants, and weighty men like that. To pay for my first month's fifty-dollar rent, I sold some worked-over gloryhole stuff, shares of the Sides, the Central, White & Murphy, the California, and the Mount Blanc, for a few dollars. The only reason these dogs had any life was because they weren't far from the Ophir. But they had been poked and probed half to death, and only the Central, hard by the Ophir, had yielded any ore, and not much of it. Later on, in eighteen and sixty-seven, some mining men combined most of these two-bit holdings into a mine called the Consolidated Virginia—another dismal prospect—but I'm getting ahead of my story again.

My landlady, Mrs. Dillon, was a Temperance enthusiast, I later found out, which caused no end of problems. Not a drop of spirits was I permitted upon pain of immediate eviction. But the place was uncommonly cheerful, with fine views down upon the business district—our new brick plant was visible—and below, the great hoisting works of the mines. The whole city lay before me, from the Chinamen's quarter in the northeast to the divide off to the south separating Gold Hill from my metropolis. In view of the number of saloons that stayed open around-the-clock, I decided that the absence of spirits in my congenial room was not too great a burden to bear.

I began to live in a pretty high style for a newspaper reporter. Barnum's Restaurant most nights, the bar at the International Hotel, Turkish baths, Moselle wine, new ready-made suits from Roos Brothers Clothiers, a trip to the Sierra. And most of it was on the cuff. I'd pay later, when I cashed in my shares.

But then one day I received a quarterly dividend check that rattled my skull. Each share had yielded $60 and I was $600 richer. I promptly paid my accounts and still had $200 left over. In three months, there would be another, and then another, and another. In the space of a year my ten shares would supply me with $2,400, or about two and a half times what my newspaper salary was yielding me.

Of course I knew that such windfalls don't last; mines emptied themselves. But who could say what the future might bring? If the Crown Point had struck an ore body of this magnitude, why not others at lower levels? I was an affluent man. I could use some of this awesome wealth to buy shares in proven mines and keep on multiplying my wealth.

De Quille cautioned me one day that it looked to him like the end was in sight and maybe I should get out. The Crown Point lode had now been pierced from end to end, top to bottom; its extent was known, its richness ascertained. Dan thought that the entire pocket might be aboveground in six months and those gorgeous dividends would drop soon after. He also thought that word was going to leak out, that management would start selling shares at any moment, and that I'd be smart to take my profit.

I disagreed. The Crown Point stock had climbed another notch or two. And after all, what the public didn't know wasn't going to hurt me. Every shop clerk on the Comstock wanted more Crown Point. But I did decide that when the stock reached $2,000 a share I'd sell out. Twenty thousand dollars for my ten shares seemed a mighty handsome and just recompense for all the time I had held onto it and paid assessments.

De Quille just sipped his lager and shook his head.

"Henry, I have served warning. I have entreated over good beer. I have given you an expert opinion garnered by years of observation and a recent trip into the bowels of the Crown Point, right to the two hundred, three hundred, four and five hundred levels. I have been a friend and counselor. But now I retreat. It is as if you cannot hear or see or consider. Be forewarned."

He wouldn't speak to me all that evening and all the next December day, while the Washoe zephyrs stung and a storm lowered on the distant

Sierras. I did think about his warning but concluded he was too cautious. Fortunes aren't won by the fainthearted.

I resolved to keep an eagle eye on the mine and on the share price, just because I valued De Quille's judgment. Thus fortified with philosophy, and employing a veteran's assessing gaze at the Comstock's bonanza and borrasca, I chose to do nothing.

CHAPTER 16

eader, you already know how this episode in the life of Henry Stoddard will end, so I won't, from this perspective decades later, try to make a suspense of it as if I were some cunning romantic novelist keeping a reluctant reader snared in his coils. It wasn't but a few days after Dan De Quille's warning that Crown Point's stock collapsed. Its managers, concluding that the jig was up, began furtive sales even while announcing—quite mendaciously—the existence of new proven reserves of excellent quality, mostly smelting ore.

Smelting ore, of course, was the variety of such richness that it could be reduced without costly milling, and thus the announcement was intended to ignite new lusts and greed, keeping stock prices inflated even as those villains sold down their private holdings. Forgive me, reader—the whole business smelt.

Worse, I believed them. I, a veteran reporter of monstrous shams and frauds, a cynic and skeptic, believed them. Those ten shares did it. Those perfidious pieces of a rich mine had blinded me to the point that my judgment was no better than a bartender's or shop girl's.

My downfall came about in this wise: a certain stockbroker I knew, George Marye, who operated from a brokerage chamber on C Street, had for years whispered inside information to me, and I in turn had made good use of it in my daily coverage of the mines. He had made a specialty of small sales to people who could ill afford to lose money, and my columns, which regularly exposed the shams and greed of the mining moguls, were of considerable value to him and his clients. It was not altruism or rectitude that inspired his tips but simple calculation. I believed that Marye was one of the more honorable of his dubious breed.

In January of eighteen and sixty-five, while the Washoe zephyrs blew the heat out of every ill-fitted building on the Comstock, he had observed an expanding flow of odd lots of Crown Point stock appearing on the market. He saw at once what was afoot and let me know.

"George," I replied, "that may be. But there are always people who get out early."

"These are being unloaded by management," he replied mildly.

"You don't know that."

He sighed. "There are things one knows and can't prove."

"Well, keep an eye on it and let me know."

But it was already too late. By the time Marye had sorted out what was happening, much of Crown Point's stock had been unloaded at enormous profit onto the unsuspecting public. During the next days the price slid steadily, falling below $2,000 and then pausing at $1,600. I breathed my relief: this had been just one of those flapdoodles, and a bit of good news would drive the price up again. In fact, I contemplated buying a few more shares on margin.

I told De Quille one sodden evening at the Old Magnolia that the decline was over, the Crown Point stock had stabilized, and, in any case, the mine had not cut its dividend, which would be the one sure sign of trouble.

De Quille responded with an angry silence, which seemed odd in so genial a drinking companion.

The next day the dividend was cut to five dollars a quarter, and the bottom fell out of the stock. It paused at about two hundred a share and then drifted slowly downward again. I thought to buy more, but when I confided my plan to Marye he was aghast.

"I will not do that," he said. "Go to some other broker. I'd rather lose a bit of business than assist you in your folly."

That was a remark I would long remember.

Stubbornly I hung on and watched my ten shares bottom at less than a thousand for the lot and the dividends vanish. That still wasn't bad, considering that the shares had been dumped in my lap. But the cold, hard reality was that I had thrown away a small fortune and had done it out of the same greed and folly that I had laughed at in others. I, a seasoned mining reporter, had done that!

It was a sobering event in my young life. I might have had a $20,000 nest egg to buoy me through life, save for my stubborn greed. The worst part of it was that I knew better. I had witnessed countless such debacles. I had watched hundreds of Washoe hustlers, from grandees to madams, make the same mistake, always driven by the hope that springs eternal. But from this vantage point, in a new century, I look back upon it as a priceless lesson—if only I had learned it. As you will see, I didn't master that lesson, and I made the same mistake again and again in the years ahead.

I was, actually, better off than I had been, resplendent in a new wardrobe, quartered in an apartment in one of the better neighborhoods, and I could look back upon innumerable glasses of the best Madeira and the finest Mumm's, the sweetest viands, the most sublime Havanas, and even the acquaintance—which had previously been denied to me— of several unattached and lovely young women, mostly the daughters of superintendents, brokers, merchants, and so forth.

I was not a happy man. And all the money I had squandered had bought me only pleasure and diversion. I had that in abundance. The Washoe district specialized in drink and cuisine and male companionship and comedy. I had enjoyed an abundance of them all, but now, in the moment of reckoning, I found myself mainly bewildered. When I peered into the abyss, I saw very little joy in Henry Stoddard and I wondered, not for the first time in my half-bought life, what I really wanted, and what good I was, and why I had been sent into the world.

I endured that bitter winter of sixty-five by performing my tasks almost by rote. I didn't carouse with Gillis or Wright or Joe Goodman but held myself apart and spent my time huddled about my parlor stove, squandering costly firewood recklessly. Most of it was provided by Chinamen who were reduced to digging out roots in the surrounding mountains because the Washoe had stripped away everything else and was consuming scores of cords a day from the distant Sierras. But I paid little heed to prices; my need to be warm overrode all prudence, so I stuffed the Chinamen's roots into my stove and bought more.

"Come on, Stoddard; we're going to feast at Barnum's tonight," Goodman announced. But I declined, saying that I wished to read.

"Henry, we've all gotten stung playing the mines. Set it aside, now. You've been wandering around the shop like a headless ghost."

I thought the allusion was apt, but I still declined his offer. He stared long at me.

The new *Enterprise* building was narrow, long, and frightfully clean— but time and black ink would improve that swiftly. Driscoll had ordered a steam press and boiler, but until then we were producing our paper on an elderly hand-cranked flatbed. We did have new fonts, and the *Territorial Enterprise* had a perky, fresh look about it that gave it an additional edge over its rivals.

I surveyed the bunks at the rear and wondered how long it would take for me to surrender my comfortable digs and start living on company beans and bunks and twenty a week, enduring snoring compositors and the foul exudations of unwashed male carcasses. Prices were as dear as ever and varied wildly with the weather and season, because every item consumed by the city was dragged up the endless grades in wagons drawn by muscle. It was a constant hazard of living on the Comstock that now and then an item couldn't be found or purchased for any price.

The town's water supply was becoming increasingly precarious and was adequate only during the spring runoff, when creek water could be diverted into the town's meager reservoirs. The rest came from glory-holes upslope that had tapped into an aquifer. The stuff was well nigh poisonous, and rumor abounded that the citizens of Washoe were treated to daily doses of arsenic or mercury or other salts that poisoned flesh and weakened bones and addled brains. I tried to remedy that by drinking as much imported beer as possible.

One overcast day, with snow spitting out of the rug of clouds locked on Sun Mountain, I decided to pack up. The Comstock held no allure for a worn-out and grumpy Henry Stoddard. The city was still in the blush of its first great boom, although anyone who knew the mines could understand that the clock was ticking and in two or three years the place would house ghosts. I would simply depart ahead of the herd.

I thought perhaps to go back to Platteville and see my father while he still lived. I had lost my mother without the chance to say good-bye, and now I feared such a thing might happen again. His letters had suggested he was ailing. A winter trip back to the States would be an ordeal, so I hesitated.

Reader, you are accustomed to thinking that the continent can be easily negotiated by catching a fast express train going a mile a minute and riding a luxurious Pullman palace car for a few days, but in eighteen and sixty-five the only thing that bound us to civilization back east was a frail and faltering telegraph line. It would be four more years before rails linked West and East. The choices were to travel by sea to Panama and risk its tropical fevers or travel the Overland Trail by marathon laps of a Concord stagecoach at great discomfort, with acute taxation of the wallet, sleep, and digestive system en route. If I sold my flagging Crown Point shares I would have about enough to take the next mail steamer to Panama and another to New York—or Yankee-held New Orleans and up the great river if the South collapsed and a riverboat could pass unmolested.

Perhaps a respite of a few weeks in Platteville, in that spacious old home looking out upon the serene valley, the hardwood-covered slopes, the rushing creeks, among stable, cheerful, industrious people who avoided excess in all things, would heal my soul.

The notion awakened a certain ambivalence in me—could a place, even an ancestral home, wreak a miracle? But I was so weary of the

Washoe that I determined to set my course for civilization and abandon the perfidious City on the Hill.

And there was another reason: I wanted a family and the prospects for starting one on the Comstock were about zero if one could offer little more than twenty a week and a hovel somewhere. I had no answer for the great metaphysical questions about my purpose in life. But on a lesser plane, I knew what I wanted: to share my life with a sweetheart and achieve some security before the long darkness.

So I gave Joe Goodman notice.

CHAPTER 17

oe Goodman surprised me. How well I remember it, because it was another of those defining moments in my life and one of those memories that refresh my soul, even now.

"Henry, I'm not going to let you walk out if I can help it," he replied when I told him I intended to leave his employ in a fortnight. "I'll give you a five-dollar-a-week raise."

"I appreciate that, Joe," I mumbled, not sure what was the best course for me. "Let me think about it."

"You do that," he replied. "Set aside this evening, because I'm treating you to dinner at Barnum's."

I agreed to that. After we put the paper to bed we would have a late meal at the best eatery on the Comstock. I took it for a little farewell send-off.

But again, I was wrong. We were late that night because of a billiard hall murder, a knifing on D Street, and a frail's suicide. She had executed herself by drinking a bottle of carbolic acid and expired in agony. Gillis had vanished, Wright had imbibed too much tarantula juice before the sun crossed the yardarm, and Rollin Daggett was busy, so I collected the information and put three stories together, scribbling them with a compositor looking over my shoulder and setting lines as fast as I penned them. That drained me.

It put me in even a lower mood and inspired dreams of flight from the gaudy, shabby, tormented city on Sun Mountain. It was an inauspicious beginning for Goodman's dinner. I noted sourly that he hadn't invited the rest of the staff, as was the usual case for a send-off, so this bare-bones farewell was a pretty good indication of what my worth was to the publishers.

It was ten before I met Goodman in the Barnum's bar and we seated ourselves. The place certainly deserved its reputation: snowy linen graced the tables, and we could usually choose from an amazing number of dishes, some of which weren't available during this midwinter period, when the passes between the Washoe and California were stopped tighter than a corked jeroboam of Dom Perignon. In fact, it had dawned on me that I would have to wait for the roads to the coast to uncongeal before I could embark for Panama and the States.

But Barnum's managed some marinaded antelope flank, twice-baked potatoes, cream of mushroom soup, Parker House rolls, and some greens grown down in Carson City by a demented florist.

Goodman eyed me speculatively, noting my dark spirits, and ordered four flagons of Moselle. He obviously was in a spendthrift mood. I wasn't in much of a mood for jabber, so he did the talking as we downed the wine and tackled the plates du jour. I liked him. Without fail, he presented the world with a groomed, trim persona and urbane countenance. Joe Goodman could discourse pleasantly about anything literary, and that is how he filled the stretching gaps while he treated his departing and rather surly employee to a little send-off. On this occasion he dilated at length about his friend Ambrose Bierce, who, I took it, was something of a literary swashbuckler.

About the time that Barnum's served up quince pies and pungent java, Joe got around to the issue. "You're not happy with the paper?" he asked blandly.

"The paper's fine; it's Virginia City that's grating on me."

He nodded. "It's like a stage set," he said.

"Yes, all illusion and no substance."

"And people are perched here ready to fly away. We all think about it. People even consider their friendships tentative because no one knows when the mines'll shut down."

"Yes. It's been hard to make real friends. I've acquaintances galore, but no confidants . . . and no prospects for a family."

"Yes, that's the heart of it. The ratio's about four men for every woman now, I've heard."

"And reporters hardly attract their attention."

He smiled. "You'd have that raise if you want to stay. I think, with a bit of effort, you could sell to some literary magazines. And the East is always hungry for correspondents. We're like Tibet to people on the Atlantic seaboard. You have to remember where we are—nowhere."

"Joe, deduct wives, children, elderly widows, and the frails from the female population, and the true ratio must be about a hundred men for every available maiden anywhere near my age. I'm tired of that."

"It's not the best place for a man with domestic instincts," he agreed. "But where there's a will there's a way—"

"I've thought about your offer and can't accept. But I would stay on for a few weeks, until the passes open and I can get to San Francisco."

"I'm disappointed, Henry. You're the most reliable man I have. The paper would really suffer if you left."

I didn't buy the flattery. "Well, thanks for bucking me up, Joe."

"I'm dead serious."

"You're being kind. I've pretty well pegged it out. You know exactly where your circulation comes from. Every time Dan De Quille signs a column, people laugh. When Sam Clemens was here, he did the same thing and people bought up the entire run of the paper."

Joe stared into space a moment. "Henry, we had three breaking stories tonight. Who got the facts and wrote them up?"

I nodded. It was good to be appreciated. I was indeed his most reliable man. Maybe my prose was meat-and-potatoes, but at least I got the stories together and could move fast if I had to.

"If you're not happy at the paper, maybe we could work something out. Take time off, something like that. When the passes clear, take a trip to San Francisco."

"I've been happy, Joe. It's the city, not the paper. This place—a lot of things bother me. No trees. No grass. Naked dirt. Bare mountains. Mean winds. Aw, none of that's the reason. I'm sick of seeing the worst of people, the lawlessness and greed, the hollow lives squandered in dissipation, the quest for loot of any sort, the shabby scheming, the crooked brokers and managers, the broken bodies of the miners who get pulled out of the pits about once a week. And the uncertainty. That's worst of all. I didn't understand how it affects everyone until my bonanza vanished before my eyes. One day I was rich, the next day . . ." I shrugged.

"Write about it, Henry. Write a piece for *Golden Era* and I'll send it to them with my endorsement."

"But not the *Enterprise*." I grinned wolfishly.

"I'm not a masochist and I like profit," Joe retorted. He signaled for a refill of the Moselle.

The wine was reaching me in spite of the hearty meal. That was fine with me. In vino veritas.

"It's worse than that," I confided. "I haven't the faintest idea why I'm alive or what good I am to anyone. When the Crown Point stock bottomed, so did I."

A Washoe zephyr snarled through town, rattling wood and gusting straight through Barnum's.

Goodman smiled. "That's not my department. If it's the paper, I can help you. Send you down to Carson to keep an eye on the politicians. Give you new assignments. And, most of all, let you know your work is valuable to us. If it's the Washoe, I can't help you. That's your monkey. But I can point out a few things. It isn't as mean as it seems. Every time a miner dies, every man in the pits contributes something for his widow and his children and his burial. Every time a man's injured, it's the same. This town's given more to the United States Sanitary Commission than any other its size. We're optimists. When we crash, we pick ourselves up, laugh, and keep on going. We're not quitters. There are people here I'm proud to know—and you're one, Henry."

We left it at that. I told him I'd think about it a day or two. I was unable to make up my mind about anything and even wondering whether journalism was the right craft for me. I knew I wasn't much of a writer. My sentences were awkward and I never hit upon the choice word, the enchanted phrase, the way De Quille and Twain did.

Goodman clapped me on the back as we braved the bitter night and told me he hoped I'd stick around. He hunkered into his greatcoat and plunged into the night, his figure occasionally caught by lamplight from windows. And then he was gone. He had tried. I felt flattered but no happier or certain of what to do.

I felt the wind howl down my neck and up my sleeves and knew I should head for my room. A black blank lay overhead, the stars snuffed by overcast. There was nothing to navigate by in the world, or in my soul. I thought of walking over to Cad Thompson's and the hell with the consequences. But I knew I would end up more miserable and lonely than I was, standing there without goal or compass on a bitter January night.

Instead, I patrolled C Street, virtually the only soul out and about, peering into yellow-lit saloons, hurrying by dark hardwares and broker- ages and dry-goods stores. Saloons were all Virginia City boasted, sa- loons by the score, of every description, the parlors and dining rooms of the miners. Take away the city's watering holes and there'd be no city, just a bleak mountainside riddled with holes.

Half-frozen, I retreated to my room, which was almost as cold as the whole outdoors, and waited impatiently while a sluggish parlor stove shot timid heat into the heavy chill. I finally wrapped myself in the blanket from my bed and settled beside the stove, awaiting some sort of hospitality. But life on the Comstock was always cold and inhos- pitable.

I sat there, thankful that Joe had made a stab at keeping me. He had made me feel better. My mind drifted. I wondered what I would end up doing after visiting my family at Platteville. I supposed I would end up reporting dog bites and truancies on some small-town weekly around there. The thought depressed me all the more.

My thoughts drifted back to wicked, lively, exuberant, sybaritic Virginia City. Yes, it was a greedy town that catered to every lust and weakness, that cruelly used and spit out the weak and innocent, that robbed widows of their mites and stole from orphans and broke the bones of young men. Yes, it was all that. And it had become the literary capital of the Far West, a gourmand's paradise, a drinker's Eden, a womanizer's Elysian Fields, and a newsman's delight. Then, suddenly, in the glow of the stove, I knew I would stay. In all of mortal history there had been no place like Virginia City. It had drawn to its bosom not only the flower of American literature but also the most brilliant entrepreneurs, the world's finest mining engineers, the most gifted miners, the most brilliant tinkerers, and all of them achieving the impossible, refining and improving the means to bring ore to the surface and extract its precious content.

The real genius of Virginia City flourished in sheds filled with blueprints, in blacksmith shops where canny men hammered out new designs, in managers' offices where pencil pushers calculated how to bring a hundred cords of wood to their boilers, in pits where men deep underground perfected the wooden frameworks that would keep millions of tons of rock suspended above fragile human flesh, in laboratories where chemists taught themselves how to milk the obdurate rock of its treasure. Other mining towns would come and go, but none would ever match the Comstock. I knew, suddenly, that I was witnessing something so magical, so rare, so awesome, that for centuries to come Virginia City would be a byword and a marvel.

The city itself, the young harridan, gaudy in its paint, shabby and beautiful, brilliant and absurd, had seduced me. In the morning I would tell Joe that the answer was yes, and yes, and yes again. And I would accept his lousy five-dollar raise.

· ·

returned to my work, determined to stay in Virginia City until the bloom in her cheeks faded and she began to rouge her face to hide her decay. But she was not decaying. Indeed, rich ores were hoisted to the surface each day from what seemed inexhaustible lodes deep under the bustling town.

I focused anew on the processes and innovations that were making Virginia City the world's laboratory of mining techniques. I'm sure all of that would seem dull to a modern reader, and yet they were exciting in their day. I will describe some of these only briefly, and largely for the record, because I know, reader, what really interests you: gossip, great men, loose women, scandals, disasters, and death.

I would quote from my own clippings, which I had pasted into fourteen big albums, but I no longer have them. Almost every word I wrote on the Comstock was lost, as I will explain eventually. So you will be spared some of those drab stories about ores and profits and equipment.

In March of eighteen and sixty-five we did have a disaster, a giant cave-in at Gold Hill, in which the upper levels of three mines, the rock above them weakened by spring meltwater, suddenly thundered down, splintering support timbers. But no one was injured, because crews were working the ores at much lower levels.

I did interview a young man sent out in eighteen and sixty-four by the Bank of California, in San Francisco, to start up a Virginia City branch and try to garner some of the lucrative lending business enjoyed by other financial institutions in our city. His name was William Sharon, and he erected a solid branch bank and hustled into the lending racket. At that time, porcine bankers were lending to mine owners and mill men at the rate of 3 to 5 percent a month—which was high even for the riskiest of loans. Mills had to work at full capacity just to pay the interest, and any slackening of ore, or loss of business, swiftly resulted in a mine or mill sliding into arrears.

The devious Sharon coolly began lending at 2 percent a month and soon had all the business he could handle. What's more, he was willing to collateralize his loans with the mines and mills themselves, even though a mine could plummet to virtual worthlessness in days and an abandoned mill could fall apart in a few months.

Soon after he arrived, Sharon found himself in possession of a failed mill. That did not faze the young man. He had grown up in a Quaker family, like De Quille, abandoned a youthful dream to become a boatman, studied law, and by a series of misadventures landed in San Francisco, where he had proved himself as an upcoming young clerk at the Bank of California. I liked the small, slim, tidy, and extremely reserved young man, although it was hard to get an ounce of news out of him.

"Now that you've a mill, what are you going to do with it?" I asked him.

He remained silent so long that I supposed he wouldn't answer. "Dismantle it," he said. "Mills are worth only about five cents on the dollar. But this one has Wheeler mullers and pans, and I can sell all of those."

Zenas Wheeler, a California tinkerer, had conquered one of the difficulties in reducing ore. Mullers and pans were giant iron mortars and pestles used to reduce the pulp, consisting of rough broken rock mixed with water and chemicals, into a virtual paste so fine that the amalgamating mercury could combine with the precious metals in the rock. Until Wheeler found a solution, the heavy, rotating muller had driven the pulp to the periphery of the pan by centrifugal force. But he had evolved a combination of mulling shoes and plates that continuously worked the pulp back under the shoes of the mullers, in the process shearing rock into particles as fine as talcum powder. This, in turn, made the extraction of precious metals from the ore more efficient, which raised the profit from a ton of ore and also increased reserves by making more low-grade ore potentially valuable. So popular had these devices become that the California foundry producing them managed an output of one a day.

I had followed this major innovation in my reporting, along with the patent lawsuit that had followed, which Zenas Wheeler won.

Those things fascinated me—there were dozens of such innovations transforming mining everywhere on earth, all of them inspired by the awesome bonanza on the Comstock. They might simply be called Yankee ingenuity, but whatever the case, most of what was developed on the Comstock in the sixties and seventies is still in use today, for nothing better has been invented.

I thanked Sharon for his time. Later he would be still harder to reach and I would have to resort to more surreptitious means to report his doings.

Be patient, reader. I know how much technology bores most people, but in eighteen and sixty-five it became my passion and I haunted the mines and mills, examining innovations, reporting them, studying the failures and successes, making myself the authority for everything that was happening aboveground, even as William Wright, or Dan De Quille—I scarcely knew which of his names he preferred—was making himself the Comstock's best informed source of what was going on down on the deepest levels, five hundred, six hundred, and even a thousand feet into the bowels of the earth. I had a good sense of what innovations would prove profitable and thus acquired a modest following among the engineers and not a few speculators who read the paper. And between us, we had turned the *Territorial Enterprise* into the paper that got it right.

But Wright was Joe Goodman's star and I the back-room man. Even though the erstwhile Quaker downed ardent spirits in amazing quantities he remained the literary light of the Comstock, regularly writing rich and comic columns for the paper, as well as *Golden Era.* Wright was in rare form that year, producing one wild yarn after another, including one that won him wide acclaim: "The Wonder of the Age: A Silver Man."

This purported to be an account of a discovery of a human body that had petrified into almost pure silver at the Hot Springs Lead in some mountains near the California border:

> In removing the body from its resting place, an arm was broken off. It was from observing the peculiar appearance of the fractured arm that Mr. Kuhlman—who is not only a good practical miner, but an excellent chemist and mineralogist—was induced to make a careful assay of pieces taken from the severed limb.
>
> When it was announced to the miners that what they had looked upon as merely a most remarkable petrifaction was a mass of sulphuret of silver slightly mixed with copper and iron (in the shape of pyrites), they were at first incredulous. But repeated and careful tests, made before their own eyes, at length convinced them that such was the indisputable fact.

Dan De Quille went on to demonstrate that the phenomenon was worldwide, and thus in Sweden a miner who had died sixty years earlier had been transformed into iron pyrites.

I could quote much more, because the piece is a long one. But my sole desire is to permit you, reader, to sample a little of William Wright's bottomless humor. Maybe someday this arsenal of wit will be gathered between two book covers instead of scattered through dozens of newspapers and magazines. I marvel that he wrote these pieces year in and year out, one upon another, and yet continued to function as the paper's editor, imbibe spirits in Bunyanesque style, and tomcat about Virginia City, sometimes with Alf Doten, who was variously an editor or reporter for most of the papers in Virginia and Gold Hill and a devotee of Bacchus.

Probably the most famous of Dan De Quille's masterpieces was penned in eighteen and seventy-four. It was, actually, very short for a scribbler as loquacious as De Quille. It is the story of one Jonathan Newhouse, who invented a solar armor intended to keep him cool while crossing Death Valley. The special attire, which included a helmet, was lined with sponge, and before crossing the burning desert the sponge was to be soaked, thus keeping the wearer cool by evaporation. Additional water could be pumped into the sponge as needed:

> Mr. Newhouse went down to Death Valley determined to try the experiment of crossing the terrible place in his armor. He started out into the valley one morning from the camp nearest its borders telling the men at the camp as they laced his armor on his back that he would return in two days. The next day an Indian who could speak but a few words of English came to the camp in a great state of excitement. He made the men understand that he wanted them to follow him. At the distance of about twenty miles out into the desert the Indian pointed to a human figure seated against a rock. Approaching, they found it to be Newhouse still in his armor. He was dead and frozen stiff. His beard was covered with frost and—though the noonday sun poured down its fiercest rays—an icicle over a foot in length hung from his nose. There he had perished miserably because his armor had worked but too well, and because he was laced up from behind where he could not reach the fastenings.

Ah, that was joy. And so was a later response from the *Daily Telegraph* in London, which had swallowed it whole. That was, of course, the occasion for yet another De Quille masterpiece, plus a gaudy celebration in Virginia City. It was regarded as no small feat to flummox one of the most august newspapers in the world.

But I have a bad habit of getting ahead of myself, this time by almost a decade. Such is my confusion that I failed to mention that we had become a state in October eighteen and sixty-four—something Joe Goodman had ardently campaigned for. We celebrated with a special edition of the *Enterprise,* and the rest of the Comstock celebrated in the usual fashion. Statehood was a personal triumph for Joe Goodman and our powerful paper. Our state motto was "Battle Born," because statehood had come to us as the direct result of the Civil War. The Union needed our silver and the Republicans needed our votes, and so the deed was done in Congress.

In eighteen and sixty-five the terrible war in the East ended. We had scarcely been aware of the war, though we had fragmentary news of it coming over the fragile line of the overland telegraph. That was the occasion for another party. I use the phrase delicately. According to later chroniclers there were no papers to be had for two days because there were no printers, compositors, reporters, or editors sober enough to publish one. That made little difference, because few citizens were sober enough to read one. I wouldn't know about that. By the end of the third day Virginia City was dangerously low on whiskey, or so I have learned. I don't remember much of it.

And then we received word of the assassination of President Lincoln. It came to us in fragments. The first dispatch read: "His Excellency President Lincoln was assassinated at the theater tonight."

The next one reported that Lincoln had died at eight-thirty in the morning and Secretary Stewart had died at nine. But that was contradicted by a later report, and then the Western Union wire was silent and stayed silent for a day.

We published an extra, though we had but little news.

Later we filed into Maguire's Opera House to hear Bishop Whitaker of St. Paul's Episcopal church read the Litany for the Dead. The war had come to us after all.

CHAPTER 19

he straight, unvarnished truth was that the great majority of single men on the Comstock were glad there were few women around. And I suspect most of the married men felt the same way.

Most of those who had flocked to the mining district luxuriated in male company, which they readily found in all of the hundred saloons dotting Virginia City. There, at tables or hunkered over the bar, they swapped yarns, shared speculations, befriended one another, and never worried much about decorum, taboo words, curfews, schedules, bringing home the bacon, nagging wives, boredom in the parlor, female shopping sprees, bawling babies, sudden doctor bills, turning down an offer to see a racy comedy at Maguire's Opera House, and all the rest.

My impression of the male saloon life in Virginia, even now, after three decades have elapsed, was one of hearty camaraderie, punctuated now and then by brawls, fisticuffs, and rowdy politics. Women would have wrecked it all. So joyous was the evening life at such spas as the Delta or Crystal Palace that most places would not even employ serving girls for fear of damping the fun. The saloons were a tonic for sagging spirits, bouts of loneliness, and even financial distress, because a broke miner or speculator or man-about-town could cadge all the drinks he wanted any night and when he was flush he would buy drinks for any man who was momentarily down-and-out.

The tinhorns ran their green-oilcloth tables, but they didn't do a big business. Why fool around with faro or monte or roulette—in which the odds ran against a player—when one could gamble on mining stocks? A man with ten dollars burning a hole in his britches could buy ten shares of a wildcat and sit back and see if the shares whelped.

So gladsome was the nightlife that even the married wretches, such as the Cornishmen, often slipped out for a few mugs of beer. They were flush, earning top dollar, and why not? But they were men apart, men who would pull out their turnip watches, stare, and vanish into the night while the rest of us were just cranking up the evening and the pianist was just beginning to loosen the ivories.

Were the men on the Comstock opposed, on principle, to the company of women? Of course not. In the back of their minds they all knew that sooner or later, after the mines wound down or when they had a pocketful of dollars, they would settle down. But oh, how they connived to delay that day. Some of them did so by sending regular checks to wives back east instead of bringing their spouses and families to the Comstock.

I imagine the majority of these gents visited the restricted district—actually, public ladies resided all over the Comstock and not just on D Street—whenever the itch overtook them. But this was something scarcely discussed. I cannot remember any such talk. Were we actually prudes? No. We saw such visits to ladies of the night as momentary departures from our male camaraderie. When any of us did talk about women, it was usually sentimentally and phrased in terms of domestic comforts: laundered and mended clothing, tasty meals, clean parlors, and never more than that. For most of the roistering, happy males on the Comstock the notion of female companionship was alien. How could any happy male befriend a woman—apart from the necessary romancing of a sweetheart?

Still, men had their hungers, and now and then they would sally—more often singly than in company—to the Alhambra Melodeon, where they could watch bawdy comedies and scantily dressed ladies in shows such as *Lady Godiva,* or to several saloons, such as the Bon Ton or Grecian Bend, that featured pretty serving girls who would usually bargain for a night if someone offered enough silver. The various troupes that played the theaters usually numbered a few tarts who were available—for a stiff price—to stage door Johnnies. These entertainers would perform private *tableaux vivants* for gents who wished to peek but not play. So male society was never enough, though we all pretended it was.

We formed what seemed warm friendships at the time, and yet I, for one, knew that the shifting tides on the Comstock would swiftly separate us all. What's more, these friendships weren't really intimate. I cannot recall one of my saloon pals baring his soul to me, or confessing the slightest joy or unhappiness, or expressing his dreams, or inviting me into the parlor of his mind.

Nor did I ever open my private thoughts to all these drinking companions who drifted through my life, a dozen names, fifty names, people who were at the bar one night and gone the next. We didn't talk much about ourselves. I don't think ten people on the Comstock could name the town or state I came from.

I can't remember a serious political discussion; enthusiasm for the Union, for the Republicans, for freedom, for getting rich, for low taxes, sufficed for conversation, sweeping us along each evening. I can't remember any serious public policy discussions even in Carson City, where our politicos gathered.

We talked about boxing, dogs, horse racing, mules, crops, stage and freight service, mine accidents, narrow escapes, wildcat mines, mining machinery, ore, and the price of everything. If we had a piece of ore, or a question about ore, we hunted down Metalliferous Murphy, renowned ore expert. Give him a bit of ore and he'd lick it, cock his head, and pronounce the inevitable verdict: "This *spicimen* is highly *mitalliferous!*" When Metalliferous thought well of a mine, he went whole hog. "That one won't run out in *tin* thousand years," he'd say.

So there was our life, and we loved it. I look back upon it with fondness. I know now that women gather in flocks in much the same manner, delighted not to have to cope with males, especially males demanding one thing and another, like laundry and meals. But back then, in the whirling evenings, drifting from the Delta to the Old Magnolia to the El Dorado to Spiro's, we scarcely noticed that our social life was unique. Truly the Comstock offered a life that could be found nowhere else.

But I remained restless. I had grown up amid pleasant domesticity in sedate Wisconsin. Evening meals hadn't been dull or hurried affairs.

My father and mother talked, joked, poured their attentions on each of us while teaching us how to hold a knife and fork and what to say and not say in company at the table. My parents were happy together. Little did I know how few married couples were happy with each other or how few husbands and wives were friends who did things together instead of going their separate ways each day.

My five-dollar raise had lifted me out of the lower classes—I now earned as much as the lowest-paid miners—and my earnings were now comparable to those of a tradesmen. Twenty-five a week plus all I could eat at the stew pots of the paper gave me some loose change. I bought a few shares of unproven mines that lay adjacent to productive ones and salted away some rainy-day dollars in Sharon's Bank of California and began, in that boom year of eighteen and sixty-six, to think about a better life. Not that I was unhappy. But I had larger social dreams than the thousands of other males swarming the Comstock. I was as randy as all the rest, but my dreams turned to sweethearts, not bawds.

I decided, one desolate day, that anything was possible, including a sweetheart on the Comstock. Faint heart never fair woman won. So, one Sunday morning, after a pleasant night in the Old Magnolia, I gathered my nerve and decided to go where the respectable women would be of a Sabbath morning. Few churches had rooted in the sterile soil of Virginia City, and in general religion was ignored. Still, the Cornishmen had their Methodist church and the Episcopalians had started up a small mission church. The Catholics had by far the largest and most active congregation, largely comprised of the Irish and German and Italian miners, not to mention the Mexicans.

I chose the Methodists, knowing the Cornishmen better than the others. I put on my only suit, wrapped a starched collar about my neck, and a bow tie, and marched myself south to the clapboard Methodist church at war with myself because I really didn't know what I would do there other than survey the females in the pews.

The Comstock's soil was pretty thin for religion. It wasn't that people opposed churches or Christianity. I never heard a disrespectful or even skeptical word, unlike more recent times, when atheists like Ingersoll hack away at the whole of organized religion, root and branch. No, most of those on the Comstock were believers of sorts and spoke well of the churches. But they really didn't want them around—not just yet. Later, perhaps. Maybe in ten years. Someday when the town was full of wives and churches that would be fine.

So the congregations were both brave and small, save for the Catholics, whose church seemed to umbrella and shelter the multitudes of ordinary sorts in the mines and mills and lumberyards and livery stables.

That was the genius of Father Manogue, who had once been a miner and spoke the special tongue of that trade. Patrick Manogue's wit and good humor and boundless faith filled his church all the while he was a priest in Virginia City.

I marched into the plain building, scolding myself for being a hypocrite. I wasn't there to worship God or improve my mind and soul but to examine—and perhaps meet—respectable young ladies. I was not disappointed. Although the status of some was uncertain, I was pretty sure that at least three were present that March Sunday, sitting between parents or beside brothers and sisters. I could not see their faces. Most of them sat ahead of me and wore extravagant hats. Nothing intrigues a young man more than a young lady whose face is hidden, and I spent half the service straining and leaning one way or another, hoping for a glimpse.

I spotted one or two of my old Cornish friends from Wisconsin, but the handful of worshipers that day yielded no one I knew very well. It was going to take some doing to meet the young ladies—probably a dozen Sundays. I surveyed the single men on hand, and oddly, they weren't more numerous than the single women, and I imagined I was onto something. In that church, the odds had evened out.

I worshiped gladly. We sang along to the music of the foot-bellow organ, we progressed through the usual Protestant service, and I dropped a silver dollar in the collection plate as a sort of tentative tribute. The circuit-riding minister, the Reverend Mr. James, dilated at length upon abstinence and sacrifice, this being the Lenten season, and that, too, was fine.

We arrived at the benediction, and fate intervened. The Reverend Mr. James announced a social that evening in the church basement, strangers invited.

Then, as the organ huffed to a halt after the processional, we rose to leave. And that was when I finally was rewarded with a few faces—including that of a demure brown-haired, brown-eyed beauty whose gaze lightly met mine and sent galvanic energy straight through me.

CHAPTER 20

ow well I remember that long Sunday afternoon. At last the Comstock was offering something other than male saloon company, and while I had always enjoyed the camaraderie, I wanted more.

I whiled away the day reading rival newspapers, as was my wont. But the minute hand was stuck on all the clocks and the day dragged. I look back upon the young and fretting Henry Stoddard with great tenderness. He had found the courage to change his life. In fact, biblical verses whirled though his mind all that spring day: "Seek and ye shall find." "Knock and it shall be opened unto you." "Ask and it will be given to you." He knew that the rest of the *Enterprise* staff had much the same dreams, but habit or discouragement or self-doubt had imprisoned his colleagues. Most bragged of being confirmed bachelors, and yet Henry Stoddard knew that the bragging was pained and hollow.

No name, a lovely and young face framed by brown hair, brown eyes. When at last the hour arrived, I ventured out, found a pastry shop and bought some sweets, and then marched myself—crawling with doubts—toward the white clapboard church and the company of strangers. Perhaps one of my Cornish friends would be on hand; otherwise, I would be on my own.

They glad-handed me, of course, no doubt thinking I was on the brink of joining the congregation. I wasn't so sure about that, having both agreements and quarrels with organized religion. I saw not a soul I recognized, nor did I spot Miss Brown-Eyes. But I introduced myself to a few who looked Cornish to me, and that proved to be accurate. A John Penrose, a Tom Trego, a Marty Trenoweth, the latter with a wife, Eloise, and small daughters. I do not remember what we discussed. Pleasantries. Of course they were curious about me and I told them my trade and employer, which evoked a certain curiosity and perhaps a faint distancing. Newspapermen were not only exotic but also known for their wanton ways and utterly heathen conduct. Had not the very owner of the paper, Goodman, and that Twain been involved in duels? Wasn't De Quille a hoaxer and drunk?

Nonetheless, I was accepted on probation and dipped into the spiced meat loaf, tinned vegetable salads, breads, and stews. One thing about Virginia City: all classes and sorts could and did put on a feed. I circulated through the rude basement social hall, met various miners in Sunday plumage, a one-armed mine foreman, a timber cutter, a few graying merchants, a number of stout and fortressed wives, and assorted little nippers imprisoned in dress-up clothing. And no Brown-Eyes. Not even the other two or three young women whom I had surveyed during the morning service.

One thing about all this: I realized that even on the hurly-burly Comstock there was a stratum—however thin—of respectable, middle-income families, the traditional middle class, poised to stay or fly as the fortunes of the mines dictated. I felt at home because these people were very like the ones who had always surrounded me in Platteville, the ones Judge and Mrs. Stoddard had entertained, associated with, and done business with.

So I felt comfortable among them, but were they really what I wanted for friends? Who among them could spin a yarn about the police, criminals, murder, the art of writing a good story, the mechanics of newspapering, the brawls, drunks, theater, and demimonde? If I had so much as mentioned Adah Isaacs Menken, the belle of the *Enterprise,* I might have found myself gently isolated and shunned. I no longer lived in their polite and pleasant world—and the world of Miss Brown-Eyes.

I did, however, maneuver the conversation around to those in attendance in the pews that morning and discovered that among them was the Stolz family. He was a senior mining engineer for the Yellow Jacket, a man of great substance. And attending with him were his wife, Felicity, and his daughter, Clarinet.

"Clarinet!" I exclaimed—this to the Reverend Mr. James. "What a name!"

"They are a musical family. Clarinet Stolz plays the harp and is preparing to study in San Francisco as soon as she finishes high school."

"She is in school?"

"A senior. Seventeen."

"Ah," I said. "Lovely name, Clarinet."

I slipped into the spring night soon thereafter feeling unusually melancholic. I wasn't inclined to rob the cradle. I felt torn by life. From the solid respectability of Judge Stoddard's home I had drifted into a wild city that never slept, where a male population roistered in saloons. I had entered a suspect profession. It wasn't that a scribbler could not be respectable, only that a certain class of people—from which I had sprung—assumed that he would not be. By degrees, I had become the unwitting black sheep of the Stoddard family.

I drifted toward the Delta, not prepared to surrender my acquaintance with a mug of beer to a church that preached abstinence from spirits, cigars, snuff, card games, coffee and tea, dancing, and most other species of ordinary pleasure. At that moment I rather envied the Catholics and their Christ, who miraculously made wine at the wedding, enjoyed feasts, liked parties, and yet taught that there were larger and more important spiritual goals to pursue. For them, what counted was how such pleasures were handled. They could become vices or not—but were not prohibited.

I pushed to the bar rail that evening, ordered a draft beer, and sank into silence, turning aside the proffered conversation of assorted males next to me. I had come to some sort of impasse in my life and couldn't resolve my feelings or find a cure. In spite of the hubbub, I was drinking alone that Sabbath night, blotting out the conversation, noise, and sights that swirled about me. I had the sinking sensation that no matter how I lived my life, I would be trapped in dissatisfaction and frustration. I hadn't met Miss Brown-Eyes in the church's social hall, but I had met her class, and a dozen women who could be her mother.

But I wasn't at home in the Delta. So I ordered a mug, and another, wandered out back to the reeking outhouse, and returned for another. A teamster—I recognized him as one of the habitués of that establishment—tried to engage me in talk, but I turned my back. He and several hundred like him hauled the cordwood that fed the mine boilers up the long slope from the Carson Valley and were an especially profane and burly lot.

"What's the matter? You too good for me?" he demanded.

"No, I simply need to be alone."

"You're too good for me, that's what."

I resolved to remove myself from that emporium and take my custom elsewhere, but as I turned, he spun me around and pinned me to the mahogany bar.

"I was just leaving," I said.

"You young snoot, putting on airs. Don't like my smell, is that it?"

"I'm sure you smell just fine. Now, if you'll excuse me—"

I attempted to maneuver free, but he had a handful of my suit coat in his clutch and I was pinned.

"G'wan, fight," he said.

I didn't. I stood quietly, waiting for his bellicosity to dissolve. It didn't.

"You're that reporter," he said. "You lift words and haul 'em around. Gives ya lots of muscle."

Men laughed. Men enjoyed this sort of thing.

"Sorry, I'm not one to fight. Especially with someone twice my size."

"Coward, eh?"

More male stuff. This sort of thing was the standard fare on the Comstock night after night.

"We are each brave or cowardly in our own way. I write things in the paper you would not have the courage to write. You perhaps are more at home pounding on people."

It wasn't the right thing to say.

"You calling me a coward! You twerp!"

He roared and gave me a mighty shove that catapulted me twenty feet across the saloon and into the foul sawdust. People stepped out of my trajectory. I arose slowly, uninjured, and found myself staring at Tom Fitch, editor of the *Virginia City Union.* His canines were bared. I knew at once that this episode would be plastered across the front page of the rival sheet in the morning and that truth would play second fiddle.

The spring air was playful, and I stood in the lamplight of C Street brushing gummy sawdust off my good suit. This sort of thing happened a hundred times a night on the Comstock, and more violent episodes, ratcheting up to murder and mayhem, occurred once or twice a night. I had covered them for years. From within the Delta I heard heightened laughter and suspected that Fitch was pounding the coffin nails into his version of the event.

That was all right, I supposed. We had done the same, time after time. But this night I resented it. I had gone peaceably enough into a saloon to have a beer and think through the feelings that were tugging wickedly in several directions. I had dodged a fight, was in no trouble with the law—but was branded a coward.

Well, that was male society for you. Walk into any saloon, any dive, any boardinghouse, any dormitory, and pretty soon there'd be a pecking order struggle of some sort. Maybe that was true of women, as well, but I was so innocent of any contact with them I couldn't say. I wondered what I might retort after reading the barb aimed at me in the morning. Or what sort of riposte I might work on silver-tongued Tom Fitch, the very man whose kneecap had been rearranged by a ball from Joe Goodman three years earlier. I'd have to wait and see, but intuitively I knew that Fitch was going to pull out the organ stops.

I debated whether to slip into another of my favorites, the Old Magnolia, hard by the *Enterprise.* I decided I needed another drink, so in I went, ordered a glass of Moselle from Gus Beerbaum, and sipped it while I contemplated my fate.

One thing was clear. That small episode had sealed my fate on the Comstock. I would not be admitted to respectable society—unless I got rich and bought my entrée. In the morning, the Reverend Mr. James and his respectable middle-class congregation would discover that the newspaper interloper at their potluck had departed their midst for the Delta, there to engage in a drunken brawl and reveal himself to be a triple-dyed coward.

. . . .

CHAPTER 21

I learned something that morning. A pen dipped in acid could balloon a minor event into big trouble. The editor of the *Union,* a bitter enemy of our rag, saw his chance and went after me. His account bore so little resemblance to events in the Delta that I didn't recognize it. I learned that I had been staggering drunk, picked a fight with an innocent and pint-sized teamster by insulting his mother, sister, family, and hometown, that the teamster had mildly deflected my mad-bull conduct until I had cracked a whiskey bottle across his shoulder, and then the wiry teamster had "discovered the yellow" in Henry Stoddard of the *Territorial Enterprise.* Such barbaric and cowardly conduct required my immediate dismissal, he informed his parishioners.

They were grinning at me around the plant. I rushed into Goodman's warren and began flailing arms.

"Calm down," he said. "I don't care whether Fitch got it right or didn't. I'm not going to give you the boot just for picking a fight."

"I didn't pick a fight!"

"Well, it don't matter."

"I didn't start it. I swear to God I was just minding my own business—"

"Sure, kid."

"Why aren't you supporting me? If it'd been Clemens or Wright or Daggett you'd be out there setting type and belching fire right now."

"Forget it, Stoddard."

"Forget it! It isn't true. I'm ruined."

"No one takes that stuff seriously."

"Some people might." Like Clarinet Stolz and her family.

"Well, write up your reply and we'll page-one it."

"Don't you want to hear my side?"

"You're taking it all too serious, Henry."

I nearly quit on the spot but got myself together and stormed into a room full of Cheshire cats. Whistling compositors, a smirky printer's devil, beaming newsmen. They had laid a yellow ribbon on my blotter. I glared needles at them and pretended to be busy. But I didn't write up anything. The damage was done. I thought maybe I'd haunt the Delta until I found some witnesses and then get them to testify even if I had to bribe them with a quart of Monongahela ... but by the end of that foul Monday I had slid into a sulk and didn't venture beyond the Old Magnolia, where I tossed shots all alone.

The next day Wright had his own fun and on page 1. "Our man Stoddard had the good sense to pick a fight with a fellow fifty pounds his junior," he began. "Stoddard is a mild fellow, except when he's into the Kentuck, and then watch out! They say it was all over a woman."

I found him lurking at his desk back in the composing room.

"Et tu, Brutus!" I bellowed.

"Well, Henry, we're glad you're turning into the top gladiator for the *Enterprise*," he said.

I stomped out.

It died as swiftly as it started, but I never got over it. I began to see Goodman and Wright and the whole damned *Enterprise* in a bitter light. Not a soul believed me or even inquired what the facts were. So there I was, sour toward my old friends and carousing companions, my allies on a combative paper, yet barred from politer society by a mendacious account that wasn't even funny.

I look back upon it even now, after all these years, with heat. To be sure, age has helped me. I know now they probably doubted Fitch's canards. They all knew Tom Fitch had a grudge. They saw my anger. They probably surmised that my version of the event was the true one—had they bothered to listen. But they were all charter members of a hazing club, all male, that told them I should have laughed it off or plotted a clever riposte or, in any case, showed that none of their barbs, or Fitch's canards, made the slightest dent in me. I had flunked. I was taking it too seriously—just as Mark Twain would take a similar roughing too seriously soon thereafter, and be remembered around Virginia as a thin-skinned sorehead. I'm talking about the famous robbery on the Divide when he returned to lecture, but I'll get to that shortly.

There it was again, a lynch mob of the ungentle sex acting with a casual cruelty that wouldn't have been tolerated in a city of families. But I should have shown more brass. Young Stoddard was something of a snob, and his companions at the bar rails had always sensed that. His daddy was a judge, his mother a cultivated, well-read woman who wrote poetry, and Henry Stoddard wasn't a man to dirty his hands. Oh, I see all that now. I haven't changed much, but at least I know how young Henry must have seemed to his drinking companions.

It reminds me now that Mark Twain's daddy was a judge, albeit an impoverished one and a bad businessman, and young Clemens thought maybe he was a tad better than those around him. He was known as a prickly man.

I worked sullenly for a few days, all the while thinking of escape. I was done with the Comstock, with a womanless society, with male company, murder, brawls, mayhem, and knifings, with greed and chicane, confidence men and bordellos and tinhorns and yeggs. With men who sneaked down to D Street or over to Cad Thompson's or the China-women held in pure mean slavery over in that miserable quarter on the northeast edge of town where one paid four bits to paw a poor yellow girl and little more for a small brown ball of opium, a slimy pipe, and a filthy pad. Sick of it all. Sick of mines, sick of gloryholes, sick of lethal water dribbling out of abandoned shafts and turned into the city mains. Sick of fires every other week, each one threatening to level the wooden town. Sick of myself.

I resolved again to get out and decided to follow Clemens to the Coast, where life was more pleasant and civilized. I didn't know what I'd do there. Clemens's occasional witty dispatches from there to our rag kept him afloat because all he could get was piecework or the most menial of reporting positions. I knew I would have even less luck than that. But anything would be better than hanging on in this miserable thatch of buildings on a barren mountain.

So I laid plans and then stopped cold: the Crown Point had hit another bonanza, and I still had those ten shares I supposed were worthless. William Wright told me. The Crown Point management had invited him to see what had yet to be announced: a major strike located at southerly crosscuts five and six hundred feet down, with no boundaries in sight. Mine managements had been using De Quille more and more that way, knowing that he was trusted and that whatever he wrote in the *Enterprise* could be relied on. So De Quille had gone to Gold Hill, gone down the shaft, taken samples, explored the pitch of the new lode, brought up the samples for assay, found that they yielded over two hundred dollars to the ton with an abnormal proportion of gold, and then approached me.

"It's a big one. Chances are Crown Point's management's laid hands on every loose share, Henry, but just in case they haven't, you should go hunting. My story won't break until morning, and you have about half an hour before the compositors vanish from their benches en masse to hit the brokerages."

I hastened to my broker. There wasn't a share of Crown Point to be had at any price, and the same went for the neighboring mines, the Belcher and Yellow Jacket. Better-informed people had gotten there ahead of me—including all of Crown Point's management, not a few miners, and every broker who had a good tipster working for him. But I had been this route before and knew that any genuine strike lifted the prices of all the mines on the Comstock. The trick was to get in and out fast, before the glow wore off. I bought a hundred shares of a treacherous old favorite of mine, Hale & Norcross, a mine then in borrasca—out of ore—and worth only a few dollars a share. I bought on margin, employing that sort of recklessness for the first time. But I liked the odds.

Well, off it went. Crown Point escalated so fast I could hardly keep track. I had dozens of offers to sell my ten shares at four, five, seven, a thousand, fifteen hundred each. It was a temptation, but I had learned something since getting burned. There comes a time when the stock falters and starts to seesaw, and that's the time to bail out. But so far, each day of trading resulted in additional gains. My ten shares were going to put me on Easy Street after all.

Hale & Norcross floated upward decorously, no one rushing for shares in a defunct mine but no one quite ready to ditch the old outfit, either. I'd probably double my money on that one, and watched, poised to sell and pay off my margin debt with a solid profit. That was how it ran that summer, Crown Point showing all the fireworks, Hale & Norcross floating along in its own wobbly way. I divided my time between my work at the paper—covering the mines—and haunting George Marye's offices. The perfidious Wright, who had embarrassed me months earlier, had become my financial salvation, and many was the evening when I bought him a glass of Moselle, his favorite, at the Old Magnolia.

He accepted these affably. So many speculators bought him booze that he rarely spent a dime in a saloon on the Comstock—and rarely showed up sober for work.

The summer rolled by and I grew itchy; why didn't I simply sell and avoid the disaster that had visited me last time? Easy to say, reader, but when you are confronting those issues in the real world, and not merely reading a Comstock memoir, you would know how excruciating such a decision can be. I hung on, haunted the brokers, sought tips from my old Cornish friends (who reported that the boundaries of the new lode were still unknown—no drift had, so far, penetrated to the far side of it), and debated selling just one share as a species of insurance. Maybe I had learned something from the prior debacle—but maybe not.

Then it happened. No, reader—assuming you have borne with me all this time—it wasn't what you think. This time, the news came from the Hale & Norcross, and it happened in this wise:

Unlike the Crown Point stock, the Hale & Norcross shares were widely available and cost a dozen dollars or so, even though there were precious few of them ever issued. The managers took a different tack. When a face crew at the 800-foot level hit bonanza ore late that summer, the shift bosses locked them down there while assays were run and management had a chance to bloat its holdings. That took two days. I got wind of the imprisonment from a Cornish friend and swiftly bought another fifty shares—also on margin, but my original hundred were worth more by then and I could afford it. So I had a fat hundred fifty when the news broke: bonanza at Hale & Norcross, and young Henry Stoddard was suddenly a Midas.

CHAPTER 22

 sold the Crown Point stock for just under sixteen thousand and then rued the decision. The stock kept rising as the mine's prospects and reserves improved. I was rich. I had safely ridden a small investment into a modest fortune. But all I could think of was how impulsive and cowardly I had been. I berated myself for being the sucker, bailing out before the rise was half-done.

Now, looking back, I am amused. Young Stoddard had a bad case of Comstock greed and hadn't learned much after all. There he was, with enough money to live in luxury for a decade even if he didn't invest it or work for a living, and yet he was wallowing in self-accusation. What made his wallowing all the more ridiculous was his holding of Hale & Norcross, which was ratcheting upward daily. A hundred and fifty shares of a Comstock mine in bonanza was a fortune.

I did pay off my margin so the brokers couldn't sink their tentacles into those shares. And I squandered a fancy sum on all my colleagues. For William Wright, a silver pocket watch. For Joe Goodman, a fly-fishing outfit. For the compositors, quarts of assorted spirits. And I let several of my old Cornish friends know that if ever they needed cash to help an injured miner, a mine widow, a sick man, to call on me. That was a part of the tradition on the Comstock. The miners, and later the miners' unions, took care of every unfortunate man who had ever descended a shaft into the cramped and black and frightening world underground. And his widow and children. They did this by assessing themselves, often donating large portions of their weekly wage. Some managements helped those who had broken body and bone and health in the pits; others didn't. But somehow, those in dire need received help, hospitalization, railroad or coach fare, and a little pocket money.

There's a notion abroad that the managers didn't care about the miners. Actually, most cared deeply and did what they could to make mines safer, the ventilation better, and working conditions more comfortable. Some of it was simply common sense: happy and safe miners worked better, produced more, laid fewer grievances before managers, suffered fewer accidents, and were more peaceable.

Even so, every mine on the Comstock broke the bones and bodies of its men, and most of the mines killed some as well. Mostly, carelessness was the culprit. Men did things they shouldn't, often well aware they were taking risks. Part of the suffering can be ascribed to primitive technology. These shafts were daily being driven deeper than ever before, into hotter rock, farther from fresh air, and deeper into water-bearing strata. Everything had to be engineered in new ways, from the signal systems telling the operator to lift or lower the cage to the eccentric spring-driven safety catches that—theoretically—stopped a cage in its tracks if its cable snapped. Gigantic pumps had to lift more water out of the mines than anyone had ever before attempted. Massive blowers had to push cool, fresh air farther than ever before—sometimes thousands of feet. Timbering had to be devised to hold up the ceilings of caverns as big as a statehouse.

It took a long time to design and build this equipment and then ship it thousands of miles. Often it had to be built back in the States and then shipped by sea to San Francisco and then freighted by ox team to Virginia City, where it was installed. There was always a time lag between good intentions and safety in the mines.

The mine managers and miners learned how to deal with unheard-of dangers and difficulties—but at a brutal price, which almost daily increased the number of graves in the miners' cemeteries north of town and filled the miners' hospital with frightfully mangled men, some of whom would live on in madness, their souls long departed. Even the best safety measures could not prevent some accidents, such as the sudden rush of scalding water released by a miner's pick or suffocation by toxic gases lurking where a drill steel went. These things happened, and no blame could be attached to them. The mines could promote safety, but much of the death and injury had to be laid to the judgment or misjudgment of the miners. Most of the deaths occurred around the shafts or in the cages, when men got careless about keeping their arms and heads and legs inside the lift or tumbled down the shafts to their doom.

I was acutely aware of that. One of my old Cornish friends from Platteville, Leo Polgar, had died when he fell down a shaft. Dangers abounded. And yet these men braved them day after day. I owed them something of my newfound fortune. They nodded, unsmiling, and let me know when they needed help. I knew it would be soon—a day, a week, a fortnight.

So I turned to my work, and my colleagues wondered why on earth I bothered. Why didn't I resign, leave the arid wastes of Sun Mountain, and go where life was intended to be lived? I had no answer to that. Nothing required my presence there a day longer. And yet I stayed because I loved my work.

I continued my prosaic life, but little changed by sudden affluence. The only thing different was my constant trips up C Street a few doors to Marye's to see how Hale & Norcross was doing. I was mother-henning that stock so much that my colleagues were getting smirky again. But what did it matter?

That fall, Sam Clemens returned briefly and we treated him badly. I was in on it, I'm ashamed to say. He had grown weary of San Francisco, traveled out to the Hawaiian Islands in the spring, wandered through the gold camps of the Sierra, written the piece that was to make him famous, "Jim Smiley and His Jumping Frog," later retitled "The Jumping Frog of Calaveras County"—and published it in the New York *Saturday Press.* We never dreamed when we last saw him what that comic yarn would do for our erstwhile colleague.

We weren't surprised, though, when he began lecturing, freely copying the humorous monologues of Artemus Ward. His first broadsheets were self-deprecating and comic, and I will reproduce a part of one I have before me, which I kept all these years:

> *A splendid orchestra*
> *is in town, but* has not *been engaged*
> *Also a den of ferocious beasts will be on exhibition*
> *in the next block*
> *Magnificent fireworks*
> *were in contemplation for this occasion,*
> *but the idea has been abandoned*
> *A grand torchlight procession*
> *may be expected; in fact the public are privileged*
> *to expect whatever they please . . .*
> *Doors open at 7 o'clock. The trouble will begin at 8.*

With this folderol he took San Francisco by storm, and soon expanded his lecture tour, speaking to full houses in Sacramento, Marysville, Grass Valley, Nevada City, You Bet, Red Dog, and then the Comstock, with appearances in Virginia City, Gold Hill, Silver City, and Dayton.

Well, his old friends lurked in waiting. I use the phrase purposefully, for we had contrived to shorten his growing stature by a head or two. He lectured first in Virginia, where we all cheered him on. The next night he lectured in Gold Hill and afterward would return to Virginia, passing over the Divide, that barren and dark ridge that divided the two towns—the sinister site of perhaps twenty murders and uncountable robberies.

We had one in mind, and enlisted his booking agent, one Mike—the last name escapes me after all this time—and thereby sprang a hoax that would overmaster all those that Sam Clemens had ever perpetrated and balance the scales of justice, so to speak. We plotted to rob him. He wrote about all this in *Roughing It,* but that version was not the true bill because it makes no mention of his distemper.

Thus it was that Clemens, flush from the pleasure of a successful evening, his purse fat with $300 of box office receipts, and accompanied by his agent, braved the Divide on a miserable windy, cold October night—and met with masked highwaymen. I confess to be among them, and if my old friend Clemens should read this he may take pleasure in my discomfort as I pen this account. We were all there, Gillis, Goodman, half a dozen others who had known Sam in his salad days.

Mike had manfully primed the pump with frequent references, every few steps, about the sinister nature of the Divide. And when they reached the Virginia slope, there we were.

Clemens's first enlightenment was the click of a revolver being cocked. The second was a harsh command: "Your watch. Your money!"

"Certainly . . . I—"

"Put up your hands. Don't you go for a weapon. Put 'em up higher!"

Sam did as instructed.

"Well, are you going to give us the money or not?"

He lowered his hands to his pockets.

"Put up your hands! You want your head blown off? Higher!"

And thus we kept him dancing, finally relieving him of his gold watch—a new and treasured gift from a friend—and his boodle. We informed him that he must keep his hands high and not follow, which he earnestly obeyed for some while after we had retreated back to the comfortable warmth of the saloons on C Street.

I have shortened this episode a great deal, reader. In fact, we kept

Sam hopping about up there for some while before we got loose of him. Later that evening we commiserated with him as he told us his woeful story. We, of course, plied him with drinks, paid for with his own cash. Samuel Langhorne Clemens was an unhappy man that cold evening. But enough was enough and we contrived to return the watch to him, saying we had gotten wind of the culprits. He eyed it—and us—suspiciously, his imagination now embracing us as the source of the night's woes. And then we returned the cash—most of it, minus the price of a considerable bottling of spirits.

But he was not comforted and was not smiling. He turned solitary, as was his wont, and froze us out. The whole joke had gone sour, and we were reminded that Clemens had always been a good one for making a hoax and a bad one if he were the butt of a hoax. I must say, looking back, that we had been a bit too realistic. A man peering into the bore of a revolver is a man facing death. Our joke had been just about as rough as jokes get, and from my perspective now I wish we had tried something a little milder to make an evening's entertainment. But that was eighteen and sixty-six, and Virginia City was still a metropolis of men, and that sort of hard edge would last another five or six years—until the second bonanza in the seventies, when at last the sexes more or less began evening up.

As for Sam Clemens, we saw him off, clapped him on the back, and made much of him, and all seemed forgotten—but he never returned to Virginia City again, even when his lectures brought him near.

CHAPTER 23

Money was a puzzle. I look back upon young Stoddard with a bit of pride because he remained levelheaded. Speculation formed the leitmotif of most lives on the Comstock. Anyone with loose change bought some shares of holes in the rock. But Stoddard resisted that, resisted the wisdom of barkeeps, brokers, managers, touts, well-meaning friends, miners, serving girls, and even mine managers, all of whom hustled this or that mine and probably got a little grease for their efforts.

I figured mines came and went. Ores were scooped out and then a mine died. I also was skeptical of investing money in other Comstock ventures, figuring these would live or die with the mines. I was partly wrong about that. I could have made a fortune in any of the ancillary businesses fostered by the mines: timbering, water, transportation, construction, cordwood, heavy equipment, and even milling and smelting. But in the larger sense, I was right: Virginia and Gold Hill eventually reached their apex and then shrank into skeletal remains.

I chose the railroad. The Central Pacific had loomed in my mind for years. The man who first promoted it, a brilliant engineer named Theodore Dahone Judah, had plotted its route over the Sierras and had even gone to Washington City to tout it. Most men considered Judah mad, and perhaps he was. But in his fevered mind he envisioned a transcontinental railroad, and he found the route through the Sierras to do it. He died at thirty-seven, as controversial as ever, and was soon forgotten. But he left behind him the whole scintillating, alluring, feasible, and elegant plan for a mighty railroad to the States.

It wasn't until four Sacramento merchants, Collis Huntington, Leland Stanford, Mark Hopkins, and Charles Crocker, took a hand in it that the Central Pacific sprang to life. In spite of generous federal grants, land subsidies, and other inducements offered by Congress, the project had languished ever since eighteen and sixty-two. Problems abounded, and the worst of them was a lack of labor in the Far West. The Union Pacific, on the other hand, building out from the East had plenty of labor, mostly Irish immigrants, to help it lay tracks across the vast prairies. The managers of the Central Pacific finally solved that problem by importing Chinamen by the thousand, mostly Cantonese, and ere long they had pushed the line from Sacramento to the Sierras, and were employing the coolies to cut the grades and build the bridges and trestles that would lift steam engines and carriages over the towering Sierra Nevada—a breathtaking proposition—and then down our arid Nevada slopes. Even as the Union Pacific raced westward across flat prairies, the Central Pacific was gearing up at the beginning of eighteen and sixty-seven to wrestle one mile at a time from the unyielding barricade that isolated California from the continent.

Leland Stanford was a wholesale grocer, Charles Crocker a dry-goods merchant. Mark Hopkins and Collis Huntington were hardware merchants. Such men seemed scarcely the types to begin a great railroad that would connect California to the States. But they shared a burning vision, and in the end the vision prevailed. They formed a stock company but were slow to subscribe to its shares themselves, buying only 800 of the 85,000 shares. Their first task was to survey a feasible route over the fearsome Sierra Nevada, and their second was to get federal funding. Eventually, they achieved both, perhaps to their own astonishment, and certainly to the astonishment of the world. And I kept close track, because the fate of Virginia City teetered on the fulcrum of a railroad.

We starved for railroads. The talk in any Comstock saloon often turned to railroads. There we were, a city of fifteen thousand, or so some said, although I doubted it, plus the additional populations of Gold Hill and Silver City—and every pound of food, fuel, manufactured goods, and all the rest came to us in wagons and carriages drawn by oxen, mules, and horses. We were, so to speak, at the extreme end of all lines of supply to California and out of reach of the East except for the briefest season of warmth. Hay and oats had become so dear that no one in town could afford a team or saddler. Not all the hay from the Carson Valley and Genoa and the flats around Reno sufficed to keep Virginia City in livestock feed, and in winter owners sadly released their stock to wander and live or die—mostly die—for there was no feed at any price.

We ached for railroads. We begged for railroads. We entered each winter season—when the forbidding Sierras cut us off from California—with foreboding, fear of starvation or lack of fuel or the lack of necessaries for the mines and mills, such as the chemicals used to break down the ores: mercury from New Almaden, California, in particular. Say the word *railroad* on the Comstock and you evoked mysticism, religion, something sacred and holy. A railroad would lower the cost of goods, assure supplies that seemed to run out each winter, give us ingress and egress from our mountain aerie. The proposed transcontinental railroad would pass north of us, and someone would build us a branch. The Central Pacific became a dream and passion on the Comstock. And I dreamed along with the others, seeing the good in it, the profits for it.

Now, of course, writing as I do from this vantage point over three decades later, I can see what young Stoddard didn't—that not even the government's subsidies and grants would make the Central Pacific solvent after it connected to the Union Pacific at Promontory Point, in Utah Territory. I marshaled all the right reasons for buying Central Pacific stock, but it was a bad decision.

The bulk of the stock was eventually commandeered by those four merchants, who made a fortune from it—mostly by paying themselves to construct the railroad and by keeping their own tangled books, which no one has ever deciphered, least of all those stockholders like young Stoddard, who could not imagine why their shares paid nothing, declined in value, and seemed worthless paper even while traffic over those thin bands of steel increased dramatically each year and the road did a lucrative business.

I purchased $15,000 of Central Pacific stock—enough to make me a significant shareholder—and sat back, knowing that railroads were the

future and my share of the future would grow. I duly received my certificate and put it in William Sharon's new California bank branch for
safekeeping. There, in Sharon's safe, it would germinate. I didn't doubt
it for an instant.

When I informed my colleagues that I had bought stock in the Central Pacific, they nodded solemnly and not one of them ventured the
slightest skepticism. I had purchased something as close to a sure thing
as was known to mortals. I scarcely even bothered to check the price of
the stock with my brokers from day to day or month to month. What
was the need? The daily ups and downs of the Central Pacific scarcely
mattered when the future was so bright. And wasn't Charles Crocker,
whose construction company was building the road, a genius?

Reader, you will tell me that all these ideas were naive and that any
fool could predict what would happen. But you have the benefit of hindsight. An investor must employ foresight, and that is what the sober and
thoughtful young Stoddard did. In the main, I will not fault him—not
now, not ever. If there was any weakness in his examination of the
company, it was a lack of understanding of greed. Stanford, Huntington,
Hopkins, and Crocker were all reputable merchants, so the young man
trusted them with his $15,000, scarcely realizing that the same lusts that
corrupted the mining securities business corrupted the railroad securities.

The four sharpers milked the Central Pacific, the government, other
shareholders, and ultimately the railroad's customers, right down to the
impoverished widow and orphan, of every dime they could extract and
then built their grotesque and unsightly mansions on Nob Hill, where
those who survive live like monarchs, purchase bad art, and buy rare
books they never read and can barely understand.

Perhaps in that respect Stoddard might have been more cautious,
but in all others he was on solid ground. Railroads! Even now they make
my heart sing, and I have invested in them over and over.

I continued to work for Joe Goodman, making the rounds of the
mine offices, talking to mill owners, examining assay results and printing
them, and reporting the accidents that more and more frequently mangled men in the pits. That became my new passion. I covered safety
issues ruthlessly. Yes, they were all for safety, but now and then some
operators, driven by their lust for bullion, cut what corners they could.
The miners' cemeteries north of town grew and grew, and we accustomed ourselves to a daily funeral down C Street, the black hearse, the
black horses, the marching of the grieved, all dodging the ubiquitous ox
teams, twenty-mule-team freight wagons, pedestrians, and stagecoaches
crowding that choked thoroughfare.

Sometimes I wandered through those desolate miners' cemeteries north of town, where not a blade of grass grew and no tree or shrub blessed the arid slopes. There, carved in decaying wood, or sometimes stone, were the records of brief, brutal lives—rarely did a miner live beyond forty. They died of injuries and disease, but I sometimes think they really died of a hard and exhausting life.

And then one day, we found ourselves reporting a death caused by something else: murder.

CHAPTER 24

e put this headline on it:

Horrible Murder
WOMAN STRANGLED TO
DEATH IN HER BED
Blood-Curdling Tragedy
Directly in the Heart of the
City

We ran the story on the twenty-second of January, in eighteen and sixty-seven. The victim, a Cyprian named Julia Bulette, was known to most of us. She lived in a cheaply built white frame crib at 4 North D Street, near the corner of Union and a few rods from the Frederick House hotel, on the edge of the restricted district.

Julia was no ordinary lady of the night. Neither was she anything like the legend that blossomed later. She had come to Virginia City in the early days, probably eighteen and sixty-three, although that isn't certain. Not much about her is certain. She was born in Liverpool or London, depending on what version you choose to believe, immigrated to Louisiana as a child, and eventually married someone named Smith, although that's uncertain as well. She left him, either separating or divorcing, depending on what version you choose to believe, and plied her trade in several California gold-rush towns, particularly Weaverville. In spite of the Creole name she adopted, she had no French blood and was not a New Orleans–bred Daughter of Joy.

She had been born in eighteen and thirty-two and thus was thirty-five, an advanced age for one in her calling, when she was strangled in her bed late in the night of January 19 or early in the morning on the twentieth. Her past is hazy, but her life on the Comstock is not, and I am more certain about what follows than what precedes.

What is certain is that Julia Bulette was a woman of some sensitivity and warmth and had none of the crassly commercial qualities one associates with women of her sort. She was, and is, remembered fondly on the Comstock as a woman who befriended males of all sorts, not just her clients, but many others who delighted in her female company in that woman-starved city. Indeed, she was an honorary member of Virginia Engine Company Number One, and the only extant photo of her shows her in her fireman's uniform. Actually, she was more than an honorary member: when the fire bells clanged she would swiftly assume her post operating the brakes of the fire wagon as it raced to the conflagrations that always threatened to devour the city.

I knew Julia, having met her on several occasions, and can testify that she was neither a great beauty nor plain, neither brunette nor blond. She exuded a pleasantness in her regular features, and her tall, trim figure was the envy of many a woman on the Comstock. The faintest trace of English enunciation lingered on her tongue, making her diction crisp and warm. I liked her.

Contrary to the legend that somehow blossomed about her, she never nursed sick miners during the periodic cholera and influenza epidemics that swept Virginia City. She was neither a Florence Nightingale nor even that sentimental legend, the whore with the heart of gold. I know of no instance in which she slipped cash to the down-and-out, although she was notably generous to her sisters in vice and helped many of those suffering women in their moments of distress and hopelessness. And they in turn loved her with the solidarity of the sisterhood.

Julia's special grace lay simply in friendship, which she offered freely and affectionately to any man she chanced to meet. She had decorated the interior of her wretched two-room establishment gracefully, with a Brussels carpet, mahogany furniture, lace curtains, and other benedictions. In her bedroom to the rear was an oversize mahogany bed, a sort of altar, primly made up with a white counterpane in the summer and an elaborate woolen one in the winter. That and a washstand with two bowls upon it and her armoires comprised her bedroom furniture. She had no kitchen and shared the one next door, at 6 D Street, with her neighbor and confidante, Gertrude Holmes.

The secret of Julia's success was her quiet, cheerful, and well-attended parties. She could seat a dozen people in her parlor and thus entertain in style, plying her male guests with wines and liquors from her ample supplies, including whiskey, ale, beer, rum, brandy, port, claret, and cognac. At the time of her murder she owed Thomas Taylor

& Company, the liquor merchant, $141.50, which suggests that she entertained a great deal.

Another of her charms was her wardrobe, which might be described as conservative, well made but not extravagant, and always discreet. It was not in Julia's nature to flaunt her profession. She won a comfortable living catering to the Washoe district's better class of males but saved little and lived just barely within her means, squandering her money on clothing and generously provisioned parties. She dressed as if she might be a bourgeois wife or daughter, and that added to the charm of her parties. For a little while, on many evenings the most fortunate of Washoe's lonely males found themselves in the company of a gentlewoman. And those of us who attended scarcely were aware that one or another might stay on after the rest of us headed into the night. She was innately a gentlewoman. All the rest is mythology.

That, indeed, is how I came to know and admire Julia. We at the *Enterprise* were frequently in attendance along with half the other newsmen of the city. I kept my resolve not to mire myself in that life–though I regretted the decision a hundred times a week–and thus I never made an appointment with Julia for something more intimate in the later hours.

I would wander there with Steve Gillis or Joe Goodman or Alf Doten, imbibe her sweetness along with her spirits, and then slip away, my feelings always mixed and moiled by the evening, because she shared her person with us, as a sister or mother would, and inquired into our lives and hopes and dreams, as any sweetheart would. It was not only Julia's body that was public; it was her gracious heart, and that wrought a different sort of pain in many males.

The events of late January unfolded in this wise: That Saturday evening, she left her cottage and walked upslope to Piper's Opera House to see the twin bill *The Robbers* and a farce titled *Willful Murder*. In spite of her dignified attire, she was denied admission through the front doors, although she was welcome to attend through the side door and sit in a special section reserved for women of ill repute. She declined and returned to her crib to await an appointment with a customer. At about eleven-thirty she said good night to her neighbor, Gertrude, mentioning that she would have a customer at midnight. The women would have breakfast together, as usual.

That was the last time anyone saw her alive. Around eleven on Sunday morning, a Chinaman who arrived each day to build her fire came and did that, being careful not to disturb her, and left. A little later Gertrude came to summon her to breakfast and found her dead in her bed, strangled and mauled. The official report said she had been struck with a pistol, beaten with an eighteen-inch piece of firewood, and smothered with a pillow. There were clear imprints of fingers and a thumb on her throat. Her finer clothes, furs, and pieces of jewelry were missing. She had died a terrible death at the hands of a brutal man.

Oh, we grieved, there at the *Territorial Enterprise,* for we all knew and loved her. Joe Goodman depicted her as "being of a very kind-hearted, liberal, benevolent, and charitable disposition—few of her class had more true friends."

Her death shocked the city. Julia had become something of an institution on the Comstock Lode, someone almost sainted, at least to those woman-starved men who contemplated her. The murder became the sensation of the hour even though violent deaths were common among Julia's class, often from suicide. The city's constabulary hadn't a clue who did it. Julia had mentioned no name to her companion Gertrude. She kept no list of regular customers that a detective might find useful. Some vicious person had descended out of the night, beaten and broken and murdered her, stolen most that could be profitably fenced, and fled into the protecting darkness. There was no imprint of a body on the bedclothes to either side of Julia. The man had not come for her favors, or at least had not taken them.

I remember how we sat about at the paper, or stood at the rail of the old Magnolia, trying to cipher it out, raking the lists of her party guests—but in the end, we were as much in the dark as the police.

We all attended—along with a great crowd—the funeral, conducted appropriately and discreetly at Engine House Number One, on B Street, at three o'clock the next day, Monday. Officiating was the Reverend William M. Martin, and I was gladdened that a man of the cloth did his Christian duty and sent Julia Bulette off with a sermon that everyone agreed was appropriate to the occasion. Julia's executrix, Mary Jane Minieri, had gotten her a fine mahogany coffin and paid for an engraved silver plate, a funeral wreath, shroud, and hearse—the whole business, all done up properly. It came, I found out later, to $149.

Well, I'll always remember what came next. How could anyone present ever forget? A throng of us marched with Julia to her grave. Leading off was the Metropolitan Brass Band, followed by sixty members of the fire department on foot and in full regalia. Then came sixteen carriages of mourners, those of us who had befriended her as well as the frails who had loved her as well. There would have been many more but for the blizzard that raged that dark day. This lengthy cortege traveled solemnly and dolefully the length of the city and then to the Flowery Hill Cemetery, behind a little hill south and east of town, actually a great distance from most of the others, which cluster about the north end of the district. And we buried her there and hurried back to warmth, feeling a chill that went to our marrow.

Joe Goodman, once again, weighed in editorially: "In her lonely grave her good and bad traits alike lie buried with her."

Her executrix offered $200 from the estate for the capture of Julia's killer even though the sale of everything she possessed would not even pay her debts.

The sisterhood intended to catch the man if that was possible.

But of her killer we knew nothing. I resolved to find out if I could. A reporter is not without resources.

CHAPTER 25

 had visions of nabbing the killer of Julia Bulette, visions that I now realize were simply the fantasies of youth. I had been on the Comstock ever since eighteen and sixty-one and thought I knew—as reporters do—where all the bodies were buried. It was a silly presumption.

I knew nothing, even though I had been present ever since Virginia City was more a shack town than a city. But what could I know of the dozens, scores, of strangers arriving each day, many of them Civil War veterans? And what did I know of the underworld of the whole district—which frequently robbed stagecoaches, stole bullion, held up teamsters and stole valuables from the freight wagons, mugged, knifed, murdered, and robbed? We had dutifully reported most of the crime—that which appeared on the police blotters, at any rate. But I knew nothing.

I made the rounds of the saloons, not neglecting the vicious dives on the Barbary Coast on South C Street, and let it be known that I would pay a hundred dollars for conclusive evidence, and maybe something for tips, too. The result was a rash of tips, nearly all worthless, but I shelled out some cash here and there for whatever seemed valuable, and also to reinforce my credibility among those slugs who lived on the nether side of flat rocks.

It came to nothing. Young Stoddard's fantasies diminished daily as eighteen and sixty-seven progressed, and I returned to my mining beat even as the memory of Julia diminished in my mind and across the Comstock.

The murder was just one more of Virginia's endless and vicious crimes lost upon a transient and uncaring male population. Indeed, one soon heard in the saloons that it was just another whore's death and public women weren't worth caring about—they all got what they deserved. That was a callous view of those unfortunates but the prevailing one in those days and little changed now, I confess that I shared it to a degree, though now, as I approach the end of my life, I view those poor wretches, often driven by cruelty and tragedy into a life they hated, with more charity than I had earlier.

The mines were holding their own that year. The new bonanzas more or less replaced the depleted lodes, and so it all evened out and the city continued its reckless transformation toward permanence—as if the ores would last a hundred years, which indeed was what some boomers and fools were saying.

Maybe the Chollar-Potosi was in borrasca, but the Yellow Jacket, Hale & Norcross, Savage, Imperial, and Crown Point were still producing at various rates. What's more, all the mines were systematically sinking their shafts or running new drifts or crosscuts looking for new bonanzas. A vast army of miners, timber men, engineers, woodcutters, ironmongers, and others earned good wages while dozens of mines, such as the Bullion—which hadn't found a nickel's worth of ore even though it lay squarely on the lode—probed and dug and blasted their way under Virginia City until the metropolis rested on a honeycomb of tunnels and chambers.

The mines began to interconnect, which improved safety and ventilation. Some shafts had uprising air; others turned into downdrafts, drawing fresh air into their works that eventually exited the mines through another company's shaft. This was welcomed, because the miners were running into more heat and beginning to work in rock that radiated such warmth that the men often shed their shirts and britches in that dark, cramped world. The temperatures on the lowest levels climbed into the eighties, and the heat and vile air often exhausted the men, forcing them to take rest breaks and drink ice water sent down the shafts by management.

It became a matter of speculation what the mining companies would do if the mines became too hot to work, and the most foresighted managers were even then ordering powerful ventilating systems—Root blowers—to pump cold surface air to the lowest levels through square wooden ventilating ducts. But no one imagined—in those earlier times—that the temperatures would rise much more. How wrong we all were.

Dan De Quille and I reported all that daily. He continued to penetrate the bowels of the mines, take ore samples for independent assay, and talk to the men in the pits, while I continued to pursue the above-ground technology, management, and speculations and financial frauds. One day that spring, De Quille chilled me with a warning.

"It's over," he announced over claret at the old Magnolia. "You realize there's been no bonanza for a year or so now, in spite of the most intense exploration the Comstock's seen—largely paid by assessments. The miners know it. I know it. Management knows it. But the public doesn't. There'll be some sucker plays pretty soon. Better sell your Hale & Norcross, Henry."

"I've been watching it daily," I replied, rather pained by his presumptuousness. It had been a stable stock, drifting upward, actually. If I cashed in that spring, I'd be a wealthy man.

My Central Pacific stock sagged, rallied, and sagged as Crocker's construction company built the railroad eastward into the daunting and terrible Sierras. It was down to pennies a share, but I wasn't worried. After the hard times, borrowing, panics, and reverses as the countless Chinamen dug and graded and bored a roadbed up the long, gentle westward slope of the Sierras, I would eventually be sitting on a bonanza: shares of the sole and crucial transcontinental railroad. How innocent I was.

The spring passed quietly—until May 24. On that memorable day, the police cracked the Bulette murder case. Or, rather, the evidence dropped in their lap. Oddly, they already had the man in jail. He was a Frenchman named Jean Marie A. Villain, but better known as John Millian. He worked in a bakery on D Street. A little earlier, a public woman named Martha Camp—a friend of Julia Bulette—had been assailed in her bed by someone who had entered her room. Martha had screamed, startling him, and as he fled she got a good look at him. Later she spotted him on the street and reported him to the police, who charged him and held him for attempted murder.

On May 24, a Mrs. Cazentre of Gold Hill reported that she had acquired a certain dress she believed had belonged to Julia Bulette. She had paid forty dollars for it to a man named Millian, who represented himself as someone selling some clothing on behalf of a miner's widow whose husband had been killed in the Ophir. Mrs. Cazentre had started to think about all that, decided something wasn't right, and went to the constables.

Swiftly everything fell in place. A dry-goods merchant, Sam Rosener, identified the dress as one he had sold to Miss Bulette and asserted positively that the dress was unique in Nevada. The police swiftly examined a trunk Millian was storing at the bakery and discovered a trove of Julia's belongings—silk dresses, muffs, coral earrings, a Masonic emblem, rings, a silver brick stamped with Julia's name, all identified by Gertrude Holmes.

Confronted with all this, Millian confessed—only to retract the story later. Indeed, while he was lodged in the Storey County Jail his fevered brain wrought story upon story about it all, which he published far and abroad. His main argument was that he had been employed merely as a lookout by two reprobates named Douglass and Dillon, who had actually murdered and robbed Julia and then entrusted the goods to Millian.

He spoke but little English and seemed confused the whole while. But we all thought he was the man, even after he began to concoct his alibi involving Douglass and Dillon. As I gaze back through the mists of time I admit that such a thing was a possibility, but very doubtful. No trace of the alleged perpetrators was ever uncovered. I believed then, and do now, that the police had the right man. But there is a bit of room for doubt.

In the ensuing trial Millian's able attorney, Charles de Long, made a plausible case that Millian had not done the deed and argued that the evidence was entirely circumstantial—which it largely was. Nothing very certain connected the man peddling items stolen from Julia Bulette to the murder; neither was the attempted murder charge, lodged in the case of Martha Camp, proof that he had murdered Bulette.

And so we debated it hotly at the paper and awaited the trial, which came swiftly, on July 2. I covered it, along with most of the other reporters in town. Two doctors described the condition of Julia's body and how she had died. Mrs. Cazentre testified at length. Sam Rosener testified that the dress was one of a kind. Gertrude Holmes identified as Bulette's the goods found in Millian's trunk. Police Chief Edwards testified about how the trunk was found and opened. Various of Julia's friends—and perhaps customers—identified these items as belonging to her. One of these was Hank Monk, the legendary Benton stagecoach driver whose later claim to fame was terrifying Horace Greeley half to death with a wild ride to Hangtown, where Greeley was to make a campaign speech. (Legend has it that Monk used to patch his clothing together with copper rivets and when San Francisco's clothing manufacturer Levi Strauss heard about the idea a work-trouser business was born.)

I don't recollect that the defense called a single witness. De Long argued circumstantial evidence, and if the jury did think Millian was guilty, he ought to be judged insane, for only a madman would store a murdered woman's possessions in a trunk at his place of employment or sell items so easily recognized.

All this took but part of a day, and in the afternoon the jury retired to discuss matters. Just before midnight they brought the verdict—guilty of first degree murder.

That seemed proper and just, as did the sentencing that followed: death by hanging. De Long appealed, of course, and as that pleading wound its way through the courts eighteen and sixty-seven unwound its skein and I returned to my coverage of the mines. If I had learned anything, it was that I was no detective and belonged exactly where fate and inclination had placed me, writing about the mines.

Meanwhile, the Bulette legend grew. The stories amaze me. It was said that she was a madam, lived in a glittering mansion, drove in a handsome carriage with liveried attendants, lavished money on the poor and helpless, that most of the miners in the city marched in her funeral, and on and on. Julia would have smiled at all that. But somehow, I prefer the legend, because it was rooted in love.

CHAPTER 26

 fell into a pensive mood that summer. I had been on the Comstock for six years, watched a shantytown turn into a solid city; I had grown up, learned a trade—I won't grace journalism with the appellation of profession; it is mere scribbling—won some money from the Wheel of Fortune, and had yet to win a woman and make a home, possess a house, or establish myself in a more fruitful and solid occupation.

Maybe that was young Henry Stoddard's fault. He was too cautious. I look back upon that young man, in his upper twenties, as someone cynical, a little morose, and hardened by a life lived too close to the wild side. He had heard too many speculators and managers swear before the Throne of Heaven and all the cherubim and seraphim that a mine was failing when, in fact, it was about to enrich anyone who owned the smallest piece of it. He had reported too many stagecoach robberies, holdups, suicides, brawls, injuries, blindings, stillborn babies, food poisonings, epidemics, knifings, and suicides. His profession excluded him from good company and shadowed his social acceptability.

I took stock again that quiet summer, wondering again whether to decamp. It was getting to be an annual habit: Stay or leave? What more could the sprawling city on the shoulder of Sun Mountain offer?

Instead, I sold a hundred shares of Hale & Norcross, saving back the remaining fifty, and bought a house. The shares were then hovering around three hundred, and the sale suddenly put me in possession of a sizable asset. Enough to take me anywhere, establish myself in New York, San Francisco, New Orleans if I chose. I could live comfortably on the interest the rest of my life if I chose. At the high rates of the day, I could have an annual income of three or four thousand.

I elected to stay and bought a house on A Street in a handsome neighborhood populated largely by superintendents, lawyers, and other substantial people. The house, like almost all in Virginia City, had been erected hastily and scarcely held its heat on a winter's day, but I had funds enough to remove the pasted cloth and wallpaper that adorned the interior planking and plaster it, thus making it immeasurably more pleasant. I bought furniture—the prices flabbergasted me, even knowing as I did that every item had been dragged over the Sierras by the power of oxen. And I advertised for a day housekeeper, finally selecting a thin miner's widow in her forties, prematurely gray.

She arrived at eight each morning and left after doing up the supper dishes each evening. I managed my own breakfasts.

Mrs. Bertoletti pleased me. She was vivacious when she sensed that I wanted company, industrious, pious, kept a good house, doubled as seamstress and manager, and was unattached, her children having left her nest. She brought tasty new foods to my table, and I acquired a fondness for olive oil and pastas and excruciating sweets.

Her husband, Marco, had been crushed by some collapsing timbers at the 300-foot level of the Savage, leaving her with several older children poised to leave the nest. That and a small fund hastily collected by the mining brethren. The sons swiftly left the area; the seventeen-year-old daughter found a husband. And the widow, on the brink of starvation, found me through a classified ad in the *Enterprise*. She spoke adequate English, embellished with a vast, rich emotional overlay upon everything she said, well orchestrated with gestures that said more than words. We understood each other famously.

"Why don't you get married, eh?" she immediately wanted to know.

I assured her the notion was on my mind.

"You're getting too old," she said. "Pretty soon—" She completed this by drawing her finger across her throat to indicate the bloody conclusion of my youth or manhood or whatever she had in mind.

I settled in, met my neighbors—most of whom I knew, having

haunted their lairs as a reporter collecting information about the condition of the mines—and thus melded into that privileged neighborhood above C Street, where those who could afford comfort usually found it.

I spread my new-won cash widely, believing that safety lay in diversity. I purchased excellent farmland just east of the old town of Genoa, originally Mormon Station, and adjacent to the old landmark Kinney home. This I leased for a share of the hay and the apples from its young orchard. Raising hay for the Virginia City market was a surer way to get rich than striking gold. I purchased shares in some of the traction companies building horse-drawn streetcar lines in Ohio and Pennsylvania. I bought railroad stock, in particular Cornelius Vanderbilt's New York Central, and diverse mining shares, including some producing gold mines around Downieville and Nevada City in California. But most of all, I bet on railroads, the future of the country. I was right, but quite a little early, and would suffer terrible reverses because of that.

Thus, as eighteen and sixty-seven drifted by, I became a man of parts. Virginia City was now home, and I abandoned all thought of moving. I continued on the paper, not for a means to survive but for want of anything better to do. I liked the work and my colleagues. But they had started to treat me differently, as if my successes in speculation separated me in some subtle way. They particularly resented any effort on my part to buy them a beer or give them any gifts or make the slightest effort to improve their lot. Proud men they were, and with proud standards. All this I found out painfully, stubbing my toe, so to speak, in my efforts to share my good fortune.

I awakened that notable summer to something else. Insensibly and by degrees too gradual to notice, women had come to the Comstock and the sexes were edging closer to some sort of numerical parity. Thus it had always been on the frontier—males first, women later, when a few comforts, amenities, and public safety had been established. I grew aware of this while attending some of the balls and dances to which I had been invited that summer. The Comstock had turned to dancing, and any excuse, such as July Fourth, would do. Bands and orchestras and quartets had sprung up, supplying the city with everything from marches to Viennese waltzes.

I attended, having surrendered myself to Fate. If a sweetheart came along, splendid; if not, I intended to enjoy myself nonetheless, for women were still a novelty and prize anywhere on the Comstock. The town lacked level dance floors, but what did it matter? It seemed every week some society or another, from the Hibernians to the Knights Templar, rented a hall and hired a band and invited all.

I faced a double problem: for one, I could scarcely dance, and for

another, I was not practiced in these social graces. But observation sufficed. At one of the first of those summery affairs I hovered about, watching young men my age boldly approach a lady—often older, married,
and with a family about—and strike up a conversation. I learned something important. Dances were to be enjoyed for themselves, and one's
dance partner needn't be an eligible female.

Odd, how buffalo-witted young Henry Stoddard was about that. The
young man supposed, until he learned otherwise, that one attended these
affairs merely to contact available women, that the dancing scarcely mattered, as if it were some rite of courtship to be gotten past. No woman
saw it that way at all; they had all come to enjoy the music, the whirl,
and the new acquaintances.

Fiddlers, of whom Virginia had a rare crop, called most of the
dances, and we found ourselves forming up for quadrilles or Virginia
reels. Anyone could join the lines or circles and follow the swings and
steps. But one daring new dance, the waltz, required taking one's partner
in hand and whirling her about, which elders frowned upon but young
people enjoyed. And that, as it happened, was how I embarked upon
my first dance of the season. I was conversing with Mrs. Penrose, wife
of one of my old Cornish friends, while the string band played a waltz.

"Come along, Henry, and we'll whirl," she said, and to my astonishment I found myself whirling Mrs. Penrose like a dervish, uncertainly
at first, but with swift-building confidence once I got the one-two-three
one-two-three hang of it. I thought it very daring to be so close to a
woman.

Well, as time went by, I found myself more and more confortable
around the punch bowl. There was always someone I knew—a reporter
gets to know all sorts of people—and pretty soon I was a regular on the
dance floor, enjoying the fair sex as we whirled and scraped about. I
even picked up a little rhythm and style, and evoked happy exclamations from my partners. Young Stoddard was stepping out in style those
summer and autumnal days and emerging from some cocoon like a
retarded butterfly.

I scarcely thought of myself as an eligible young man. But my new
home, a housekeeper, and all the other subtle trappings of substance
apparently alerted the women of the Washoe that Stoddard was a man
to be invited, examined, and considered acceptable company. I was
reminded of my lifelong propensity to end up in the middle. I was not
the sort of dashing gent who attracts women, but on the other hand, no
one of the fair ladies I met at the balls that year rejected me. They still
were a minority, and the eligible ones had unusual choices and the
chance to be as picky as they could ever wish. Stoddard, presentable

but without flair, comfortable without wealth, a newsman but not drawn to a higher calling, fell in the obscure center.

For my part, I didn't exactly find the maiden of my dreams—but then, I wasn't sure what that was, or just what sort of nature, character, face, figure, hair, eyes, laughter, beliefs, voice, spirit, and inner self I might fall for. In morose moments I suspected I was doomed to a life of bachelorhood, and then I would retreat to my new haunt, Ward & Heffron's Argentine Saloon on South C Street, to balm my spirits and try to make sense of being a social butterfly. This high society was quite a departure, and I seesawed back and forth about it, sometimes vowing to return to my comfortable beat and other times ready to step out and try something new.

The truth of it was that young Stoddard, in the waning months of eighteen and sixty-seven, wasn't quite at home anywhere and hadn't the faintest notion what to do with his muddled self.

CHAPTER 27

 have had a lifelong propensity—let's call it a vice—of nursing my woes instead of setting them aside. That spring of eighteen and sixty-seven I was doing just that in spite of the changes in my private life: the house, the sale of stock, the new investments, and my attendance of balls and galas.

But the Comstock was nothing if not lively, and there were always diversions and entertainments. One night it would be Lotta Crabtree or Fay Templeton at Maguire's. Another night, Lawrence Barrett or Tom Keene or Frank Mayo or Joe Jefferson or Nellie Gilson, "the California Diamond," at Piper's. And I must not forget Victoria Loftus's British Blondes. And if not that, then an evening at one of the melodeons, sampling broader and bawdier humor.

Virginia City had won a reputation as the best theater town west of Chicago and east of San Francisco, and theatrical troupes and entertainers and showmen flocked to our precincts, knowing that the quality of the show made little difference. Miners were so delighted by dramas, female pulchritude, good monologues, and magical acts that they usually showered the performers with coin during the curtain calls. Occasionally some of these missiles beaned or bruised a comely artiste, but who was she to complain when the boards were littered with cash?

And so Virginia City diverted me, swiftly undermining any tendency of mine to dwell morbidly upon my misfortunes, real or imagined. We continued to review all these performances at the *Territorial Enterprise*, often in scathing terms, and relations with Maguire and, later Piper were so strained that we no longer were given free seats or other perquisites. So we bought our seats and wrote what we chose about the performances. Our reviews tended more and more toward the sardonic. It didn't matter to the troupes; they uniformly won the adulation of the miners, filled the opera houses, and walked off with heavy bags of silver.

But that spring of eighteen and sixty-seven was notable for other reasons. Things were again changing on the Comstock, and these matters were directly on my beat. In short, it was up to me to keep abreast of more mining news than I had ever dealt with previously. I was reporting at full tilt, barely aware that the Comstock was seducing me once again.

One of the players in that real-life drama was Adolph Sutro, the owner of a quartz mill down on the Carson River, a keen observer of the mining scene, and a true visionary and genius. For years Sutro had observed the difficulty of hauling ores downslope and supplies upslope from the Comstock to the Carson River, a dozen miles distant, though the river and the Comstock were much closer as the crow flies. He had also been aware of the acute water problems in some of the mines, most notably the Gould & Curry, which in eighteen and sixty-six encountered severe flooding it could not control.

His particular idea was breathtaking and unprecedented. He proposed to build a tunnel from the river up to the Comstock mines, on a gentle gradient, terminating at the Savage mine shaft about sixteen hundred feet down. Laterals to the other mines would drain nearly the entire mining district and thus obviate the need for enormous pumps, monstrous supplies of cordwood to run them, and the expenses of hauling ore downslope. Ore cars would take ore directly down the tunnel, employing the benefits of gravity, to the mills at Dayton on the river. He would charge a small fee for that—two dollars a ton—but the costs would be lower than those of hauling ore by mule team.

What's more, if the mines themselves purchased shares in the giant undertaking they would acquire its profits, and these would assure them of cash during their inevitable periods in borrasca. One or another mine might be exhausted, but the tunnel would earn steady profit because the producing mines would continue to use it. Mines might come and go, but the tunnel would serve the Comstock for decades and yield a rich reward for investors.

The length of the tunnel would be 20,498 feet, or nearly four miles—

a length never before dreamed of. It would cost, he said, around $3 million.

Sutro—an earnest, plain, bulky Jewish man born in the Rhineland—took his scheme to the state legislature in eighteen and sixty-six and won a charter to build the tunnel, with the proviso that it must be fully capitalized by May of eighteen and sixty-seven. But Sutro immediately ran into legal problems. The state of Nevada did not have the authority to grant an easement across federal lands; indeed, little of the land that even the Comstock mines stood on was patented.

So the indefatigable Sutro hied himself all the way to Washington City, there to lobby Congress for the necessary charter. And it was to his credit that he won his charter and that he was able, at the same time, to interest some wary eastern capitalists in the venture—providing, they said, that the core investment be achieved in San Francisco, where financiers wiser to the pitfalls of the district and more familiar with western mining might be the first to subscribe.

I had covered all this in the course of my reporting, sometimes traveling down to Dayton to consult with the shrewd mill owner, sometimes catching him in Virginia City while he was selling his vast undertaking to skeptical mine managers. I remember him well—a nattily dressed man who exuded conviction and intelligence. The entire project was feasible, he said over and over; everything about it was practical and financially rewarding. I wondered about that. The Comstock had a history of tumbling such schemes to dust.

Whenever I expressed my doubts to him he would stare, smile, clap me on the arm, and say, "You just vait. Stoddard, you vill see when Gott gives you eyes."

I never knew him to take offense, and perhaps that was why he managed, one skeptic at a time, to win over the majority of mine managers to his cause.

Now, in May of sixty-seven, he seemed on the brink of success. He had won the support of most of the Comstock mines, whose combined production totaled 71 percent of the district's output. He had raised $600,000 and won a year's extension. He was in the process of petitioning the Nevada legislature as well as the United States Congress for funds to pursue this valuable work, because the Comstock's output would improve the entire national revenue. And then, suddenly, it mysteriously fell apart. The Comstock mines canceled their subscriptions of the stock of the Tunnel Company, thereby annulling the promise of eastern capital.

Sutro was devastated—for the briefest while. But I soon realized that the feisty man wouldn't take no for an answer. When I interviewed him that spring he insisted the mighty project would go forward because it made economic sense. To be sure, he had been forced to raise his estimate to something like $5 million, but that didn't explain why the bottom dropped out from under him or why Nevada's powerful senator William Stewart, whose fortunes had come from the Comstock, had suddenly deserted Sutro and resigned as president of the company.

One day Sutro was the trusted and brilliant entrepreneur who would lead the Comstock to new wealth; the next day Sutro was said to be untrustworthy. In January, the Nevada legislature had cordially commended Sutro for his "great service" and expressed confidence in Sutro's ability to see the project through; not long after, Sutro's plan found little support among any of the state's politicians.

I found myself wondering just why Sutro's plans had come a cropper, and I didn't have to look far or conjure up some obscure explanation. Right there on C Street, the briefest walk from the paper, stood the mighty Bank of California and that manipulator of Fate, young William Sharon, the compact, silent financier who had ended up banking for most of the mines and mills in the district by offering lower interest rates and easier collateral than his rivals.

I had always had trouble digging news from Sharon, who usually was unavailable for interview, always terse, and offered me something only when it was in his interest to do so. And yet I had known for two or three years that Sharon was the most powerful and shrewd man on the Comstock and his will prevailed. He had the leverage—debt instruments—to bend mine owners and managers to his will and did not hesitate to do so.

Sharon had, from the beginning, accepted flimsy collateral for his loans to the mills. In the early sixties over seventy mills had been erected to reduce the rich ores of the Comstock, but most of these swiftly vanished, while the surviving and more efficient mills increased their capacity. Mills survived only when they had ample ore; let a mill enter a slack period and it could not earn enough even to service its debt, much less earn a profit. The effect of the swings of fortune on the Comstock was to put one mill after another out of business—and these often ended up in the hands of Sharon and his Bank of California.

They were bad collateral. An unused mill deteriorated with breathtaking speed. The giant batteries, pans, and mullers swiftly rusted and locked tight. The rude mill buildings, constructed of green lumber, twisted and warped and fell apart. Sharon once told me that he was able to salvage only $3,000 from mill equipment that had collateralized a $60,000 loan. I had reported the case of a mill in the White Pine mining district that had been built for $200,000 and later offered for $5,000 with no buyers in sight.

Sharon and his bank acquired its first mill by default in May of eighteen and sixty-six. It was the Swansea, in Lyon County. By May of the following year the Bank of California held seven failed mills and had little prospect of recovering much from any of them. But the wily Sharon was not daunted by this threat to his fiefdom or his bank. He reasoned that these liabilities could be turned into an asset, and that is exactly what he proceeded to do.

The bank's principal owners agreed to Sharon's proposition to create a separate corporation, the Union Mill and Mining Company, to purchase and manage the failed mills. By June, the corporation was a reality. Its charter members were Darius Ogden Mills, William Sharon, Alvinza Hayward, Thomas Sunderland, William Chambers Ralston, Charles Bonner, Thomas Bell, and William E. Barrow.

These gentlemen, as it happened, were principal shareholders of Comstock mines and quite capable of pressuring the managers to send their milling ores to the mines of the new corporation. There had never been much competitive bidding on the Constock; the selection of mills by mine supervisors had largely been a matter of gifts, pressure, and bribery, rather than costs, efficiencies, and purely economic factors. And the mines themselves had been reluctant to build their own mills unless the case for milling their ores themselves was blatant. For the most part, the relationship was an old-boy network that often left outsiders, including the smaller stockholders, with far smaller dividends than more efficient managers might have won for them.

Well, reader, it comes clear now, doesn't it? The new combination swiftly became the powerhouse of the Comstock. William Sharon, the arachnid at the center of the web, began to extend his control over the remaining mines and mills until he was within sight of complete domination of the entire Comstock.

And as for Sutro—little did he realize that Sharon and his banking friends were contemplating a railroad that would largely eliminate the need for the tunnel. I didn't realize it either until it was announced. That was how silently they worked. And I had become the fool, failing to break the most important stories of all. But who was Henry Stoddard when pitted against a crafty genius like Sharon?

. . . .

CHAPTER 28

Joe Goodman, wearying of what in Virginia City was strenuous sport, appointed Rollin Daggett to replace him as editor of the *Territorial Enterprise* and turned to his accounting. It was an inspired choice. Daggett was already a fixture on the Comstock, having found gainful employment at various rags.

Others have described him far better than I could hope to, so I shall rely on them. Wells Drury, editor of the *Gold Hill News,* called Daggett the Cyrano de Bergerac of the Comstock. A later editor of our sheet, Judge Charlie Goodwin—not to be confused with Joe Goodman—limned Daggett thusly: "He had no more form than a sack of apples and his character, from a Christian standpoint, was a good deal shopworn in spots."

I prefer my own version, that Daggett was Don Quixote, for if there was any windmill to be assaulted, lanced, or skewered Daggett found it, and if there wasn't he found one anyway. He was a famous fighter. In fact, he was famous in every branch of endeavor, and no more so than in his editorial brown study, which consisted of a trip to the Old Magnolia, where whoever tended bar automatically poured him a decanter of Steamboat gin, which he proceeded to demolish until he was sufficiently ripe to perform his editorial duties.

That was Daggett. I welcomed him. The *Territorial Enterprise* had a way of collecting unique specimens, save only for the plodding Henry Stoddard, who had become a back-room fixture, like an old type case, known to all but invisible. But by then, eighteen and sixty-eight, I was more or less content in my niche. I wrote about machinery, hoists, ore tenors, and stock prices, whilst the rest wrote about people.

Daggett left me alone. Someone on the paper had to do the sort of thing I did, or write obituaries, or take church news, or list the band concerts. Besides, rumor had it I was rich and not hungry.

Like most editors of that period, Daggett could double for a compositor if need be and was no stranger to the type stick and fonts. One could find him, of an evening, at the office annex, otherwise known as the Old Magnolia, where he, if humored properly, would sing "Slug Fourteen":

"He leaned upon the stone and swore:
By Jesus Christ as I have said before
And you have often, often heard me tell
Brevier won't justify with nonpariel."

Now, if you don't know fonts that ditty will fly by you, and I will leave you in darkness. Suffice it to say, Nevada's leading newspaper was better than ever. Better than when Clemens was aboard. Better than when Dan De Quille was more or less—actually less—editor. As for De Quille, he continued to turn in his curious pieces, and I always enjoyed them because he didn't have a mean bone in him, unlike Clemens. A quick examination of De Quille's titles in that period will show you what the venerable humorist was up to: "The Washoe Zephyr," "A Bug Mine," "Ever Prospecting—Always Behind," "Munchhausen the Second," "Traveling Stones," "A Singular Kind of Fish," "A Ghost in Ophir," "The Local Editor—His Duties and Delights." Oh, I could go on and on. With Daggett drumming and De Quille fifing, we had the best paper in the West, no doubt about it.

Reader, do you detect a small thread of envy? You are right. I sometimes wished I could join the illustrious of the Washoe, but I had come to know Henry Stoddard pretty well by then and knew I could no more produce a masterpiece like "Traveling Stones" than I could improve on Shakespeare.

On April 24, 1868, Daggett assigned me to cover a hanging, which was not something I wished to do. In fact, he assigned three of his reporters to cover the hanging, because this would be no ordinary one. The lengthy appeal proceedings of Julia Bulette's murderer, John Millian, had run out after the Nevada Supreme Court upheld the conviction. A gallows had been constructed in a small amphitheater north of town near Geiger Grade. The main event was scheduled for noon. I felt queasy about it, not wanting to observe a man plunge to his death, not even a man with a black hood over his face.

I had no particular quarrel with the death sentence. I thought Millian's guilt was beyond reasonable doubt even if the evidence seemed circumstantial. And Millian's wild stories about two ruffians named Douglass and Dillon were mere fantasies, supported by not one piece of evidence. Most of the press was present. I spotted Alf Doten of the *Gold Hill News* and people from the *Virginia Chronicle* and various San Francisco papers. The killer of Julia Bulette was going to depart from us in very public fashion.

In due course, Millian was brought out of the jail and put in a closed carriage, along with Father Manogue. A second carriage transported the attending physicians and the reporters. Our conveyance was followed by a third, which carried the coffin and undertaker. This procession was escorted by the National Guard and deputies, all armed and in uniform. Behind us came a mob of three thousand people, on foot and horse, spectators to an execution.

We of the press were gathered scarcely a dozen feet from the scaffold, which was closer than I preferred to be. Millian seemed steady enough as he mounted the gallows. He thanked those who had visited him in his cell or otherwise helped him, speaking slowly in a tongue he had barely mastered, and launched into a fretful speech— almost as though the talking might delay his doom a snatch or two longer, claiming gross injustice and that the police chief had perjured himself. But Millian ended up expressing his forgiveness of all concerned.

Then, after a short prayer with Father Manogue, Millian shook hands with all and sundry up there on that raw wood platform, stood calmly while the noose settled about his neck, and then the hood, and went instantly to his doom. After two minutes a shudder ran through his body. He was cut down after twenty-five minutes.

I did not like what I saw and reported it badly, barely able to scribble out what I had witnessed. The tone was stiff and colorless. I no longer have the story, or I'd quote it as an example of bad writing. There have been moments when I wanted to be anything other than a reporter, and that day was one.

But I had my consolations. It fell to me to report one of the great stories of the Comstock, and but for my diligence the *Territorial Enterprise* might well have been scooped by its busy, busy rivals. I had made it my daily duty to keep an eye on William Sharon, the crafty black widow spider whose web was closing around the Comstock. I visited his office in the Bank of California as often as I deemed sensible, given his distaste for the press, for publicity, for anything other than total silence surrounding his machinations.

But I had evolved my own spiderweb of tipsters. Many of them were clerks in law offices, employed at writing fair copies of contracts and documents and woefully underpaid, a condition I sometimes remedied when I was given certain information. Likewise, courthouse clerks provided fat tidbits, in addition to what I could glean from public records, tax notices, and all the rest. Likewise, my friends the stockbrokers and speculators were good sources and welcomed whatever silver crossed their palms. And thus I discovered that Union Mill and Mining, Sharon's little corporation, was not content to operate seven mills and run the bulk of Comstock ore through them; no, it was going to own every mill in the district and mill all the ore. In short, Sharon intended to own the Comstock.

When I discovered that Union Mill had purchased another mill, and another, and another, I saw the picture and began announcing these acquisitions in the paper. That irritated Sharon, who at first refused to see me but then capitulated when I reported that, too. But now I reversed the tables, and on the occasions when I penetrated his silent, dark, wainscoted offices, where he worked in a miasma of gloom, it was I who was the bearer of news. For I would tell him what I knew, and he, always curious about what I knew, would question me, often seeking to find out who was sliding information to me—which evoked my most charitable of smiles.

These seances became something of a sport and joy for me, because I learned to fathom the importance of my information by the degree of irritation in him. The visits became more frequent, and I got more out of him because he could scarcely refuse to see me. And I have no doubt that I shocked and vexed him from time to time.

Sometimes he studied me with hooded eyes and I knew he was pondering ways of abolishing me from the rolls of the paper. But both Goodman and Daggett fully understood what I was bringing to the front page—almost always ahead of our rivals—and assured me of their support.

Sharon wasn't any more evil than any other financier on the Comstock, just more shrewd, and possessed of the gift of secrecy. In the end, we used each other. I had learned to gauge my news by his reaction to me; he had learned to confide the things he wanted known. And so we spiders did our dance, and in my reportage in sixty-seven, sixty-eight, and sixty-nine I described the purchase of more mills, until Sharon's company owned seventeen and had a controlling interest in most of the mines. The Comstock was changing, for good or ill. Ill, I thought, because powerful combinations usually cut wages of employees and began to dictate to merchants.

I missed one important event, and William Sharon relished telling it to me. That was the railroad. There had been, over the years, various charters issuing from the state legislature, but none had ever resulted in rail and crossties and roadbed and locomotives and rolling stock. One of these charters was the Virginia Carson & Truckee Railroad Company, with the authority, as my friend Eliot Lord put it, to run spider legs of rail in various directions. Perhaps the reason that it, and its successors, failed was that the Central Pacific had yet to top the Sierras and enter Nevada. Crocker's construction company had to fight for every mile up the long, gentle western slopes of the Sierra Nevada.

I should pause here to explain that Sharon's railroad project was doubly daring. The output of the Washoe district was declining steadily, and no new bonanzas were improving the picture. To build a railroad just at the time when the Comstock mines seemed to be playing out was, in the eyes of some, a folly. The product of the district in eighteen and sixty-seven was about $13,800,000. In eighteen and sixty-eight it had declined to $12,418,000, and in that terrible year of eighteen and sixty-nine, when work on the railroad began, it declined to $6,683,000.

No new lodes were in sight, save for one small, rich seam in the Yellow Jacket at the 900-foot level. Even so, that mine's product had fallen from $2.6 million in eighteen and sixty-seven to $682,000 in eighteen and sixty-eight. The great Savage mine had paid its stockholders over one and a half millions of dividends in eighteen and sixty-seven, but only ninety thousand the following year. The mighty Gould & Curry was all but exhausted. Worse, the explorations for new ore had run into a gangue of carbonate and sulphate of lime, while the productive quartz had all but vanished. And yet that genius, that willful gambler Sharon, plunged in.

It did not seem so daring to him, for he gazed upon the world with an entrepreneur's eyes. What he saw was that the timbering of the mines was becoming astronomically expensive because the massive logs, cut in the distant Sierras, had to be transported thirty or so miles by mules and oxen. What he saw was mountains of low-grade ore in heaps beside the mines, uneconomic to haul down the slope to the mills on the Carson River by muscle power—but a source of vast wealth when hauled cheaply by rail. He saw mines failing for want of heavy equipment, water pumps, boilers, engines, most of it too heavy to be hauled, even in pieces, up to Mount Davidson by muscle power.

What he saw was a city economy built on exceptionally high prices because every item on the Comstock had been drawn there by muscle power—and the prospect that prices, and no doubt even wages, could all be reduced 20 or 30 percent if there was a railroad that would eventually connect to the Central Pacific and California. His vision was better than mine in all matters except the wages. The skilled miners would not budge from their four dollars a day, no matter what pressures the managers and financiers brought to bear upon them. And when the railroad arrived and commodity prices did plummet in the stores, the miners of the Comstock enjoyed happy times, the equivalent of a large raise.

In December of eighteen and sixty-eight, I ran into Sharon on C Street. He was wearing his usual stovepipe hat and Inverness cape and calculating look. He paused, caught my attention, and told me he had hired a man named James to locate a roadbed and determine the feasibility of the railroad project and that the survey was to include a route to the mills on the river and a line to Carson City.

I reported the news, which met with disbelief—and hope. Sharon had fathomed something I hadn't: that most of the mines had reached only the 700-foot level—mere gouging of the surface as far as he was concerned. He intuited that farther down in the mysterious rock lay untold riches, giant bonanzas, incredible wealth—and he was right. I give him credit for that. He, almost alone at that point, believed in the Comstock, believed the best was yet to come. The rest of us, whose eyes were jaded, believed that his Virginia & Truckee Railroad would be completed just about at the time when it might haul the last of the low-grade ore down the hill.

The surveyor, I. E. James, turned out to be a genius. His daunting task was to plot a railroad from a site on a mountain slope, 6,205 feet above sea level, to a river valley 1,575 feet lower and only thirteen and a half miles distant. The route would require trestles over ravines, tunnels, and bridges at every hand, almost beyond counting. He located a twenty-one-mile right-of-way, with a grade that averaged 2.2 percent, a maximum of 116 feet to the mile, and curvature that equaled seventeen full circles, which would make it the crookedest railroad on earth.

CHAPTER 29

he two gentlemen who largely organized and financed the Virginia & Truckee Railroad were largely beyond my reach, and I now draw my depiction of them from the published sources available to me. They both were prominent San Franciscans with a keen eye for profit and opportunity, especially such opportunity as William Sharon presented to them during a trip he made to the City on the Bay, in eighteen and sixty-eight, to lay before them the idea of a railroad. I can well imagine the skepticism Sharon met in the Bank of California presenting such a plan at a time when the Comstock seemed to be in sharp decline.

But the bank's presiding officer, Darius Ogden Mills, and its cashier, William Ralston, were not ordinary men. Mills was a calculating plunger who had occasionally risked the bank's assets—or, rather, its depositors' assets. I have before me a tintype of Mills, a plain, saturnine man with black muttonchops and a regal nose. He wears a Prince Albert frock coat and a brocaded vest and stands with one hand inserted into his vest, Napoleonic and formidable. But, in truth, he was largely a puppet. The real genius—and organizer—of the Bank of California was William C. Ralston. Although the bank was really Ralston's, he reserved for himself the title of Cashier, from which cockpit he could maneuver in utter secrecy with Mills as his storefront.

Ralston, a man of regular features, trimmed beard, and a receding hairline that gave him a noble forehead, was, in fact, the man who drew the Comstock into the hands of his bank. By that year, his Union Mill and Mining Company had mined and milled 95 percent of the ores coming from the Comstock. He had achieved this by first appointing his wily and like-minded agent, William Sharon, as his regional manager and then acquiring properties one by one.

Unlike Mills or Sharon, Ralston was a romantic and visionary, and dreamed of a San Francisco that would become the cultural capital of the West. He could be impulsive and occasionally ruined men who opposed him. He could also be generous, was usually loyal, and had the great virtue of accepting responsibility for errors when things went wrong.

When consulting with his business associates he habitually ripped a sheet of paper into smaller and smaller pieces, and when he had reduced one sheet he would reach for another and demolish it—a habit that unmoored all but the most doughty of those he conferred with.

In eighteen and sixty-six Ralston had purchased the villa of Count Lussetti Cipriani in Belmont, south of San Francisco, and turned it into a rambling mansion. One of Ralston's whimsies was to board his four-in-hand carriage in downtown San Francisco and promptly, at 5:00 P.M., race it to Belmont—twenty-two miles south—in a contest with the commuter train. Usually, he won.

William Chambers Ralston, like so many of California's geniuses, was a self-made man. He had devoted his youth to the riverboat business on the Mississippi and Ohio Rivers. In eighteen and forty-nine he joined the gold rush, but at Panama City he ran into friends who were engaged in shipping and went to work for them. By eighteen and fifty-one he was captaining a 1,100-ton steamer, the *New Orleans,* from Panama to San Francisco. In eighteen and fifty-four he became the San Francisco agent for the Independent Opposition Line, Commodore Vanderbilt's riposte to the Pacific Mail Company. After that, he plunged into banking, eventually forming his Bank of California along with Mills and Louis McLane, of Wells, Fargo & Company. From that vantage point, Ralston began financing everything from sugar refineries and silkworm farms to watch factories and theaters.

The Virginia & Truckee Railroad was actually his creature.

He and his partners began by persuading the Nevada legislature to renew one of the old railroad charters. He and Mills and Sharon had the uncommon good sense to employ, as general manager of the new railroad, Henry M. Yerington, a muttonchopped, hard-driving genius who knew how to turn an idea into a going enterprise. So popular was this gent that later a township once known as Pizen Switch changed its name to Yerington. He had reason not to like the Bank of California crowd, having seen his mill squeezed out by the monolithic competition. But he was one to set aside grudges, and took over what became the most celebrated little railroad in the nation. Not only did he build it, but he ran it so successfully that it became, mile for mile, the most profitable short railroad ever operated. He remained its manager all the rest of his life.

On September 27 I caught the stagecoach to Carson to cover the launching of construction, scheduled to begin early the next day. But when we of the press arrived for the ceremonial hammering of a silver spike we discovered that Yerington's crews had been hard at work for half an hour, and we all had to fabricate the official event by consulting various witnesses. Three hours later, Yerington had a locomotive running on new track. At once I liked Yerington. He was a doer. From that moment on, the *Territorial Enterprise* carried railroad news in virtually every issue, eagerly reporting the daily progress. On October 3, the great Crown Point trestle near Gold Hill was completed and a route to Carson was imminent.

We were carrying other news, as well. The Central Pacific had long since passed through northern Nevada on its way to Promontory Point, Utah, and on May 10 the Central was joined to the Union Pacific and a transcontinental railroad became a reality. Soon Virginia City would be linked by rail not only to California but also—improbably and wondrously—to the States.

But Virginia City was thirty-some miles south of the Central Pacific, and every crosstie, rail, and spike arrived at our doorstep by mule or ox power. Likewise, the rolling stock Yerington and Sharon ordered arrived in the same manner. Sharon swiftly ordered three engines from Booth and Company: the "Lyon," "Storey," and, later, "Ormsby." These were fine 2-6-0 types, or Moguls, with forty-inch drivers, two weighing 44,000 pounds, while the "Storey" weighed 54,000. At the same time, he ordered two others from Baldwin Locomotive Works, also Moguls, the "Virginia" and the "Carson," to be used as work engines building the road. These were bigger brutes, with forty-eight-inch drivers, each weighing 55,000 pounds.

We awaited them breathlessly, the papers reporting their progress daily. When the Booth locomotives arrived at a spot on the Truckee River that would soon become Reno, they were dismantled and hauled in pieces to Carson City. But Yerington wished to put the two Baldwins in immediate service, building the road from both ends. That meant hauling them intact, up the Geiger Grade, to Virginia City by ox team.

All this I covered for the paper, sometimes taking lengthy trips to watch the progress. The Baldwins caused trouble almost from the start. On the Truckee Meadow, south of Reno, a wooden bridge adequate for wagons turned out to be inadequate for a 55,000-pound locomotive, and the teamsters were forced to ford a creek. Then, when the straining oxen began to haul the monster up Geiger Grade, they hit a pothole, bogging the "Carson" for days while the hole dried out. But the "Virginia" eventually arrived.

What a moment that was, when those panting bovines dragged the monster onto the northern reaches of C Street, thereby very nearly provoking a riot. Every office, every shop, every saloon, and most every household discharged its occupants, who crowded the street to see the behemoth. We celebrated, as usual, with a several-day binge, and my recollection of the following days is a bit hazy.

In San Francisco, meanwhile, the Kimball company was constructing our rolling stock, including two coaches and a mail car. In Carson City, the railroad's own workmen were building the freight cars.

The normally taciturn and secretive Sharon had, in the space of a few weeks, metamorphosed into a showman. The Bank of California had begun to wine and dine financiers and other captains of industry, and Sharon never hesitated to pull a cork on vintage wine when the occasion demanded. The railroad had been funded in part by bank money, but most unusually, massive sums from its partners as well as contributions from Storey and Ormsby Counties, which taxpayers cynically presumed—and rightly so—were a public contribution to a private business, with little or nothing asked in return. The financiers also wrung $700,000 from the mining companies on the Comstock.

But Sharon never stopped courting financiers, knowing that the railroad would require vast amounts of additional capital to run rails from Carson City to the Central Pacific. I have to say this about Sharon: he was a cultivated man who could quote Shakespeare, orate, and name the vineyard just by smelling a cork. He shamelessly employed all these graces when courting the moneybags he brought out to the roadbed to see the sights.

By the middle of April of that momentous year, Yerington had 750 laborers grading roadbed, building bridges and trestles, and tunneling, and this was soon expanded to 1,200, mostly Chinamen, housed in thirty-eight camps, so that progress was being made at every point of the route simultaneously. Meanwhile, the company had ordered rails from England and had engaged woodcutters in the Sierras to supply crossties. As the result of all this planning and enterprise, it took only six weeks to spike down the forty-pound steel rails from Carson City to Gold Hill, the temporary terminus. From that momentous silver-spike morning on September 28 to November 12, Yerington's hard-driving crews had built a railroad.

And oh! How we celebrated.

The honors, on the bunting-draped occasion, fell to the smaller of the V & T engines, the "Lyon." We gathered there in Gold Hill on that November day and waited the arrival of the first train from below. Eventually it showed up, belching smoke from its tall Dolly Varden stack, steaming across the last and most formidable trestle, and hissing to rest before our half-believing eyes at the new red station. The Gold Hill municipal band struck up lively airs and every whistle of the surrounding mines and mills began to howl like a mad bagpipe, joined by the "Lyon's" own cat's meows. In due course, William Sharon stepped out of the cab of the "Lyon" and the celebrating began in earnest.

Sharon knew his Comstock citizens. Was not the Comstock the drinkingest place on earth? He uncorked some champagne resting in a tub at trackside, and after a few bottles had been demolished by the dignitaries he invited the thirsty crowd to partake of the barrels and barrels of beer he had laid up for the occasion. We all did. And only much later, after we had been properly anointed, lubricated, and baptized, were we treated to mellifluent oratory celebrating everything from faster transportation to lower prices, oratory that rendered afternoon into evening before it was exhausted.

What no one celebrated on that day was the line's awesome profitability. Sharon and his associates had built that stretch of the V & T for $1,750,000, or $83,333 per mile, but that didn't include the rolling stock, shops, and other works still under construction. Not long after, they were dividing among them a hundred thousand dollars of pure profit each and every month. The road was repaying, each year, approximately what the three owners had sunk into it. That was not a bad investment.

. . . .

CHAPTER 30

The readers of this memoir have no doubt sensed by now that something has been missing from my account of life in Virginia City. I have not dwelled much upon the lives of the miners and their families, the very souls whose daily toil under difficult circumstances produced the glittering wealth that was transforming San Francisco into the Athens of the West Coast.

In the course of bringing my reader up to the present, I must step back a bit to eighteen and sixty-seven. That was the notable year when Sharon formed his combination, the Union Mill and Mining Company, and began buying up every property he could lay hands on at a bargain price. Scarcely two months after that behemoth had come to life, the quiet and industrious miners organized a union. They achieved this notable milestone on the Fourth of July, and they had one primary objective: no man, they said, should work underground for less than four dollars a day. It did not matter to them that their skilled members were far more productive and worth much more than the apprentices and new men who largely mucked up ore with shovels. Four dollars for an eight-hour shift for all who entered the stygian darkness was their battle standard, and they meant to enforce their will.

Most of the mines agreed at once, but one firm, the Savage Mining Company, held out. In August, the union quietly resolved to send a committee to visit the mine and request that all those who worked underground should receive the proper wage. But the "committee" consisted of 300 doughty men who marched to the Savage works and parleyed. In short order the foreman agreed to hoist the working miners so that the committee might discover who were earning less than the proper wage, and the committee soon discovered that fourteen of the seventy on that shift were not earning the standard.

To no avail did Superintendent Charles Bonner explain to the assembled miners that those experienced men working on the breast, or face, surely earned that amount, but unskilled laborers produced less and therefore were paid less, which he considered only fair. But he failed to persuade that formidable committee, and in short order the Savage capitulated. From that time on, four dollars an eight-hour shift became the standard on the Comstock, and the district enjoyed a remarkable labor peace compared to what came later, in other districts, in more recent times. Four dollars was no pittance even in a district where prices were high owing to the difficulty of transporting everything to those barren slopes of Mount Davidson, as Sun Mountain was increasingly called. It had been renamed after Donald Davidson of San Francisco, who had purchased Comstock ores and sent them to England for reduction.

Later, when the full impact of the Virginia & Truckee Railroad began to be reflected in the plummeting prices of food and commodities— which fell once the railroad began operating—the miners were even better off, their hard-won dollars purchasing a third again as much as they previously had. Cordwood, a large item in the budget of any mining family, immediately dropped from $15 to $11.50 and by the following year had fallen to $9. Comstock miners had become the kings of American labor, and no workers anywhere else on earth were better paid.

I don't mean to suggest that all those in the class of toilers were noble while those in the countinghouses were villainous. Plenty of miners, especially those operating under contracts, were brimming with chicane. A contract outfit might be engaged by a mine to extend a drift ten feet for a fee of $300. The mine super would then drill a small hole at the side of the face and drive a wooden peg into it, from which to measure the contract work, and then retire to his office.

In due course he would be ushered into the drift and find that the head was indeed ten feet farther than the peg and pay out the cash to the contract outfit—which would vanish from sight. Only later would the super discover that the miners had blown out the company's peg and inserted a new peg ten feet back. Then they had lollygagged around for an appropriate time and collected their booty for doing exactly nothing. In time, the managements learned to measure from the start of the drift to its head.

Laboring underground was fraught with danger. Unknown and toxic gases sometimes burst from seams of clay, nauseating miners. Water constantly menaced them and the more experienced among them learned not to thrust their picks into a certain type of blue clay for fear that they would loose an explosive cataract that would drive them back from the breast of a drift, in peril of drowning or being scalded. Timbers collapsed suddenly, trapping men behind them, while rescuers dug frantically to free them—more often failing before the oxygen gave out and the doomed men suffocated.

The mine managers purchased enormous amounts of timber cut in the Sierras, much of it in the Lake Tahoe basin. Large and well-manned companies built giant flumes that shot the sawed timbers into the Carson Valley or Washoe Meadows, where the wood was hauled by ox team to the mines, at least until the Virginia & Truckee took over. A single mine might have more wood in it than a large community aboveground. Thick posts supported floor upon floor of thick planks, and between the floors were wooden steps and wooden chutes, while a type of planking called lagging braced up weak rock.

It was inevitable that such massive amounts of wood deep under the surface would catch fire, and in April of eighteen and sixty-nine the thing most dreaded by miners came to pass. A fire in the Yellow Jacket, which swiftly spread to its neighbors the Crown Point and Kentucky, caught a new shift of men just heading into the works early in the morning and murdered thirty-six. Those were days that haunt me still, and even now, thirty-one years later, I write with difficulty, the images refusing to turn themselves into words by which I might share this terrible occasion with you.

I remember that morning as if it were yesterday. It was my custom to rise late and reach the editorial sanctum of the paper around ten, my theory being that nothing important or newsworthy happens before then, while many stories erupt in the evenings. Around midnight I usually called it a day. On that morning of April 7, I could scarcely have been more wrong about the occurrence of news. I awakened to the cacophony of whistles wailing dirges. I hastened through my toilet, neglecting the razor, and headed into a springtime morning filled with dread. All about me people were racing toward Gold Hill, beyond the Divide, where the sky lay leaden with a gray pallor. A fire wagon raced by, and another, and I knew trouble of the worst sort was at hand.

It's a considerable distance to Gold Hill, but I made it in twenty-five minutes, and there beheld the nightmare I most feared: smoke billowing in sinister columns from the shafts of the Yellow Jacket, Kentucky, and Crown Point mines while about these three mines a wailing crowd milled restlessly. I knew that some of those poor women, whose children clutched their skirts, would likely be widows soon. I worked my way through to the shaft of the Yellow Jacket, where firemen in their great hats were directing a stream of water down the shaft and engineers in the hoisting works were raising and lowering the cage in the vain hope of bringing men up. But no man came.

I caught the attention of a mine clerk I knew who was watching morosely from behind the rope that cordoned all of us back from the shaft. "What happened?" I asked.

Bainbridge—that was his name—explained it thusly:

"As far as we can tell, when the night shift left the pit at four this morning someone left a candle burning in its holder, and it caught the mine on fire. This was at the eight-hundred-foot level. With no one in the pit, it went undiscovered until the day shift went down at seven. No sooner did men reach that level than they were driven back by violent fumes, smoke, and heat." He sighed. "Some got back up in a cage so jammed that some had nothing to hang onto. The others . . ." He let the rest remain unsaid.

The fire had swiftly engrossed the Kentucky and then the Crown Point, whose connecting crosscuts and drifts had improved ventilation for the miners, and the story had been much the same in the other mines as well. Men were still down there, but little could be done because of the ferocious heat, smoke, and fumes rising from the shafts, enough to kill any fireman venturing downward.

Men had been rescued from the other mines as the engineers worked the cages as swiftly as possible, but the fire overwhelmed the underground crews before all were lifted to safety. And the very last to come up were so suffocated they were barely alive, and took a long time to recover as they gasped for air aboveground. Some of the last were so weakened that they could not hold on and fell to their deaths as the cages ascended.

So we waited in dread, while the wives gathered, the mine foremen attempted to discover who had gotten up and who was left down there, and firemen played their hoses down the shafts, almost helplessly. No one wished to seal the shafts to suffocate the fires—not with men down there. The smoke billowed upward, rising high in the blue sky, a harbinger of grief. The waiting was terrible and prolonged.

At the Crown Point they sent the cage down to the lowest levels, well below the holocaust, with a lamp on its floor and a message written on pasteboard:

> We are fast subduing the fire. It is death to attempt
> to come up from where you are. We shall get you out
> soon. The gas in the shaft is terrible and produces
> sure and speedy death. Write a word to us and send
> it up on the cage, and let us know where you are.

When the cage came up, the lamp was extinguished and no word appeared on the pasteboard.

I noticed that the Reverend Father Manogue was hurrying about with some of his fellow priests, doing what he could to comfort the women, but even their kind and powerful presence did little to allay the tears. I swear that those women already knew, somehow, which of their men they would never again see alive.

Then, miraculously, a shifting of the fire far below emptied the Yellow Jacket shaft of smoke and fumes, and it became the downdraft shaft, sucking fresh air into the works while the smoke billowed all the higher from the Kentucky and Crown Point. Swiftly those brave firemen wet the shaft to cool it, and toward noon some firemen descended to the 800-foot level and recovered the bodies of four miners. As each body was lifted out, a terrible wail erupted from the crowd as wives and children strained to see, and in each case a heartrending cry informed us that someone's husband and father had been recognized.

The firemen continued to bring up the dead from the Yellow Jacket until all but one of those known to be below had been accounted for. Only superhuman effort enabled them to do this, for at every hand they were fighting fire and every breath they took weakened and nauseated them. But they persisted, and won their way to the lowest levels.

Things were even more desolate at the shafts of the Crown Point and Kentucky where noxious fumes and smoke prevented any efforts at rescue and all firemen could do was flood water into the shafts while the engineers in the hoist works pumped air to the lowest levels in a desperate effort to fill the lungs of the living. But not I, nor anyone else who beheld that cataclysm, possessed any hope that live men remained below. Only the wives continued to hope, and I am glad they did, for hope is the greatest of God's gifts.

By nine that night it became plain that the fires in the mines were advancing from one level to another. Nonetheless, the firemen continued to hunt for bodies. They found several around two in the morning, in the sump or water-filled hole at the bottom of the shaft. These they brought up.

I wrote my story, slept briefly, and returned the next day. By that time, twenty-three bodies had been recovered; no living man had been brought out of the mines that night. And so the hours and days passed. By the tenth it became plain that no one alive was in the mines. Because the fires were still expanding, eating one level after another, the fire crews decided to seal the shafts and suffocate the flames. So the shafts were covered with planks, wet blankets, and earth and the various conduits and pipes stopped up. That morning, steam was directed into the works but to no avail. The fires smoldered on, and on.

On the twelfth, the shafts were opened and more bodies brought up—these too decomposed by heat and fumes to be recognizable. The firemen had to load them upon tar-impregnated canvas to lift them up.

But the fires reignited and began devouring new quarters of the mines. The mining companies abandoned the idea of extinguishing the blazes with steam, which carried too much air with it.

At that time, five men still remained in the mines. Three more days elapsed and the shafts were opened again and firemen were able to probe a little. But the heat was unbearable.

Thus the rest of April passed, with the fires still smoldering and ready to explode again if given the slightest dose of air. Occasionally another body was brought up, and some of these were scarcely identifiable as mortal remains at that point. On May 2 the fire worsened, and at that time the three mines sealed off the shafts more or less for the duration, and not until May 18 did anyone descend. The work of shoring up the ruined mines began even while miners and firemen built bulkheads to seal off the still-burning sections of the works. And the heat they encountered was barely relieved by the volume of fresh air the mines were pumping below.

I wrote that story each and every day and thought it would never end, and in a way it never did, because Virginia City was never quite the same.

Nor was I the same. I wondered whether wealth was worth it.

CHAPTER 31

 wrestled each day with loneliness. The Comstock deposited innumerable acquaintances, drinking friends, newsmen, in my daily life, and yet I felt terribly alone. Such is the nature of a mining town that it discourages intimacy. No one plans to stay, and therefore no friendships run deep or endure. We were all lonely; it wasn't just me. We all thought from time to time about leaving. More and more I could meander into the old haunts and find myself sipping claret and feeling apart.

Sometimes I had a drink with William Wright, who was running those days with Alf Doten, the Gold Hill editor. That pair chose a wilder and woolier recreational life than suited me. Dan De Quille and I were bored with each other: I knew his whole history, philosophy, and virtues and not a few of his less savory facets. He had heard my story and my outlook and was just as bored with me. We had been together on the paper since eighteen and sixty-one. A new man was a diversion, and for a while I did some sociable drinking with Rollin Daggett, the romantic, the dreamer, the jouster. His appetites were Falstaffian and I could never keep up with him as he drained his usual decanter of Steamboat gin. But pretty soon we drifted our separate ways.

Virginia City had finally found a way to socialize apart from its hundred saloons, and that was with balls. These were staged by every manner of host or hostess or club or society, from social butterflies to bawds. In fact, the whores' balls were among the gaudiest and best attended on the lode and made a fat profit for the dance halls. But most of the balls were held under better auspices, by miners' unions or the firemen—the firemen's balls were perennially popular—or the Sons of Norway or Hungary or Sweden or Italy, for the town had organized itself along ethnic lines.

I attended many and danced to fiddle music, string orchestras, pianos, quartets, brass bands, and even once a calliope when a small circus blew through the lode. I danced with miners' wives, older widows, a smattering of single girls, and a wide variety of serving wenches, Cyprians, and kept women, sometimes in masks. That was about as close as I managed to get to the fair sex, and while I enjoyed whirling a buxom lady about the boards and I enjoyed pleasantries with all sorts of attached women, these events did not stave off my loneliness and sometimes plunged me into melancholia.

I resolved, in desperation, to take some time off and visit San Francisco. Travel to that fabled metropolis had suddenly become much easier. The V & T did not rest on its laurels upon completing the line to Carson City but began building a line northward, up the Washoe Valley to the Truckee River valley, where one would, someday soon, catch a westbound Central Pacific train to the terminus at Sacramento and then embark for San Francisco on a river steamer. In short, Virginia City would be connected to the world. But not just then.

We had been able for some while to make an excursion to Carson City and return the same day on one of the thirty or forty trains run by the V & T. In fact, the railroad was running as many trains day and night as the system would bear, and even those were scarcely enough to handle the volume of goods and passengers going up or down the slope.

I took a month's leave—Joe Goodman frankly wondered whether I would return, though I promised solemnly that I would—and set forth for the cosmopolitan City on the Bay, suspecting I was something of a rube and ought to be careful lest I lose every double eagle in my purse or, worse, find myself enslaved on a slow boat to Singapore.

Travel lifts the heart, and it lifted mine. I found a seat in one of the

Kimball-built coaches operated by the railroad. These first coaches were a far cry from some of the luxury coaches that soon would be drawn up the slope and down in the eighteen-seventies, carrying nabobs and potentates such as President Grant, General Sherman, and Leland Stanford (whose ornate car, the Stanford, cost $30,000). Phineas Barnum would come to Virginia City by rail, as well as Helen Modjeska, Edwin Booth, Maude Adams, Salvini the Younger, and David Belasco. Baron Rothschild arrived in a splendid car, and that inspired Henry Yerington to ask Darius Mills for one of his own, which was eventually built in the railroad's own shops.

But I am getting ahead of myself, as is my wont. Those first coaches were austere, but when I settled onto the hard coach seat I found myself buoyed up by the sheer pleasure of going somewhere as the Mogul engine easily towed us down the curving rails, past Silver City and Dayton, and then into Carson. Getting away from Virginia was tonic and elixir to a man who had idled away so much of his young life in that straitened locale.

I rode a stagecoach up the Washoe Valley, past enormous compounds where Sierra timber was gathered to be transported to the mines. We passed Steamboat Springs, with its geysers, and finally wound into that desolate flat where a crossroads called Reno was rising. The shacktown served no purpose but to connect Comstock passengers to the Central Pacific, and I could see it had no future and no amenities worth noting. I boarded the Central Pacific evening westbound and felt the doubled-up engines begin to drag us over Donner Pass and into fair California. But of that part I saw little because night had descended.

On occasion I stepped onto the platforms between coaches to smell the sugar pines or observe ancient snowbanks rotting down to nothing. I needed to escape a portly patent medicine drummer who considered himself a connoisseur of wine and women but knew nothing of the latter nor anything about happiness or love or even friendship. I could take him only in small doses, and then I retreated to fresh air.

We roared under long snow sheds that echoed hollowly and rode along perilous grades with unfathomable deeps plunging off one side or another and crossed alpine trestles over rushing rivers. But then, gradually, the air warmed and the scents of pine gave way to spiced fragrances, and we settled into a swift run down a gentle grade and into the great central valley. By dawn I sensed I was ripping across another nation, for nothing I saw on the great rolling hills east of Sacramento reminded me of anything I had ever seen in the East.

We clanged our way to a halt, with a great hissing of steam, and the conductors dropped the iron stools to earth and began handing us down.

The paddle-wheel river steamer *Sausalito* was waiting, so I barely had a chance to examine the waterfront city, with its brick merchant and warehouse buildings and a solidity about it that suggested that much of the gold from the Sierras had stopped right there. I boarded, along with a flock of passengers, and ere long I was embarked upon my first boat ride down the mighty river that would carry us upon its shoulders to San Francisco.

I was, frankly, glad to escape Virginia and was tempted to go back on my word to Joe Goodman and leave the Comstock behind. Everywhere, onboard the humming side-wheel boat, on the sunny streets of Sacramento, in the uncomfortable railroad coaches, I beheld women, brightly dressed and bonneted women, in a proportion equal to men. I thought I had arrived at the Pearly Gates. I circled the deck and finally stood at the rail beside a fair maiden, flaxen-haired, carrying a formidable wicker basket, its contents blanketed. Ah, what a perfect specimen of high-grade ore. Her fitted suit, her gloved hands, her wide-brimmed hat with daisies upon it, stirred a boldness in me that had all but vanished on the Comstock.

"Is this your first trip to California?" I asked as we both watched the waters we were plowing and the circling gulls.

"Oh, no, I live in the Mission District," she said.

I wasn't quite sure what that was. "Ah, and what do you do there?"

She surveyed me distantly. "Keep house," she replied.

That was fine with me. "I'm from Virginia City myself," I said. "It's not as pleasant as this. You must live in perpetual warmth."

"San Francisco's cold," she said.

"I'm a reporter for the *Territorial Enterprise*," I replied. "I report on the mines."

"You're a writer?"

"Oh, not particularly. Some newspapermen are real writers."

"What's the difference?"

"Well, ah–"

The blanket in the wicker basket began to throb. I stared, fascinated by a light woolen cover that had come to life, so to speak.

An infant squalled.

"Oh, dear," said my traveling companion. She pulled back the blanket to reveal a squirming baby.

She smiled. " 'Fraid you'll have to excuse me," she said, and vanished into the nether regions of the vessel. I watched her go, watched the gracious sway of her body, watched her soothe the infant with her kid-gloved hand. I had the feeling that California was not going to be any better than Virginia City when it came to certain matters of the heart. Henry Stoddard was doomed. I knew it then, and the notion never left me after that.

I watched the great city loom large in twilight as the paddlewheeler eased into its slip at North Beach. From the bay the city seemed to be nothing but steep hills, one upon another, all of them covered with a dense mass of wooden homes, mostly in light hues. The lady was right: the whole place was distinctly chilly. I could see the Golden Gate to the west, half-lost in fog. And I could smell the sea, iron on the breeze.

In short order I set foot on the peninsula, smelled fish, found a hack, and caught a ride to Portsmouth Square, where there would be some hotels I could afford. The place excited me: it seemed warm and alive, affluent if not rich, and cosmopolitan, just as my small city on a mountainside had gathered into it people from all over the world.

I knew, suddenly, that I was going to make this a working vacation: here were the very men who had siphoned off most of the wealth of the Comstock, and also those who had siphoned off most of the gold in the Sierras. Men like Huntington, Stanford, Hopkins, and Crocker, who had started as gold-rush merchants in Sacramento. Or perhaps Ralston and Mills, whose corporations dominated the Comstock. The Bank of California seemed a good place to start.

Joe Goodman would receive some telegraphic dispatches soon. I intended to interview the nabobs who owned my city, who ran the railroad in which I had some shares, and whose names were known to almost everyone on the Comstock. I wanted to see where our silver and gold had gone.

CHAPTER 32

I ended up at the venerable Russ House on Montgomery Street, a place convenient to the banking district. I settled into my austere room and awaited an earthquake. In a city reputed to be sybaritic, Russ House seemed an anomaly. I supposed that if this city had welcomed Sam Clemens with a good, sharp quake it owed me one also. Clemens had wandered the streets and scribbled furiously and gotten a good deal of cash and satisfaction out of this, and I imagined that San Francisco should do no less for me. With even a small quake I could enhance my reputation and my purse.

But I was out of luck. The city sat serenely on its haunches and never so much as hiccuped during my sojourn there, to my great disappointment. Clemens was born under a fateful star, but Stoddard was doomed to obscurity. My general impression was of a place that had abolished weather. The climate regulated itself at a cool level, and disruptive storms and heat and cold were scarcely heard of and an astonishment to the city's pampered citizens on the rare occasions they showed up. One could as well live in one of those paper houses of the Japanese as in a solid building in a place like San Francisco. There was, of course, a winter monsoon, but its severity was greatly exaggerated by local bartenders, and in all the while I sojourned there I found no employment for overcoat or glove.

I thought maybe that would be a bore after a while, but the citizens didn't seem to mind the drone of seasonless weather. Nothing ever stayed them on their appointed rounds. So that, apparently, was the bargain struck with Mephistopheles: mild weather spiced with a hard shake now and then. The odds were sporting, and the city always rebuilt in a week anyway.

Had I come from Platteville to this urbane locale, I would have felt the rube. But Virginia City was no wallflower when it came to cosmopolitanism, and I entertain the notion that it was, in fact, a notch above the Bay City. I found myself at home in every pub and saloon in sight and found the mixologists the full-blooded brethren of those on the Comstock—which is to say, engaging and full of fancy. I had always trusted bartenders and saloon keeps to give me the lowdown, and as soon as I had settled myself into my room I headed into the streets to wet my whistle. I suspected that a day or two of patronizing the watering holes would equip me for whatever else I chose to do.

I had divided this expedition into thirds: one was sightseeing; another was to examine, and if possible meet, those single San Francisco maidens who might consider a swain from the hinterland; and third was to write and transmit heated dispatches to Rollin Daggett, lucubrating upon the venalities of the City of Saint Francis.

I didn't achieve all three. I saw the sights, largely by heeding the counsel of the dispensers of spirits and advice. Thus I ventured to the various wharfs, there to sample crab and other delectations from the sea; took the ferry to Marin County; and gazed raptly upon the choleric joy of the stock exchanges in full heat. I did not neglect the attire of those on the streets, nor their plumage, equipage, livery, and bloodlines. The gents of San Francisco were no better attired than those on the Comstock, where we habitually wore suits and bow ties and attended to our grooming.

The women were more numerous but less attractive, tending toward avoirdupois and wrinkles. Ours on the Comstock were better dressed and more fashionable. I discovered almost no churches, except a Catholic one on the border of Chinatown. When it came to Orientals, San Francisco had it all over my town. In Nevada the Chinamen lived in cottages on the edge of the city. Here they settled themselves in noble if cramped edifices and on the whole seemed a better class.

The manses rising on Nob Hill were fine scandals, the work of lunatic architects, the purpose being to spend as much money as possible being as tasteless as possible. I admired them at once and felt right at home. We understood those things in Virginia City and applauded. I would have been sorely disappointed to see a railroad nabob ensconced in any residence resembling, say, the work of Christopher Wren.

I stood there atop that steep mound, and saw those châteaus a-building and thought to myself, *Ah, there you see before your eyes some of the wealth of the Comstock, ripped out of the bowels of the earth by brave men and filtered to other purses by craftier ones.* I was glad to see Comstock wealth somewhere. What I saw had not been built with railroad money, for the railroads were still miserable, debt-ridden creatures at that time. No, I was seeing Sierra gold and Comstock gold and silver.

I had gotten the idea in Virginia City that the gold and silver were lifted from the pits only to vanish, maybe to another planet or sphere. I was glad I had come to San Francisco, for without seeing these castles and the rococo banks in the financial quarter, or the stock exchange, I would never have known what purpose Virginia City served. There we all were on the slope of Sun Mountain, furiously creating wealth, and yet none of it stuck there, and that seemed a mystery: a river of silver and gold, going–somewhere else. Someday, when this City on the Bay had sucked the last ounce of silver out of my town, Virginia City would be ruthlessly cast aside as a worthless thing, and these nabobs would milk something else.

As for meeting damsels, I did best while attending the various opera houses, most of them on Market Street or close by. These gaudy theaters flocked with maidens fair, and it was no difficult matter to meet fair women and their escorts, sip claret, ascertain the status of all those ladies with gloved hands, and engage those who wished to discuss whatever had occurred before the most recent curtain. San Francisco celebrated its theater and music and welcomed every passing troupe and orchestra just as we did on the Comstock.

I exchanged a few cards, scribbled a few more addresses, and received several invitations to call at tea time, which I promised to do. I met so many Marguerites and Joannas and Helens that they all ran together like wet watercolors on paper, and I knew I'd be lost until the Right One struck my fancy. Still, here was a surfeit of women, a novelty so far beyond my ken that I scarcely knew how to behave. I set aside late afternoons for tea and set about earning my keep in the mornings.

The Bank of California seemed the logical place to begin, so I penetrated its portals one morning and by means of various inquiries found my way to the suite of the cashier, William C. Ralston. There a clerk stayed me.

"I wish to see Mr. Ralston," I said. "I'm Henry Stoddard, with the *Territorial Enterprise.*"

"The what?"

"Nevada's leading newspaper."

"A reporter."

"Yes. I am doing a story on the men who built my city."

The clerk, a fragile fellow who was unfamiliar with sunlight, vanished a moment and then returned.

"He's busy, Stoddard. He really has nothing to contribute, other than what he's already said: the Comstock is nothing but a hole in the ground with gold and silver in it."

"I'd like to talk with him about his railroad."

"Some other time."

"Would you please ask him?"

"No, he's not accessible now. However, our president, Mr. Mills, occasionally responds to the press."

I was thus railroaded out of the suite. I recollected that Sam Clemens had not interviewed nabobs for stories but got most of them from boardinghouse ladies and bartenders. Even so, I hurried to the offices of Darius Ogden Mills, President, but discovered he was otherwise engaged and I could not expect to see him that fortnight. I later read in the *Alta* that Mills was hosting various Boston and Philadelphia capitalists, hoping to extract funds with which to purchase one or two of the Comstock holdout mines, such as the venerable Ophir, whose shares were largely in the hands of Lucky Baldwin. The Bank of California was clearly run by absolutists. If there was yet a blade of grass on the Comstock they didn't own, they would attempt to mow it.

Well, perhaps that was a story in itself. I would boil it for a few days and see about the flavor of those beans.

The problem with extracting stories from landladies and bartenders was that I lacked Sam Clemens's wit, and the three or four I attempted to pen at Russ House ended up in a parlor stove.

So I turned to the more important objective of this interregnum on the bay and began attending four o'clock teas, chez Driscoll, chez Dilworth, chez Carpenter, chez Bodenheim, hoping all those Marias and Letitias would separate themselves into definable colors. These affairs, it turned out, were something of a San Francisco mating ritual for those of a certain class. The hostess usually camouflaged herself in the company of half a dozen matrons for some reason and opened her doors to assorted swain, some in straw boaters and high-collared shirts and jaunty white shoes. If they were not employed, that was a definite plus because it implied independent means. Whereas a man like myself, toiling at a trade—newspapering, of all quaint things—was at a disadvantage. No sweet Paula or Belinda would dream of marrying a tradesman. But I had acquired a certain social ease clear back at Judge Stoddard's capacious home, so I was welcomed by mothers, sisters, rivals, and squinty brothers who supposed I was imagining all sorts of dishonorable things about their sisters.

I wasn't. These social butterflies were bright and gaudy and plumed in pastel and ostrich and served us tarts and scones from Comstock silver, but they had pastel minds as well, and I waited in vain for the afternoon's tea sipping to generate anything such as regularly issued from my colleagues. So that was a disappointment. But I kept at the whole business: theater evenings, meeting ladies in the green rooms and salons, teas in the afternoons, sightseeing in the morning. After a fortnight I discovered I had not written a story worth the name and had improved Joe Goodman's paper by not one word.

I kept praying for an earthquake or typhoon or cholera epidemic but had no luck. I thought to venture to the Barbary Coast—the real one, not the ersatz Virginia City version—and thought better of it. Shanghai might be an interesting place to visit, but I didn't wish to live there. What was left? Some of the most elegant bordellos in the world, the barkeeps told me; a few nights in Chinatown toying with the exotic; a trip down the peninsula on the Southern Pacific; sailing on the bay; fishing the rich waters just west of the Golden Gate; or committing suicide.

Instead, I fell into my ancient routine, navigating from one saloon to another from midafternoon until shut-eye. I didn't much care for San Francisco. It was a gaudy cold fraud. I didn't much care for that city, or for myself.

I returned to the Comstock early, halving my sojourn on the bay. I could say this much about it: I had discovered what I didn't want from life. That made Virginia City more comfortable but didn't make me one whit happier. I distributed a gross of favors to my colleagues at the paper, who remained remarkably uncurious about my excursion, but I knew that later Rollin Daggett would strong-arm me to the Old Magnolia, order his customary medicinal of Steamboat gin, and question me closely about the city, the octopus bank, why I failed to dispatch a single story, and my luck or lack of it with women, which was becoming the bane of my existence. Daggett, at least, had bottomless curiosity, which is why he was a great editor. As for me, I stared into space.

CHAPTER 33

ell, reader, by now you have acquired some insights into young Stoddard. He was something of a plodder, wasn't he? Yes, of course. He wasn't born under any lucky star, nor was he particularly gifted. Sam Clemens went to San Francisco and promptly produced memorable literature, fashioning it out of the most amazing things, such as house moving. Consider this, from the *Morning Call:*

> For several days a vagrant two-story frame house has been wandering listlessly about Commercial Street, above this office, and she has finally stopped in the middle of the thoroughfare, and is staring dejectedly at Montgomery Street, as if she would like to go down there but really don't feel equal to the exertion . . .

That house was good for two more columns on subsequent days. The next began:

> That melancholy old frame house that has been loafing around Commercial Street for the past week got disgusted at the notice we gave her in the last issue . . .

And the next day:

> If you have got a house, keep your eye on it, these times, for there is no knowing what moment it will go tramping around town . . .

Clemens got three funny stories out of a house on rollers; poor Stoddard lacked the wit to write one story about anything in the whole town.

Clemens went off to the goldfields and wrote the story that made him famous, "Jim Smiley and His Jumping Frog," while Stoddard wandered about, trying to interview important men who could not be reached even by the savvy reporters of that great city.

And Stoddard's efforts to meet women and find a sweetheart were beclouded from the start, as if women found in him something that hastened their desire to be elsewhere. Nor was it for lack of trying. The young man diligently pursued all openings, thinking that eventually lightning would strike, but it didn't.

All this reinforced his ripening conviction that he had been born to be a man lost in the deck. He could look with pride upon his reportage of important mining news and knew absolutely that these less-than-sprightly accounts formed the backbone of his paper. That is what saved him when he looked into a mirror. A plodder he might be, but not a dunce.

So he returned to Virginia City, found comfort in its familiar venues, poured drinks with his editor, Daggett, and returned to whatever he was doing before he broke loose of the traces and went on a lark.

Peace, stranger, and patience. Later in this narrative you will learn that Henry Stoddard ended up living a rich, fulfilled, adventuresome, happy life and enjoyed the companionship of the loveliest woman on earth and the joy of seeing his children mature and prosper and begin lives of their own. We will come to all that eventually.

Mining and business news there was aplenty, and I renewed my determination to make the *Enterprise* the cyclops of the Comstock. I interviewed Adolph Sutro about his aborted tunnel project, finding him subdued, bitter toward the mine managements that had welshed on their commitment to the tunnel when the railroad was building, and acidulous about Sharon's growing monopoly but still determined to continue with the tunnel, because it made economic sense as the means to drain the mines and carry ore down to the mills. But the consensus was that Sutro was finished; Sharon's octopus had whipped him.

"When the mines flood, they will come again to me about ze tunnel," Sutro told me, probably wishing for enough water to float Noah's Ark.

Sharon himself had turned to ancillary ventures. His mines depended on timber and water, and both were growing increasingly short. He and some partners had long since purchased the Gold Hill and Virginia City water companies and reorganized them into one supplier of potable water. Drinking water had become extremely scarce on the Comstock, perched on the arid slopes of Mount Davidson.

Ample water existed in the mines and was a nuisance there, but it was foul and not potable, especially after collecting in the sumps. It could not be used in the mine boilers because it was so mineralized that it corrupted the pipes with scale. The sources of the Comstock's supply were horizontal shafts driven into the mountain above Virginia City to locate ore. These usually ran into barren quartz, so the shafts were abandoned for that purpose—but happily served another. Many of them had been drilled into aquifers that offered pure water in limited amounts—barely enough to supply the two cities. In the spring, when the aquifers were charged by snowmelt, water was adequate; by fall there was an annual water famine.

Sharon and his partners in the water company—including four modestly heeled gents who would soon become well-known on the Comstock, Messrs. James G. Fair, James C. Flood, John W. Mackay, and William S. O'Brien—used the scarcity to charge astronomical rates and thus enriched themselves. There had been rival water companies, each driving shafts into the mountainside below the previous shafts in order to commandeer a commodity more valuable than gold, and this had led to lawsuits and maneuvering in tycoon style, but Sharon et al. triumphed. I covered all this with deepening anger. Many householders who couldn't afford the dollar-a-month tariff for piped water survived by bucketing water from the flumes bringing it to the city. No one blamed them, nor did I.

The Virginia & Truckee swiftly put hundreds of teamsters out of work. A few tried valiantly to survive and delivered awesome wagon-train loads of ore—one running 90,690 pounds all told—to the mills. But they couldn't compete with the sturdy engines of the railroad, which dragged trainloads running over four hundred thousand pounds down to the mills. The engineers enjoyed setting records. Thus one day Engine 7, the "Nevada"—a 55,000-pound brute built by Baldwin, hauled 112 tons. Then the mighty Engine 6, "Comstock"—a twin of the "Nevada"—delivered 401,200 pounds to the mills and later beat itself by delivering 434,120 pounds. The teamsters tried to compete, but after a terrible accident on Geiger Grade, caused in part by overloading, they abandoned the game, and we no longer saw their giant wagon trains on our streets in such plenitude, nor was so much livestock feed hauled up to the flanks of Mount Davidson.

All this I covered each day, filling obscure corners of the *Territorial Enterprise*. I usually found my stories under the obituaries or next to the classified ads or used as filler on the gaudier pages, but that was all right. A good murder or scandal would always beat a story about hauling ore. I was at peace, at last, with my status on the paper and believed the stories were being placed exactly where they deserved to be placed.

The water company was small potatoes compared to Sharon's efforts to control the most important subsidiary industry of mining—timbering. Every tree in the whole area had been massacred to support the mines or build the city or burn for firewood, and the whole commerce of the Comstock depended more and more upon wood brought from the distant Sierras, where good rainfall had produced abundant forests.

Imagine, if you will, two goodly cities and a smaller one, totaling thirty thousand in population, utterly devoid of any other source of energy than wood. No coal was to be had at that time, though later, near the end of Virginia's heyday, some valuable lignite deposits close at hand were found and exploited. But coal was wanting throughout the region. San Francisco imported its coal from places as far away as England, Australia, Chile, Japan, Seattle, and Coos Bay, Oregon, because it had none apart from some minor deposits on Mount Diablo. And it commandeered all that was available, consuming 331,000 tons in eighteen and sixty-nine and 434,000 tons in eighteen and seventy-two.

So the Comstock relied largely on wood and what little coal it could get. And that wood came from the east slope of the Sierras at first, until an area perhaps sixty miles long, from the Truckee River in the north to the headwaters of the Carson River in the south, was denuded. And then the lumbering interests crossed the divide and began harvesting the plentiful timber of Lake Tahoe, all of it destined for the mines and homes of boilers of the Comstock.

This was no small business. The district burned eighty to a hundred thousand cords of wood each year in its boilers and stoves. This cordwood was usually floated down the Carson River just following the spring flood, in a giant flotilla running fifty miles in length, gathered near the mills on the river, and taken by train or wagon up the slope to the cities.

But that is only what was taken for fuel. Much more timber was cut to support the stopes and drifts and for construction. The square-set timbering that had become standard in all the mines required fourteen-to-eighteen-inch-square timbers, erected in cubes, to prevent the ceiling of these giant galleries from collapsing. In some weak areas the timbers had to be much larger, as much as thirty inches square. And heavy plank floors turned these underground caverns into a species of skyscraper. Those who operated the lumber companies could enrich themselves faster than those operating the mines—a reality that did not escape the men in the countinghouses and offices.

I am quite aware that this awesome enterprise exacted a frightful toll on the surrounding country, denuding slopes, ruining water supplies, affecting weather, and wrecking the exquisite hills around Lake Tahoe. And yet I say without hesitation that this enterprise was magnificently organized and executed with the technical and entrepreneurial genius that we Americans alone possess. Express your horror if you must, but do not neglect to admire what was accomplished by the boldest race of mortals on the planet.

The wood was cut by lumbermen using axes and two-man crosscut saws, dragged by oxen and horses or mules to Sierra mills, and there sawn into the mine timbers and planks, the local mills using the available wood to fire their boilers. This gigantic enterprise employed thousands of men during the eight-month season when the Sierras weren't snowed in. They erected cunningly built V-shaped flumes that could float these square-cut timbers downslope for miles on a small charge of water. In the Carson and Washoe valleys, these were collected at trackside or riverside in giant lots and transported to the Comstock.

Sugar pine was a favorite wood. It grew to a hundred-sixty or eighty feet and had trunks four to six feet in diameter on the whole. It was soft, clear, and easily worked and thus favored for construction. The yellow pine and Jeffrey pine were also treasured and abundant. These grew to three-or four-foot in diameter and rose a hundred-twenty to forty feet.

The Douglas fir, most prized for its strength, was not found on the eastern slope but was harvested at Lake Tahoe in great numbers. There the giant logs were shot by flume into the lake, gathered by steamboats into giant skeins that were pushed to the mills at Glenbrook, sawn into usable wood, carried up to Spooner Summit, and then flumed into the Carson Valley, where the sawn lumber was loaded on the trains and taken to the mines.

The scale of these operations was awesome. Imagine it. I believe now that if the Comstock's mines hadn't given out around eighteen and eighty all of the Tahoe basin would have been reduced to unsightly stumps and naked hills. As it was, the entire eastern flank of the Sierras for sixty miles–some say a hundred–was denuded by the Comstock Lode and now, as I write at the turn of the century, has barely begun to reforest. One of America's great scenic gems survives only because the Comstock died. I offer no apologies for any of this, for I wish to sing of bold men, a race of geniuses, who wrought a fortune from a virgin land. So save your moralistic clucking for another time.

As part of my humdrum duties for the paper I recorded the daily shipments of wood that arrived on our arid slope, little knowing that soon entrepreneurs would be scrapping with one another for that source of wealth: in mergers, in the counting rooms, in land purchases, in creek diversions to power the flumes, in the labor markets, and in the courts, just as fiercely as they had fought over the mines. And at the heart of it would be, as usual, the octopus: William Sharon, the Bank of California, and their friends.

CHAPTER 34

T he beginning of the eighteen-seventies marked the oddest period on the Comstock. Everything was paradox. The Bank of California had invested $3 million there just at a time when ores were exhausted and reserves dwindling. A railroad had been completed, which served only to stay the execution by making low-grade ore profitable because it could be hauled cheaply to the mills on the Carson River. Exploratory work in the mines, around the thousand-foot level, was coming up with nothing, and, accordingly, mining stocks tumbled. The vaunted Crown Point, of which I once held a small stake, was trading for as low as two dollars a share, and the value of the mine was thus far below the cost of its surface works.

The mighty Yellow Jacket, Hale & Norcross, Savage, Ophir, Kentuck and Gould & Curry were all on their deathbeds and could scarcely assess money from stockholders to continue further exploration. The Comstock's ore was not located in continuous veins, or sheets, but in pockets, like raisins in a pudding, as one observer put it, and the district was out of raisins.

Miners and their families were pulling out. Shopkeepers and saloon keepers were calling it quits. I expected the paper's revenues to shrink and gave myself a year, at the most, before I would get the pink slip from Goodman. The paper had been a bonanza for Goodman and would continue to pay him handsomely until the lode slid into real decline.

Yet one group, William Sharon's powerful Bank of California combination and its allies, remained optimistic. I have to give them credit: it took steely will and sheer nerve to continue to expand their hold on every crucial aspect of Comstock commerce—the mines, mills, water, timber, railroad—just when the mines were playing out. They either knew something I didn't know about the mines, or else they were mad. The only explanation I could come up with was that the bank was in so deep that it had no choice. If the Comstock died, so would the Bank of California, ruining all its depositors.

My own mood that beginning of a new decade was just as paradoxical. I had been on the Comstock nearly a decade, and that fact amazed me. The other item that amazed me was that I was thirty-one, unmarried, no longer young, and apparently doomed to bachelorhood. During my nine years away from my family, I had missed two weddings, acquired two nephews and a niece I had never seen, missed a funeral for my grandmother and another for my uncle, and had yet to see the homes and farms of my siblings.

Then, in February, I received the telegram I had, in the back of my mind, been dreading for over a year. My father had died. Peacefully, in his sleep, my sister wired. Would I return to help settle the estate? There wouldn't be much. His last years had actually drained his reserves. But the capacious house and grounds would bring something. Maybe a few hundred per sibling. Some furnishings and mementos would be divided, and which of them did I want?

I grieved. Judge Stoddard had been a noble gentleman who had imbued me with certain qualities, one might call them checks upon unbridled appetite, that had served me well all my adult life. Now he lay beside my mother in a family plot on those very acres, a corner fenced from the world. He had been failing for a year, had suffered several small strokes, and had succumbed suddenly to a hardening of the arteries. After the attack, he had not lingered more than an hour.

Even before his death I had learned most of what his future foretold from our sporadic correspondence. He himself had written frankly to say he was failing, had puzzling blank spots when he lost track of things, and it would pleasure him to see me one last time. But that was before the Union Pacific and Central Pacific had linked together in Utah, and the states were a strenuous stagecoach ride away.

I contemplated a trip east. I now could board the Central Pacific and eventually end up in Omaha, where I could transfer to connecting lines east and north and then, mostly by stagecoach, reach Platteville in two weeks. It would be a brutal winter trip. Except for those thin bands of iron rail and the fragile telegraph, nothing lay between Virginia City and the States—as we called the East—except vast, lonely prairie.

Of course I write from the vantage point of the new century. But in eighteen and seventy the continent was largely unsettled: the slaughter of the buffalo had barely begun; tens of millions of them roamed, and were often shot at from coach windows. The Sioux, under Red Cloud, had just won their war with the United States and wandered freely. It would be more than half a decade before they would defeat George Custer and another year or two before they would be put on reservations. Likewise, to the south, the Comanches lived in freedom and would continue to do so for another half a decade, and the Apaches were as wild and fierce as ever.

Looking back, I marvel that Virginia City, which was really the acme of industrial progress, had boomed for years so distantly from all the manufactures of the States and without a rail link to the East or to California. But there we were: a metropolis built of iron and steel, wood and muscle, digging deeper than mines had ever gone, extracting more ore than any other district, coping with water, heat, and other problems that had been thought to be intractable. There, in the middle of nowhere, was a city of such brilliance that it imported the best wines, whiskey, seafood, theater companies, furnishings, and other manufactures from every corner of the world, a city whose hotels and restaurants rivaled those of Paris and New York. If you do not marvel at this, reader, than your ears are separated by hardwood.

I decided, in that time of paradox, not to attempt the trip, and wired my sister to proceed without me. I longed to go but saw no compelling reason for it other than a sacred one: I wanted to stand at my father's and mother's graves. I did request the most recent tintypes there might be of them, and eventually I received two in the posts. I spent that day staring at those images, heartened, full of loss and love, promising them I would make my life count for the good and would not slack.

I'm not sure my family understood the scope of the journey; they seemed a little miffed, and not even my explanation of what was entailed allayed their unhappiness with me. So I resolved to heal that as best I could with frequent correspondence and focused on my work and on the strange, dying city that was now gobbling investment rather than pouring gold and silver out of its cornucopia mines.

The saloons had gradually become quieter and dreamier, men less inclined to roister and carouse and more inclined to stare at distant horizons seen only in their minds. It was as if Virginia City lay waiting: for life, for death, or for slow strangulation. But it was not to die. Not yet. For in that memorable year, just as it had in the past and would in the future, Virginia City struck bonanza.

The man responsible for all this bore the ordinary name of John P. Jones. He had been born in England near the border of Wales, but his parents crossed the Atlantic when he was two and he grew up in Ohio. He came to San Francisco during that famous gold-rush year, eighteen and forty-nine, and pursued various mining enterprises in the goldfields. He held several public offices but was defeated in his race for lieutenant governor, which, as fate would have it, was to benefit the Comstock. He arrived in Nevada almost without means, having exhausted his funds in politics, but found employment with the Kentuck mine and was deemed so gifted that the Crown Point—my old friend—hired him as its super-intendent. There, during the mines' waning days, he searched for ore, running drifts relentlessly but without success.

In June of eighteen and seventy, the Crown Point lay recumbent, exhausted, and hopeless. Nothing at the unprecedented 1,000- or 1,100-foot levels showed any sign of ore. He abandoned a drift running east and tried one running south, without any sign of success the first 200 feet. By November, Crown Point stock had slid to around two dollars and no one wanted any. At that gloomy juncture, the miners noted a change in the rock. The hard gray porphyry diminished, clay and quartz appeared, and the quartz was friable and decomposed, a very good sign. Red lines of iron rust appeared, another good sign of mineralization. At 239 feet from the shaft, the miners hit a clay seam and found on the other side white quartz, which contained pockets of ore.

Jones traveled to San Francisco with his news and presented it to the directors, and as a result speculators began to buy up the dirt-cheap stock. At that point he had to abandon California briefly and attend to a very sick daughter, and the stock collapsed and the speculators de-nounced Jones, thinking the sick daughter was Jones's excuse to unload worthless stock at the crest of a boomlet. But Jones stuck to his beliefs and impressed not a few speculators, one of whom was Alvinza Hay-ward, one of William Sharon's partners and part of the California bank circle. Hayward bought 5,000 shares at under five dollars, Charles Low bought 1,000, but William Sharon controlled over 4,000.

Meanwhile, the news kept getting better. A new crosscut at the 1,200-foot level hit the same moderately rich ore body. Hayward bought Low's thousand, wanting control of the mine, and then only Sharon opposed him. But Sharon knew he was defeated and, in that fateful year of eighteen and seventy-one, sold his 4,100 shares to Haywood for $1,400,000, which was then the largest stock transaction in the history of mining. Haywood and Jones had a rich mine. So the Crown Point bloomed, independent of the powerful combination that ruled the Com-stock. In November of eighteen and seventy, a share was worth $7. By the following June, a share was worth $340.

And as a result of Mr. Jones's perseverence, almost every stock on the Comstock skyrocketed. Mills were suddenly valuable. The Bank of California's loans were suddenly collateralized. And Virginia City breathed a sigh of relief—for the moment.

I wrote the stories day by day, but privately I remained skeptical about the city's future. One strike scarcely revived the bonanza days when a dozen mines were in the silver.

CHAPTER 35

Not a few people on the Comstock were ready to call it quits, and I was among them. The city had gone sour. A vigilante group called the 601 started to roam the city. In late March 1871, masked men pulled a murder suspect named Heffernan out of the county jail and hanged him in the night. In July, they hanged a desperado named Kirk who had been warned to leave. They operated at night, wore sheets, and seemed to function with utter impunity, which suggested to me they were powerful men.

My city oozed fear. There was an immediate and salutary decline in our usual epidemic crime, but the price was terror. Newsmen are particularly vulnerable in such times, and I worried that I might find a 601 notice on my door, a mandate to leave town, and at the moment that didn't seem a bad idea. For a while, Virginia City wasn't itself. But all that passed, and no one ever found out who the self-anointed avengers were. But I had my suspicions.

Those were gloomy times in all respects. It wasn't obvious that Virginia City was any better off from the strike at the Crown Point mine. Some additional ore had been discovered at the Hale & Norcross, but none of this compensated for the swift-encroaching doom of the other mines. The Savage had stopped paying dividends in eighteen and sixty-nine, and the Kentucky stopped in March of eighteen and seventy. The Yellow Jacket was all but exhausted. The Gould & Curry paid a last small dividend in October. The other mines, from one end of the Comstock to the other, had paid nothing since eighteen and sixty-eight.

I took the Crown Point strike for what it obviously was—a curtain call, after the last encore. It was time for me to be thinking about heading elsewhere. In a few years Virginia City would be mostly empty, its sagging buildings harboring ghosts. The paper would let go of most of its employees, turn itself back to a weekly, and supply a few hundred die-hards with news. I didn't want to be part of that. I didn't want to see the city when the Washoe zephyrs blew dust and trash through empty streets and the throb of the mills and the hiss of the boilers had been stilled.

But there was something else murdering the city, and that was the want of potable water. What a paradox it was that the mines could barely stay dry and employed enormous pumps, larger than any other in the world, to drain them while we who perched high above the pits could barely find potable water to drink. The existing water was heavily min-eralized and included arsenic. While the ladies claimed that arsenic made their cheeks rosy and improved their complexions, no one much cared for some of the other minerals, which acted as purgatives.

Comstock people gazed longingly westward, across the great Washoe valley and into the Sierras, where water was abundant. Or we gazed down to the valley floor, at the Carson River, seventeen hundred feet and seven or eight miles below, and pondered the cost of pumping so much water so great a distance. I quoted engineers and supervisors who were certain that water brought at such cost to the city would be the final blow. The troubled mines could not bear that additional ex-pense, and the struggling merchants and citizens of Gold Hill and Vir-ginia City would abandon the place rather than see ordinary water—the ultimate staff of life—rob them of their livelihoods.

The Virginia and Gold Hill Water Company, one of William Sharon's pocket enterprises, wrestled with the problem to no avail. An entire decade of exploration had yielded no water. Economical water was not available in the Virginia Range. Shrewdly, Sharon sold a con-trolling interest in the company to some young entrepreneurs named Mackay, Fair, Flood, and O'Brien, who thought they could deal with the problem. But the trickle of water only diminished as the tunnels ran dry.

Then came one of those turning points that still leave me marveling. In the summer of eighteen and seventy-one, the company's directors decided to bring water from the Sierras via an inverted siphon that would form a gigantic U. High in the Sierras, and fourteen hundred feet above Gold Hill and Virginia City, a small diversion dam would be built across Hobart Creek; water run into a flume that would take it to a point above a saddle called Lakeview that divided the Carson City basin from the rest of the Washoe valley. There it would enter a pipe that would carry it down to the valley, across its floor, and clear up to the vicinity of Gold Hill, whose elevation was lower, so that gravity should do the entire job. The outlet end of the pipe would be 351 feet below its inlet. A reservoir would be constructed near the mining towns to hold reserves and permit pipe maintenance and repair.

It sounded practical enough, but it wasn't. The static head, or the pressure of the water in the pipe as it crossed the valley, would be much greater than had ever been experienced before, and it was not at all certain that a water pipe could be constructed that would resist a static pressure of 1,720 feet, or 800 pounds to the square inch, and not spray water from every joint or simply rupture. Nothing like this had ever been attempted in the entire history of hydraulic engineering. When all this was announced and the engineers explained to me what they had in mind, I was amazed. The mines were dying. The engineers were attempting something never before done, and barely feasible, and at a cost unimaginable.

The chief engineer, German-born Herman Schussler, had engineered similar lines and had settled in San Francisco, where he had designed much of the Spring Valley Water Works system. He was the ideal man, having built a legendary thirty-inch-diameter line in California that operated under 887 feet of pressure. It was his pioneering work that made the Washoe project feasible. Surveys determined that flumes at both ends could convey the water much of the distance, but it would be necessary to construct seven miles of high-pressure pipeline from a spur of the Sierras to a point in the Virginia Range above the thirsting cities.

The eleven-and-a-half-inch-diameter pipe was to be manufactured of English wrought iron and riveted together at the Risdon Iron Works in San Francisco, with two or three rows of five-eighths-inch rivets sealing the longitudinal joint. The thickness of the metal would vary, the thinnest, of course, being used high up, near the inlet and outlet, and the thickest across the valley floor. At the lowest elevations the walls of the pipe would be five-sixteenths of an inch thick and could be stressed up to 13,500 pounds per square inch. Each length of pipe would be about twenty-six feet.

The weight of this pipe would run 700 tons, all of it to be dragged into place with livestock. The segments of pipe would be joined together with five-inch-wide wrought-iron rings, of a diameter somewhat larger than the pipe, so each joint could be caulked with lead. The designers purposed to use thirty-five tons of lead to caulk the 1,524 joints. Inside each joint, another ring would be riveted to the butted ends of each segment to hold them together. At places where sharp bends were necessary the iron works would make up specially riveted sections.

Nor was that the end of it. It would be necessary to bleed air from the line, and additional valves were needed to blow off water and sediment. These were to be placed at low points while the air valves, intended to release air compressed by the force of the water, would be located at high points. The plans called for fourteen air valves and sixteen water valves. To protect the pipe from rust and other wear, the segments were to be dipped into a mixture of coal tar and asphaltum heated to 350 degrees to form a weatherproof coating.

I marveled when I saw the blueprints. This pipe would lie about two and a half feet under the surface, and the line would snake along slopes, cross thirteen gulches, and dodge obstacles such as points of rock. So the work was contracted and the iron works began the gargantuan task of manufacturing all those segments of pipe, while the mining towns suffered perpetual drought and dearly priced water and arsenic in their drink—and waited.

Do you begin to grasp, friend, why I began this narrative by saying that the real hero of this memoir is the City on the Hill? I am telling you of wondrous things, of feats and daring and genius beyond all the world had known. I am telling you of a great city that rose in arid wasteland, a thousand and more miles from the westernmost settlements of the States, isolated by dry prairie, monotonous and empty lands, naked savages, gigantic herds of buffalo, and utterly ignored by the nabobs of Washington and New York and Philadelphia. I am telling you of men so bold and purposeful that they would bet a bank on their vision. I did not much care for William Sharon, but he had my utmost admiration for his daring. Without him and his bold associates, the Irish quartet who took over the company, the rest of Virginia City's fabulous story might never have unfolded. I counted myself among the skeptics, believing the Sierra water would arrive just about the time when no one needed it.

After I left the water company offices, where all this had been announced, I scribbled out my story and laid it before Rollin Daggett.

"They must know something that we don't," he said. "No sane investors would risk so much on a dying burg."

I could scarcely argue with that.

"It will not affect me in the slightest," he continued. "My liquid intake is supplied to me by the decanter at the Old Magnolia, and I am perfectly comfortable washing my carcass with slightly blue water from the Ophir mine. See the color it gives my skin?"

He thrust a bare wrist at me, but I could see no alteration from the weary gray that had been the hue of his flesh from the time I'd met him.

"I would suggest that you rewrite the lead on this tale," he said. "Something along these lines: 'Virginia's lovely ladies are going to lose the rosy hue on their cheeks.' That's the way to tackle one of your lengthy, technical engineering stories."

It wasn't a compliment, and I was taken aback. But it made sense. Daggett always made sense. I was one of the only souls in all of American journalism who cared about such matters as engineering, pipe thicknesses, pressures, mechanics, locomotives, and matters of that sort. Daggett wanted to sell papers to ladies, while I was hoping that shrewd men in the mining offices would read my daily output. There it was: on the one hand, entertainers like De Quille or Twain, or Daggett himself, who could find comedy and delight in a story like this and, on the other, the balding Henry Stoddard, who could work up a passion about iron and rivets. I rewrote the story.

CHAPTER 36

By eighteen and seventy-one I was considered a veteran of the Comstock and was now the senior reporter at the *Territorial Enterprise.* I had entered my middle years, and my hairline had receded accordingly; indeed, I was more bald than hirsute, and I took it as another signal that I was unlikely to succeed with the ladies. I looked to be just the sort I was, a man in a rumpled broadcloth suit, slender, absorbed with a variety of mechanical and technical matters of little interest to women and society, a reliable reporter of such things as the amount of water pumped daily from the Ophir or the diameter of ventilation pipe being installed in the Savage mine or the dropping price of Hale & Norcross shares on the San Francisco Mining Exchange.

I wasn't resigned to bachelorhood, but my fits of social enterprise grew fewer, and the comfortable habits I had formed on the Comstock seemed likely to be the ruts I would follow for life. I did not lack for stories. Indeed, I had scarcely enough time in any day to cover the mining news. I had broad and excellent connections among managers and owners, and these fine sources gave me—and my paper—a pronounced advantage in the coverage of the mines.

One of these was Adolph Sutro, who was as indomitable as ever. Even as Sharon and his railroad had defeated the great tunnel project Sutro was petitioning Congress for a cash grant, and got as far as a favorable committee report before the politicians abandoned him. In eighteen and sixty-eight they were largely absorbed in impeaching Andrew Johnson, so the measure died. But that didn't stop Sutro, who patiently argued that the tunnel would drain the Comstock of its pesky water and would be the salvation of the mines, which could profitably ship their lower-grade ore down the tunnel to the mills on the river.

Much to my amazement, Sutro raised about six hundred thousand dollars from European investors and started boring the tunnel. He soon acquired another infusion, this time over a million dollars, and continued his project, now having something concrete—lengthening bores, one from the Savage shaft and the other from the river bottoms—to show potential investors. Sharon's combination fought hard, pressured the mines to resist, but the remarkable little Sutro wouldn't quit.

I wonder how many yards of copy I wrote pursuing that story. There were others. Mine managements continued the ploy of locking miners underground for several days when they were on the brink of breaking into a bonanza. But this ploy had become so well-known that speculators began to discount it.

Where the news that miners were being held underground once drove stocks upward, by the turn of the decade the reverse was true, and stock prices began to fall. What's more, the unions had grown tired of this business, and now they were obtaining a writ of habeas corpus, alleging that the miners were being held against their will. I covered each of these conflicts, my own views strongly on the side of the miners and against the manipulators who were trafficking in human bondage for the sake of financial gain. I like to take credit for eliminating the practice, for I did not shrink from reporting the issue in all its noisome detail until at last the mine managements surrendered.

I had started to monitor yet another phenomenon. The deeper the mines pierced into the rock of Mount Davidson, the hotter they became. Most of the shafts on the Comstock Lode in that period were about a thousand feet, and the temperature was climbing with each additional hundred feet. Miners at the lower depths had begun to work in air well above room temperature, heated by the very rock they were penetrating. Mine managements were sending down ice water and improving the ventilation, because the heat was subduing the vigor of the miners. So I would regularly include in my reportage the temperatures at the lowest levels of the Savage or Best & Belcher or Kentuck.

One of my best sources in that period was a young man named John Mackay, a Dubliner by birth, born in 1831, a veteran of the California goldfields, and most recently a speculator and mine manager, along with some partners we at the paper knew little about except that they owned the water company. Mackay was a thin, quiet, shrewd gentleman who knew a great deal more about practical mining than most of those in the stock brokerages or superintendents' offices. He had once been a hard rock miner and knew exactly what went on down in the bowels of the earth. He was not, then, a man of means but had made a little money from the shares he owned of the Kentuck.

In the late eighteen-sixties, he and his partners, James G. Fair, James C. Flood, and William S. O'Brien, had taken a hard look at the Hale & Norcross mine, which was then in failing condition. William Sharon had made an attempt to control the mine when it was still producing ore and seemed to possess reserves. The contest for the stock reached such intensity that shares were driven as high as $10,000. Eventually Sharon won, only to find that the mine's reserves were about exhausted, so he sold the stock at a frightful loss rather than be stuck with assessments and expenses on a dying property. I think it may have been the worst beating Sharon took. The stock languished while the mine lost money and continued to assess its remaining stockholders such sums as the managers thought they might extract from the unwitting shareholders.

This mine was splendidly situated on the center of the Comstock Lode, and there were those, including Mackay and his partners, who didn't believe it was done for. That, as it turned out, was the beginning of one of the greatest transformations ever to visit the Washoe mining district. Mackay's close partner and colleague, James G. Fair, was also a practical miner with plenty of experience, but his other two partners were simply brokers—indeed, former saloon owners—dealing in Comstock shares on the San Francisco Mining Exchange.

Surreptitiously Flood and O'Brien began buying shares in small lots, concealing the enterprise for as long as possible from the cyclops eye of Sharon and his far better financed colleagues with the Bank of California. Of the four, only Mackay had enough to pay for his shares. The rest did it by borrowing or, in the case of Fair, agreeing to superintend the mine as part of his repayment.

Now, I must confess that I did not get wind of this and was truly and fairly scooped by my rivals over at the *Gold Hill News*. In October 1869, they wrote that because this foursome possessed over four hundred shares of the Hale & Norcross they would likely control the mine at the time of election of officers the next March.

They were right. The newcomers had whipped Sharon, the king of the Comstock. And that was the beginning of some ferocious struggles, between the California bank crowd and the upstarts, that would preoccupy the Comstock for years. But I will come to that in due course. Upon gaining control, the Mackay group canceled an $8,000 assessment,

and under Fair the mine economized its operations and began a relentless search for new ore. I had long since sold my few remaining shares
rather than sit still for the brutal assessments, but as all this transpired I
wished I hadn't.

Fair turned out to be a brilliant manager, spending as much time in
the pits as Mackay, unlike the bank crowd. In 1869 the mine paid out
almost $200,000 in dividends, and after locating a new deposit in 1870
the mine paid out $500,000. But then the high-grade ore ran out and
the profits fell off swiftly. Assessments were resumed so that Fair could
probe for more ore.

Meanwhile, not wishing to send all their ore to the California bank's
array of mills, the new combination organized its own milling company
to reduce its ores, thus further weakening the mighty bank's hold on the
Comstock. It all made sense to me: Mackay and Fair were practical
miners, while the opposition operated from plush offices on California
Street in San Francisco and never lowered their august selves down the
shafts and into the works for a close look.

In a way I had become like the bank crowd, trusting too much in
my sources and developing no new ones. Stung by the *Gold Hill News*
scoop, I began paying more attention to what the outsiders and newcomers were up to, in particular John Mackay. I must say straight off I
found him to be a most likable man, always cheerful and patient, and
willing to see me, certainly as open as any man in his position ever is.
Unlike Fair, whose affability depended on his mood and who could
rebuff me as suddenly as welcome me, Mackay became a staple in my
quest for news. I never was put off by his clerks, and on the rare occasions when he couldn't candidly respond to a question he would smile
and confess it and not hand me some malarkey. The Hale & Norcross
became an open book, the only mine on the Comstock whose management let me in on everything.

Mackay and his family lived modestly in the better neighborhoods
above C Street, and he worked long hours operating his own mine as
well as studying other prospects, because the foursome now had some
profits in hand and were examining other possibilities. Just what they
were about they wouldn't tell me, nor did I press them. They needed
their privacy in order to acquire shares at the lowest possible price.

And so the years passed.

In eighteen and seventy-two William Sharon, still in control of the
mightiest engine of wealth the world had ever known, ran for the Senate
on the Republican ticket for the seat vacated by the retiring William
Stewart, the first of the Comstock's succession of millionaire senators.
The office had never come cheap, and Sharon, with the might of his

California bank behind him, began the usual wining and dining and electing of the legislators who would decide his fate, spending freely in Carson City, sharing the good times, and riding toward the United States Senate with a force irresistible.

Except for the *Territorial Enterprise.* Joe Goodman abominated the compact and scheming Sharon and resented all the wealth he and his colleagues had milked from the Comstock. Goodman's paper was then the mightiest voice in Nevada as well as the Comstock, so Goodman set to work.

Upon the arrival of Mr. Sharon from the balmier precincts of San Francisco, my amiable publisher loaded his cannon and lit the fuse:

> Your unexpected return, Mr. Sharon, has afforded no opportunity for public preparation, and you will consequently accept these simple remarks as an unworthy but earnest expression of the sentiments of a people who feel that they would be lacking in duty and self-respect if they failed upon such an occasion to make a deserved recognition of your acts and character. You are probably aware that you have returned to a community where you are feared, hated and despised . . . Your career in Nevada for the past nine years has been one of merciless rapacity. You fastened yourself upon the vitals of the State like a hyena, and woe to him who disputed with you a single coveted morsel of your prey . . . You cast honor, honesty and the commonest civilities aside. You broke faith with men whenever you could subserve your purpose by doing so . . .

Sharon lost in spite of his bottomless purse. And little did we know at that time what the impact of that editorial would be upon the *Territorial Enterprise* itself.

CHAPTER 37

 had been a decade on the Comstock, but was I a happy man? I might have been but for something that was galling me. I had been with the *Territorial Enterprise* all those ten years, was its senior man—and yet I had not

been advanced in salary for many years. I was still receiving the twenty-five a week that I had wrung out of Joe Goodman. In the whole period, I had won only a five-dollar advance, and every other man on the staff had long since passed me by. Even newcomers were earning thirty.

Other men would have quit, especially having seen others advance with regular improvements in their wage as they proved themselves. But when it came to promotions the publisher managed to stare at me with a blind eye. To be sure, I had made a minor success with mining stocks years before and had invested it and bought a modest house. But that had slowly declined. Some of my investments, such as my railroad stocks and streetcar companies, went bad, and others reduced dividends, and I had occasionally eaten into my resources for one sound reason or another. I had always assumed that Goodman would reward me for the sort of reportage that formed the beef and beans of his newspaper. I was not far from penury.

But it just didn't happen. I might have understood and forgiven it if the paper had been in trouble. But it had been coining money and was Goodman's little gold mine. Each issue burst with advertisements, circulation stayed high, costs remained constant, and Goodman pocketed a fat profit each week. He did not hesitate to pour cash back into the paper. We had crisp new fonts to work with, the best steam-driven presses money could buy, and every modern device known to printing. With the advent of the railroad we finally had adequate newsprint and no longer worried about what our next edition would be printed on—if it got printed at all.

Goodman had long since bought out his partner, Denis McCarthy, so the paper was his alone. I could see no reason at all for denying me some reward for the faithful service I had provided him. At times my bitterness took the form of envy, as when Gillis passed me by at forty dollars a week and De Quille continued to receive regular boosts, or at least annual bonuses. I told myself that Goodman had an eye for flashy wordsmiths and couldn't get it through his skull what reporting was all about. I was the only one among his staff who wasn't regularly selling to *Golden Age* or one of the East Coast journals, and that was simply because no one in the East cared about new milling machinery or the percentage of gold to silver in the ores of various mines.

I didn't know what to do about all this. A man hates to beg and likes to be recognized on his merit. I so dreaded a confrontation with Goodman, and so yearned for him to call me into his sanctum and honor me with an increase, that I did nothing month after month and year upon year. But that did me no good. Some nights I was so rankled that

I ached to pour my woes out upon my colleagues, especially Daggett, who might just take my message to Goodman and recommend an improvement in my pay.

But I am a proud man, and I didn't, so the matter festered in me, sometimes making me sharp-tongued toward my rivals. They began to examine my mood before inviting me to join them at the Old Magnolia, and I can scarcely blame them.

To make matters worse, I discovered that our smaller rivals were paying their better men more than I was getting. Here I was, on the biggest and richest paper in the state of Nevada, and there was Alf Doten over at the *Gold Hill News* getting fifty a week and all the reporters at the *Virginia Chronicle* were getting at least thirty. McCarthy himself was now editing the *Chronicle* and making fierce war upon the Bank of California crowd. I thought maybe I ought to talk to him. His paper's circulation was but a small fraction of ours, but he was waging a splendid fight against us.

One summer day in eighteen and seventy-one—exactly a decade since I had alighted in the Washoe district—I resolved to pull this thorn from my flesh no matter how painful the result. If Goodman didn't oblige, I would quit. I would, by God, take a decade's worth of expert knowledge about mining over to the *Chronicle* and let Goodman stew.

I did some heavy fortifying that afternoon at the Old Magnolia, staying off by myself. Goodman usually toiled in his lair until eight in the evening, overseeing the next morning's edition, and then hied himself to Barnum's or some other eatery for a decanter of Moselle and the dinner du jour. I sipped ordinary claret and planned my attack, which I fathomed would work best at about seven-thirty. Long before then, though, my thoughts had become sufficiently lubricated by ardent spirits so that I deemed it wise to proceed to the task at once or slide into incoherence. So, my belly roiling, I abandoned the editorial annex, tramped next door with fateful steps, braved the busy compositors and junior scribes, mounted several stairs, and presented myself to my publisher.

"Yes, Henry?"

"I've been here ten years and done a good job and you never gave me a raise except for that lousy fiver years ago."

He stared at me to see whether I had been drinking and satisfied himself that I had. "Sit," he said.

I declined to sit. I had heard somewhere that a standing man has it all over a sitting one, so I stood.

"I want a raise. I've earned it. I've given you the best mining news on the Comstock."

I knew my truculent tone wasn't winning any smiles from my publisher, but this thing had been bottled up too long in me and now it was pouring out like muriatic acid.

"They come and go," I continued. "All these smart, clever reporters stay a month and depart. They don't know the town, they make mistakes, they have no loyalty, they can hardly spell, but you give them raises and ignore me."

"Henry, you never asked for one."

"I'd like to think you admired my work enough to offer one."

"Well, we all know you're better fixed, after that nice little stock market gambit—"

"And what has that to do with my worth to you?"

Goodman blinked and stared into space. I didn't much care what he thought. He smiled suddenly. "I was just about to pull out of here. Let's go over to Barnum's—my treat—and talk about this. All right?"

I wanted just to yell at him, but I swallowed my bile and nodded.

He pulled on his suit coat and hat, and we ventured out into a hot evening. The thump of the mills affirmed the vitality of the city, along with the rattle of ore cars, hiss of steam, and clatter of wagons on C Street. The street was crowded, as usual, with an amazing flow of mostly male humanity.

At Barnum's Goodman turned solicitous, inquiring what sort of spirits I might enjoy. I could see his mind whirling faster than a roulette wheel as we ordered. He avoided the Topic, but I knew about the time we got around to some brandy and a Havana he would bring it up. I sensed I had embarrassed him, and I privately gloated. I was not on my best behavior that hour, and if I could have made things more painful for Goodman I would have.

We had medallions of California beef, California carrots and broccoli, California salad, and breadstuffs made from California flour. The Washoe was little more than an arm of that state.

"You're a valuable man," Goodman said, broaching the subject at last. "I don't quite know how this happened. Of course I'll advance you. How about thirty a week?"

"That brings me up to the *Chronicle*'s minimum standard," I said, letting the irony show through.

"Yes. Well, you see, we thought that you were comfortably well off—"

"What has that to do with my worth?"

"Yes, of course, Henry. Actually, you haven't developed a following the way De Quille has."

"A following! I'm read by every mine and mill manager and stockbroker and speculator in the city. I'm read by the union men, the financiers. I know good and well that William Sharon and his bunch read every word I write."

"Yes, yes, of course. But we seldom hear about it. No letters, you know."

"Are you saying that I never was worth any more than a cub on the *Chronicle*? Thirty a week is their bottom wage."

Goodman was growing agitated and manfully concealing it. But I knew him too well to be fooled, and I was as reckless as I'd ever been.

"Yes, you're worth more. You're my old standby, Henry, the man I've always counted on, the man who got out the story, the man who didn't get drunk or sick or just vanish for a spell."

"Then how about thirty-five a week and another raise soon?"

Goodman stared, sighed, and nodded. He never did say yes.

"Thank you," I said, the tartness still in my voice. "I'm finally doing better than a cub."

The whole business actually disappointed me.

Goodman made short work of paying the tab, found an excuse to vanish, and left me standing on C Street.

I did not feel good. His offer of thirty a week simply offended me. I felt bad because he had forced me to ask for more. He as much as said the reason he hadn't raised me was that I wasn't very good, had no following, as he put it, and therefore didn't bring readers to his paper. I remembered back to the first weeks on the Comstock, when I learned that Goodman had a literary streak in him, had been closely associated with *Golden Age* in San Francisco, had been a bon vivant and cultural arbiter. All these years he'd viewed me with a blind eye, seeing his dutiful mutt at work.

I remembered the star I had been born under: not bad, not good, the sort who got lost in a crowd. I stared at the stars above, wondering why Fate had fashioned this iron jacket around my life, and had no answers.

Now I had my raise, arm-twisted out of him, and I had bound myself to stay with the *Enterprise*–for a while.

CHAPTER 38

. . . .

I liked John Mackay. He and his partner James Fair had gotten hold of the Hale & Norcross and made its low-grade ore pay out a last gasp. But there wasn't any future in that mine, and the partners had started to gamble on sucker properties. Mackay got a hold of the Bullion mine, which had tantalized investors for years because it was located in a prime spot on the lode, right between the Exchequer and Potosi, both of them paying propositions. But the Bullion treated John Mackay as badly as it had treated everyone else: more assessments, more drifts to locate ore, and more defeats. Not a nickel's worth of ore was ever lifted from that hole in the rock.

Fair didn't do much better. As manager of the Hale & Norcross he cut expenses, mined low-grade, explored ruthlessly, made some money that largely went into new exploration, and finally got wise and took his skills next door to the Savage, where he did much the same thing. The pair of them, in the beginning of the seventies, didn't seem any different to me from dozens of other Midases who turned out to be little more than bad poker players. But they did have one advantage over the herds of speculators. Both knew mines and ore.

Mackay liked to box and frequently showed up at Bill Davis's gymnasium on South C Street to go three tough rounds. I liked to watch him. He wasn't fast, but he was dogged, and depended on sheer perseverance and aggressiveness to win over his stronger, swifter opponents. He never panicked or quit under a barrage but found his openings, and what he learned inside the ropes is what he took into business.

I never had any trouble getting a story from him, nor did he ever convey to anyone any snobbishness or condescension. He was incapable of both. His English was shaky, and later, when his wife acquired social status, he spent hours studying an English grammar. His language was homespun, and it was always "me and Fair" and not "Fair and I."

Mackay and Fair were good for a few lines now and then. Little did I know what lay just over the horizon. I should have guessed; it was all there in the gym if only I had eyes to see. I might also have guessed from Mackay's moves in business. The partners didn't like to ship all their Norcross ore to the Bank of California's Union Mill and Mining

Company mills, so Mackay and Fair bought a mill of their own, and then another, once again driving wedges into the powerful combine that had pocketed the Comstock Lode, and further loosening William Sharon's stranglehold. Mackay was boxing with Sharon the only way he knew how: exploiting every small opportunity and avoiding Sharon's haymakers. But I knew it wouldn't come to anything. That's what I told De Quille and the rest of my colleagues. Small potatoes.

In eighteen and seventy-one Mackay and Fair made the biggest sucker move of all, and I got a good chortle out of it. With the Hale & Norcross and Savage mines running out of low-grade, the Irishmen needed ore to keep their mills running, and began a desperate search for some milling ore—they no longer believed the Comstock would yield a bonanza—to keep going before the mills bled them of their slender profits. (Fair changed his tune later and said he knew all along that he'd strike bonanza, but I remember how he talked back then, when I was worming stories out of him. He was looking for some milling ore and nothing more.)

The partners settled upon an arid stretch of the Comstock Lode, a miserable, cheating, seductive, perfidious, evil stretch of 1,300 feet lying between the played-out Ophir on the north and the dying Best & Belcher to the south. To be sure, that footage lay squarely on the lead, but it had busted the dozens of speculators, wildcatters, and entrepreneurs who had tried to squeeze a nickel out of its barren rock. Mackay and Fair were hardly the first to rest their gazes on that naked stretch of Mount Davidson, some of which lay directly under Virginia City. To make matters worse, the titles to much of that rabbitbrush slope were clouded and a speculator could scarcely imagine what sort of trouble he'd get into if he hit ore.

None of that deterred Mackay. What intrigued him and Fair was that the property lay between the two richest mines on the Comstock: the fabulous Gould & Curry and the Ophir. Between them, those two mines had produced $20 million of silver and gold.

Originally, those 1,310 feet had been held by six companies: the Central had 150 feet; the California had 300 feet; the Central Number 2 had 100 feet; the Kinney had 50; the White & Murphy had 210; and the Sides had 500. By the late sixties these outfits had honeycombed the whole area with drifts as deep as five hundred feet and had gotten little for their trouble. Only the Central, which had a piece of the ore body that enriched the Ophir, had hauled any ore to the surface.

In eighteen and sixty-seven some entrepreneurs had folded most of those barren mines into a new company, the Consolidated Virginia, intending to go down to 1,500 feet. The Consolidated Virginia possessed 710 feet on the lode. That company proceeded to drive a shaft over six hundred feet and then ran an exploratory drift from that depth—to no avail. After $160,000 in assessments had yielded only barren rock and floods of hot water, the project faded and the whole operation was written off. The California mine possessed the remaining 600 feet. Its fate had been no better than its neighbor's. In eighteen and sixty-nine that mine's managers had made another major effort only to hit more water. That's where matters stood when Mackay and Fair began to examine the properties.

The price of Consolidated Virginia shares had dropped to around a dollar in July of 1870, rose a bit during another bout of exploration, plunged again to about a dollar and a half in February of 1871, and then rose somewhat when the partners began to buy up shares in that and the California mine in eighteen and seventy-one. All through that year, the partners bought Consolidated Virginia and California shares, and on January 11, 1872, they took possession of the decrepit mining companies. We who kept track of such matters calculated they had spent less than fifty thousand dollars for the lot.

Immediately they put lawyers to work to examine the clouded titles and establish undisputed ownership. The task proved difficult but was finally achieved, and the partners possessed clear title to a parcel of ground that had defeated some of the best minds on the lode. The depot and yards of the Virginia & Truckee Railroad had been built upon the easterly surface of the Consolidated Virginia mine, complicating the whole venture and limiting the area where a new shaft could be sunk.

I was curious about what they would do next, and for a change they weren't saying much. But I did get the drift of their plans one time in Davis's gym, after watching Mackay go three rounds against a bigger, heavier, faster man and still come out fine. Mackay regarded exercise as the key to health and has stayed active all his long life. As I write, he is still going strong at age sixty-nine, having outlived all his colleagues, Fair, Flood, and O'Brien, by many years.

But I digress. It's an old man's habit, each thought leading to another memory, and pretty soon a man full of memories is wide of his mark. I caught Mackay that 1872 day at the gym just as he was washing up after his bout, and I asked him what the partners intended to do with that bleak stretch of rock.

"Go deep," he said simply. "The others barely scratched the surface. Most of the shafts on the Comstock are below a thousand feet now, and ore's down there."

Then, suddenly, he clammed up, having no doubt said more than he intended. And that was what I reported in the *Territorial Enterprise*. The paper had opined, years earlier, that the way to get at ore in that area was to start a new shaft well east and downslope from the line of mines, simply because the strike of the Comstock fissure—the gap in the country rock that had gradually filled up with mineral salts over aeons of time—ran easterly. But no one had heeded a mere newspaper, and I wondered if Mackay would heed us now.

He did, but Fair didn't. James G. Fair had his own notions about how to explore that patch of desert, and for a while we were kept in the dark. All I could report was that the partners were up to something, and all we knew for sure was that the exploration for ore would be conducted down, down, down in the hellfires of the Comstock.

In fact, the partners were debating behind closed doors just what to do that spring of eighteen and seventy-two. One possibility was to continue driving the existing Consolidated Virginia shaft deeper until they either hit ore or ran out of money. Another intriguing idea was to use the Ophir's 1,100-foot shaft and drive a drift southward into the California and Consolidated Virginia property at that level.

The third and wildest plan was to begin drifting north from the 1,200-foot-deep Gould & Curry mine shaft, clear through the 700 feet of the Best & Belcher mine but far below that company's works, and into the Consolidated Virginia ground. That idea had been proposed, I later learned, by Pat McKay, manager of William Sharon's Gould & Curry mine and no relation to John, who was always looking for a way to fatten his profits. For a nominal fee he would let John Mackay and James Fair lift the rock out of his shaft.

Down on California Street, in San Francisco, Sharon licked his chops and approved, figuring he would get back some of the boodle he had lost trying to control the Hale & Norcross. Thus the wily Sharon suddenly became the very soul of cooperation. He didn't at all mind having a Mackay crew drifting northward, eating up Consolidated Virginia cash, and paying him a steady little stipend for hauling out their rock through his shaft. He cheerfully told his colleagues that he would help those Irishmen spend their cash—or so I heard much later, because all this maneuvering was carefully kept from the press.

Fair liked the idea and came to claim it as his own, which was his nature. He was not a man to deny himself credit. So the work started in May. All that summer the Consolidated Virginia crew bored north, working across the entire 700-foot length of the Best & Belcher, deep below that mine's works, gasping for air as the drift progressed farther and farther from ventilation. One of my old Cornish friends from Platteville, John Penrose, told me about it over ale.

I listened to his stories about barren rock, near-suffocation so far from fresh air, acrid powder smoke lingering in the narrow, cramped drift, and Fair's manic three-shift efforts. I concluded the jig was up. The lucky Irishmen had no more four-leaf clovers.

C H A P T E R   3 9

s I look back from my perch upon the cusp of a new century, I realize that there are a few myths that need to be dispelled. Reader, if the miracles by which you get the metals you use are not your favorite reading, skip these paragraphs. I have reported the dull precincts of technology most of my days and understand your reticence. There are other parts of this memoir that you will find more entertaining, especially if your brain has been softened by trashy novels.

Not the least of these myths is the notion that the mines employed dynamite to blast out the rich ores of the Comstock. It is true that dynamite did arrive on the Comstock and was swiftly put to effective use, but that didn't happen until the midseventies.

It had been invented by Alfred Nobel in eighteen and sixty-seven as a safe means for employing the explosive power of nitroglycerin, the notoriously unstable and lethal "blasting oil" that proved too dangerous to use. Nobel simply mixed nitro with an inert clay and then rolled the moist mixture into waxy paper cylinders. The result was a stable product that could take jolts and abuse without detonating and could scarcely be exploded without the help of a fulminate of mercury cap.

Of course it had its own drawbacks: it was useless when frozen, and old dynamite tended to decay, leaking the nitro from the clay until the whole mess was unstable. Even so, its use greatly improved mining along toward the end of the heyday of Virginia City. DuPont acquired the license to manufacture it in this country, and soon its famous brand, Hercules, became a staple of the mining industry.

But that wasn't how things were done during the times I have written about. The miners used black powder as they always had, except that it contained sodium nitrate instead of potassium nitrate, which made it a little more powerful but prone to absorb moisture. That, too, was a

DuPont product. At the beginning of each shift, the man responsible for the blasting loaded his paper cartridges from the powder barrel, always in solitude and in a place apart from the rest of the mining works.

Then, with his charged paper cylinders and his roll of Bickford fuse, a marvelous cord with a core of powder wrapped in jute that burned a steady thirty seconds a foot, he proceeded to the face, or breast, where muckers were shoveling the rock loosened by the previous blast into the one-ton ore cars and the double-jackers were steadily battering their hand-held steel drills into the face, gouging deep holes in the rock that would receive a charge of powder.

If the air was bad, the residue of smoke and fumes from the previous charge seared their lungs. Later, when the Burleigh drill—a heavy drilling device that operated on compressed air—partially replaced the muscular task of jacking holes into the rock, the vicious dust, actually sharp-edged minuscule fragments of rock, lodged in miners' lungs and gave rise to miner's lung, or silicosis, which shortened the lives of men who worked underground, though we little understood that back then.

But that, too, came later. In eighteen and seventy-two the Savage mine experimented with the new drills, but not until eighteen and seventy-four, when Adolph Sutro introduced the technique in his gigantic tunnel, did the compressed-air drill come into general use. The men in that endless tunnel welcomed the new drill more for the fresh air it released than for the work it saved them.

As you know, I could barely stand to go into the pits, for I could not cope with the terror of those dark, cramped quarters or the knowledge that just above my head lay the crushing weight of tons of rock. Dan De Quille laughed at me and continued to be the paper's eyes and ears underground. Later, when Fate played a wry prank on me, I had to overcome my fear, and eventually I learned to descend to the River Styx almost as readily as others, though to my dying day I will fear it.

Perhaps I knew too much. Those massive timbers that looked so capable of propping up the ceilings actually began rotting the day they were installed because of the extraordinary dampness and heat and the fumes rising from the mineralized water oozing from the native rock. Dry rot sapped the strength of those timbers, and soon they were a fragile hulk, their strength gone. If one could poke the blade of a jack-knife well into them they were as good as useless.

I knew, from years of covering those mines, that the mining companies spent enormous sums replacing the worst of those timbers, that the roofs of those caverns were unstable, the rock fractured and shifted, in constant motion. The mines had tried to build support columns out of the rubble from the faces, by planking up and filling those square-set cubicles, but to little avail. Nothing on earth could prevent those ceilings from collapsing when the conditions were right.

Fair and Mackay's face crews descended down the Gould & Curry mine shaft in the company's splendid two-deck cages, which could drop or lift dozens of men, or tons of ore, and come delicately to a halt at the appointed level, the genius of the operators being no small part of this magic. (They were a far cry from the early days, when miners got to the workings by descending a ladder, sometimes two or three hundred feet, at great peril to themselves.) There, at the bottom of the shaft, they trudged north through a cramped, dark drift barely wide enough for an ore car to pass and barely high enough to permit them to stand erect, carrying their candles, or candle-lanterns, with them, along with their tools if there was no ore car handy to transport them. The farther they got from the shaft, the worse the air became. The fumes from the detonated black powder had no place to go and simply lingered there, evil and sulphurous, making the candle flames dim to small blue dots. If black powder fumes were bad, the miners would soon discover that dynamite fumes were ten times worse, so harsh and vicious that they scoured lungs, reduced throats to raw flesh, and stung eyes and nostrils.

I have always thought that their four-dollar wage was modest compared to the dangers and torments they endured, but it was princely compared to the dollar sixty-five, or its equivalent, that miners earned in England and positively kingly compared to what miners earned in Germany or the rest of the Continent. Once the fresh crew reached the face, it confronted a pile of rubble that lay between it and the breast. The more experienced men studied the area carefully to ascertain whether there had been a misfire, leaving an unexploded charge in the face. The telltale mark was usually a hump in the rock indicating an area that had not been blasted loose. More than one careless miner had been blown to bits because he had failed to spot a misfire or failed to smell a "hanging" charge that was still smoldering but not yet detonated.

It was up to the muckers, the least skilled among the crew, to reduce and shovel this rubble into the ore cars, using sledgehammers and shovels, first clearing the rock closest to the face so the drilling teams could begin their double-jacking. Other men, working behind the muckers, erected the timbering used to support the drift, usually fourteen-inch-square posts that supported a crossbeam of similar thickness. These had to be wedged into place, and if the ceiling consisted of decomposed or dangerous rock, a plank ceiling, called lagging, had to be built. If water threatened, drainage ditches had to be chopped to remove it.

In addition to all this, the rails for the ore cars had to be extended every little while and ventilation pipe—if there was any ventilation—had to be lengthened. All this took place while the double-jackers hammered their holes in the face, switching drill steels as their cutting edges dulled, each steel slightly smaller in diameter than the previous one. While one man rotated the drill the other hammered with the rhythm of a pulse, never missing a beat when they traded tasks.

The muckers were greatly aided by a heavy iron sheet that had been pried into place by the previous crew before the blast. It offered a smooth surface from which to shovel, speeding up the whole process.

In addition to the foul air, noise fouled the mind. A miner could not escape the constant clang of hammer on steel, the rattle of ore sliding into a steel ore car, the scrape of shovels, or the chatter of the Burleigh drill as it battered the face of the drift. The Comstock heat, which increased as the shafts sank, sucked sweat and strength out of the miners, and not even buckets of ice adequately cooled overheated men. Many of the mines found themselves shipping tons of ice into the pits, at great expense and with little effect. The deeper the shafts, the costlier the mining, and the less productive were the miners. Eventually those shafts pierced deeper than any other on earth, and there were those who suspected they were approaching the very roof of hell.

Then, toward the end of the shift, the powder man would tenderly charge the holes hammered into native rock. There would usually be seven of these, the cutholes, relievers, edgers, and lifters, each with a purpose: to blow out the middle of the face, and then the top and bottom and sides in a manner that would extend the drift about three feet farther in approximately the same rectangular shape. Gently—for ungentle powder men tended to vanish from this world at a young age—the powder man cleaned out the holes with a tiny scoop on a wire, twisted the paper cartridges until the paper broke so the powder would pack better, and then tamped each cylinder home, using a wooden rod—never an iron or steel one, which might spark. To the final cylinder he tied a precisely measured piece of Bickford fuse, tamped that into place, and sealed the hole with a bit of muck that would contain the explosion a fraction of a second and greatly increase its muscle.

These fuses, each carefully measured, would hang like rat tails from the face. The holes nearest the center of the breast, or face, would have the shortest fuses because they had to blow first, opening space for the charges around the periphery. Then the powder man would cut a length of Bickford fuse called the spitter, which was always shorter than the shortest fuse hanging from the face. Then he would shout the traditional warning, "Fire in the hole," and light the spitter with his candle or a lamp, working carefully and deliberately, with nerves of ice, to ignite all the dangling fuses. When the spitter began to scorch his fingertips, he knew it was time to go—walking deliberately, because it would not do to stumble at such a moment. Then, from the safety of the vestibule of the junction of another drift, he would count the blasts, or the puffs of air, and leave a report for the next shift saying whether all, or not all, of the charges had ignited. If he wasn't sure, it would be up to the next shift to beware.

Out of all this brutal labor came awesome wealth, ore rich with silver but sometimes so laden with gold that its value transcended that of the silver. All across the Comstock, two or three thousand human ants crawled down those frightful holes, twenty-four hours a day, shift upon shift, disemboweling Sun Mountain of its minerals to the metronome of the howling mine whistles.

I often sat in the office of the *Territorial Enterprise* contemplating the contrasts: the hard, exhausting, short lives of the miners in the dark pits—for whom sunlight was a luxury and sensuous pleasure—and the lives of the well-padded magnates and brokers and financiers who harvested the wealth clawed from the earth by those sweating, half-naked toilers who braved smoke, poisonous gases, heat, collapsing timbers, deafening noise, and suffocation day after day.

Why did those brave men descend to the gates of hell six days of every week? I've asked myself that a thousand times and have partial explanations but no real, all-embracing answer to one of life's enigmas. Money was the primary lever. Many of those who descended into the pits had only recently arrived in the United States and were penniless. Recruiters in the East steered them west to the mines.

Four dollars a day seemed a king's ransom to men who had found no work at all, or worked for a pittance, in the old country. In Saxony, miners earned less than two dollars a *week,* so the Comstock wage seemed miraculous to them. The wage would be enough so that a man could get ahead and in a year or two move on to something better. Four dollars a day would soon bring his brothers and sisters, or his parents, or his wife and children across the sea to the New World.

The mines were merely the way station en route to a dream. And so they came: Irishmen fleeing famine and oppression, Bohemians, Czechs, Germans, Poles, Danes, Swedes, Finns, Italians, Jews, Frenchmen, Hawaiians, Chinamen, Filipinos, Australians, and all the rest, all of them beginning a new life, becoming their own sovereigns, in the free soil of a young country. How often I heard a foreign tongue on C Street, or D, or down in the drab, square boardinghouses, frame cottages, and shanties below, hard by the mines.

Most never achieved their dream; they died of a hundred diseases, or were mangled and broken by the mines, or failed swiftly from miner's lung or consumption, or were destined to live as cripples, in grinding poverty, the objects of charity. But they came to Virginia City, and the magical city rewarded some of them handsomely with opportunity and nurtured its bonanza legend by making millionaires of a few. And in all those years I scarcely heard a word of regret, even from those who had lost. They considered it a worthwhile gamble.

C H A P T E R   4 0

 had known James G. Fair since the midsixties and didn't much like him, although I respected him. He had arrived on the Comstock in eighteen and sixty-five, having made some success of various mining and milling ventures in the California goldfields. His failures in the Golden State had taught him what not to do and had prepared him for the rough-and-tumble of the Comstock Lode. Within a year he had become the superintendent of the Ophir, which he operated shrewdly, never wasting a cent, unlike other operators.

That's how I got to know him. My daily rounds took me to most of the mines, and I visited Fair regularly. He had been born in Dublin in 1831, and he was a Protestant. He didn't lack blarney and could employ it at will, becoming the soul of camaraderie when he wished, which was when he intended to use me for some purpose or other. He had a genius for ingratiating himself with those who might help him and often wrapped an arm and a smile about me. That's when I knew to be wary.

Fair was a big, husky, black-haired Irishman who had spent plenty of time underground and patrolled every cranny of his works daily. He and I had in common an appreciation for mining machinery. There wasn't an innovation that Fair hadn't tried, and he boasted that he knew machinery better than anyone else on earth. He was probably right. He claimed to have been born to it, coming from a family of mechanics. Actually, after his parents immigrated to Iowa he had spent his youth on a farm before heading for the goldfields and freedom of California.

But it was plain to me that Fair had a repellent side. He criticized everyone, including his partners, blaming them for whatever went wrong but taking credit himself for whatever they did that was beneficial. He had no friends and wanted none, and was incapable of friendship because his entire instincts focused on himself. He let it be known that everyone else was a knave or fool.

He lived quietly in a pleasant house on South B Street, in a good neighborhood, with his wife, Theresa, who was Catholic, and their four young children: Theresa, Virginia, Jimmy, and Charley. But Fair was as bad as a husband as he was as a friend, because he notoriously cheated on Theresa and was a constant visitor to the bawdy districts of Virginia City, barely being discreet about it. Judging from the way his sons, in particular, turned out, I don't doubt that he was as miserable a father as he was a husband. The fact is that James G. Fair hadn't the slightest care about any mortal other than himself and hadn't the slightest intention of ever letting law, ethics, decency, kindness, or charity interfere with satisfying his own lusts and whims. Of the four bonanza partners, Mackay, Fair, Flood, and O'Brien, Fair was truly the greedy one.

Long before he had struck it rich he manipulated the mining stock market as ruthlessly as any man alive. At one point he had a large holding in the Gould & Curry at a time when he knew privately that the mine was failing and its reserves were almost depleted. What he did then so perfectly characterized the man that it is worth repeating.

Theresa had, at that time, about seven thousand dollars she had squirreled away and guarded carefully. Fair advised her to buy Gould & Curry with it, promising that she would get rich. So Mrs. James G. Fair bought the stock, whispering to various friends that her husband had recommended it. That started a boomlet in Gould & Curry shares, for what man would bamboozle his wife? As their price rose, Fair quietly unloaded his own massive holdings, coming out handsomely on the rising tide. When the news of the mine's actual condition finally permeated the market, the Gould & Curry stocks dropped, wiping out Theresa's money.

In tears, she asked him why he had recommended such a disastrous investment to her. He consoled her, wrote her a check for $7,000 out of his enormous profits, and never paused to consider how he had used and abused his own wife. "My dear," he said, "you'll never be a speculator."

That was "Slippery Jim" Fair, as the world came to know him. And he had other dark facets of character. He so distrusted others that he never delegated responsibility, zealously performing what should have been the routine work of clerks and foremen and purchasing agents, working himself to exhaustion and going without sleep. He was never known to compliment anyone and constantly rejected the efforts of his partners to reward a valuable employee with better pay.

And when trouble brewed in the pits he invariably blamed Mackay for policies that were Fair's own doing, broadly insinuating to his own miners that he couldn't change Mackay's unreasonable rules. Thus was Fair not only self-centered but also villainous, and the more I was thrown into contact with him, the more appalled I became. Was there no decency in him? Would he earn his millions and never give a dime to anyone in need? Yes, that was his nature.

And yet he was a mining genius, and I would be the last to rob him of his deserved reputation as a brilliant operator of mines and mills. Fair was the first to innovate, the first to economize, the first to invent new and better methods. During the prebonanza years when he was managing the Hale & Norcross, and then the Savage, he squeezed out a profit where other managers had failed and kept going on low-grade that defeated lesser men. He claimed to have a nose for ore, but that notion, like so many of his boasts, was buncombe.

A reporter usually knows when he's being used, and it wasn't difficult to plumb Fair's intent. That hot summer of eighteen and seventy-two he became almost garrulous when I dropped by to inquire about the quixotic drift that each day was being pushed under the Best & Belcher toward the Consolidated Virginia, at enormous cost.

"Glad you dropped by, Stoddard," he said affably, doling out a cigar. "I've a question for you. You know, Mackay, he's an old hand with the mining, and he's the one that took to that notion to drift from the Gould & Curry's shaft, and you know, Flood and O'Brien, they ain't ever been in a mine—too fat to fit, I'm thinking, and too tidy to get dirt on their britches. They're just along for the ride, and it's up to John and me to make the decisions.

"It was all Pat McKay's idea—he's the super over at the Gould & Curry, you know—though I don't doubt old Sharon was the spider in that web, trying to milk us to haul out our rock. Now, my old pal John Mackay's no fool, one of the best men around when it comes to practical mining, but I've been wondering if he got took on that one.

"I've been down there about three times a day, and all I see is more and more diorite, no ore in sight, and yet the partners shell out hard cash every day to drive that drift and pay off Sharon to use his shaft and lifts, and I'm thinking, Stoddard, what's the sense of it? Eh? Does it make sense to you? It don't to me; that's for sure. But how do I turn this machine off? Mackay, he's the man running the show, and I'm wondering, Henry old man, what I should say? He's wrong, you know. That's a dead-end hole, and I'd like to get sensible and work from the bottom of the Ophir shaft—that's eleven hundred down, and we could head straight into the California—but John's wisdom is such that my thoughts are no contest. What do you say, Henry boy?"

That took interpreting, but I knew my man and I had more than an inkling what this was about. This was classical Fair, fobbing off blame when things looked bad. He'd obviously concluded that the northbound drift from the Gould & Curry was a trip to nowhere, and he wanted the blame pinned on his partner John Mackay and the Gould & Curry's manager, Pat McKay.

It didn't matter that Fair himself was the original enthusiast for that approach. Now that it was going sour and the face crews were gasping for air at the breast of a drift eight hundred feet from the shaft, he wanted me to put his doubts on public record. And as usual, he was complimenting John Mackay in his left-handed style while doing it.

I nodded cheerfully, my way of avoiding uttering large or small lies, smiled, and beat my way back to the *Territorial Enterprise,* formulating my story as I hiked upslope from the Savage, where Fair's writ still ran. I decided not to let myself be used. Much later, I wished I had, because if I had published what James G. Fair wanted me to publish he would have been singing quite another song when success arrived.

The story I did write that roasting August day simply said that the Consolidated Virginia crews had encountered not the slightest sign of ore, that boring much farther would no longer be practical without costly ventilation, and that the whole project looked like a dud. I didn't even mention Slippery Jim Fair, nor did I even hint that he was blaming John Mackay. The story drove down the price of Consolidated Virginia shares and irked the partners, but I didn't much care.

August folded into September without the slightest change: the drifting continued through country rock, and the partners were all restless, threatening new assessments, and on the brink of abandoning the drift. Later Fair would concoct a whopper to describe what happened next. According to his version, just about then, when everyone was about ready to quit, he discovered a vein, as thin as a knife's edge, elusive in the flickering candlelight, too thin to mine, but a promise of something grand. He was, he explained, almost living in that drift, shift by shift, day by day. And because his keen eye for ore had seen this, he flogged the partners onward, flogged his face crews forward, and gradually that knife-edge seam of ore widened to an inch or two, and then several inches, and then a foot, and finally several feet, fairly good ore assaying at sixty dollars a ton—and the bonanza was on.

It didn't happen like that. Comstock ore usually didn't lie in seams or veins, but in pockets. You hit a pocket or not, but you rarely chased a vein. When, in fact, the face crew did strike ore, it was suddenly, as it broke into a fissure. On September 12, a face crew, actually under the supervision of the Consolidated Virginia's supervisor, Capt. Sam Curtis, struck a fissure crammed with low-assay silver-bearing quartz, clay, and syenite, the east-wall country rock of the Comstock. James G. Fair was nowhere in sight when it happened. Curtis, a gifted mining veteran, followed the vein northeasterly, the fissure widening and the assay values improving with every foot.

The partners didn't know what they had found, but they did know they had some low-grade ore and promptly used it to finance a new shaft on Consolidated Virginia ground, which would allow them to raise the ore more efficiently and provide desperately needed ventilation once it connected with the long drift from the Gould & Curry. Feverish three-shift, twenty-four-hour work began on the new shaft, and in short order the shaft reached the drift and the partners began lifting low-grade ore from the new works.

I have the advantage of hindsight. The Mackay-Fair partnership thought it had found a modest pocket that would keep the Consolidated Virginia and the California mines afloat for a while.

Little did they or I know that history was being made.

CHAPTER 41

've been neglecting to tell about my friend and colleague Dan De Quille, or William Wright, though no one except perhaps his family called him that anymore. De Quille had become a fixture on the Comstock, making it home except for periodic visits to his wife and children in Iowa, where he had conveniently parked them so he could live the life he enjoyed as an imbiber of intoxicants and a devotee of other of life's great pleasures.

Wright is often given credit for a literary skill probably larger than Twain's, but no one, to my knowledge, has ever credited him with perfecting many a married man's furtive fantasy—a life lived in sublime and free bachelorhood about fifteen hundred miles from his wife and children. Now there was his transcending genius.

De Quille continued more or less regularly, or maybe I should say irregularly, as the reigning literary monarch of the *Territorial Enterprise.* His output depended inversely on his input of spirits. I note, looking over his oeuvre, that 1869 was a fallow year for De Quille, with only "Letter from Donner Lake" reaching publication. I suspect he was off fishing, fly rod in one hand, bottle of Bourbon County, Kentucky's best, in the other. Whatever the case, he did much better in 1870 and 1871, generating for the *Enterprise* such jewels as "Mule Gives Birth!" (If you do not know about mules, you will see nothing in such a story.) Also, the citizens of the Washoe district were treated to "A Big Injun Takes de Gas," "The Washoe Shoe Fly," "Perkins' Ghost Appears to a Bootblack," "A Melon-Choly Affair," and "Last of the Great Expeditions. The Mighty Hunters All Dead."

In addition to all this, he continued his normal reportage—whenever he was around—including his regular forays into the pits to examine ore and shaft, square-set timbering, and sanitary facilities (usually a two-holer ore car that could be run up the shaft and emptied). This he continued to do in large part because of my unconquered dread of descending to the nether regions of the district. He had become, over his long career on the Comstock, the recognized authority.

It was precisely because of my reticence to descend into the pits, and because of De Quille's long history of doing just that, that De Quille, and not I, became one of the darlings of history.

That fall of eighteen and seventy-two word bruited about that the Mackay-Fair combine had hit some ore, though its extent and value were unknown. John Mackay did not conceal the event from the watchful eyes of a thousand greedy speculators but casually minimized it, usually in what he reported to me.

"Yes," he would say during those fateful weeks, "me and Fair have found some pockets and we're exploring a bit to see what we've discovered. First assays are running seven to thirty-four a ton, mostly from silver, but it's too soon to say anything else. We're going to sink a shaft over the new lode as swiftly as possible to improve ventilation. If there's ore, we'll haul it up that way."

The stocks of the Consolidated Virginia and California mines rose modestly on news like that. Veteran Comstock speculators knew better than to leap in with both feet. But the four partners were quietly buying what they could, paying a modest price a share even as they kept largely mum about what was transpiring down at the end of that long drift. They ended up with three-quarters of the stock of both mines.

What actually was happening down there, though neither I nor the world knew it, was steady improvement of the ore. The face crews drove into a body of ore that grew thicker and thicker, from seven feet to twelve, to twenty, and finally an amazing forty-eight feet. All four sides of the drift consisted of ore. But it was still low-grade, milling at twenty-three dollars a ton, and little hinted of what was to come.

The partners, realizing they had struck moderately valuable ore, began their new shaft. But even as the shaft was being sunk twenty-four hours a day by three shifts, face crews working in the ore body were trying to find the outer limits of the thickening vein by drifting and crosscutting, and in March 1873 the firm uncovered some high-grade.

Mackay, largely through me, continued to tell the world that yes, some reserves had been found. But by then I was skeptical. Word swirled about, of course—one could usually find a miner who would open up after an ale or two. But the miners kept uncommonly quiet, which meant they were being well paid to keep mum. I scarcely knew what to believe, and my thoughts pendulumed between bonanza and borrasca. I had my brokers check the performance of those two stocks, but I could read little or nothing in the modest upward movement of both, classical performance on some tentative good news. The firm's ore, still being raised through the Gould & Curry shaft while work continued on the new Consolidated Virginia shaft, was then milling at about thirty-four a ton.

Meanwhile the firm, working though James Flood, issued new shares of Consolidated Virginia stock, raising the total to 23,600, and then in March they brought the shares up to 108,000. The result was to make the shares affordable, so that people of limited means could invest in the mine. By then the company was lifting 200 tons of ore a day through its new shaft and the Gould & Curry.

I took it all to mean that Virginia City had won a reprieve from the death sentence that visited all mining towns and thought maybe I'd be around another two or three years. That was how most people took it. The merchants and saloon men thought much the same thing: business as usual until this pocket wore out.

No one supposed that Mackay and Fair, and their San Francisco partners, would be kings of the Comstock or enter the social universe occupied by Ralston and Sharon as well as bank president Darius Ogden Mills or any of the San Francisco railroad nabobs. No, this would be a fine, compact little boom for the lucky Irishmen, and it would not turn the world upside down.

That spring of 1873 the partners quietly explored what would become one of the greatest strikes the world had ever known, paying for their explorations with the lower-grade ore they were pulling out of thick seams above and around the massive bonanza pocket. Ore values increased sharply and the company ran a new drift south and east for 200 feet without running out of solid ore. The shaft work continued through the summer, and the drifts being run from it a hundred feet lower were still hewn out of solid ore. Through all of eighteen and seventy-three, the exploration continued, financed by the ever-expanding body of rich ore that drifts, winzes, upraises, and crosscuts revealed to the astonished owners and managers.

Eliot Lord, of the United States Geological Survey, put it this way:

> The wonder grew as its depths were searched out foot by foot. The bonanza was cut at a point 1167 feet below the surface, and as the shaft went down it was pierced again at the 1200-foot level; still the same body of ore was found, but wider and longer than above. One hundred feet deeper, and the prying pick and drill told the same story; yet another hundred feet and the mass appeared to be still swelling. When, finally, the 1500-foot level was reached and richer ore than ever before met with was disclosed, the fancy of the coolest brains ran wild.

The partners, persuaded at last that they had struck an ore pocket beyond description and that most of it still lay beyond their frenetic explorations, decided the time had come to tell the world. The upper ore body was thirty to forty feet wide, with rich streaks separated by mineralized porphyry, which itself could be milled profitably. And no one knew how deep it ran.

San Francisco speculators had gotten wind of a strike and were furiously seeking information by fair and foul means. They could not be put off any longer.

The task of telling the world fell to Superintendent Fair, not Mackay, and the way it happened still reminds me of how modest a role I continued to play at Joe Goodman's newspaper. The partners had always come to me with their routine stories. But when it came to breaking the biggest mining story in history, they turned to the paper's celebrity.

De Quille tells the story better than I could:

> One day [Fair] drove up to the *Enterprise* office and came in.
>
> "Those city papers have been abusing us long enough," he remarked; "I won't stand for it! Where's Dan? I want him to go down to the mine. I'll show him what we're doing."
>
> Fair spoke pretty loud, as if he only wanted to shut up the city papers, but probably he had all the stock he wanted and had just got ready to tell the truth; I don't know. Anyway . . . we drove to the mine and went down to the richest place in the bonanza.
>
> Fair said, "Go in and climb around. Look all you want, measure it up,

make up your own mind; I won't tell you a thing; people will say I posted you!" And so he went away. That just suited me. After I was through I went to the *Enterprise* office and wrote two articles . . .

Dan spent half a day down there, chipping samples, measuring the feet and yards and rods of ore from top to bottom, from one wall of the enormous pocket to the other. At the same time, another reputable mining man, Philipp Deidesheimer, graduate of the legendary Freiburg School of Mines, inventor of square-set timbering, supervisor of the Ophir and other great mines, and acknowledged mining genius, was invited in to have a look. A veteran newsman and a veteran mining superintendent would tell the world.

I remember the strange mood Dan De Quille fell into upon his return to the paper that afternoon. Instead of writing, he stared out the grimy window at October skies.

I asked him how it had gone.

"I'm waiting for the assay reports," he said.

"What did you see?"

He stared at me and shrugged.

I thought maybe he had been sampling the wares of the Old Magnolia, and so left him alone. But his conduct puzzled me. I hadn't ever seen De Quille behave like that, as if he had received a visitation from the Devil or a brace of angels. I resolved to hustle him off to a doctor if his trancelike condition worsened.

I was itching for news and prodded him, but he just stared at me as though I didn't exist. And for the next several hours I no doubt didn't exist in his mind.

Then the assays from his seven samples came in, and these ranged from $632 to $93 a ton, the average being $443. At that historical point, the average milling ore on the Comstock was yielding $40 a ton. He showed the results to me. The ore was uncommonly rich, but I still had no inkling of what he had seen, what had made him so moony and afraid to set pen to paper.

For once, De Quille wasn't in a social mood. He was having a bad time describing what was beyond description. What they had shown him down there was a chamber gouged from solid ore that lay in vertical rifts between the inclining foundation rock of Mount Davidson and the overhanging wall of diabase, or porphyry. De Quille had entered a chamber supported by six to nine sets of timbers (five feet each) wide, four floors, or sets, high, and found high-grade ore mixed with shattered porphyry composing every face, floor, and ceiling. He saw, as well, a 54-foot-wide gallery running lengthwise (north and south) for 140 feet, bored through black ore that glistened with native silver crystals and free-milling gold, but was also mixed with barren rock. There was so much wealth in sight that he could scarcely grasp what he was seeing.

What Dan was actually trying to do as he mooned about the paper was put a price tag on what he had seen. He finally came up with the figure of $230,000,000 for what was visible in that one area, which was only the top level of the ore body, but just to be cautious he cut that in half for publication, proclaiming he had seen $116,748,000 of "the finest chloride ore filled with streaks and bunches of the richest black silver sulphurettes." And that was just the top level of the Consolidated Virginia and didn't include its neighbor, the California. His story appeared on October 29, 1873, under the heading: "Consolidated Virginia—a Look through the Long Forbidden Lower Levels . . ."

But his calculations were modest compared to those of the temporarily deranged Deidesheimer, who some time later announced that he had seen one and a half billion dollars' worth of ore—yes, all of that—in the bonanza mines and would base his considerable reputation on that figure.

I could not believe what I was reading and hearing and thought De Quille was smoking something in the China quarter, and I told him so.

He just bared his yellow teeth back at me.

In February, Congress had demonetized silver, unmooring it from its historic $1.29 an ounce, or one-sixteenth the price of gold, which meant that just at the moment of the bonanza discovery silver prices were beginning to decline. Although the ore in the Consolidated Virginia proved to be rich in gold, the demonetization threw a cloud over any calculations. Further clouding the estimates was the highly variable nature of the ore, which ran in rich streaks, mixed inchoately with low-grade, and worthless country rock.

The result of all this folderol, which occurred across the fall of eighteen and seventy-three, was nothing. Few serious investors believed a word of it, and there was no run on the Consolidated Virginia. I myself believed that De Quille had gone overboard, mesmerized by the high-grade, his eyes not noticing that tenors varied sharply. But until I overcame my fear of descending into those pits I would never see it firsthand—to my ultimate sorrow. I bought no stock.

· ·

Water! That memorable night of August 1, 1873, sweet Sierra water gushed into the new reservoir above Gold Hill and Virginia City while fireworks bloomed in the sky, dignitaries made speeches, bands played lively airs, people lined up with buckets and bottles to capture some of the precious stuff, and the whole Comstock gave a sigh of relief.

The new system drew freshwater from a mountain source twenty-one miles distant, carrying the water of Hobart Creek first by flume to the head of the pipe and then down and across and up the Washoe valley in seven miles of pipe capable of withstanding the static pressures of about eight hundred pounds a square inch—an engineering marvel—and then into another flume that delivered the precious water to the thirty thousand people scattered through the cities on the Comstock and to the mines that would use it in their boilers. The whole project cost $2 million and involved engineering never before attempted.

How proud we were that night, each of us with a cup or tumbler in hand, sipping sweet cold water from the distant blue wall of the Sierras, proud of the Comstock, proud of the water company, grateful to its visionary directors, Mackay, Fair, Flood, and O'Brien, for this bonanza. Once again, the foursome had whipped William Sharon, who had sold them the works in eighteen and seventy-one, believing he had escaped a bad investment and stuck some Irish fools with it. But it was Sharon who played the fool; the longer he ruled the Comstock, the more he antagonized us all. Not even the braggart Fair came close to matching Sharon when it came to outsmarting himself.

I believed that as that freshwater percolated through the city's cast-iron pipes and mains and into the bodies of its citizens some of the terrible disease that afflicted the Comstock would decline, though I've seen little proof of it. But people said they felt better. The city's evil mineral-poisoned water had sapped health and strength from all who imbibed it, including myself.

Thus Mackay and Fair became public benefactors, doing what Sharon didn't have the courage or vision to do, and that is one reason why Sharon is not remembered happily on the Comstock even to this day, while Mackay and Fair—whatever their faults—have their champions and always will whenever the story of the Comstock is told.

Only Rollin Daggett professed to like the old species of water better.

"It flavored my Steamboat gin and tinted my flesh blue," he complained. "Now I'll be the same color as everyone else and imbibe the tasteless at the old Magnolia."

Nonetheless, his flesh remained gray, and I ascribed it to his character, imagining that a man's flesh ultimately becomes the color of his soul.

The water company didn't stint on the price of water, having invested so much in the works, but people paid it readily enough, and those who couldn't afford it could always walk up to the reservoir and bucket out a pail or two. Mackay and Fair's company never begrudged a poor man a little water. The mines paid readily enough, for now they could use water that didn't deposit scale on the boilers that required periodic shutdowns and cleaning. Nor did the miners have to husband the drinking water sent down the shaft for thirsty miners working in vicious heat.

I wrote the story, dwelling on the technical marvels. I pasted it in my scrapbook, along with my other stories, but later I lost all my clippings, and I have little to show for years as a reporter. De Quille wasn't interested because he didn't have an instinct for modern technology, and Daggett eyed freshwater with jaundiced eye. Indeed, he put a front-page story inside just to let the world know what he thought of sweet water.

If Twain had written the story, it would have had a comic twist: maybe three dead fish, a bottle with a message in it, and a defunct cat arriving from the Sierras. Daggett would have displayed it on page 1. There were times when I thought Stoddard was a bald, superannuated hack and ought to cut the umbilical cord to that paper.

Actually, the water supply was not my preoccupation that fall. The shares of the Consolidated Virginia mine had risen modestly on the news of some low-grade ore, and I was contemplating making the plunge. I had largely gotten out of Comstock mining stocks, having suffered the ignominy of bad selections, assessments, and the machinations of rapacious manipulators of every Comstock mine. My paltry income, such as it was, derived from the occasional largesse of a street traction company and other foolish investments. But I kept eyeing the Consolidated Virginia as its price crept upward, wondering whether to buy a share or two.

The price had reached $110 in July and then declined to around

$100 and finally down to $80. I itched to take the plunge, but I was by then a Comstock veteran who had seen hundreds of people lose everything they possessed on some steamy tip or another, so I dithered. I knew that in March of 1873 the new shaft had reached the main body of ore and was being sunk deeper, still entirely in ore, and that the partners had become uncommonly silent after that. But that didn't mean anything. Mine owners used those silences as often to sell out as to buy up shares. Some wild instinct, which I could barely control, prodded me to buy every share I could find, but the sober and cautious Henry Stoddard resisted. I'd made a little on the Crown Point and Hale & Norcross; I should be satisfied at that.

Then one day I ran into John Mackay at the gym.

"You might want to buy some Con. Virginia, Stoddard," he said blandly.

"So you can sell it out at a profit?" I was only half joking.

He smiled. "We've been on the Comstock too long, you and me," he said. He always spoke slowly and carefully because, I had learned, that was how he had overcome stuttering as a young man.

That did it. I hiked over to my current broker, George Marye, a man I had, through long association, come to trust, and told him to sell everything I possessed and buy Consolidated Virginia.

"Do you know something I don't know?" he asked.

"No, but John Mackay said I should."

"You'd do it on that?"

We had talked many a time about the gulling that mine managers routinely gave small stockholders like me, and Marye's response was a raised eyebrow. He sighed. "All right. I'll wire the eastern exchanges."

Thus he sold my miserable shares in the Central Pacific, the Flint & Pere Marquette Railroad, the West Philadelphia Passenger Railway Company, the Orinoco Steam Navigation Company of New York, and a new mail-order mercantile firm, Montgomery Ward and Company, and bought eighty shares of Consolidated Virginia at seventy-nine dollars. Because of the Panic of that year I took a beating on every stock I sold, but the Panic was also reining in the price of the Consolidated Virginia. I had cast my fate, and only time would tell how foolish I was. At worst, I might be reduced to living on my thirty-five-dollars-a-week reporter's salary once again. At best, I might make enough in the next few months to improve my lot.

But I was not solaced by the continuing decline in the share price, which reached sixty-seven dollars in December in spite of Dan De Quille's initial revelation of the Big Bonanza. Plainly, no one was believing it. I knew then that I'd been misled and rued the day I had run into John Mackay, whom I thought had been my friend. I sulked my way into eighteen and seventy-four feeling angry and betrayed.

I look back upon that as wildly comic. Here was the richest strike on earth, but not even the respected De Quille could sway skeptics. I see it now as just desserts. There it was, a bonanza beyond description, but the world's petty schemers figured it was sucker bait and left it alone. Fair and Mackay didn't mind. As cash became available they increased their holdings and began buying into the neighboring mines—just in case this incredible ore body reached into the Ophir or the Best & Belcher or the Gould & Curry.

So I possessed my eighty shares. Not long afterward I wished I had bought on margin everything I could and mortgaged my little house and bought every share I could that way. But hindsight is a wondrous thing. One is less wise trying to see what lies ahead.

That fall of eighteen and seventy-three the world ignored the news. De Quille had obviously been sampling the Old Magnolia's wares. Or maybe it was another of his famous sketches, like that one about the sun armor that worked so well the poor wretch froze to death in Death Valley. I resolved to take De Quille out on a bender and see whether his sober version of what he saw underground matched his six-drink version.

The next time I saw John Mackay, I grumbled that my shares had dropped steadily ever since he steered me to them. This time he didn't smile.

"Stoddard, I would not treat you that way. What Dan De Quille wrote is pretty much true. Come on down into the works and see for yourself. I'll arrange it."

There it was, a direct challenge to the terrors that inhibited me. I could go look. I could see whether my every penny had been squandered on a foolish investment. I had not been down in a mine since Dan De Quille took over that task, and the terrors of being in the belly of the black rock overwhelmed me.

"All right, John," I said, itching to flee.

"I'll take you down myself, Henry. It's safe. New timbers, the best methods, new hoist and lifts. You bring along a hammer and take your own samples."

I agreed to meet him at the headframe in an hour. When I arrived, John handed me a miner's jumper and felt hat, a candle lantern, a pick-hammer, and a canvas sampling bag. Then we stepped into the cage. My heart hammered and my pulse raced.

Mackay eyed me. "If it's beyond you, Stoddard, we'll haul you right up. Just a matter of ringing the bell cord. You hold on now."

Then, with a sickening speed, the cage dropped deeper and deeper until the tiny square of light above dimmed to nothing. We did not pass well-lit stations because this shaft descended directly to the 1,200-foot level where the first of the ore appeared. It connected to that long drift from the Gould & Curry and was well ventilated on that account, which comforted me. I knew that there was an escape out that tunnel if fire or some other calamity beset us.

But nothing untoward happened. We did, finally, pass the Gould & Curry drift and continued downward, reaching the underground cavern De Quille had written about. I could barely breathe. The weight of the whole earth pressed on me, stopping my lungs, halting my breath. I swallowed hard and stepped into the hot cavity, which was lit by numerous candles, pinpricks of light that turned the massive square-set timbering into a shadowy forest.

"You all right?" Mackay asked.

I wasn't, but I nodded.

"It gets easier, longer you're here. You'll do fine, Stoddard."

"Yes," I responded hoarsely.

"Good. Remember, we can summon the cage anytime. You're just a few moments from grass."

He led me quietly into a noisy chamber where scores of miners shoveled ore from numerous faces into ore cars while others worked at the breasts, double-jacking the holes into which the next round of powder would go.

"You've seen plenty of ore in your day, Stoddard. What do you see here?" Mackay asked, pointing at a black face glistening with streaks of sulphurets and some free silver.

I saw ore. In fact, ore is all I saw. As we traversed the cavern, circling around each planked floor, one level after another, *ore was all I saw*. Black and glistening, streaks and seams, massive boulders of it. I forgot the weight of the rock above me, for this was Aladdin's cave, and what I witnessed was more ore than had ever been seen before in one place, ore of incomparable richness. I needed no assay to tell me that and took no samples.

"The worst of it runs ninety dollars to the ton," Mackay said. "But look closely: don't look at the ore; look at the waste rock, the porphyry. It's all over. There's high-grade, but it's mixed with other stuff. This is all mixed and fractured rock. Don't estimate too high." That was my friend, talking about the worst of it rather than the best. That was the language of trusted and trusting people.

"And the best of it?"

"We don't know. It keeps getting better and better. Let's say six hundred to the ton just to be conservative."

I spent, in all, an hour with Mackay underground. My heart and pulse settled, and while I still was edgy and taut down there, I had come to accommodation with my terrors. We talked about many things: the heat, the hot water, the high ratio of gold to silver, the ease by which this ore could be reduced, the partners' plans, the probable size of this body of ore—which remained unknown. All the while Mackay was smiling at me, enigmatic, his expression saying things he didn't speak, such as, *Do you trust me now, Stoddard?*

I did, and thanked him.

The terror never quite vanished, and I was more than happy when he suggested we go back to grass. We shared the lift with an ore car and two other men, visitors like myself. The world still didn't believe, but I was now a believer.

The world seemed different when we returned to it. The sun shone in a brilliant blue heaven; the city lay upslope; the Virginia & Truckee's yards and station stood close by. But it was not the same. Nothing would ever be the same. I had an inkling of how De Quille felt that October day.

"Satisfied now?" Mackay asked.

I nodded.

"How many did you buy?"

"Eighty—every cent I had."

"I imagine that'll multiply like rabbits," he said. "We've bought all we could afford and still sink capital into this. You'll do just fine, Stoddard. And feel free to write this up. We're not keeping it a secret. In fact, we want to share it with the world."

I did just that, tempering my observations more than Dan did, but my account was little noticed.

CHAPTER 43

indsight. If I had but known what the future would bring, I would not have purchased Consolidated Virginia at all but would have sunk everything in the stock of the California, then languishing in the thirty-dollar range.

But it didn't make sense. No exploration had been made of the California at these new depths. No ore was known to be there. The great body of ore struck at the Consolidated Virginia probably extended that far north, but who could say? So Henry Stoddard did what a prudent man would do and bought shares of a mine whose new ore reserves were only beginning to be understood and shied from speculating on the California. True, its shares had risen from almost nothing to quite a bit on the strength of the discovery next door and one might ride that speculative wave. But I had a firm rule in those days not to speculate at all.

So I nursed my eighty shares of Consolidated Virginia, watched its value ebb and rise and ebb in the fall of seventy-three, never advancing very far, and returned to my reportage at the *Enterprise*. Nothing in Virginia City changed. When I asked the man on the street, or the man next to me at the bar rail, the sagacious fellow would allow that, yes, it was good that the Irishmen had found some ore; the city would prosper a while more. And that was that.

Then, in December, the partners reorganized, creating a new corporation embracing both the Consolidated Virginia and the California mine and dividing the two properties so that the Consolidated Virginia held the southern 710 feet and the California held the remaining 600. To compensate shareholders of the Consolidated Virginia for the loss of footage, the directors voted a stock dividend of seven-twelfths of a share of the California mine for each share of Consolidated Virginia.

Thus I found myself the possessor of about forty-six and a half shares of the mysterious California. There were now 108,000 shares issued of each. So, willy-nilly, I got a piece of both mines, much to my own good fortune, though I had no perception at that time the California would be an even finer investment than the Consolidated Virginia.

The two companies at once began to sink yet another shaft farther east of the Consolidated Virginia shaft and straight on the ore. This they called the C & C. Meanwhile the Consolidated Virginia shaft reached 1,300 feet and drifts were run south and east into the ore body, which had increased to 300 feet of length and 50 feet of width. And the tenor had improved as well, milling at fifty dollars a ton.

Now, as I look back from the turn of the century, I play the foolish game of what I should have done in the light of history. But Henry Stoddard didn't know what the future might bring, and eighteen and seventy-four turned out to be a year of shocks.

For thirteen years he had toiled at the *Territorial Enterprise* for Joe Goodman, who had become its sole owner and proprietor and publisher. Then, suddenly, that changed, and it happened in this wise:

William Sharon, after taking his licking during the election of eighteen and seventy-two, retreated to San Francisco to continue to do the
bidding of his Bank of California masters, Ralston and Mills. Sharon
had accumulated a great fortune, but his soul was not content. He
wanted to join that rich man's club, the United States Senate, just as had
various Virginia City magnates. The venerable attorney William Stewart, who had made his bonanza during the period of litigation, was retiring, and a Senate seat was there for the taking—for anyone rich enough
to purchase it.

The process was lengthy and venal. A candidate stumped though
the legislative districts of the state, greasing many a palm, the ultimate
purpose being to elect those legislators who would then, in January, elect
him United States senator. Sharon had expended a vast sum in eighteen
and seventy-two doing just that while running against John Jones, only
to be foiled by Joe Goodman's famous editorial barrage reminding the
citizens of Nevada that the candidate had ruthlessly and coldly employed easy terms followed by the sharpest usury and other dubious
practices to drive mines and mills into bankruptcy, where they were
easily collected by the octopus bank.

What the estimable Sharon learned from that was that he needed
his own mouthpiece, and as long as the *Enterprise* opposed him he could
spend a fortune on an election to no avail. Joe Goodman's paper, published in Nevada's preeminent city, dominated state politics. And that is
how it came about in the election year of eighteen and seventy-four that
he bought the paper, reputedly for the astronomical sum of half a million
dollars, enabling Joe Goodman to retire to the pursuit that had fascinated
him for a lifetime: archaeology.

Half a million was an incredible price to pay for a small daily
newspaper in a town of barely twenty thousand. During good times it
had been chocked with ads and no doubt filled Goodman's coffers. But
there had been long bleak stretches when the ore was running thin
and merchants cut back their ads and people let their subscriptions
lapse. The *Territorial Enterprise* wasn't worth half a million—except to
one man.

I don't suppose I'll ever forget that memorable day when Goodman
summoned us to the Old Magnolia, that being the only imaginable place
to break such news, and bought us all a drink.

"I've sold the paper," he said.

There followed a pregnant pause. I could scarcely believe it. No one
of us dared ask who would be our new masters. I myself thought—for a
whirling moment—perhaps Goodman's old partner, Denis McCarthy,

might have bought it because some long-forgotten dogs and cats he had stuffed in the safe had come to life.

McCarthy had purchased the *Chronicle* with his unexpected loot, and it made sense to me that he might want his old sheet, too.

But I was sorely mistaken.

"Who?" asked a man new to the paper, Charlie Goodwin, our amazing jurist turned journalist, curiosity screwing his pudding face.

"Ah, to a new corporation called the Enterprise Publishing Company."

At that point, my nose detected a faint odor. Within a few seconds it had reached skunk proportions.

"Owned by?" I asked.

"Several corporations. The Virginia & Truckee Railroad and some bank holding companies—"

"The Bank of California."

Goodman smiled.

"So William Sharon owns it."

"Oh, I wouldn't say that. Yerington's going to keep an eye on it as well as his railroad."

After that no one had anything to say. We would learn how the guillotine blade fell soon enough. I wondered about my job. I suppose we all were wondering.

So we drank a final round with Goodman, halfheartedly, for the sellout was treason. After he left that day I scarcely saw him again. He cleaned out his papers, abandoned his office, and vanished to the Coast, having shaken off the dust of Virginia City.

I owed him eternal gratitude. Long ago he had hired me when he had little reason to believe I could write. He had given me a new life, one that suited me. He had been slow to advance me, but I had come to understand my limitations and didn't begrudge him that. In fact, I would have preferred Goodman a thousand times more than the new management.

Goodman gave us a long leash, had a great eye for talent, published some of the most notable material ever to appear in any newspaper anywhere, had started Twain and developed De Quille and Daggett, fought some hard battles, never wavered from his mission of civilizing the Comstock, had stood up for decency and liberty, and had even fought a duel with a rival editor, thus risking his life for his beliefs. He had hired a sixteen-year-old tramp printer named Fremont Older (who lost his first week's salary playing faro in Gentry & Crittenden's), and what Older learned from Joe Goodman was to make him the doyen of

San Francisco letters some years later. The *Enterprise,* under Joe Goodman, had become one of the best papers in the world. To my mind, we were every bit as fine as James Gordon Bennett's *New York Herald,* the great paper that had sent Henry Stanley to Africa to find the lost missionary David Livingstone. Suddenly, as Joe packed up, I found myself choking back a tightness in my throat.

I caught him at the boardwalk just as he loaded the last of his stuff in a buggy.

"Joe?"

"Good times, Henry. You've been my mainstay, the solid man all these years. You made this paper."

"Joe? What'll become of us?"

"I've owed you more than I've ever acknowledged, Henry. I think the new owners will do better for you. Yerington—"

"He's Ralston's lackey."

"I don't think they'll interfere. They're keeping Daggett editor, and Daggett's not a man to sit down and take it. And Judge Goodwin's going to stay on."

But we both knew it wasn't so. Sharon had bought the paper to make it his slut.

"Joe? Come back and see us." That was all I could manage.

He nodded, shook hands silently, climbed into his black buggy, and steered his dray into the traffic of C Street. I watched him go, feeling the earth had fallen from under me. For the first time in several years I wondered what my future would be. But I wouldn't quit. Not yet. It had all been so sudden, so shocking, that I had scarcely considered my own life, my own options.

So Rollin Daggett was Sharon's editor. I returned to the sanctum and studied his shapeless, gluttonous, half-inebriated mass. He must have known, because he seemed not a bit surprised. Later I knew for sure that Daggett had known and that, indeed, there had been some negotiations beforehand with the bank crowd.

The proud *Enterprise* made a U-turn.

Mr. Sharon has lived in Nevada for ten years and by his sagacity, energy, and nerve, he has amassed a fortune. This is his crime. He has done what he has done without once breaking his plighted word, without once violating one principle of business honor. While he was doing this he has carried, with his own, the fortunes of hundreds, and has never once betrayed a trust or confidence . . . The present prosperity of Western Nevada is more due to him than to any other ten men, and could his work here be stricken out, with it would go two thirds of our people, improvements, and wealth.

Sharon could not have said it better. There was even some truth in it. Not long after, and with the expenditure of another quarter of a million spent enlightening the electorate, the Nevada legislature sent him off to the Senate. As for me, I reckoned my days on the proud old paper were numbered.

CHAPTER 44

 stayed at the *Enterprise*. No one fired me, and I was loath to leave Virginia City, which I loved all the more with the passage of so many years. It was Sharon's paper, but no one crimped my style when it came to mining news.

By way of making amends for Daggett's editorial, I paid closer attention to the dealings of the bank crowd, as they were called everywhere. The Irishmen were not yet kings of the Comstock—though that was about to change. The bank people still managed the Union Mill and Mining Company, a consortium of the lode's better mines and mills. They owned the lucrative Virginia & Truckee and tens of thousands of prime acres of Sierra timberland to supply wood and fuel to the mines. They ran Comstock banking and lacked only the water company to empty the pockets of most of the city's citizens and businesses.

I did not neglect Mr. Sutro. Somehow or other, the doughty entrepreneur raised enough capital, mostly in England, to continue boring his tunnel. Around-the-clock, his face crews working from both the Carson River and the shaft of the Savage mine, drove toward each other, day by day narrowing the long gap. But it was clear that hand-drilling would not complete the task until the mid-eighteen-eighties, probably well after the tunnel would be useful to drain the mines and take ore to the mills on the Carson River.

Sutro, ever willing to try new methods, experimented with Burleigh drills, which swiftly proved themselves, and the boring increased from around one hundred thirty feet a month to three or four hundred. And as the shafts drove farther from air—a mile, then two—the miners welcomed the air released by the drill. The original plan had been to ventilate the works with four shafts, but only the first one was completed because the others ran into hot water.

I interviewed Sutro repeatedly, enjoying writing those stories because every additional foot of his tunnel threatened the bank crowd's railroad along with some of its mills. Sutro saw it the opposite way: every ton of ore going out of the Comstock on the railroad was two dollars lost to the Tunnel Company. So I took a certain wicked delight in reporting Sutro's progress, and I trumpeted the news that the new drills meant that the tunnel would be completed in the foreseeable future. I knew that would upset stomachs down on California Street, so I wrote a lot of it.

But I pitied Sutro's miners, who toiled in hot, wet conditions, in air that choked them. They proved loyal to the rotund little man and worked furiously, the shifts rivaling each other to set records and drive the tunnel farther and farther. I pitied as well the mules that dragged the heavy trains of ore cars out to the riverfront, where a pile of waste rock grew each day. The mules suffered from the want of air as badly as the miners and could scarcely be induced to enter the mine or work in it and stopped dead at every point where fresh air was vented into the lengthy tunnel. They could hardly be whipped ahead, so badly did they need that air.

I don't know that Daggett ever realized how much attention I was paying to these tunnel proceedings in the very pages of Sharon's paper. Daggett was enough of a newsman to know that if we didn't cover it, Denis McCarthy's revamped *Virginia Chronicle*—ferociously anti-Sharon, with daily diatribes against the "bank crowd"—surely would scoop us. So I maintained my small beachhead deep in hostile turf.

As for Charlie Goodwin, eminent jurist turned scribbler, he knew, winked, and smiled. Dan De Quille saw it, too, and followed suit, so the *Enterprise* retained a modicum of its independence.

As for the bonanza partners, as they were beginning to be called, the work of exploration continued. I eschewed dealing with "Uncle Jimmy" Fair, as he liked to be called, and went daily to Bill Davis's gym, where Mackay—then a trim forty-three—continued to box three tough rounds with anyone who wished to step into the ring. Mackay had leveled with me from the beginning and still leveled with me long after he had achieved some success.

The contrast between the pair fascinated me. Both were born in Dublin in eighteen and thirty-one and both were experienced miners and entrepreneurs, but there the resemblances stopped. Mackay lived quietly in a pleasant middle-class home on Howard Street, three steep blocks above C Street, with his wife and sons. He kept to himself, drove an ancient and unpretentious black buggy, and seemed a little astonished at his good fortune. Fair was even then becoming a flamboyant figure, putting on the dog, mythologizing himself, and living the life of a bounder and cad.

Mackay knew himself to be an unlettered and uncultivated man and decided to do something about it. He soon was immersed in magazines and books. He had developed a taste for theater and music and attended every play and concert that came to town. He loved poker and played constantly, his approach the same as his boxing—slow, careful, methodical, and these traits often defeated more mercurial players. In time, when he was earning most of a million dollars a month, poker paled, and he irritably abandoned a game that had been robbed of its risk-taking savor by his wealth.

"Why bet?" he asked me plaintively.

I caught him at the gym almost daily and regularly asked how things were progressing. He would smile slowly and allow that everything was fine. That was my signal to ask specific questions.

They were sinking the Consolidated Virginia shaft lower, still in solid ore, and the drifts continued to reveal ore and more ore as the body widened. The ore lay almost vertically in an inclined crevice, with the diorite of Mount Davidson forming its floor and the diabase of the east wall forming its roof. All through early eighteen and seventy-four the miners drove deeper and deeper. At fifteen hundred feet the ore was richer and the walls of the body still farther apart. There seemed no end to it.

All this had awakened curiosity from one end of the country to the other but no great run on the stocks of either company. The Consolidated Virginia management gladly showed the entire works to anyone who wished to descend to them. A few took up the offer, and then more and more, so many that the troupes of spectators, squired around by company factotums, seriously interfered with the mining. But Mackay and Fair had deemed these inspections necessary and important.

Most of those who descended the cages and wandered about by lamplight hadn't the faintest idea what they were seeing, but that didn't matter. They were seeing something, and they were free to take samples and have them assayed. So, by the score, people rode the Virginia & Truckee up to Virginia City, checked in at the International Hotel, and had themselves taken into the bowels of the earth. Word, obviously, was spreading, and yet it still had little discernible effect on stock prices, which seemed glued to the range they had occupied for months: at about forty for the unexplored California, in the eighties for the Consolidated Virginia. In May, the Consolidated Virginia began paying a dividend of three dollars a month. Thirty-six dollars a year was not a bad return on each of my eighty-dollar shares.

I puzzled over the whole business. In the past, such news as was now plain to the world would have shot Consolidated Virginia shares through the roof. My only explanation was that fifteen years of speculation of Comstock shares had so jaded the world that no one quite believed anything. I could well understand that. I had talked to washerwomen and clerks, hostlers, telegraph delivery boys, ice dealers, and bartenders who had sunk every cent they had into a mining or milling company upon the optimistic reports of managers, only to lose it all because the managers were manipulating the market or assessments bled them into surrendering the stock.

Still, the prices did drift upward slowly, negligently, with retreats and hesitations, and I knew that down on California Street some shrewd men had come to their own conclusions and were buying. I wondered if Ralston, Sharon, and Mills were among them.

Marye obliged me occasionally with news "from below," and I learned that Sharon was buying shares of the Ophir, which lay next to the California and might contain some of the new bonanza ore. Sharon had been living quietly in California, getting richer and richer on his profits from the Union Mill and Mining Company, his third of the railroad, and his dividends from the Belcher. But the Ophir was then largely owned by E. J. Baldwin, and if Sharon wished to control it he would need to buy a great deal of stock. Baldwin held out, and the Ophir stock rose higher and higher, driving up the shares of most of the Comstock mines.

That was how things stood until late October, eighteen and seventy-four. No one can ever explain just what happened then, but the common explanation was that the good news coming from the new drifts at the 1,500-foot level triggered the run on those bonanza stocks. I have always thought it was but one of several factors, not least of them the hundreds upon hundreds of visitors Mackay and Fair sent through the mines.

Whatever the case, in November the run started, with hysterical speculators in San Francisco kneeing and elbowing their way into owning Comstock shares—at any price, in any amount, of any sort. And not just the two bonanza mines, either. Any proven Comstock mine would do. The San Francisco Mining Exchange spiraled into bedlam and tumult, hysteria and madness. The entire supply of capital on the West Coast vanished from its normal niches into the maw of the exchange, leaving banks without money, savings accounts depleted, ongoing California businesses bereft of operating funds and buyers for their product.

In Virginia City, George Marye and other brokers opened their doors around-the-clock. People emptied their mattresses, dug up their hidden coins, sold off real estate, furniture, and old clothes, pawned rings and jewels, and bought, sometimes only a single share of an obscure mine.

So did William Sharon. In San Francisco, on December 12, E. J. Baldwin, thereafter known as Lucky Baldwin, sold 20,000 shares of the venerable Ophir mine to Sharon for $135 a share, or $2,700,000. Quite a price for a worked-out mine whose only claim to future profit was being next door to the California. But Sharon, who was determined to become a Nevada senator, jacked his new stock higher through manipulation virtually until the legislature elected him on January 12, 1875. He wanted to go to Washington with cash in his pockets, and he had seen a way.

In December the price of a Consolidated Virginia share climbed to $610, only to rise to $700 early the next year. That put the market value of the mine at $75 million, and my eighty shares were worth, at least on paper, $56,000. The unproven California, which had been selling at $37 in September, leaped to $520 in December and reached $780 in January, thus valuing the unexplored mine at $84 million, and my forty-six shares were worth about $36,000. On paper. In December, the San Francisco Mining Exchange sold Comstock mining securities worth $50 million in spite of the fact that only $20 million of investment capital was available on the whole West Coast.

By early January, I was worth, conservatively, $90,000. On paper.

I watched and reported all this agog, for no one had ever seen anything like it. And as I hinted earlier, the Big Bonanza changed me, changed my life, changed my view of the world, changed my ideals, changed my very soul. As you shall see.

CHAPTER 45

ild times. They whirled by so fast I barely remember them. Not all my years as a mining reporter on the Comstock had inured me to the daily sensations that crashed over us all hour by hour. I would examine George Marye's chalk board one hour and discover at a later hour that I had earned another thousand dollars. Everything went up; half-dead mining stocks revived.

I began to think what I might do with my fortune. California beckoned. Real estate. Stocks and bonds. Invested conservatively, at 5 percent, I might have four or five thousand dollars of annual income for life, and live in affluence. My most immediate instinct was that I could leave the *Enterprise* any time I chose, and with that in mind I reported the mining news with renewed candor, not caring whether Goodwin or Daggett rebuked me.

Then, starting on January 8, 1875, it all came tumbling down. The fevers of December cooled, and sobriety returned to speculators. In but a few days the Consolidated Virginia had dropped to the middle four hundreds and the California had plummeted even further, into the two hundreds. I did not suffer loss, having bought much lower. What is more, both mines would pay heady dividends, as was the custom of Comstock bonanza mines. But the return to sobriety bankrupted many, including the esteemed Philipp Deidesheimer, who had speculated recklessly. Another was William Ralston of the Bank of California, whose speculations on the Comstock and elsewhere began to open up fissures in the solid California Street bank that would soon shatter that powerful institution.

But I will come to that in due course. I was absorbed with the bonanza news, and my daily columns were stuffed with facts and figures. The Consolidated Virginia shaft had reached the 1,500-foot level, and drifts indicated that the ore ran fully 900 feet longitudinally, while crosscuts indicated that the width reached 200. This stunned me. The bonanza kept growing and growing. And while a lot of country rock was mixed with the crushed quartz of the bonanza, lowering the tenors overall, some of the richer veins of stephanite and quartz impregnated with argentite and gold assayed at thousands to the ton. It may not have been the richest ore wrested from the Comstock, but its sheer magnitude awed anyone who contemplated it. And the Consolidated Virginia was milling it, bad and good rock, for a yield of about a hundred a ton.

Virginia City changed overnight. The International Hotel groaned with guests, many of them notables who were arriving by the coachload to tour the mines. Mackay and Fair still welcomed selected people into the pits but not so many as to interfere with the mining. The city acquired a cosmopolitan air, and one could hear any tongue on the streets and in the cafés and discover people in exotic garb in any saloon.

Somehow the dowdy city accommodated them all, fed them spectacular meals—the Comstock was becoming famous for its viands—politely took their money, and ushered them back to civilization. For underneath it was still the same rowdy, raucous, roaring frontier town set in an arid wild, and many of those who first saw it were shocked by its ugliness.

I found myself coping with a constant stream of visitors who were seeking out the paper's mining reporter for advice. If I had charged for the information I dispensed freely as a matter of goodwill for the paper, I would be rich. I told them all, simply, to buy no share of an exhausted mine—which they disputed, citing the indisputable bonanza found in the exhausted Consolidated Virginia—and sometimes told them prices were much too high and not to buy at all. It wasn't advice they cherished.

My own world expanded at a lightning pace. I had wealth. I could do whatever I chose to do. The odd thing was, after all those years on the paper, writing was all I could imagine doing. I was the old dray horse, broke to harness, docile and happy in my limited life. Unlike so many, I liked the whole Washoe district. I even liked those bleak desert wastes and sometimes hiked in them just to be alone.

Those weeks of boom had produced a whole new crop of millionaires, which the *San Francisco Chronicle* gladly touted as proof of the Bay City's affluence. One R. N. Graves, who held 8,000 shares of the Consolidated Virginia, was $2 million richer, as was Gen. Tom Williams. A pair of Virginia City lawyers who had gotten stock in the old Central No. 2 in exchange for unpaid legal services ended up selling their Consolidated Virginia shares at the height of the boom for $3 million. The lawyers were smart enough to put their boodle into California real estate. In those days, at least, the Comstock in general, and the bonanza partners in particular, could do no wrong.

Poor Deidesheimer. On December 21 he proclaimed to the *San Francisco Post* that the ore in the Consolidated Virginia, California, and Ophir would reach one and a half billion dollars. And that was from a veteran superintendent. "Nothing like these mines has ever been seen or heard or dreamed of before," he said. A few weeks later he was bankrupt. On January 5 my colleague Dan De Quille published in the *San Francisco Chronicle* yet another piece in which he described the bonanza ore as going through all three mines at the 1,550-foot level, and he again proclaimed at least $116 million of it was in sight. That actually was modest compared to the $300-million estimate that Sharon and others were bruiting about.

The *Chronicle* started boasting in response to an admiring piece in the *Chicago Inter-Ocean,* which observed that "many of her citizens could sell out at a month's notice for $5,000,000 each":

That was true enough three months ago, but the *Inter-Ocean* is one of those old fogy journals who do not keep pace with the times. Lick, Latham, Sharon, and Hayward are all poor men. Worth $5,000,000? Well, yes, they may be worth that paltry sum. So are Reese, Mills, Baldwin, Lux,

Miller, Jones, Ralston, and Stanford. These are our well-to-do citizens, men of comfortable incomes—our middle class. Our rich men the *Inter-Ocean* has not named. They are Mackay, Flood, O'Brien, and Fair. Twenty or thirty millions each is but a modest estimate of their wealth.

I watched, mesmerized. After a Christmas break, the market resumed on January 2 and the madness continued. By January 7, the thirty-one leading Comstock mines were valued at $262,000,000, and the remaining 65 increased the total worth to three hundred million. How much was that? I have before me a report of the assessed value of San Francisco real estate at that time. The whole city was worth $190 million.

And there were those who believed the Consolidated Virginia would reach $3,000 a share.

Then, on the eighth, the Comstock shares spiraled downward when William Sharon shorted his Ophir stocks. I watched, astonished, seeing my own paper profits vanish in smoke. I had waited too long myself— as usual—and could only stand at the sidelines. On that day, the leading mines depreciated nearly eighteen million dollars. San Francisco short sellers moved in and reaped their own bonanzas while driving the stock lower. I corralled John Mackay at the gymnasium, seeking answers, and found that his wealth had not altered the man an iota.

"Sell out?" he asked.

"No, I got caught," I confessed.

"Don't sell. They're great mines. Just let the speculators have their way. The mines were overvalued and the prices will settle. It's the biggest silver discovery in the world, and you'll see those mines produce. Stoddard, just hang on and don't play the fool and sell. As for me, I'm a miner, not a speculator, and I'll see to it the mines are run right. We don't know how much ore's down there—no one knows—and we won't know for years. But there's plenty. People keep asking what it's worth, and I won't say, because I plain don't know."

I took him at his word and hung on. But the relentless collapse wiped out large and small speculators and virtually everyone who had bought on margin. When it was over, my Consolidated Virginia shares— multiplied to 400 by the stock split—were still worth $450 each. My 46 California shares, multiplied to 230 by a similar split, were worth $50 each. I was rich. I calculated my worth as almost $200,000, which I took pains to conceal from my newspaper brethren. I did not forget that it was all paper profit.

And that spring the Consolidated Virginia upped its monthly dividend to $10, so each share was bringing me $120 a year, or $48,000 into my coffers per annum. All this brought little change to my life. I reported the mining news, lived quietly in my modest house on B Street, and wondered what to do with so much money. Henry Stoddard could afford most anything life offered.

One of those things was the opening of the Washoe Club in elegant quarters on B Street, not far from my home. Somewhat timorously, and with John Mackay's help, I applied for membership, and the sixty founders admitted me after surveying my worthiness and assets. I wasn't sure I wanted to belong to a club composed of brokers, managers, superintendents, speculators, and entrepreneurs, all men of much larger means than mine. Nor was I sure a newsman belonged in such a place, but I found a business reason. There, under its crystal chandeliers, beside the handsome bar and back bar or in the billiards room or library or dining room, were the very men from whom I drew my stories. There were Fair and Mackay, Senator Sharon and Senator Jones, Darius Mills, I. L. Requa, superintendent of the Gould & Curry, George Marye, Adolph Sutro, and all the rest who had made the Comstock what it was.

I confess I did not particularly enjoy my sojourns there, especially when these great men of finance turned silent in my presence, aware of the reporter in their midst. At those moments I yearned for the Old Magnolia and a good bibulous evening with Daggett and Goodwin and De Quille, rather than these lofty heights. I felt I was the imposter.

Still, the millionaires' club had its attractions, especially on the occasional ladies' night, which I never failed to attend, still hopeful of mending my bachelor ways. I do not know why so many rich women are beautiful, but it is a plain fact. Some of it has to do with their tailored and elegant clothing, the best of grooming, and the reality that nothing is lacking in diet and comfort. But that doesn't explain it. I have observed for years that a plain woman can marry up and emerge the swan. I have also observed that some rich women, who cannot by any stretch of language be called beautiful, become handsome. I have met my share of handsome and formidable dowagers, *presences* in a room. Their money has something to do with it. Women and money amalgamate like mercury and precious metals.

But a reporter, even one comfortably fixed because of the bonanza, wasn't what the ladies set their sights upon, and I well knew it. There were upper and lower professions and castes, and reporters weren't among the anointed.

By the midseventies, Henry Stoddard was mostly bald, owlish, wore spectacles, and supposed he was doomed to a life of bachelorhood writing about ore and machinery. I wasn't much different from the hundreds of thousands of unwed farmhands and grimy mechanics and bachelor clerks across the country, the unmarried brothers and uncles one could find in most every family. It wasn't my preferred fate, but I had been compensated by a lively life in a lively town and a treasure chest full of memories, and overall, I was happy.

CHAPTER 46

O ne of those first nights at the Washoe Club will remain in my mind forever. Among those present that spring night was John Jones, at that time Senator Jones, an affable full-bearded Englishman—some would say Welshman—who had succeeded in both politics and mining, having been a capable superintendent of the Kentuck and Crown Point mines and then beaten his former employer, Sharon, for the Senate seat, always calling himself a "common man."

I always enjoyed my moments with Jones because he could spin a yarn better than anyone else I'd ever met and extracted yarns from a day's events with all the skill of a Twain. But on this fateful night he introduced me to a slim brown-haired, hazel-eyed matron, Catherine Iliff. Mrs. Iliff struck me as an uncommonly handsome woman, somewhere in her thirties, her nature studious, or perhaps it was her small gold-rimmed spectacles that made me think it. Unlike so many others at the Washoe Club, she wasn't quite coiffed. Strands of rebel brown hair drifted from her head, perhaps by design. I thought to myself that here was a woman who would bend no knee to Parisian couturiers.

It proved to be a correct assessment. I learned swiftly that Mrs. Iliff was a devotee of literature and knew all the latest works of Twain, among many others. I cannot, from my perspective at the turn of the century, reconstruct exactly what happened between us that evening. But it had to do with Twain.

"Oh!" she said. "You're with the *Enterprise*? Did you know Mr. Twain?"

"Yes, Mrs. Iliff, both sober and less so, Clemens, Josh, Mark, and otherwise."

She laughed. "Tell me about him. Was he always so . . . crusty?"

"Thin-skinned," I replied, "but with such an eye for comedy, for the bizarre, and telling that he was destined for greatness. I envy and admire him."

"Well, fame certainly came to him," she said. "I read *Roughing It* last year and *The Gilded Age* just last winter. Were you in *Roughing It*?"

"No, Henry Stoddard isn't the sort to show up in literature," I replied, slightly sourly. "I fade into the background. I'm the reporter who writes about ores and pumps and milling equipment."

"I thought it was terrible, what you people did to him when he came back—that put-up robbery."

"So did he," I said. "That was the last we saw of him, but De Quille keeps in touch."

Well, that was my introduction to Mrs. Iliff, and all the while we talked I was growing aware of an uncommonly magnetic woman. She surveyed me alertly, her eyes questioning and conquering, and I realized she had a lively curiosity. I was just as curious about her, but the gold ring bearing a fine blue diamond on her finger told me I must rein in my questions. That was Stoddard's luck: he lived in a city with a woman shortage, and when he did meet a woman who set his spirits soaring she was attached.

"And where is Mr. Iliff?"

"Oh, Peter? He died of consumption two years ago. He was a mining engineer, and we were in Potosí, Bolivia . . ."

I don't remember hearing the rest. I don't even remember what happened that evening at the glittering Washoe Club, surrounded by handsome and very rich people. I do remember a melting sensation that reduced stuffy old Stoddard to butter.

Somehow or other, I discovered that she had been born Catherine Taylor in New York City, had married Peter Iliff and adventured to various mining towns in Mexico and Peru, had two young children, Peter, Jr., and Caroline, and was staying at the Joneses' home in Gold Hill for the summer to take the air.

I learned also that she had become bookish whiling away her time in strange Spanish-speaking frontier towns with the comforts of books, which she ordered wholesale. I gathered that Iliff had left her little, because he could not work during his long and painful decline. The cold, barren plateau at the foot of Bolivia's legendary and mystical mountain of silver, the Cerro de Potosí, and life at thirteen thousand feet above sea level had exacerbated his consumption and hastened his doom. I learned, too, that it had been a good marriage and his death had drained all the joy from her life, save for her blossoming children, now nine and seven.

"All summer? Here?" I asked stupidly.

"All summer. Do you like this city?"

"I love the Comstock, and I can't say why. It has something, an air, a history . . . a humor."

"Yes, I should like to hear about it. I'm glad it has at least one saving grace."

We laughed. She thought the surrounding bleak hills were oppressive and sad. But she hastened to say she had spent a decade in just such surroundings, for metals were wherever they were found and one could not mine them from the comforts of a great city, though Potosí was a large one.

She pumped me for more about Twain, De Quille, Joe Goodman, and everyone else at the *Territorial Enterprise*, and the more I told her of life at a mining-camp newspaper, the more intrigued she became. She hadn't known that Mark Twain had continued to send contributions to the paper from San Francisco or that most of us wrote pieces for the *Chronicle* or *Call* or *Alta* or *Post* to supplement our limited salaries.

"Are you a member of the Washoe Club?" she asked.

"Yes, I was admitted."

She discreetly didn't say what was obviously puzzling her: that a newspaper reporter could scarcely afford these elegant digs. And I didn't enlighten her, perhaps because I still suspected my sudden wealth was a chimera, paper that would blow away with the next Washoe zephyr.

And that was how it began and the main reason eighteen and seventy-five was the most memorable of all of Henry Stoddard's years. I could not imagine what she saw in me, a balding, squinty, bespectacled, uninspired scribbler of obscure ability, neither flamboyant nor unsocial. But I squired her to dinner, often with Mrs. Jones as chaperone, and met her sweet children in residence at the senator's house—both solemn and quiet, perhaps too much so.

She grilled me knowledgeably about mining, what stocks to buy, what sort of ores existed straight below where we sat, sometimes at the International, sometimes at Barnum's, sometimes in the club. She had absorbed her husband's business. I had the oddest and most marvelous feeling that these meetings were leading us somewhere. Sometimes I was afraid—of succeeding, of losing, of surrendering a middle-aged man's perfect liberty—but in the end I knew I must court her ardently, for my heart would have no other.

I enjoyed showing her Virginia City just then, when the half-moribund city had leaped back to life and was brimming with a strange buzzing vitality that affected everyone. Only two mines—the Consolidated Virginia and California—were producing, but their yield was greater than each previous bonanza period. And all those dead mines were feverishly sinking new shafts well east of the earlier ones, hoping to strike the same incredible ore that had fallen to the Irishmen. So coin jingled in pockets, bachelor miners had ample to spend on entertainments, and even miners with families had cash to spare. Piper's Opera House boomed, and troupe upon troupe crowded into the city that showered actors and actresses with silver dollars at curtain call.

They were saying Virginia had reached twenty-five thousand, but I knew it wasn't so. The three towns together—Virginia, Gold Hill, and Silver City below it—came to less than twenty according to carefully done directories. The transients who had flooded in pushed the numbers higher, but old Virginia wasn't significantly larger than it had been for years.

Mrs. Iliff spent most evenings with me, but sometimes she opted to devote an evening to her enlarging circle of matrons or to participate in one of the Joneses' dinner parties or to engage in other activities unknown to me. I suspect the senator did not see Stoddard as an appropriate match and was introducing her widely. On those evenings my agonies demolished me and even my pals at the old Magnolia took umbrage at my sulky behavior. But the next day she would gladly respond to the card or note I expressed to her and we'd be together again.

I was in a state such as I never had been, and Judge Goodwin asked sharp questions, first about my health and then about visiting the dark and noxious opium dens run by the Chinamen in their north-side quarter.

"Actually, Judge, I've become a drunk," I said.

"That explains it, then. You have not been yourself."

"That's because I have too much money."

"Well, that'll do it. I can tell you offhand, I am free from such burdens."

We laughed. On the Comstock, that explained everything.

The market held. The new mines disgorged awesome amounts of ore, and amazing dividend checks accumulated funds in my accounts. That summer we had important visitors. The new bonanza had not escaped the attentions of the entire world, and especially the United States Congress, where serious men worried about what such awesome floods of precious metals would do to the money supply. Great Britain and India were largely on a silver standard, and the pound sterling was threatened. The Comstock was steadily eroding the value of both gold and silver.

To answer these questions, the director of the United States Mint, Mr. H. A. Linderman, decided to undertake a personal inspection and eventually ventured forth to the wilds of Nevada accompanied by the eminent professor R. E. Rogers of the University of Pennsylvania, to examine the works, assess the bonanza, and report to the world.

Accompanying them was a *New York Tribune* correspondent, whose name eludes me after all these years. Such was the importance of this visitation that Flood arrived from San Francisco and Mackay and Fair made themselves available to escort the director and his expert through the works.

The *New York Tribune* correspondent was shown the mines along with the others and saw 110-pound bars of gold and silver bullion—each worth $3,000 to $4,000—stacked in towers. He didn't know gold from iron pyrites, but it didn't matter. He was impressed:

> Here is a city of about 25,000 inhabitants, about 7,000 feet above the level of the sea, with inhabitants in the garb of laborers, but with the habits of Parisians. Here are restaurants as fine as any in the world, though not so extensive as some, nor as elaborate in appointments; here are drinking saloons more gorgeous in appointment than any in San Francisco, Philadelphia, or New York; and here are shops and stores which are dazzling in splendor. The people here seem to run to jewelry. I have never seen finer shops than here, and the number of diamonds displayed in the windows quite overwhelms one's senses. The Washoe Club is nearly as well furnished as any in New York, except in pictures, books and bronzes, and the manner of living of the inhabitants is generally upon a high scale . . . I have never been in a place where money is so plentiful nor where it is spent with so much extravagance and recklessness.

I thought he exaggerated. All that ore lurking underground bent men's judgment and distorted their vision. I myself considered Virginia the most amazing little town in the world but not the match of any cosmopolitan one. He departed our precincts along with Director Linderman and Professor Rogers, boarding the Virginia & Truckee coaches for Reno and the Central Pacific, and we awaited the verdict. Would the official estimate deflate the wild notions that grew like opium poppies around Virginia? Given the speed at which federal bureaucracies moved, we expected the report to appear about when the boom had become a bust, which proved to be the case.

It didn't matter much. More important to me was getting to know Mrs. Iliff's shy children, who had suffered from a want of friends in distant Bolivia and then the want of a father.

inding is the road of love, and much of the summer of that memorable year I caromed between exultation and despair. Catherine Iliff eyed me candidly, gave no hint of her designs, and let me wonder.

I did not know if she was interested in a union. And if so, whether Henry Stoddard filled the bill. I heard no expressions of love or endearment but still was encouraged by her frank, assessing gaze whenever we met and her questions, which pierced to the core of life's purpose.

I did learn one thing that exhilarated me: her adventuresome life with Peter Iliff, in wild Latin mining camps, among exotic races and peoples, had given her a taste for adventure. She confessed one afternoon at tea that she found nothing appealing upon the eastern seacoast. Mining camps offered the sort of bold and rambling company she had learned to enjoy.

She had not closed the door to other swain, either, and I received wind, now and then, of yet another mining man or lawyer or superintendent squiring her to dinner. That's when I despaired. Henry Stoddard had been born an obscure man, of obscure intelligence and skill and courage, a man who evanesced to invisibility in a crowd. I could not think of a thing about myself that stood out or that was particularly admirable. Worse, I had become set in my ways, an aging bachelor with the usual raft of dubious habits. What could such a fine woman see in a hairless, newly bespectacled man? Well, she wore gold-rimmed spectacles, too, so she might forgive that. I gave serious consideration to a toupee.

But then, in the summer's heat, things subtly changed. She began asking more about my family and told me more about hers. She weighed my religious and moral and ethical convictions. She discovered that I was not poor and had profited from the Big Bonanza. She brought her children with her on our forays to the countryside for a picnic.

On one occasion we all went to a circus, and there was John Mackay, having a grand time passing out silver dollars to urchins who ached to get into the tent.

"Well, hello, Stoddard," he said. "This is something. When I was a lad I hadn't a shilling for a circus."

He laughed, patiently slipping the coin into the hands of dozens of clamoring boys, who shrieked, corralled their friends, and headed for the admission gate.

"I want you to meet my friend Catherine Iliff," I said.

Mackay paused. "Peter's wife. He was one of the best men in mining, Mrs. Iliff."

"Yes," she said, a tremor in her voice.

"You're at the Joneses'," he said. "You've a good man on your arm. Stoddard, here, is as true as they come."

She smiled at me, and Mackay withdrew to his battered old buggy for another bag of Carson-minted dollars, a vast smile across his taciturn face. In all the essential ways John Mackay had changed not at all, but in one way he had changed a great deal. Largely gone were his gaucheries of speech. He had seen the deficiency and studied grammar with all the determination that he had employed to succeed in mining.

We talked a little more, and then we treated the children to the clowns, elephants, trapeze artists, jugglers, and tigers obedient to a master in a silk stovepipe hat. I had little use for circuses but found myself delighted by the exclamations of the Iliff children, and that made the August afternoon glow.

That evening Catherine and I dined at the International, and something ineffable fell upon us. Emboldened, perhaps by John Mackay's kind endorsement, I paused before dessert, took her hand, and proposed.

It was an ordinary sort of proposal, neither romantic nor inspired nor clever. But if it lacked novelty, it offered sincerity. "Catherine, I've loved you ever since I saw you, and love you more each hour. You're the one. I wish to marry you. Would you be my bride? I can support you, be a father to your orphaned children, and be–"

"Yes," she said, and squeezed my fingers in hers. "I thought you'd never ask."

"Never ask?"

"I'd given up hope."

I sat there, flummoxed and wondering why she had chosen me when there were scores of richer, more personable men in Virginia City. And then I thought I knew. It went straight back to that first conversation when we talked about Twain. She was a reader and interested in the life of the mind. I was a writer. The only writer she had met. I found out later that wasn't the whole reason at all, but I could think of no other at the time.

The waiter brought cherries flambé, but they were not a hundredth as sweet and promising as the kiss that came at the Joneses' doorstep.

The next day, August 26, the Bank of California collapsed. I had heard rumors, as soft as cottonwood fluff on the breeze, but had discounted them. William Ralston, William Sharon, and Darius Ogden Mills had between them money beyond counting. Or so I had supposed. Suddenly the branch at Virginia City closed its doors, leaving us all without access to our funds. My own had been piling up there, month after month. In wild alarm I rattled the locked doors just as scores of others did, calculating my losses, which came to twenty-some thousand, most of it the dividends of the Consolidated Virginia, which I had negligently permitted to amass instead of reinvesting in sound businesses.

I was almost too heartsick to grasp the story as it arrived on the noisy telegraph keys at the wire office. Ralston had been speculating with depositors' money for months. One of his schemes was to buy the Spring Valley Water Works for $5 million and sell it to the city of San Francisco for $10 million—but he failed, and had sunk a fortune into that rathole. Another, worse, mistake had been to plunge into the frenzy of the Big Bonanza, along with his banking partner Senator Sharon. Reasoning that the massive ore body under the California mine would extend next door into the Ophir, the banking crowd began buying Ophir stock, quietly at first and then madly, finally winning an enormous block of it from Lucky Baldwin.

But unknown to Ralston, the perfidious Sharon had concluded that the ore didn't reach the Ophir and was preparing to short-sell the Ophir stock at the time Ralston was paying ever-higher prices for the same stock. The bear attack had its effect: the panic of January had shot the Ophir shares down from $315 to $35, leaving Ralston and his bank holding $3 million of investment in an exhausted mine.

There was more. John Mackay and James Flood had organized a new Nevada Bank as a rival to the hated Bank of California, underwriting it with five millions of dollars. Thus was the old bank crowd dethroned, driven out of the Comstock by the new kings, who controlled the mines, the mills, the timber and water. Ralston and Mills had been outsmarted and outmaneuvered at every hand.

The upshot of all this was to leave Ralston ten million in debt with only four million secured. And while Ralston once could have guaranteed all of that and more, the Panic of '73 and the collapse of the Comstock shares in January of that fateful year eighteen and seventy-five had destroyed his collateral. He had taken desperate measures, surrendering his third of the Virginia & Truckee Railroad, selling vast real estate holdings in Kern County, raiding his bank-owned smelter of other companies' gold and silver, which he sold to the mint. All to no avail. Senator Sharon had come out fine; the rest of us, including his Nevada constituents, had lost nearly everything we had deposited. As the dust settled and I licked my financial wounds, my perception of Sharon darkened.

It was to darken still more when I heard about that fateful afternoon of the crash. Ralston spent those hours rewriting his will and conveying the deeds to all his properties to Sharon, who was expressly instructed in the will to reimburse depositors. Ralston tendered his resignation to the bank's angry board and walked out Sansome Street to the bay for his usual swim. He didn't return. They found his body later. Some said it was suicide. Some said it was a heart attack.

I always thought it was a species of murder, done by the nerveless, soulless Sharon during those wild hours he was short-selling the Ophir while helping Ralston buy the same shares at record prices.

I had to give the efficient Senator Sharon credit, though. Within weeks he reorganized the Bank of California, injecting over seven million into it, finding large amounts of capital among his friends. Sharon, Mills, a stockbroker named Keene, and Baldwin each subscribed a million. I never got my deposits back, but San Francisco people got something.

The bank reopened on October 2 and survived in a modest way, but never again as the premier financial institution of California. The branches in Virginia City and Gold Hill reopened, but my applications for my deposits fell on deaf ears. As usual, the people of the Comstock came last and least, thanks to our very own senator. He had, as usual, turned events to his profit and had scarcely heeded Ralston's will and last wish.

I opened an account with Mackay's Nevada Bank and licked my wounds. I had lost over ten years of newspaper salary. There were a few solaces. My Consolidated Virginia shares, which had fallen to $240 the day the bank failed, slowly climbed to $320. I was not poor.

My thoughts wandered back to the day Joe Goodman had sold out and left the paper in the hands of the California bank crowd. I remembered Rollin Daggett's fawning endorsement of Sharon. And I wondered whether, by selling out, Joe Goodman set the stage for the disaster that followed, for as long as the *Territorial Enterprise* stood between Sharon, with his lusts for money and power, and the people of the City on the Hill we were safe.

None of this bothered the raffish folk of the Comstock for long. They were used to risks, shrugged, and went on enjoying life in the wildest place on earth. I loved them for that.

As for me, I was about to enjoy a new kind of life. When at last we plighted our troth, Catherine and I began to melt into one another, finding happy companionship, forming a new family with my new son and daughter. I gave Catherine a gold engagement ring with a cornflower blue sapphire in it because we both loved blue the most.

Then we set a day: October 30, 1875. We would marry that evening at the Joneses'. The senator would be present and give the bride away. The Joneses would take care of the children while Catherine and I would retire to the International Hotel that night and entrain for San Francisco in the morning for a week of bliss.

CHAPTER 48

U nlike most veteran bachelors, I did not look upon wedlock with dread, but only with profound joy, and with determination to accommodate my bride every way I could so that our hearth might be the haven of sweet domesticity and peace.

I chose Dan De Quille as my best man. I had known him for what seemed an eternity, since I first arrived on the Comstock. He knew me as well as any man could. I added my new friend Wells Drury, editor of the *Gold Hill News,* a great and cheerful rival in the art of scoop, as one of my groomsmen, thus adding an ecumenical air to the newspaper fraternity. De Quille had just gotten back from Hartford, Connecticut, where he wrote *The Big Bonanza* while a guest of Mark Twain.

By now my colleagues at the paper knew I had made a tidy sum in the bonanza stocks, but I sensed no envy or distance. Most of them had cashed in, too, and half the staff of the *Enterprise* were flush and would remain so until the Old Magnolia relieved them of their mining profits. De Quille hadn't profited; he scorned speculations and spent his wage satisfying whim, occasionally dispatching some of it to his wife and children in Iowa.

Catherine and I invited our families but knew that we would not see them on our wedding day. Hers, in New York, would require weeks of travel on several railroads, while mine would require two weeks by coach, riverboat, and railroads. We were linked to the States by thin bands of steel, yet the rest of the nation still seemed an eternity away.

We would be married in the Joneses' parlor that Saturday evening and receive guests and well-wishers at the Washoe Club. Catherine was all smiles and secrets, and I knew she was busy with seamstresses, creating a trousseau.

I devoted time to Peter, Jr., and Caroline but did not succeed in breeching their reserve. No trips to the soda fountain, no matinees at the variety shows, no hikes up Sun Mountain with a picnic basket rewarded me with their trust. For them, I was the stranger who might take their only parent away, the stranger who would lessen the time and attention their mother devoted to them. I knew of no way to heal it other than with respect. I would respect their bonds and not attempt to be the father I could not be or to impose any sort of adult discipline, for it would only embitter a child. I felt inept, too long a bachelor. I suspect my beloved Catherine saw it all and worried about it, but she withheld her concerns from my ear, striving only to complete my joy.

So the weeks slipped by as Virginia City put itself together again after the crash of the bank. The town had a certain insouciance, a penchant for shrugging off such things, but my own losses galled me and festered cancerously in my heart. The madness of wealth had driven Ralston, the arrogance of power and money had driven Sharon, and between them they had bled me of much of my money. Not even the Consolidated Virginia's solid ten-dollar-a-share dividend consoled me, though it kept me afloat and lit my future. Our future. I was giving thought again to leaving the *Enterprise* and even leaving Virginia City for the sweeter climes of Northern California and thought to make our honeymoon an exploration of life on the Coast.

I gazed upon the city with an ancient ambivalence once again: the City on the Hill offered a wild and joyous life to a bachelor, while the same city reduced high-minded men to greed, deviousness, disloyalty, drunkenness, and desperation. I had come a long way from the capacious village home of Judge Stoddard and wondered whether I had grown or was now corrupted or both. I needed to take stock, examine my soul and mind, see what corrosion had eaten away the virtues of Henry Stoddard, see how I must change if I was to assume the heavy responsibilities of marriage and family.

We had not yet picked a minister or judge to officiate, and I took the opportunity to inquire of Catherine what she believed in, what eternal verities governed her temper.

"I grew up an Anglican," she said. "The Taylors are English. In Bolivia the people were either pagan, nothing, Catholic, or some mixture. The rulers, the jefes, were nothing. They were charming, gracious, and utterly unscrupulous, especially in their treatment of the workers. I should like to believe that if a man is not obedient to God, then he is obliged to obey a higher ethical order or become a beast. Let us be married by a judge."

I puzzled that out, and liked it.

If she was to become the mistress of my manor, then she ought to decorate it to her tastes, and I told her to come like a whirlwind and spin her will upon my pleasant B Street home. Little did I grasp–bachelor that I was–what license I was providing my betrothed. Out went all my favorite pieces, some of them Queen Anne, some Sheraton. In came massive Greek Revival–I would not know the proper word for such furniture–along with doilies, heavy drapes, and a new kitchen.

Fortunately, I was in a position to enjoy her efforts. I had been the possessor of two bedrooms, and we partitioned a third, one for each child, and converted an alcove into servant quarters if the need should strike us. I believe the whole of it kept the building trades prosperous in Virginia City for two months. I knew from the species of gleam in Catherine's hazel eyes that this gesture cemented our relationship for life, or two or three lives. She was mining the house for beauty and comfort as artfully as Mackay and Fair mined mines. My bachelor digs had been prestidigitated into an *establishment* and all for the price of one month's Consolidated Virginia dividend. I was amazingly happy.

And so we drew close to the appointed day. Jones would have no less than a state supreme court justice do the honors, so we arranged his passage from Carson City on the Virginia & Truckee. I turned Catherine loose upon florists and caterers, wine merchants and dispensers of spirits, engravers and livery stables.

My colleagues at the *Enterprise* announced that my presence was required at a small bachelor soiree the evening of the twenty-fifth, at which time, no doubt, they intended to make sure that I repeated my vows with a hangover. Thus was arranged an eve at Barnum's that would no doubt rival the night upon which we bid adieu to Artemus Ward so many years before, in a pile of shattered glass. My colleagues were not going to surrender me to domesticity without putting up a noble fight. Later I heard that they had even wired Sam Clemens, luring him with the offer of a free ticket, but he could not be shaken loose.

Roos Brothers Clothiers, directly across the street from the *Enterprise,* fitted me up in a natty tuxedo until I hardly recognized myself in the looking glass. I suppose I should have had a tailor do me up, but the Roos people were heavy advertisers and occasionally shared the oysters at the Old Magnolia, and so my choice was made for me.

Thus did matters progress in true Comstock Style, which is to say entirely out of my hands or control, which is the only way to perceive life in a mining town. Then, the morning of October 26, everything changed. A fierce Washoe zephyr was whirling icy air down from Mount Davidson in the predawn, at a moment when the city was at its most somnolent. An hour later, with the changing of the shifts, the city would have been alive to the danger that crept stealthily through a dubious boardinghouse on B Street, not very far from my neighborhood. A coal oil lamp fell; the house ignited. The winds whipped the flames into a raging fire in minutes.

The fire bells clanged at last, but no one responded. We citizens—I include myself—rolled over sleepily. Then the wail of the mine whistles joined the chorus and it dawned on me, and thousands of others in that tinder-dry, rainless city, that trouble was afoot. By the time the hand-pump fire engines and even the steamer operated by the various fire brigades arrived, the fierce west winds had blowtorched the fire down-slope into the heart of the city, lifting flaming shingles and sailing them into adjoining buildings, igniting them by the dozen. By the time I shook the dust from my brain and peered out my window, I saw a city falling into ruin and a wall of flame rolling in my direction, scarcely half a block distant. Windows began to explode, drawing flames into houses.

I drew trousers over my nightshirt and jammed bare feet into my shoes, and that was all the time given me: an eerie roar embraced my block, and my small, fragile house quivered and vibrated in anticipation of its doom. I fled, half-dressed, worried about Catherine, her children, and the Joneses in Gold Hill. I shouldn't have; the west winds preserved that city while driving the rampaging flames straight through my town. I saw my house catch, and in a trice it and all it possessed were ash. I saw the Washoe Club vanish in moments. I watched people congregate in the streets, dumb with horror, retreating as the inferno leaped across streets and blocks, blistering wood until it burst into flame.

Even now, from the perspective of a new century, I remember that dawn as vividly as any memory in my head. That morning, much of Virginia City burned, including the *Territorial Enterprise*, the Catholic, Presbyterian, and Episcopal churches, the International Hotel, the splendid hoisting works and mill at the Consolidated Virginia; the hoisting works and 400 feet of shaft at the Ophir; the railroad station, plus the rail yards, trestles, and bridges; the entire business district on North C Street; one and a quarter million board feet of mining timbers at the Consolidated Virginia, along with tons of cordwood for its boilers; and about two thousand buildings in all, making refugees of thousands of half-dressed people on a bitterly cold October morning.

I gaped as the fire crews futilely directed miserable trickles of water toward the blistering flames—most of which turned to steam. Then I heard the heartbeat of giant powder as mining crews carrying crates of dynamite rushed from building to building, blowing up whatever lay in the path of the monster—all to no avail.

My house vanished in a yellow ball. I watched, mesmerized, as a thunderous flame devoured everything I was and had been, including my scrapbooks filled with fourteen years of clippings, everything I had written, all of it forming a daily chronicle of my life. I felt bereft, as if my past had been stolen from me.

Someone yelled at me, and I realized I had put myself in harm's way, so I fled at once, confused, unable to grasp what all this was and what it meant. I had to head south and over the divide to Gold Hill to find Catherine, and that was no small task amid the rambling, chaotic crowds, each soul hurrying nowhere, directionless, for no one knew where to go or what to do to save himself. Most were half-dressed, like me; most silent, too, too absorbed by this monstrous upheaval in their sedate lives to think or speak.

I saw below me the business district consumed, fed by spirits in every saloon. I saw fireproof brick buildings suck flame into windows and collapse into rubble. I saw flaming missiles, wallpaper, shingles, clothing, tumbling like Greek fire through the heavens to start new conflagrations downwind.

I hurried along a roundabout route that I hoped would take me to my beloved, walking past stupefied people sitting in the middle of a street, past weeping children, tear-streaked men, stoic women, and not a few angry, half-demented men cursing every flame and defying the murderous heat.

A series of explosions shook the city, and I saw a row of houses crumble. The dynamiters had, for the moment, stopped the southward spread of the flames, but now the mines themselves were besieged. Down in the bowels of the earth were a hundred million board feet of timber, enough wood to build several large cities. If those caught fire and the fire burned its way from mine to mine through the connecting drifts, there could be no more mining and it would be years before the fires would die. Those fabled ores in the Consolidated Virginia and California would not be touched, at least not in my lifetime.

But of that I paid little heed. Determinedly I climbed upslope, avoiding streets altogether, crossing the divide until I reached the Jones home, and there I found my bride, on the Joneses' porch along with the others, staring into the glowing skies just over the Divide.

"Oh!" Catherine cried. "Oh! Henry! I was so afraid for you!"

And that was as sweet a declaration of love as I had ever heard.

CHAPTER 49

. . . .

am confused about what happened next. Those hours and days following the great fire were so chaotic and desperate that even now, at the turn of the century, I am unable to put them in proper order or even say where I was.

Two thousand of us were homeless. Food, clothing, and blankets arrived from Carson City and then from San Francisco, expressed to us by the railroads. We did not want for something to eat. Many wandering people simply left on the railroad, and some were never seen again.

The Joneses made me comfortable, though my only bed was a hardwood floor. Senator Jones's brother also lived there, and the house was crowded. I comforted my beloved, who was also bewildered and beside herself, and did what I could to lift her spirits and those of her children. But I could do no more. I had no access to funds and existed in my trousers, shoes, and nightshirt, my face stubbled over and my body halfwashed.

The fire had demolished a half-mile square in the heart of the city before valiant crews of dynamiters finally caged it. I found out later that Mackay had made truly heroic efforts to save the Consolidated Virginia shaft. First he had lowered the cages to a few feet below grade, and then he had sprung the safety clutches to hold the cages in place. Then he and his miners had poured ore on top of the cages, followed by layers of dirt, then timbers over the shaft, followed by more ore and dirt until a massive rock-and-earthen dike separated the wood-lined shaft from the fires, which swiftly consumed the shaft buildings and mill, feeding on the massive supply of stored mine timbers and thousands of cords of firewood. The heat knocked over brick buildings and warped nearby railcar wheels.

The Ophir mine's managers had taken the same tack but weren't so lucky, and the fire burned down four hundred feet into the mine before they got it under control, thus averting the ruination of that great mine.

As part of his efforts to save the Consolidated Virginia headframe and shaft, Mackay's crews had dynamited nearby St. Mary's Church, because its burning shingles were flying like missiles toward the mine buildings. Mackay promptly promised to rebuild the church, and he kept his promise.

By noon the fire was out, stopped on the south by the brick Odd Fellows Hall and George Marye's new brick offices. A city had been reduced to ash in little more than four hours. They were saying that ten million dollars went up in smoke, but over the years I've come to doubt it. I do believe that fire destroyed five million dollars.

But all this I learned later. I had taken that week and the next as a vacation, but now I thought perhaps Rollin Daggett needed me—wherever he might be. The daily *Enterprise* did not publish that twenty-sixth day of October. I had a hunch where I would find my colleagues and, bidding my shaken Catherine good-bye for the moment, hiked down the slope to the *Gold Hill News*, where indeed I found Daggett, Goodwin, and some of the compositors. Alf Doten and Wells Drury were graciously allowing us to print our next editions in their plant.

There were stories to be gotten, but I scarcely knew where to find them. Go to the fire crews? But the station houses had burned. Find the mine managers? They were as much adrift as the rest of us. Look for Mackay in the gym? What gym?

We finally divided our task, with Goodwin covering the railroad—which was boarding passengers at Gold Hill—while Dan De Quille, Daggett, and I sought stories on the streets and in the remaining superintendents' offices. I correctly guessed that I'd find Mackay and others at the Gould & Curry's brick building, and that proved to be the case.

So we assembled a paper and collected news off the wire, which Doten shared with us. It was from those wires that I learned that the news of the fire had panicked the San Francisco stock markets and dropped my Consolidated Virginia stock to a hundred a share while lowering all the others. So the fire had cost me a house and rich new furnishings and sliced my assets by three-quarters. I considered the bleak news and wondered how it might affect my forthcoming marriage, but then I did what I could to write the myriad stories that we collected.

Mackay heard about the panic in the streets of San Francisco, where people were unloading Comstock shares at any price, to anyone, and counting themselves lucky to salvage pennies on the dollar. He came to us at the *Gold Hill News* to say something to the world: the Consolidated Virginia had been saved and would be hoisting rich ores as soon as it could.

"I have been through all the mines this morning, and they are all right. There is no gas or fire in any mine connected with the Gould & Curry." Regrettably, he added, 700 miners would be laid off until a new hoisting works could be built, but meanwhile 300 tons of ore a day would be lifted from the Gould & Curry shaft.

That quieted the markets in San Francisco and heartened the doughty citizens of the Comstock.

Somehow we put our paper to bed, printed it on Doten's press, and swiftly sold out. The *Virginia Chronicle* staff was doing exactly the same thing, everyone amicably helping to write the news and set type. I remember doing that for three days, Wednesday and Thursday and Friday. Somehow, I had acquired some clothing, though I haven't the faintest recollection of where it came from. I fear that Catherine saw all too little of me in that time of crisis, though she said not a word when I reported to the paper each morning.

The Virginia & Truckee proved itself a priceless asset just then, carrying in supplies for a city of twenty thousand and taking out destitute and homeless people. Yerington put on every engine and car he could, running forty-five trains a day with clockwork precision.

I supposed Daggett was shorthanded, so it surprised me that on Friday, after we had somehow put another paper out, he pulled me aside.

"Henry. Take the week off. Get married tomorrow."

I stared at him.

"You deaf or something?" he asked.

"But you're shorthanded—"

"No, Dan is back, and that helps. We're sharing with Drury and Doten, and we've got Denis McCarthy's staff, too. They're using our stuff, and we're using theirs. We're covered. Each paper's getting out, and all are full of news. Goodwin's already saying we'll be in a new building in sixty days, new presses, new everything. So, beat it, Henry. You and your bride tie the knot and take a honeymoon."

My spirits began to soar. I hiked over the Divide, shocked as always by the black, bleak spectacle that met my eyes. But even before the timbers had stopped smoldering, crews were crawling over the charred ruins, cleaning away debris and preparing to rebuild just as fast as the Virginia & Truckee could bring in lumber and nails and bricks. It was a mining camp's insolence at work, the fatalism and determination that inspired a community to pick up the pieces after each disaster and make things better then ever before. By that Friday, frames of new buildings were everywhere visible across the Comstock, and the sight of them heartened me.

I approached the Joneses' home apprehensively, wondering how I could propose to my shaken fiancée that we proceed as planned, the very next day, right on schedule. But I had underestimated Catherine, for she had more heart, more spirit, more love, and more zest for life than a sort of man like me could ever imagine.

The fact of it is—and I'll never forget that moment—when I arrived on that porch she was waiting for me with a certain gleam in her hazel eyes, and I knew something very pleasant was about to transpire.

"I've been thinking, Henry," she began in that practical tone of voice that hid velvet-sheathed determination, "that we've scheduled a certain ceremony for tomorrow, and we ought to have it. We can post-pone the honeymoon. Can you get a few hours off?"

I laughed. Then I got crazy, that's what. I lifted her up and whirled her recklessly until her white skirts caught in the porch swing and she and I both capsized into it. I told her that I had gotten time off and we would be free to travel after all.

"I would like to take the children with us," she said. "School's closed. No one knows when it'll open." She took my hand gravely. "I know how you must feel. I feel the same way. But we'll have a lifetime of privacy just for ourselves. . . ."

I assented at once.

"The fire . . . the children need me—need *us* now. They haven't had much of a home. . . . And I'm sure the Joneses need to cope with all this. No one even knows when a butcher or grocer will open up again."

So I set aside certain of my honeymoon dreams, and Catherine and I swiftly made plans. We'd enlist the nearest clergymen or justice of the peace, get married—I would not even possess a suitable suit of clothes—gather our little family together, and catch the V & T. In San Francisco I would obtain a wardrobe.

We laid all this before Senator and Mrs. Jones that very hour, and they responded enthusiastically. So it happened that at eleven the next morning my beloved Catherine and I were united by the Presbyterian minister in the Joneses' parlor with no guests at all. The bride managed a wedding gown, but the groom appeared at his nuptials in a mis-matched assortment of rags, things shipped up to the Comstock in a boxcar by charitable people in Carson City. I had no ring for her be-cause the one I had purchased for this occasion had perished in the fire along with everything else. But that only made the event the more tender and memorable, and however lacking in beauty and ceremony our wed-ding was, it was nonetheless sacred and joyous.

Peter, Jr., and Caroline watched quietly, uncertain about me, about their fate, no doubt wondering what else would befall them. I was de-termined in my own mind to make our little trip a happy one for them if that was possible. And in San Francisco I intended to steer my bride into a jeweler's store and buy her a wedding ring.

It was all so odd, the city in ashes, the mines shut, noxious fumes on every breeze, dazed people still wandering about trying to salvage possessions. The future seemed dark and the city in peril in spite of John Mackay's assurances. There were quiet congratulations, but it scarcely seemed like a wedding at all, and I suspected that Catherine in particular felt bereft because we had no reception, no guests, no celebration of our union. But we had already decided that when the appropriate time came and we had a new home on the Comstock we would receive all those we had invited to our wedding.

"I don't know how long we'll be gone," I said to John Jones. "But we'll be back to continue our lives here."

"Take your time, Henry. It'll be many months before things settle down."

His prophecy was wrong. Within sixty days the phenomenal city had largely rebuilt itself and its mines, devouring awesome amounts of lumber, shingles, nails, glass, and other supplies in the process.

That nuptial afternoon a hack obtained by the Joneses drove us to the Virginia & Truckee station in Gold Hill. We boarded the crowded coach knowing we would have to stand in the aisles as far as Carson City. I held Catherine's hand in my left hand and Caroline's hand in my right, and soon enough the whistle shrilled, a blast of steam escaped the pistons, and we felt the couplings jolt and the coach ease forward, taking Henry Stoddard and his bride and children into a new life.

It did not matter that my home and all within it had perished, my newspaper's plant had perished, my city had perished, my assets had largely perished, and the future was clouded. I was the happiest I had ever been.

CHAPTER 50

e took a suite at Lick House. It wasn't the honeymoon I had expected but was in some ways better. I had married, after all, a family and not just a widow. The children needed a father, and I had no experience in that department but resolved to learn. My first and most blessed instinct was to leave parenthood to their mother and require nothing of them. If there was any good in our sudden fire-wrought arrangements, it was that they learned I was not taking their mother away from them, even for the week Catherine and I had planned. I knew that blessings would come of that.

I had fire-related business in mind and approached a San Francisco building contractor with an idea. I knew it would take months to rebuild my house on the Comstock because every available carpenter and joiner and mason would be deluged with work, much of it urgent, most of it for the mines, which were eager to resume production, and the merchants desirous of opening their doors again. So the question I posed to the builder was this: could he construct a house in pieces that could fit onto a flatcar and be taken by rail to the Comstock?

The response pleased me. Not only would he do that, but he would also send a crew to assemble the pieces. I wired Dan De Quille to take the measurements of my foundation, and when I had those in hand and we had sketched out a plan the builder set to work. I would have a house ready to travel in a fortnight and could expect to move in a week or so after that.

I wired Judge Goodwin that I would return to work in three weeks. He returned the news that the plant would be completed in two months and until then the joint production of the three papers made my presence unnecessary. But he was desirous that I should string for him while in San Francisco, dealing especially with the mining stock markets and what the new Nevada Bank and the Bank of California were up to. That would keep my hand in the business, and I agreed at once. For the first time in my adult life I could enjoy a lengthy holiday without financial care. And we would be returning to a city a building, instead of a dead black desolation.

Catherine took the news joyously, her eyes agleam with the prospect of buying an entire houseful of furniture along with drapes and kitchen and china service.

All that relieved me of a heavy burden. The other thing that lifted my spirits was that the Consolidated Virginia declared its regular $10 dividend, and I would have $4,000 in cash coming to my depleted coffers. John Mackay was showing the world that the Consolidated Virginia was the greatest of all mines and mostly unhurt by the fire. The shares rallied upon that news.

We explored the great city, sampling its seafood and patrolling the wharves, where Peter, Jr., discovered the majesty and glory of sailing ships. One Sabbath afternoon we inveigled a kindly master into letting us tour his China clipper, and I am sure it was Peter's most glorious hour. But honeymoon or not, I found myself so busy that most of the time I turned Catherine and the children loose in the mercantiles while I attended to business.

One of my first stops was at the new Nevada Bank Building, which had opened its doors on October 5. I wished to interview James Flood, one of the Bonanza firm's partners and least-known to me, because he rarely visited the Comstock. Flood and his partner O'Brien handled financial and investment matters for Mackay and Fair, and I intended to inquire what designs the new firm had upon Virginia's mines and mills, now that the California bank crowd's power was waning.

Flood welcomed me immediately. He proved to be a trim-bearded man of medium build and height, with heavy features. He had been many things in his life, most particularly a carriage builder, and after trying two or three businesses that collapsed under him during depressions he had turned to saloon keeping on the intelligent ground that the demand for spirits was constant, no matter how hard the times. He and the other Bonanza Firm partner, William O'Brien, had started the Auction Lunch a few yards from what would soon become the Mining Exchange, and it had been a smooth and inevitable progress from plucking tips from brokers pausing for a whiskey and a sandwich to trading on the floor of the bustling exchange next door.

All this I knew before I met him, and I also knew he would be extremely private, unlike John Mackay or even "Uncle Jimmy" Fair when loquaciousness overtook him.

But Flood surprised me. He really didn't know me enough to trust me, but he talked candidly about the fire and the future of the mines. He even told me about a disagreeable meeting that morning with a disgruntled stock trader named Dewey, who had inquired of Flood just after the fire how much cash the company had on hand and had decided to sell his shares when he learned that the Consolidated Virginia lacked the funds to pay the usual ten-dollar dividend. Dewey professed to be astonished and angered when it did pay a dividend.

"I told him the exact truth, but he would not believe it, and accused me of manipulation of the market," Flood said. "More and more, I am finding that no matter what we do there will be those who'll blame us for their private misfortunes."

Little did he know how true that would be, and in the ensuing months and years I would remember that prescient observation. But that was the future. For the nonce, he was pleased to announce that the company's rebuilding efforts were proceeding at full speed and as fast as could be expected and that the new hoisting works and new mill would be larger and more efficient than the ones that had succumbed to the fire.

All this I duly reported, along with whatever news he could spare about the California mine, which was not yet in full production. Flood struck me as urbane, well-groomed, well aware of his bonanza, and enjoying every dollar of it. If he was not an affable or social man, he was certainly a straightforward one. I was to discover later than his lack of affability, of camaraderie with San Francisco's elite, would cost him the esteem of the whole city and create the venom of nearly all of its newspapers.

But for this last, shining moment, the press of San Francisco was still lauding the Bonanza Firm for rescuing the Consolidated Virginia and paying the regular dividend—and salvaging the fortunes of half the rich men in the city, whose wealth was intimately tied to the Comstock. I liked Flood. I also believed, and still do believe, that he was an honorable man. In the end, I would be almost the only one who did.

He purposed to live handsomely, which was the custom among men of means, and had acquired the costliest carriage on the market, with horses to match and a coachman in livery. He had purchased Fair Oaks, an estate down the peninsula, from former mayor John Selby, and was engaged in enlarging and remodeling that when I met him. Later nothing would do but that he owned the fanciest estate in Menlo Park, which he called Linden Towers. On this fenced thirty-five-acre tract he erected a baroque palace, bristling with turrets and towers, which became known as Flood's Wedding Cake. On the grounds were such items as a private racetrack, a sixty-foot fountain, a lake stocked with game fish, and stables for twenty horses.

When the local gentry, such as the Athertons, Parrots, and Howards, sniffed a bit at him and his family, he bought a city block atop Nob Hill and began a forty-two-room town house with walls of Connecticut sandstone and an eighty-foot tower, which he surrounded with a gaudy bronze fence. He lacked an education, like the other bonanza partners, and could think of nothing to do with his awesome wealth but show it off. As I write now, from the turn of the century, I hear the Pacific Union Club is interested in the property. But I am getting ahead of my story.

I don't know how my San Francisco correspondence was received by Daggett and Goodwin, for they never said, but neither did they complain. I like to believe that it set the *Territorial Enterprise* apart and gave it a certain cosmopolitan air. I whiled away hours in the two stock exchanges, mastering what had always seemed mysterious and arcane to me from the vantage point of Virginia City. In this matter, the other bonanza partner, O'Brien, affably assisted, showing me about, introducing me to traders, and occasionally making a small trade himself. But he conveyed none of the drive, canniness, wisdom, or ambition of his partners, and it did not surprise me to learn that he never even tried to fulfill his obligations and duties in the firm. He was the cipher, the lucky man riding the genius of his colleagues.

So my honeymoon turned out to be business as usual, but no less pleasant for that. Catherine devoted many hours to tutoring the children so that they would not lose a grade, and that made the long hours at Lick House go faster. San Francisco's winter climate remained mild but unpleasant, and we were rarely warm. I do not know why people live there.

As promised, my contractor had my house loaded onto two flatcars in a fortnight and sent his crew off to the Comstock with it. The want of wagons and teamsters, as well as masons to repair the fire-damaged foundation, delayed the erection of my home until I authorized double wages for a day or two, and then it got done, but ten days later than I expected.

I had trouble securing cordwood for the house because the Virginia & Truckee groaned under the traffic, running trains just as fast as they could traverse the miles from Carson City. But not fast enough. There were long delays. Not even a railroad could supply a city bent on re-building itself at breakneck speed.

We returned in time for Thanksgiving, glad to be back. The transformed city amazed us. Some burnt-out stores had reopened, and other structures were well along. We waited impatiently for deliveries of furniture and service, but just about when Catherine was ready to remove to the bay for another stint we would receive some badly needed piece or other, which served to salve our unhappiness.

I traipsed over the divide to Gold Hill, where we continued to produce our paper. The chaos of the early hours had given way to efficient operations in which three shifts of compositors and printers worked around-the-clock to produce the *Gold Hill News,* the *Virginia Chronicle,* and the *Enterprise.* My paper had established business offices with Driscoll and Tritle, stockbrokers at C and Taylor Streets, at the edge of the burned district, and then had moved to the paint store next door while we awaited the renovation of our fire-gutted plant. By November 16 the paper was using its familiar typeface and employing its usual four-page format. That issue announced that the business offices would remove to the Odd Fellows Hall for the duration.

Our revived plant at 24 South C Street was trimmed with ginger-bread, and the interior was restored. It was fitted out with a new press and compositors' equipment, and we moved in toward the end of the year, oddly melancholy instead of rejoicing. I think, as I look back, that was because it now looked institutional, almost like a bank, and all its racy memories had vanished into brick and mortar. Was this the same place, the same paper, where Twain and Goodman and De Quille and Gillis and I and a grumbling Chinaman and a mean printer's devil named Noyes had comported ourselves? It looked so new, so clean, so improbable, that I dreaded even to carry a glass of Monongahela into it.

This was the California bank crowd's version of a paper, Senator Sharon's pet, and I sensed the old *Enterprise* rested in a grave burdened with memory. Indeed, the fire had destroyed our entire files, and now nearly all the early editions of the paper had gone up in smoke. Most of Mark Twain's pieces had vanished, many of mine, most of Goodman's and Gillis's as well. No full account of the murder of Julia Bulette remained, nor the paper's joyous celebration of the events at Appomattox. What survives in the Bancroft Library, the Mackay School of Mines, and elsewhere was recovered from unburned parts of the city, exchange papers, and other sources. I grimly saw something fitting in it: the paper now belonged to Senator Sharon and was operated by a railroad superintendent, and the death of its irreverent files seemed proper.

Now, decades later, I can't imagine how I even thought such a terrible thing.

That winter I returned to my old news beat, but with little taste for reporting and restless again. That winter saddened me. The mean Washoe zephyrs drove the heat out of the rebuilding city and filled me with foreboding. Had the city rebuilt only to die in a year or two or three?

But if my joy in the newspaper had declined, my domestic joys had multiplied. For at last Catherine and I had become lovers, and when I returned to my hearth each evening my gaze would catch and hold her, following her in her transports, my soul never having enough of her. I hoped devoutly that she was as blissful as I, and I believed she was. I saw it in her sweet face, her lingering glances, and the melting smiles when we were alone each night. The raucous high-mountain town suited her, which can scarcely be said of other women there.

A second dividend and then a third arrived on schedule, and I marveled that the Consolidated Virginia had not lost a beat, somehow finding, each month, $1,080,000 to distribute to those who held its 108,000 shares. I banked the dividends, paid for our extravagant purchases, and tried to spread the surplus funds into real estate far from the booms and busts of a mining town.

It was not that mining itself wearied me. On the contrary, the painful struggle to extract valuable metals and minerals from the guarded vaults of the earth had never fired me with more excitement or fascination. Here was the Consolidated Virginia, installing the first triple-deck cages in history, using giant hoists and thick, flat woven cables to lift and lower so much weight. There was the new stamp mill, a wonder that was extracting as much as 80 percent of the assayed values of ores from pulverized rock. Here were miners, ever wilier and more productive as they mastered the Burleigh drill, the diamond-tipped drill, air compression, Root blowers, Nobel's dynamite, and square-set timbering to prop up millions of tons of rock just over their heads. I had learned, in the course of fourteen years, almost as much as the managers and foremen themselves.

And that proved to be one of several reasons my life was soon to change once again.

CHAPTER 51

 have dwelled too much upon my domestic life and thus have deprived my readers of the important things. I include something of my personal affairs only to afford the reader some grasp of how Henry Stoddard lived on the Comstock, surrounded by mining titans, geniuses, speculators, and a devil-may-care recklessness. Even the toiling miners bet their day wages on the mines. A chalk board at each headframe listed the latest prices for the benefit of the men in the pits.

There had never been a place like the Comstock or a city like Virginia or a gathering of brilliant men such as those who assembled there. Quite unintentionally, those men of large affairs who controlled the mines or manipulated the stocks sent shocks through the entire economy of the West Coast. The Comstock sucked up all the capital available in the West, often depriving other businesses of much-needed funds. This occasioned the collapse of some businesses elsewhere, hard times, sudden impoverishment, fortunes won and lost and won again in days or weeks. It occasioned malice, especially toward the bonanza partners.

When the Bonanza Firm explored and developed the new mines, San Francisco breathed its relief, for the city's liquidity rested squarely on the mines at the foot of Mount Davidson. The new bonanza was the salvation of the Bank of California, the Virginia & Truckee, the gigantic timbering enterprises, and countless merchants and wholesalers whose products found their way to the tables and homes and restaurants and livery stables of the City on the Hill.

No paper was more fulsome in its praise of the genius of Fair and Mackay and Flood and O'Brien than the *San Francisco Chronicle*. But now, after the collapse of the Bank of California, the destruction of dozens of San Francisco fortunes, the fire, and the gyrating market that made and destroyed Californians wholesale, the *Chronicle* began to criticize the bonanza partners.

I watched, dismayed. It did not matter that the firm had been fairer to the public than any other, that it permitted any qualified person to enter the pits, take assay samples, and see with his or her own eyes. It didn't matter that Fair and Mackay had not kept the developments a secret, had not imprisoned miners in the pits while they scurried to buy shares before they rose. It did not matter that the Consolidated Virginia continued to pay its ten-dollar-a-month dividend after the fire, at considerable hardship to itself, because Mackay wished to calm the markets and assure the world that the fire would not destroy the stability of the Comstock or permanently reduce the value of its mines. Nor did it matter that in spite of the devastating blaze the Comstock produced a record twenty-six million dollars of bullion in eighteen and seventy-five and was lifting a thousand tons of ore each day.

None of that mattered.

What mattered in San Francisco was that the gyrations of the market had left wounded everywhere, not least the California bank crowd, and they were angry. Capital was short; banks had none to lend because it had all vanished into the Comstock. And suddenly all this misfortune was laid upon the partners, with the *Chronicle* leading the assault.

As it happened, manager James Fair's Consolidated Virginia annual report for that year, issued on December 31, did exaggerate the amount of ore underground, in terms of both the dimensions of the known body on levels below 1550 feet and those of its tenors. That report would come back to haunt the partners. Fair, a trickier and more opportunistic man than Mackay, had attempted to inflate the value of the mine.

The next year proved to be the apex of life in Virginia City, though we didn't know that. The California went into full production and began paying a ten-dollar-a-month dividend also. I harvested the money, scarcely knowing how to reinvest it.

Many of the mines were sinking new shafts well east of the old works, attempting to tap the same bonanza ore. Their workers toiled in desperately hot rock, in temperatures reaching over a hundred degrees, sometimes hitting water that could scald their flesh. No amount of fresh air or ice could sustain them for more than a ten-or fifteen-minute stint in that murderous heat that sucked strength out of them, made them faint, raised rashes, and incurred headaches.

In eighteen and seventy-six, the centennial of the Republic, Virginia City rebuilt itself, using the fire as the opportunity to make everything bigger and better. A new International Hotel rose, this one higher than the previous one and boasting the first elevators in the Far West. The city remained two-thirds male and with a permanent population slightly under twenty thousand. But transients crowded the boardinghouses, clogged the streets, and filled the saloons, adding to the numbers. The Bonanza Firm alone kept twelve mills humming, the two largest—the Consolidated Virginia's and California's—reducing an incredible 630 tons of rock into powder every twenty-four hours. Lawlessness declined to minimal levels; it was simply too easy to make money legitimately. But of the 135 Comstock mines on the San Francisco exchanges, only 3 were paying dividends. The rest were assessing their shareholders to finance deep exploration.

My Consolidated Virginia stock had risen again, reaching $385 in December. The California, which had again split five to one, was listed at $61. So my losses had been recovered and I was doing better than ever, able to lavish anything upon Catherine that her heart desired. But she seemed pleased to keep a thrifty house and except for a maid added little to our domestic expense. I showered Catherine with extravagances, which she accepted with a wry smile and a soft sigh, not because she cared for ostrich-feather hats or London bonbons, but because these things were tangible expressions of her husband's adoration.

Fair, whose loyalties extended no further than the tip of his nose, amazed the world by criticizing Mackay's operation of the Consolidated Virginia during a brief period that spring when Fair was absent. Mackay, he said, was gutting the mine. Mackay kept his silence and would not give me a response for publication. But I knew he was troubled. I also surmised that he had his private opinion of "Uncle Jimmy" Fair and it would only be a matter of time before that opinion would become public. Fair had steadily maneuvered to blame his partners for whatever failed. By blaming Mackay, he was simply burrowing his way into the graces of disaffected San Francisco investors and speculators whose hatred of the firm deepened as the months slid by.

I resolved then and there to defend Mackay whenever I could. Mackay was a good and decent man, not warped by wealth, and the most generous of the partners. After the fire he had swiftly rebuilt the Catholic church, St. Mary's of the Mountains, and in brick, quietly supported numerous charities in Virginia City, offered help to countless people, and genuinely hoped stockholders would profit from his enterprises.

In March, the Consolidated Virginia produced an amazing

$3,634,218 of bullion, but that served only to whet the appetites of the bears, who purposed to drive down the stock and profit thereby, howling that the mine had been gutted. Fair played along with the bears, letting it be known that the best ores on the 1,500-foot and 1,550-foot levels would be exhausted by year's end—thus pitting himself against his own partners, including Flood, who was trying to support the price of the stock on the exchanges.

The bears won, reducing the value of Consolidated Virginia shares from $440 in February to $240 in July, and once again I saw my fortunes melt away. One day I would be rich; the next I would be merely affluent. Several times I had slid into near-ruin. I knew I was on Fate's whirligig. So far, I hadn't been pauperized. In July, the *San Francisco Chronicle* unloosed a new barrage against the Bonanza Firm, which only served to depress prices further.

But as often is the case, I am getting ahead of myself. Far out on the Great Plains, something occurred that reminded us all that our booming and cosmopolitan industrial city was barely connected to the States and that nothing at all lay between us and the farms east of the Missouri and Mississippi Rivers.

On July 6, the Associated Press wires reported a military disaster on the northern plains, in which a command led by Lt. Col. George Armstrong Custer had been wiped out by the Sioux and Cheyenne on June 25. The steamer *Far West* had arrived in Bismarck on July 5 with the story. As the news ticked in, we stared, aghast, at the yellow flimsies.

Rollin Daggett, who knew the plains well, discovered pleasure in it. "Big fellows. Roman noses, fighters, those Sioux! I'm proud of them!"

That so astonished Judge Goodwin that he simply stared.

Daggett specialized in being offensive. Senator Sharon once ran into Daggett outside the International and invited him to breakfast. Daggett, or so the story goes, had already eaten but agreed to have a glass of something or other. Sharon ordered broiled quail and a pint of claret while Daggett ordered the "Miner's special"—a huge sirloin, fried eggs, and a bottle of Steamboat gin.

"I thought you already had breakfast," said Sharon.

"I had, but the way you eat makes me hungry."

"I'd give half my fortune for your appetite."

"Yes," Daggett retorted, "and the other half for my nobility of character and youthful figure."

It probably is apocryphal, but the exchange was much admired by us all.

I began defending John Mackay in print, veering from news into open opinionizing. I had grown weary of the assaults on his good name that spring and summer and purposed to retort in full measure. Then, suddenly, my stories were cut, reshaped, or killed. I did one about the California mine's five-for-one stock split, which made the price of its stock, now down to sixty-one dollars, affordable for small investors. The Bonanza Firm, which consisted of men who had risen from humble backgrounds, always remembered the clerks and shopkeepers and scullery maids, a company philosophy I considered admirable, and I said so in my story. But that part of the story never appeared. I stormed into Judge Goodwin's lair and confronted him, but he uneasily passed me off to Daggett. So I confronted Daggett, who smiled and said he had made some editorial decisions.

For the first time in my fifteen years with the paper I could not say what I wished to say. I saw Yerington's hand in it, and that hand was directed by the senator's. I stepped out onto C Street, hiked past all the shining new stores and saloons, walked around the block three times, made up my mind, returned to Goodwin's lair, and tendered my resignation.

CHAPTER 52

Catherine, who had become sensitive to my ways, surprised me that night.

"I'm proud of you," she said. "You stood up for what you believe. That paper's nothing but a mouthpiece."

"I didn't do anything very courageous. If quitting meant giving up my living, that would have required moral courage. But we're well fixed—for now."

"Even so, you were there fifteen years. And you had the courage to leave when things changed. What are you going to do? I don't think you'd be happy just doing nothing."

She was right about that. I had spent a lifetime in harness, and my daily output of news had ingrained itself in my life. "Look for another paper, I suppose," I replied. "Maybe Alf Doten would have me over at the *Gold Hill News*. He and Wells Drury put out a good paper."

"But not the *Chronicle*."

"No, not that." That was the opposition. Denis McCarthy and his minions were engaged in a vendetta against the *Enterprise* and all its people. I didn't mind his assaults on the paper's ownership, but I minded his libelous attacks on Judge Goodwin and Rollin Daggett and its new managing editor, George Daly. Daggett and McCarthy were a whisper from dueling, and I could scarcely imagine going to work for Rollin's ferocious enemy. Later they reconciled at Barnum's, an entire case of Mumm's Extra providing the necessary lubrication, and I might have joined the *Chronicle* staff without causing bitterness. But it never happened.

I purposed to become an independent correspondent—a stringer, as such were known in the trade—for a variety of papers, most notably those in San Francisco. Virginia City had become one of the most important burgs in the republic, and I knew I could sell everything I wrote, if not to the San Francisco papers, then to New York ones, which had voracious appetites for any news of the silver kings and the mines, especially in that golden year of eighteen and seventy-six, when the mines were producing bullion in dazzling amounts.

So I made the rounds, talked to my old sources, scribbled my copy, and mailed it or sometimes wired it. But it wasn't the same. I didn't belong. And my sources proved more difficult now that I was no longer associated with Nevada's greatest and most powerful newspaper, the only one with fangs. I made a point of staying away from the *Enterprise,* but that didn't help my growing despondence. I felt like an old dray horse who had been put out to pasture—except that I had put myself out to pasture and I could blame no one else for it.

For not the first time, I thought about leaving Virginia City. I think almost everyone there considered leaving that arid slope at one time or another. The glittering town with its hundred saloons wasn't proof against a landscape so bleak that it induced melancholia. Those who dug silver and gold out of the bowels of brooding Mount Davidson paid for it one way or another, foregoing gardens, gentle climates, the sea, waving fields of grass, tree-lined boulevards, rivers, and forests. We lived in squalor, huddled tight together to fend off the ugliness not only of nature but also of the mines, whose grim heaps of tailings and skeletal headframes and weathered planks smote the eye.

The only good thing about the fire was that it scorched away much of the tawdriness and most of the jerry-built structures in one violent and merciless cleansing. The new buildings at every hand were handsome, many of brick, all of them better suited to cope with the mean Washoe zephyrs that had eddied into the old buildings. The fire bought us comfort. The fire bought me a windproof house, and we no longer huddled around parlor stoves when the bitter winds off the peaks around us needled through our defenses.

I could go anywhere, build a home upon stately lawns, settle in a mild California climate, become a man of leisure—if that was what suited us. It didn't. The harsh discomforts of mining towns had, perversely, wound their way into our lives. Catherine found some unfathomable delight in Virginia City. I had spent my entire adult life there and relished its every haunt, from Barnum's, to the rebuilding Washoe Club, to the solid and comfortable superintendents' offices of the mines.

But we were restless and felt our discontent. I knew I must get myself out of the house so Catherine might have some peace. Then, unexpectedly, my problem was resolved for me, not by any exertion of my will but by Fate. I was reminded that I had gotten my first job largely by Fate, when Joe Goodman hired me almost intuitively. And now it happened again.

John Mackay summoned me. He had made a bachelor home for himself in the solid brick offices of the Gould & Curry, his wife preferring other locales to a burnt-out city. I had not seen him for some little while, the large affairs of his life as a silver king having occupied more and more of his time. I found him quite the same that autumnal day of eighteen and seventy-six, but changed in one respect: he spoke now in standard English, a workaday English that no longer revealed his origins. He had worked diligently on this, having felt the need, and now his past had vanished save for the lyrical lilt that is the special gift of the Irish.

"You left the *Enterprise,* Stoddard. I won't ask why."

"You probably know why."

He smiled. He rarely did, being a man of unusual sobriety except when his instincts for blarney came to the forefront.

"You've elected not to join other papers," he said.

"I am loyal to my old friends and my old paper—but not to its current owners."

"Loyalty has been the hallmark of your life, Stoddard. It's something I admire. How are your investments?"

"Thanks to you, I am doing well. I don't know how you managed the Consolidated Virginia dividends at a time when you were rebuilding. But you did, and it was a blessing to the whole district."

"That's why we did it. Borrowed from our own bank against our bullion, but it was a secure loan. It hasn't slowed the criticism any. I am a miner, not a speculator, and jobbing the stock markets isn't my field or my interest. But some there are who believe that's how we manage our affairs."

"I'm not one, and the criticism's unwarranted."

"Mostly," he said, staring at something beyond me.

I wondered where all this was leading and soon found out.

He examined me intently, as if registering the nature and spirit of a man he'd only just met. "Are you interested in a position?" he asked.

The question startled me. I had so cast my life as a scribbler and reporter that I hadn't imagined myself as something else.

"Why, yes."

"I need a personal secretary. A confidential secretary. And one in my own employ, not in the firm's employ."

I nodded, astonished, and waited for more.

"The man I need would not necessarily be a practical miner, but he must know mining—just as you do. John Jones was never a practical miner; he never spent a shift underground mucking ore. But he knew mining and became a fine manager, as good as they come, and now a senator."

That, I knew, was quite a concession from a man who prided himself on his life in the pits before he rose to his present estate. "Yes, sir. I know mining, having covered it for fifteen years here. I knew something of it from the Cornishmen in the lead mines where I grew up."

"That's why I'm interested in you, Stoddard. But the man I employ must have no fear of going underground. I won't have a man in my outfit who won't go down in the cage. If I want him to take a message to a shift boss on the fifteen-hundred-foot level, he will do it, without question, and without passing along the task. Are you up to it?"

His riveting gaze held me and I knew that this was a crucial qualification.

"I don't much like it, but I'll do it. I did it when you opened the Consolidated Virginia and mostly subdued my fears. Yes, sir. I'll go down whenever I'm asked."

"Good. If you find you can't, I'll require that you tell me so. It's safe enough. We do everything possible, spend whatever we must, to make the mines safe. I could not live with blood on my hands due to neglect of safety or trying to operate on the cheap."

That was true in spite of what some people said. Both Mackay and Fair had mined ore deep in black holes in the rock, and both knew that safety was crucial, not only to the miners and their families but also to the firm itself. Only recently Fair had fired some miners he caught smoking in the pit, where there were millions of board feet of timber.

"Your allegiance would be to me. You would take no direction from Jim Fair. You would handle the things I lack time to do. Some of it would involve meeting important visitors and shepherding them through the works—which is one of the reasons you must be willing to go down in the cages. Keeping my appointment books. Handling some of my finances. Fulfilling Mrs. Mackay's requests." He paused. "And sometimes keeping me posted on what others are doing."

He meant Fair, who was increasingly the wild card in the Bonanza Firm, almost out of control of the others. I nodded.

"I would expect unswerving loyalty and confidentiality, including a silence about all delicate business matters, even with Mrs. Stoddard."

"You would have that, Mr. Mackay."

He smiled broadly. Those rare smiles always illuminated him and betrayed his true, generous nature. "Then let us discuss a wage. Would five hundred a month suffice?"

That was princely. He was making me, in essence, an executive of a bonanza enterprise.

"That would be generous, Mr. Mackay."

"Then we have an agreement."

And that was how I became the confidant and secretary of the most powerful man on the Comstock in the autumn of the most successful year the district had ever known.

CHAPTER 53

So I walked through a fateful door, leaving one life behind and embracing another. I was now the private assistant of one of the world's most powerful men. If John Mackay was the same man I had known for all those years, I would have no difficulty, but if wealth had altered or corrupted his kind and unassuming nature, this new employment might not last.

That very night I walked through yet another of life's doors. Catherine clasped me to her in our privacy, before retiring, and I sensed something was amiss.

"Henry . . . ," she said, so mournfully that I braced myself for bad news.

"Yes, Catherine? What is it?"

She seemed to exude fear, and I couldn't fathom why.

"Henry, you're going to be a father."

"A father? Me?"

"Who else?" she asked archly.

"You are going to be a mother?"

"Henry, you are being an idiot."

"Are you all right? Is everything all right?"

"Don't you want—"

"Want! I've waited a dozen years for this!"

The veteran ex-bachelor Henry Stoddard somehow hadn't quite mastered the idea that his union with Catherine would produce off-spring. But once I chewed on the idea a little bit, my heart leaped. I took her hands in mine and sat beside her on our bed and told her no man had ever been so fortunate and that I would welcome the child and nurture it as best I could, as my parents had nurtured me. A pang pierced me; both my parents had died before they could see the grand-child.

"I have never loved you so much, or felt so blessed," I whispered.

Catherine was relieved. "I'm glad," she said. "I wondered."

I don't know why she wondered except that I was still the old, stolid Stoddard, forever reluctant to bare my feelings, even to my wife.

In the stillness of that night I lay awake, rejoicing. I was thirty-eight when I married and had despaired of having a family, passing along something of myself to new generations, seeing my own flesh and blood grow and reach adulthood and begin their own lives. I wasn't young, and children would not be easy, but in that quiet, with Catherine lying beside me, I knew that Henry Stoddard, born to be an anonymous man, had been given an exceptional life.

So my life was being transformed in several sudden turns, and looking back, I believe the timing was perfect. I had reason to be grateful for my new position. That fall, the bears in the San Francisco stock exchanges had mounted new assaults on the bonanza stocks on the news that the bonanza lodes were smaller than previously believed. By December my shares of Consolidated Virginia had dropped into the mid-thirties, while the California shares had dropped to the low forties. My quarter of a million had largely vanished. I had some dividend income, but my paper fortune was mostly gone. Suddenly that $500 a month looked like manna to me, especially with a growing family.

John Mackay was batching on the second floor of the Gould & Curry offices, which stood just beyond the burnt area, and planned to stay there until the International Hotel was rebuilt. Mrs. Mackay, the gracious and socially ambitious Marie, had long since fled the Comstock for San Francisco and with the first blush of wealth had purchased a house on O'Farrell Street, only to find the neighborhood too modest for both her ambitions and her wealth. Just a few blocks distant the mansions of Nob Hill were rising. In the early seventies, a brief sojourn in Paris had persuaded her that she should remove to the Continent, and that she did in the fall of eighteen and seventy-six, along with her children and assorted relations.

I could never tell for sure whether Mackay welcomed that or it troubled him. Probably both. At heart he wanted only hearth and home, but Mrs. Mackay's extensive social life had cut deeply into time he needed to run the mines. And he didn't exactly approve of the hoity-toity company she was keeping. Whatever the case, one of the richest men in the country lived a solitary life, most of it in the Gould & Curry apartment, the rest of it in San Francisco's Palace Hotel, where I often accompanied him. I had not realized how much I would be torn apart from Catherine and my own stepchildren, whom I was in the process of adopting, by my new position. So there would be a hidden price for my bonanza salary after all.

I could argue, from the vantage point I now enjoy at the turn of the century, that I joined Mr. Mackay at the very hour of the very year when the Comstock reached its apex and that all that followed was decline of one sort or another. It's true in a way. By the following year, the Consolidated Virginia had begun its decline, and eighteen and seventy-seven saw real hardship in Virginia City, with thousands pulling out for other silver or gold strikes, particularly at Bodie. But the great California mine was just reaching full production, and its awesome flood of bullion overmatched the decline elsewhere. And there would be new bonanzas as a result of the intensive exploration across the Comstock—or so we believed. Virtually every mine was sinking new shafts or running drifts at deep levels, and surely these would produce yet another bonanza.

During those years, the price of silver edged lower, because Congress had unmoored it from its monetary price of $1.29 an ounce. Silver had become merely a commodity, declining steadily toward a dollar an ounce as the Comstock flooded the whole world with it. Fortunately for the Bonanza Firm, its profits were based almost as much on gold, but in the end the decline in silver cost the silver kings many millions of dollars.

My first business for Mr. Mackay—in all my years with him, I never addressed him as John, because something in his person required the *Mister*—was not what I had expected. I had little realized how besieged he was by people importuning him for money. He told me that his daily walk from the Palace Hotel in San Francisco to his office in the Nevada Bank cost him five hundred dollars.

On my first day at the Gould & Curry apartment, he braced me:

"My philosophy is this, Stoddard. Most of those who press me are simply opportunists looking for money. And when it comes easily to them, they spend it unwisely and do not grow. But among all these are truly desperate people, ones on the brink of grave trouble—and if I help a few of those, then I have done something good.

"What I want you to do is sort all these out. From now on, you'll be hearing hard-luck stories and shielding me a little from these pressures. I don't mind giving money away, but I regret the loss of privacy and time.

"These people have pride. We'll call these things loans, even if they're not. Many people have already paid me back—but oddly, not the most substantial ones I've lent money to. The others, the truly destitute, have often returned the cash. Keep a record, Henry. When I make a loan, prepare a note and have the man sign it. Put this all in good order and you'll be a great help to me."

I felt uneasy but up to the challenge. I was going to have to say no to some people and use my judgment and shield my employer from abuse. I didn't doubt that John Mackay would follow my suggestions. But I heartened as I pondered my adequacy: I had spent fifteen years as a reporter and had learned a thing or two about the human beast. If anyone could sift through these requests, a veteran reporter could.

I was soon to discover that John Mackay's charity had woven through the life of the city. Men and women and children alike have enjoyed his largesse, and many is the man who blesses John Mackay in his prayers. As I write this, he is industriously expanding his Postal Telegraph Company in New York, and I can only trust that he will forgive his confidential secretary of thirty-some years past if I share a few of these things. His passion for anonymous charity makes him admirable among philanthropists.

I discovered in his ledgers that he was sending a monthly $500 check to the sisters' hospital in Virginia City. That he had enabled about two thousand people, made homeless and destitute by the fire, to leave the city on the Virginia & Truckee, their passage free. He had rebuilt St. Mary's in the Mountains, making it the landmark church so beloved by that city today. One day, when he encountered a barefoot boy weeping in snow, he gave the child five dollars for boots—and thus was born another of his charities. He bought boots for hundreds, maybe thousands, of barefoot Comstock boys.

His books contained countless "loans," which were, in fact, gifts, and it pleased me that some had been faithfully repaid. Let any man be injured in the mines, and Mackay was at hand to pay the hospital and doctor. If a miner died of accident or disease, there was Mackay, paying for the funeral and materially assisting the widow and children.

All of this earned only scorn from James Fair, who considered

Mackay daft, soft, and reckless. At the height of his fortunes, Mackay drove himself about town in an ancient black buggy, while Fair had himself driven in the handsomest carriage money could buy, with liveried coachmen. In the winters, little boys loved to hook onto Mackay's buggy and get themselves a free sled ride upslope, while Fair's footmen beat off the children.

John Mackay was not without a certain wry humor when it came to all this. "I have a sensational story for the press," he said one day. "Tell them that Jim Fair has donated a box of apples to the orphanage in Carson."

Thus it was that I interviewed schemers and pleaders. I soon found myself able to distinguish between a widow in desperate need and a cadger looking for an angle. But often I took those stories home with me, fretted them through the night while Catherine worried about me, and came to a hard decision in the morning. A widow got her mite. An injured miner got capital to buy a saloon. A schemer who wanted Mackay to join him in cornering the supply of mercury got the door.

My other occupation in Mr. Mackay's employ was escorting visitors through the mines. The Bonanza Firm had always invited investors and speculators to see the works for themselves. The crush of visitors often slowed production and was absorbing so much of Mackay's time that he turned over most of that to me. So the man reluctant to plunge deep into the dark bowels of the earth became the escort of hundreds, if not thousands, of investors.

They came from all over the world: East Coast magnates in gilded private cars drawn up the long slope by the Virginia & Truckee, Russian nobles, English dukes, French royalty, Wall Street financiers, and San Francisco princes such as Charles Crocker. Car after car they came, and usually I was anointed to show them about. The most demanding of them insisted that Mackay or Fair take them, but Mackay would plead various excuses and turn them over to me.

They strained his considerable patience, and when they crossed a certain line—which they frequently did—he told me, quietly, to see them to the *newest* diggings. That was a signal for a little fun.

I would take my assorted magnates, artistes, poets, governors, merchants, dukes, counts, and tycoons to a special visitors' changing room, where they could garb themselves in a mining jumper, pullover trousers, felt hat, and boots—if they chose. Many didn't, supposing they could wander about that subterranean hell in their broadcloth suits, starched white shirts, cravats, polished shoes, and waistcoats and return to the surface as dapper as when they left it.

"It'll be hot," I warned. "Your clothing will be soaked. You can leave it here in the lockers and wear what we provide."

But they weren't about to heed a lackey, which is how many viewed me. In such cases, I would shepherd them onto the lift, tell them to hang on during the long, sickening plunge, and escort them to the very bottom level of the shafts, where the moist, foul heat smacked them with brutal force. From the dripping vestibule I would lead them relentlessly through the hottest drifts, past miners drinking ice water while they rested forty-five minutes out of each hour, past rivers of water so hot they could swiftly boil an egg, through steam that materialized around the air vents, past rock too hot to touch with bare hands.

On the rare occasions when I was required to escort a woman, I sent word ahead, because the miners worked in their underdrawers, any additional clothing making them all the more miserable. But nearly all of my visitors were men, and their flinty mission was to assess with their own mistrusting eyes what lay in the pits. They rarely took samples. After a few minutes they were so boiled, so wilted, inside their soaked suits that all they could think of was hurrying the visit along.

The effect of these plunges into fierce cauldrons was to hasten the trips, and ere long they would be begging me to take them topside, professing that they had seen all they wished to see. But I took my time. When the Bonanza Firm wanted to sweat some of its obstreperous guests, I made sure they were sweated. But that happened only rarely.

I myself learned to leave my street clothes behind, wear some light cottons into the pits, and shower afterward. But the mining tours always enervated me. I marveled that miners would willingly mine in such circumstances, but they did, and that was one of many reasons that John Mackay watched over them as a faithful shepherd, and watched over Virginia City as well.

CHAPTER 5 4

 cannot explain my continuing love of Virginia City. Nor can I explain why Catherine shared it or why we reared our children on the barren and forbidding slope of an arid peak.

It became the vogue in those days to take the Virginia & Truckee to Washoe Meadows for a picnic day at Sandy Bowers's mansion, where Comstock children could see emerald grass, carpets of flowers, stately pines, and laughing creeks. Few of them had even seen such things, and they marveled at a vegetated and watered world.

What did Virginia City have that the rest of the world didn't? I suppose it was an attitude. There we were, isolated and apart, even though the railroad connected us with silver rails to the outside. There we were, surrounded by stony slopes so hostile to life, so devoid of beauty and grace, that we instinctively drew close, gathered in our saloons, joined every imaginable club or society, attended every performance of every troupe that alighted at Piper's rebuilt opera house, drank more spirits per capita than anywhere else on earth, gambled recklessly on the whole panoply of Comstock mines, most of which were sucker bait, and shrugged off disasters as part of the life of a mining town.

But that doesn't account for it, either. Sensible people fled. The wives of most of the superintendents and speculators and directors of the mines had removed to the shores of the Pacific, where they could enjoy all the amenities of civilized life. Mrs. Mackay fled to Europe.

Maybe it was the humor. We had a way of distilling comedy from every calamity and reducing tribulation to the thousand stories that swirled through the saloons each day. Maybe it was the bonds we forged, isolated as we were. We had a way of helping one another. The unions offered to the miners security, help and hospitalization in times of trouble, and comfort on the job. Maybe it was a certain pride. No low-down speculators and skunks in San Francisco were going to break the backs of our mines and our economy. Maybe it was the sheer energy we all radiated.

Money abounded. In that year of eighteen and seventy-six two mines were paying rich dividends while scores of others were sinking shafts and hunting new bonanzas, using cash garnered from assessing the shares. Even though new people flooded in and could find no jobs, the town flourished.

Eventually we rebuilt our burned area, macadamized the streets using rubble from the mine dumps, lit our streets with gas lamps, added a second water line to the Sierras to accommodate the mounting demand for freshwater, and imported fine foods from everywhere, so that our restaurants boasted the best cuisine in the United States.

We had grown cosmopolitan. The Irish were especially numerous, as were the Cornish and other Englishmen, but we had our complement of citizens from most every country on earth, especially China. These people worked in the pits, opened shops, became skilled artisans, supplied produce or ice or firewood, and sometimes fed our vices. The ladies down on D Street made that quarter the most cosmopolitan of all.

The newspapers were jovial. They outdid each other to provide the comic anecdote, praise the great city, and boast of our monthly production of ores, which now scaled improbable heights, and rarely had a negative word to say about anything.

I once proposed to Catherine that we remove to San Francisco because I could continue as Mr. Mackay's private secretary as easily there as on the Comstock.

"Why?" she asked.

"Opera, climate, trees, flowers, rain, seafood, libraries, comforts . . ."

"But San Francisco would swallow us up."

I pondered that, uncertain what she meant. Maybe it was simply that a resident of Virginia City possessed a certain cachet, a certain reputation, that was the envy of lesser mortals in great, anonymous cities.

And so we stayed, Catherine delighting in our giddy life as much as I did. San Francisco might offer flowers and mild weather and more amenities, but we felt we were in the center of the universe. Maybe we in Virginia City stayed there because we had banished boredom from our lives, along with doubt and despair, the quiet vices of city people. We entertained a little, especially my old newspaper friends, and our dinners out and theater trips were usually foursomes.

But early in eighteen and seventy-seven an acrimonious stockholders' meeting of the Consolidated Virginia sent shocks through me, and I suspected that the idyllic moment on the Comstock had passed and would not return. That proved to be correct.

The great boom and bust of Comstock shares the previous year had wounded large numbers of Californians and disrupted the entire West Coast economy. There were more and more who laid the blame on the Bonanza Firm, and gradually the very men who had been the darlings of Fate were considered the demons who had ruined California. The *San Francisco Chronicle,* once the stoutest defender of the bonanza partners, redoubled its vitriol, perhaps because the de Youngs, who owned it, had lost badly during the wild gyrations of the mining stocks. Worse, that a disgruntled stockholder named Squire P. Dewey was threatening to sue, which he eventually did. He employed any handy switch to lash at Mr. Mackay and Mr. Flood and, with his allies at the *Chronicle,* unleashed such abuse that both partners grieved, although neither Fair nor O'Brien cared one way or another.

No sooner had that burden fallen on us than other troubles crowded in, among them rising unemployment that left numerous Comstockians cold, hungry, and desperate. These were largely the transients who had arrived looking for a chance to get rich, and now as winter advanced they roamed the streets, haggard and penniless, unable to find jobs or shelter or food. The relief committee swiftly exhausted its resources. The mining unions helped as much as they could, at least among the argonaut brotherhood. In the midst of plenty, peak production, a deluge of dividends, we had an army of paupers.

It fell to Mr. Mackay, the burden of keeping people from starving, and he sent me around to grocers, saying that he would foot the bill for anyone genuinely hungry and desperate and unsheltered. He cautioned me to keep his charity anonymous at all costs, so I simply informed grocers and bakers and butchers and cordwood and coal merchants that a benefactor would feed and warm the needy. They knew who it was, of course, but kept their counsel, and the city's hungry were well fed. I presented Mr. Mackay with bills totaling three-thousand a month during those times. He studied them keenly, perhaps looking to see whether any grocer was padding his accounts, and then paid without a quibble. A man could be fed for two bits a day, so Mr. Mackay was supporting a small army during those bad times.

Early in my employment with him I had come to understand that I was working for an extraordinary man whose penetrating gaze, quiet manner, sobriety, determination, and courage set him apart. Perhaps that is the usual attitude of confidential secretaries and such admiration may be much exaggerated in most cases. But mine was no ordinary case, and Mr. Mackay was no ordinary mortal.

The pressures on him grew, especially when the Bonanza Firm began purchasing substantial interests in most of the producing mines on the Comstock and began sinking exploratory shafts well east of the old works. The staggering burden of running all of them sometimes stretched Mr. Mackay thin. And once in a while his hot temper surfaced, usually in a burst of cussing that startled those who thought of him as a sober-minded, well-spoken man whose hallmark was a judicious tongue.

He had come to despise speculators and manipulators and told me over and over that he was a mining man, not a stock jobber, and he wanted only to be left alone to develop his mines. I suspect he wasn't entirely happy with Flood, who kept plowing the firm's cash into Comstock shares at exactly the wrong moments, buying into mines at their peaks, and unloading them when the fevered speculation broke and the stocks slipped toward oblivion. But he said nothing, at least in my presence, and I admired his forbearance when it came to the firm's own tribulations.

"Henry, slow down the charity," he said one day, and I wondered about that. But later he questioned me sharply about all the supplicants I was turning away.

I will always remember those years with Mr. Mackay as the time we enjoyed the theater. Not a show or play or musicale opened at Piper's but that we saw it, sometimes more than once, and often from Mackay's box, which nearly overhung the stage. Mr. Mackay had the theater bug, had befriended John Piper, and ended up subsidizing the losers while Piper pocketed the profits from the winners. Not a bad deal for the impresario.

But John Mackay loved the footlights and counted the cost as nothing compared to the sheer delight he received from hobnobbing with these performers and watching them from his box. Often he included Catherine and me, so we watched the great Modjeska, Edwin Booth, Lotta Crabtree, and so many others and had the chance to mix with them afterward in the green room. That was simply a perquisite of working for Mr. Mackay, but it delighted Catherine and made us feel we were living in the center of the whole world. I don't suppose I've ever met a man more stagestruck than Mr. Mackay.

Much later I discovered that he had lent various performers large sums—they were an improvident lot whose fortunes rose and fell—and usually got it back from them, though he had lent larger sums to assorted businessmen and gotten little of it back, even from those who could well afford to repay.

What a whirl life became in that glittering city! We never lacked entertainment, and a dozen prospects awaited us each evening, ranging from balls and concerts to lectures and dinners with friends at the world's best restaurants. I look back upon that period as one in which I had yet to achieve true intimacy with my bride, because the whirligig of Comstock life spun us about so recklessly that we hadn't even discovered what qualities we possessed. I supposed that would come later, when the Comstock turned stark and Piper's went dark.

I should have known, though. Mr. Mackay told me early in the year that the Consolidated Virginia would not lift as many tons of ore or earn so much as it did in eighteen and seventy-six unless a new lode was uncovered. And even after relentless new exploration not one mine other than the Consolidated Virginia and California was paying a dividend. And yet I pushed my mind past such obvious realities, whistling my way past the gravestones.

These things had not escaped the brokers and speculators in San Francisco, who were bearish by nature and never more so than now, driving my stocks lower and lower. Both mines had again split their stock five for one, thus multiplying my shares, and I was getting two dollars a share each month, so I scarcely noticed. Virginia was still rebuilding; the new International Hotel was nearing completion. How could a town decline if it was still expanding at a breathtaking pace? And when the mighty California was just reaching full production?

So I fooled myself. Virginia City was feverish.

CHAPTER 55

I discovered that Dan De Quille was in the hospital again, and I resolved to visit him. I hadn't seen much of him, in part because his periodic bouts of drunkenness took him out of my usual circle of friends, especially since my marriage. The man born William Wright had fallen a long way since the early days, and the *Enterprise* periodically suspended him, though so far it had not fired him. The paper simply waited him out, and when he was sobered up—usually after a hospital stay—he might be a useful correspondent until the next debauch.

His carousing companion for years, Alf Doten, had eventually married, and the initial effect of that was to improve Dan De Quille's own conduct. With no comrade in debauchery at hand, he sometimes worked. I don't quite know when I realized that Dan was a sick and desperate man, but probably well before Catherine and I were married. I knew, late in my reporting days, that I was producing most of the *Enterprise*'s mining news and that De Quille was scarcely about.

But the Big Bonanza seemed to have revived him, and for a while there he seemed to have conquered his demons. Not only had he been inspired by the sudden flows of energy wrought by the bonanza, but he began producing those comic masterpieces once again. I remember one, in eighteen and seventy-four, that tickled my fancy and led me to believe that old Dan was in rare and good form. As usual, he spun a story that sounded so logical and persuasive that a credulous reader could plow all the way through it without grasping that it was a great leg-pull.

The one I loved, and still do, was called "The New Rock of Horeb," and it purported to be an account, discovered in the archives of the Pacific Coast Pioneers, about a party that had headed to the goldfields in eighteen and fifty-two, only to run into desperate circumstances.

According to this imaginative account, a party of young men signed on with a wagon owned by a cantankerous old gent named Abe Skinner, who suffered an acute case of dropsy that had blown him up to the size of a hogshead. One of the party was a doctor, whom Abe had included to treat his malady en route.

At Skinner's insistence, they took a shortcut through the wastes of Nevada and ended up in a parched land, dying of thirst, their horses dead, far from help, within hours of expiring. It was then that the doctor realized that right there, in those stony wastes, they had five or six gallons of water on hand, but it would take the combined efforts of the dying party to get it.

In short, the doctor proposed to tap Skinner. The very thought horrified the others, but desperate men do desperate things, so they laid violent hand on the vicious old man, tapped him, filled a barrel with five or six gallons, sampled the awful stuff, found it palatable, and supposed they were safe. But Skinner's response was to perch himself on the barrel containing his own water, armed with a six-gun, and hold off the newly thirsting party until they contrived to ambush him for the rest of his water.

It was one of the wildest and most imaginative stories I had read, a masterpiece comparable to the best of Twain's work.

De Quille, during his sober moments, had started to come to me for mining news, since he could no longer reach Fair or Mackay, who were less and less available to the press. So I would see him now and then— but in truth, the *Chronicle* and the *Gold Hill News* were regularly scooping the *Enterprise.*

De Quille had spent a year or so in the East writing a book about the Big Bonanza, a guest of Mark Twain in Hartford. With Twain looking over Dan's shoulder and inspiring him and offering countless suggestions about marketing the book, Dan had stayed sober and industrious long enough to write of the bonanza, including numerous sketches of life on the Washoe and concluding his book with the big fire of 1875. Twain arranged publication, and De Quille drifted back to the Washoe certain he would soon have a fortune. Wasn't Virginia City the talk of the nation? Wasn't its Big Bonanza the most absorbing event in years? Wasn't the promotion by Mark Twain's own publisher a guarantee of the book's success?

But it never happened. Not only did the book sell poorly on the East Coast, which just didn't understand the lively life in the world's premier mining town, but it also did badly on the Comstock for unfathomable reasons. That must have cut Dan De Quille's heart out of him, because after he got back in seventy-six he sank into virtual uselessness, constantly being suspended by Goodwin and getting himself dried out in hospitals. It was a sad case.

I hiked over to County Hospital, determined to cheer him up and try to reconnect with my old newspapering friend. I hadn't been in the Old Magnolia for months and suddenly hungered for the camaraderie of reporters. I found Dan out of bed and staring blankly out the window, which opened on the Gould & Curry hoisting works. One glance told me he wasn't well; he'd drunk himself into another of his sicknesses, and only a long drying out, good food, and respite from his bachelor ways could bring him around.

"Oh, Henry, it's you," he said.

"I heard you were here. How are you doing?"

"I drink too much." He smiled wanly. "Beats writing for a living."

"Does it?"

"One of my daughters is coming out to stay with me. They're all grown-up, you know."

The news faintly astonished me, but time had flown by and my perception of his family was a decade old. Once, years earlier, he had gone back to Iowa and tried to settle there with his wife and children but found life impossibly sedate, if not boring, and soon was back at his post on the *Enterprise*. He couldn't stand the Midwest but never really wanted his brood to butt in on his carefree life there in Virginia. And all those years he had faithfully sent them a monthly check, supporting his distant brood.

"Which one, Dan?"

"Mell. She's twenty."

Mell Wright was his oldest daughter. The idea that she had reached twenty astonished me. Where had my own life gone? "She'll make a good companion for you, Dan."

"Make me behave, I guess."

The conversation tripped along, and Dan did not spare himself. Newsmen were realists, and if a man could call himself a drunk, then he could see the world with a clear eye. But Dan soon veered the talk away from himself.

"How are you doing now that Mackay owns you?"

I started to tell Dan that no one owned me but changed that. I knew exactly what they had all been saying in the newsroom of the *Territorial Enterprise;* I'd been bought. I suppose they were right in a fashion, but they were ignoring the reason why I left: their paper had been bought and was regularly saying preposterous things about Senator Sharon and malevolent things about a very good man named Mackay.

"I think John Mackay's less demanding than Judge Goodwin or Rollin Daggett," I replied. "I can't think of anyone on the Comstock, way back to the time you and I were just getting going, who's been fairer with stockholders and the press."

"He's pretty square. Now Fair, that's another case."

For a while there the talk glimmered on, almost like the old days, but Dan De Quille wasn't the same, and some ineffable sadness afflicted him. I wished he hadn't made that devil's bargain, keeping a family fifteen hundred miles away. I ached to tell him to bring the whole family out and start over—that's all he needed. But I couldn't summon the words.

The shocking thing to me was age. We were both getting on. I would soon have my first child, but I was old enough to be a grandfather. De Quille and I had squandered our adult lives there on the Comstock, and I wondered once again what necromancy held us there.

In a subdued mood I left him and hiked over to the Old Magnolia, needing to draw my friends around me. Daggett was there, systematically wrecking his decanter of Steamboat gin, so I parked myself beside him at the bar. He eyed me, gestured, and I poured one for myself.

"Haven't seen you for a spell," I said.

"All the better for me," he retorted. The insult meant I was on a good footing with him.

"I just saw Dan," I said.

"And what's your verdict?"

"No verdict."

"I have a theory." He paused, quaffed mightily, and let the Steamboat percolate through his shapeless carcass. "The best thing that happened to Sam Clemens was that he got out of here right in front of a warrant. The worst thing that happened to William Wright is that no warrant ever pursued him."

That sounded intriguing, so I sipped and waited for the editor to unburden himself.

"You don't even ask me why. You go to work for a plutocrat, and six months later you've lost your reporting instinct."

I ignored the jibe. Daggett was like that.

"What did that warrant do for Sam? He went to San Francisco, worked for assorted papers, learned to survive, peddled pieces to *Golden Era*, wrote his famous jumping frog story, began his monologues—after stealing the art from Artemus Ward—and then began writing, including *Roughing It* with its chapters about life here and in San Francisco and his trip to Hawaii. Neither thee nor I are in it, which I take as a mortal offense, but that doesn't apply to my point, which is that the emerging Mark Twain soon was a national figure, while old De Quille, who's the real master if you want my opinion, is entombed here and probably always will be.

"You see, he pulled it off. He got himself a family, children, wife, and all, but kept them in Iowa while he caroused. That's clever of him but also his tragedy. I'll tell you right now, Henry, that if Dan De Quille had gotten booted out of the Washoe instead of Twain, he'd be the toast of the nation. So it was all Fate."

"I don't know that I agree with all that, Rollin," I replied. "Dan never had Twain's drive or his yearning to be somebody. Talent he has, but what good is it when his carousing means more to him than a literary reputation?"

"Quibble, quibble, Stoddard," Daggett retorted, and I was reminded that Daggett was not exactly driven either.

We drank and talked and it was good to be with an old scribbler. As far as I could tell, Daggett didn't even hold my job or income against me.

CHAPTER 56

hat strange summer of eighteen and seventy-seven Mr. Mackay suddenly inquired whether I still held shares of the Consolidated Virginia. I assured him I did and intended to hang on because the dividends were good.

"Henry, it's time to sell them," he said. "Flood's selling most of ours. We're selling most of our California shares also."

That didn't surprise me. Crosscuts and winzes at the 1,650-foot level of the Consolidated Virginia revealed the bottom of the Big Bonanza and a huge "horse" of porphyry in the middle that further reduced the amount of ore. It had not been secret. The Bonanza firm had always made its operations public. What's more, spies abounded in the pit, paid by speculators, brokers, and enemies of the firm.

"Sell everything?"

"At least half."

"That cuts into dividends."

"Yes, and for how long? Unless we hit new ore . . ."

"Is that what you're doing?"

"We're hedging. Jim Flood's buying the controlling stock of the other mines one by one. We'll run deep shafts along the third tier, well east of the old works. If the bonanza formation exists anywhere on the lode, we'll find it."

That was incredibly ambitious, and I marveled. "Should I own a few shares of everything?"

"Wouldn't hurt if you can stand the assessments. We're going to assess for all that exploration."

"I'll think about it. And thanks, Mr. Mackay."

But his mind had already turned to other things.

I didn't sell and I didn't buy. Eventually I paid the price for that. No doubt the reader will again rebuke me for my blindness. But hindsight is the cheapest sort of wisdom, and I pay no heed to those who tax me with my mistakes.

What matters is foresight. At that time, there was good reason to believe that systematic exploration would yield more bonanzas along the same geographic line as the Big Bonanza. The firm was spending millions doing just that, driving shafts well east of the old tier and going deeper than ever before. It had struck incredible riches doing just that, and why should anyone doubt that it could be done again?

Virginia City was a gambling town. We bet on the mines, the managements, and sometimes sheer wildcat luck. By the middle of that year, the whole burnt area had been rebuilt better than ever, with structures that would last for generations. Everywhere were banks, saloons, drygoods merchants, clothiers, and brokerages, a solid phalanx of them along C Street and more on B and D Streets. From every hoisting building smoke issued from the boiler stacks.

Over three thousand of the world's finest miners were employed either sinking new shafts or in the bonanza mines. Now and then they found pockets of good ore, and with each strike hope bloomed and the stocks rattled upward again no matter what the bears and cynics could do. Here was a city and district a quarter the size of San Francisco, the largest in Nevada, its banks as solid as any in California.

People dressed handsomely, the men in black broadcloth, the attire of both sexes the wonder of the world. We thought nothing of it, smoked the best Havanas, sipped the finest claret, and supposed it would never stop. I could see the virtue of hedging a bit, but not throwing away my chances a week or month or quarter before another fabulous Golconda was uncovered. The patient and canny Irishmen were spending *eight million dollars* to drive shafts and drifts from the northernmost extreme of the Comstock to its southernmost boundaries. That sort of methodical searching had never before been undertaken because of its enormous cost.

The city brimmed with people who expected to get rich, if not in a week, then in a month or so. The Big Bonanza had lured them there. The famous Comstock wage, four dollars an eight-hour day, drew hundred of miners from California, where the wage was one third of that. They jammed the city, spent their last two bits in saloons, and drifted away.

What I am saying, reader, is that there was no earthly reason for Henry Stoddard to suppose that just one year later the city would plunge into an abyss and never recover. And who would imagine that, except for a good though limited strike in the Ophir, all that exploration would come to naught and not a ton of additional ore would surface because of it?

So Catherine and I delighted in our life in the most brilliant of American cities, attending Piper's Opera House whenever a new troupe arrived, dining at the new International, eating in restaurants that were the envy of New York. We saw several Hamlets, done by Edwin Booth, Lawrence Barrett, John McCullough, and Tom Keene, and when we tired of Shakespeare there was always *Camille,* or *Lucretia Borgia,* or *Ticket-of-Leave Man,* or *Led Astray,* or *Rip Van Winkle,* starring Joe Jefferson. And if we wearied of drama, there were always Gilbert and Sullivan companies, bringing *The Pirates of Penzance* and other standards.

I must not forget the minstrel shows, especially Haverley's Mastodon Minstrels, forty blacks who captivated us all. Piper's was never dark. If no troupe was on hand, an orchestra was or the house was rented for a political rally. And I must not forget the lecturers who filled its thousand seats: Henry Ward Beecher, Henry George, Col. Robert Ingersoll, and even the famous phrenologist Prof. O. S. Fowler. Often Mr. Mackay gave us his own box, so we saw all these performances virtually hanging over the footlights, and afterward we headed for the green room, where we met these notables. Oh, those were the days, and the city and the lights and the universe was ours! Was there ever so glittering a city?

On occasion I escorted these thespians and lecturers into the mines. The showgirls, trimly dressed in pantaloons, boots, and felt hats, never failed to stop production while the miners gawked, but Mr. Mackay didn't seem to mind. He loved theater and music and would do anything for the performers who paraded through our fair city.

The arrival of a troupe of beauteous women occasioned celebrations in Virginia, and usually the route along Union Street to the theater was lined with cheering miners—and even Henry Stoddard—as the carriages passed by, each one brimming with the fairest of fair ladies, exchanging compliments and jests with the happy gallants who gathered to glimpse the flower of the fair sex. Bring in a coachload of beauties and John Piper had a sellout, for Virginia was still two-thirds male.

We continued to enjoy this dazzling life until the time Catherine chose to stay at home and await the birth of our firstborn. She glowed, and seemed filled with unearthly beauty, her eyes throwing light and her spirits so buoyant that her mere presence beside me set me soaring. During those weeks we achieved perfect intimacy, our union borne along by love. Our good doctor, Melville Bliss, found nothing amiss, and we had only to await the great day.

Numerous of our friends showered Catherine with baby things, and the consensus was that she would produce a girl. Whatever the child might be, I was prepared to love and nurture it to the best of my abilities. Catherine had been through all this before and took the discomfort in stride. I never heard her complain, even through periods of nausea and backache. The look in her eyes told me that this was what she lived for; this was the purpose of our union and its fulfillment.

We arranged with neighbors to take care of our older children when the moment came, so Catherine might be free of care for a week or two. I would move into one of the children's rooms for the duration, leaving Catherine our bed for the closeting. We contracted with our midwife, Hannah Daley, and after that all we could do was wait for nature to choose the moment. We knew only that we could expect a child in the middle of October.

Mr. Mackay moved into the International Hotel, taking a suite on its top floor, which perforce became my office as well. That suited me, for I was closer to home and had all of C Street's saloons and restaurants on hand. My employer divided his time between Virginia and San Francisco, and it often was my duty to accompany him. So I was a frequent traveler and a frequent guest at the magnificent Palace Hotel in that great city. We would board the Virginia & Truckee, transfer at Reno, take the steamer at Sacramento, and arrive at our destination in time for breakfast and business.

The *Chronicle*'s constant assaults on the Bonanza firm worried Mr. Mackay more and more. The paper was now blaming Mr. Mackay for all that was going wrong with California's economy, no matter how irrational it seemed to us. Worse, the tone had turned vicious and personal and the assaults came closer and closer to damaging Mr. Mackay's good name.

"I don't think it matters what I do or say; they're going to assail me no matter what. I suppose it's a price one pays for wealth," he said one day.

"Shall I answer them? I could say much in your defense."

"Not a word. I don't believe in that sort of thing. Let there be silence and let my conduct speak for itself."

"A list of your charitable contributions would help, Mr. Mackay."

"That would be the last thing I'd resort to," he growled, genuinely displeased with me. He had never trumpeted his generosity, didn't believe in it, and wouldn't stoop to it. But the reality was that he was giving away tens of thousands of dollars a month and calling these handouts loans to salve the pride of the indigent, and all the while doubting that charitable gifts did much good for the recipients, who rarely benefited from the funds or grew past their weaknesses.

The telegram that reached me at the Palace October 14 informed me that Catherine had begun labor, Mrs. Daley was present, and all appeared to be well. There would be no need for me to rush back to Virginia. I fretted, regretting my absence, and informed Mr. Mackay.

"Go back, Henry," he said. "I can get along just fine. I'll make use of Jim Flood's staff."

I took him up on it, caught the steamer, boarded a California Central train, slept through the night, transferred to the V & T at Reno, and began the last fifty-odd miles back to my bride. At Reno another wire reached me, saying I was the father of a girl and all was well except for a little bleeding, which Mrs. Daley had stanched.

So it was a girl after all I sat in the V & T coach treasuring the news written on that yellow flimsy.

But when, at last, I reached my home, I found a tearful Mrs. Daley at the door, along with Dr. Bliss, who painfully told me my bride, my darling, was dead of a sudden utterly unstoppable hemorrhage. And the infant lived.

We had been married less than one year.

CHAPTER 57

I t is said that memory is merciful and we blot out the things most painful to us. But mine was not merciful. Now, after the passage of decades, I remember that vista of horror as if it were only just happening.

The midwife fled the parlor, unable to cope, but Dr. Bliss resolutely sat me down on the settee and began to pace, his exposition of terrible events coming in spasms.

"She called me at dawn . . . bleeding . . . couldn't stop. Packed in towels, didn't even slow down. Been a little at birth, an opened vein, torn . . . she'd checked Mrs. Stoddard at midnight, sleeping peacefully; at dawn your wife stirred, she wanted to nurse . . . then blood, too much, too fast."

I sat numbly, absorbing this even though my mind seemed a thousand miles distant. Mrs. Daley had sent Peter, Jr., for help. It took too long. My dear Catherine soon lay in a crimson pool, her flesh waxen, his heart racing.

"Wanted to cauterize, last-ditch, but couldn't even find the hemorrhage, couldn't clamp on anything . . ."

"Did she say anything at the last?"

"Yes. 'Tell Henry . . .' That was it."

" 'Tell Henry I love him.' I have that much, anyway."

"Child's a healthy girl. I got her over to Mrs. Trenoweth, two blocks, patient of mine, wet-nursing a son; the baby's fine. You want to see her?"

"No."

I suppose some readers will fault me for that. I did not want to see the baby, at least not just then. My heart cried for Catherine, and I had little interest in the infant. Even after all these years I know I did the right thing, staying right there.

They took me upstairs at my insistence, but reluctantly. I had expected to find Catherine in a sea of blood—bloody sheets, counterpane, pillows, piles of crimsoned linen. But they had taken all that out, thank God, and I beheld only a waxen image of my bride, still and silent, her eyes closed, her face toward the ceiling, a fresh comforter over her. I did not know how to say good-bye. I did not even know what to do, what arrangements to make. I would have to do something about a funeral.

"She was a lovely and beautiful woman, Henry," Bliss said. "It is a great loss, for all of us, for her children, for you."

"The children—"

"They are next door. We have not summoned them, knowing you were coming."

"Get them. I must tell them."

Then my heart did break. Peter and Caroline had lost both father and mother and had only a dubious acquaintance with their new stepfather, who had adopted them. Poor things. Stuck with a lifelong bachelor who knew nothing about rearing the young. I feared for them and for me. An infant and two bereft children in the middle of their school years. I felt a weight so oppressive that I could scarcely breathe.

How transitory is life. Lying there was Catherine, young, vital, at the very pinnacle of her life, suddenly and forever gone. I stared at her silence, willing her to live, to breathe, but she had departed, and that cooling flesh no longer held Catherine, or even a memory of Catherine. For Catherine had gone away.

We are born, live, and die, scarcely choosing any moment of it all. How fragile and transitory are hopes and dreams, loves and passions, cities and empires. I have no great insights about death and the beyond, and my views are quite conventional. I'm just an ordinary man, bewildered by loss. The love of my life had died; her young children were as needful of her grace and warmth as I. We would eventually remember her in her glory, vibrant and warm and giving, the light in her hazel eyes as she beheld those she loved and nurtured. I would remember the gentleness of her hand, which often spoke to me in ways that words could not.

I turned away, unable to bear that sight, trying to hide the tears that flooded up.

"I'm sorry," Dr. Bliss said.

I felt his hand on my shoulder, drawing me away, comforting me. I stumbled down the stairs, too confused to plan or cope. The doctor said nothing but puttered about, not wanting to leave me in the midst of crisis. I stood numbly in the parlor, frozen in grief, until Mrs. Daley shepherded the children through the front door. They seemed so cheerful, so unaware, that I was at a loss for words. I addressed them without preamble and brusquely.

"Peter and Caroline, your mother's gone. She died this morning," I said, not knowing how I summoned the courage to say it.

"Gone away?" asked Peter.

"Gone to God in heaven."

Peter looked panicky. I saw tears slide from the eyes of silent Caroline, but I could not comfort her. I could not comfort myself. Mrs. Daley wrapped an arm about the girl.

"If you'd like to see your mother for the last time, we'll go upstairs," I said. "We'll say good-bye together. We're together and you'll always have a father to care for you."

They stared mutely, only then comprehending that they had been orphaned. They were too young to grasp it fully, but soon enough they would weep.

We went up the stairs hand in hand, stared, and then down the stairs into our catacombs.

The next hours were fraught with pain and desolation. Dr. Bliss stayed awhile, until he felt certain I could cope. Then he executed a death certificate, stating the cause as hemorrhage following parturition. Mrs. Daley stayed on and mothered the children. I knew I had several tasks but was not up to them at first, until Mrs. Daley lit a fire in the stove and served me tea.

I had not prepared for death, having put off all such matters and supposed that it would stay away from me for many years. Now I needed to make funeral arrangements, notify her relatives, buy a burial plot, consult her will, which I knew left all her worldly goods to her children but listed only the first two. There would be few worldly goods. I would need to find a lawyer. But I did none of these things.

Instead, I asked Mrs. Daley to watch over my numb children and sought from her the address of the wet nurse. I did not want to leave the house, my children, the silent cold flesh in our bedroom. But it was time to see my firstborn. The sun shone warmly, belying my grief as I hiked south and then east to the proper door. Mrs. Trenoweth met me, took me in with one sweep of glowing brown eyes, and nodded. I entered a genteel parlor with Currier and Ives prints on the wall and brown horsehair furniture. The sturdy woman reappeared with a tiny, fretful infant, her face hardly larger than my hand, her flesh red. She was not a beautiful child, but she was mine, and probably the only one I would ever have. Mrs. Trenoweth smiled sadly and handed the swaddled infant to me. She had no weight. She barely moved in my arms.

"I am sorry, Mr. Stoddard. I've met Mrs. Stoddard a time or two, socials, you know. . . . I have enough milk for two babies, and she'll be fine. Ah, what shall I call this wee thing?"

A name.

I held this little thing, this child whose passage into life took Catherine from me. I did not love that little creature, at least not then, for she was the source of my sorrow, or so I imagined. Later I realized that was wrong. She had not caused the death of my beloved and was utterly innocent.

"I don't know," I said.

"If ye don't mind, I'd like to call her Catherine," said Mrs. Trenoweth.

"No!"

"Very well, sir. But she is so sweet an infant I thought you would like to name her for the one you loved."

I wept and rocked the infant in my arms while Mrs. Trenoweth stood quietly, her hand on my arm.

"Yes, yes, she must be Catherine," I said. "Catherine Iliff Stoddard."

"Oh, Mr. Stoddard, that pleases me so much."

We visited a little more, and she assured me of her devotion. I asked her what she would charge, and she simply tossed the question back at me. "Whatever you wish to pay me, sir," she replied.

I thought of the toil, the night feedings, the diapers, the baths, the suckling, and said I would reward her well. Old bachelors knew little of such things. "I will get back to you as soon as I can," I said lamely.

She smiled gently and touched my hand.

A squall arose from another room, and I knew my hostess was being summoned by her own infant.

I handed her the child, and my arms suddenly felt empty, as bereft as my heart. Mrs. Trenoweth pulled the swaddling blanket about little Catherine in a practiced manner. I noticed, for the first time, two little Trenoweth boys peering from the kitchen.

"I . . . have so much to do," I said, taking leave. "Is there anything you need?"

"Yes. Whatever clothing and diapers Mrs. Stoddard had ready for the arrival of this little sweetheart."

That wrought tears. I bid her good day and promised to send what was needed.

So that was how that October day went. Before it had passed, I had purchased a cemetery lot, arranged for a funeral at the Methodist church, hired an undertaker, purchased a simple casket, because Catherine would have loathed a fancy brass-furnished one, cut a lock of her hair and slipped it in an envelope, and watched the funeral man, Broadbent, and his flunkies carry my beloved down my stairs and through my parlor and out my door and down my walk until Catherine was no longer present in my small dominions.

No sooner had the clop of the black horses faded that afternoon than I received a wire from John Mackay, sharing my grief. And then things started happening and I knew Mr. Mackay's hand was behind them. Relief came for Mrs. Daley, and she was free to leave. The new lady, a Mrs. Torleone, swiftly took charge, feeding the children and preparing tea. Food appeared. Neighbors came. Flowers flowed through my front door. My children were comforted and touched and patted and encouraged. I stayed in the parlor as long as I could, overwhelmed by the great generosity of my employer, and then excused myself and closed the door of the bedroom and lay down, with no one beside me.

· ·

have nothing profound to say about life and death, funerals and grief. I was heartened by the numbers of
friends who attended Catherine's funeral. In her brief
sojourn in Virginia she had made the acquaintance of
so many.

My newspaper friends all came, which pleased me deeply. Judge
Goodwin, Rollin Daggett, Wells Drury, Alf Doten, and most of the compositors, including Fremont Older, who was then making a name for
himself in San Francisco. Denis McCarthy came and even Joe Goodman, all the way from the bay. Mr. Mackay arrived and represented the
Bonanza Firm. Twain wired his condolences, and Senators Sharon and
Jones did not forget me, either. Dan De Quille hovered about, making
himself an instant father to my children, telling them gentle tales and
talking as much as he could about death and loss and grief, reaching
their young hearts and minds in ways I could not, and releasing their
pent-up fears and anguish.

So many people came that I cannot remember them all: Henry
Yerington, John Piper, former governor James Nye, and Adoph Sutro.
They filled the pews and sang the hymns and watched quietly as the
pallbearers, my newspaper friends, carried Catherine to the shining
black hearse, drawn by black dray horses, and then followed out the
long, lonely road.

I had wired the Iliff grandparents of my adopted children and Catherine's New York family, the Taylors. The funeral was fine, more flowers
than I had ever seen amassed in the barrens of the Washoe, and we
buried Catherine in a new plot in the Pioneers Cemetery, down near
Six-Mile Canyon, well east of town. She would rest there forever, her
spirit lost to the naked slopes.

I was especially heartened by the presence of my newspaper colleagues, who came to grieve with me and be with me in my hour of
darkness. They lingered on afterward, coming to the house, sitting quietly, not letting me be alone, and I was moved almost to tears by this
affection. Some of us had been together almost from Virginia City's
inception. I had more beloved friends than I ever knew, and they stood

by me, even though I had left them for a new and more domesticated
life.

The *Enterprise,* the *Chronicle,* and the *Gold Hill News* gave Catherine
long and loving obituaries, and I was pleased. But the sun set on that
October day, and one by one, as the stars popped into the skies, my
guests left, and then we were alone, my children and I and the stranger
keeping house.

Mr. Mackay gave me a fortnight off, and at first I intended to spend
it at home, fearful of disrupting the fragile connections of the children
even more and of course wanting to be close to that strange and wondrous infant at the bosom of Mrs. Trenoweth, my very own daughter.

But I abandoned that in a day or so. There came upon me as vio-
lently as a thunderclap a need for greenery and trees and water, a place
where I could see nature's cycles of life and death. I could not bear the
barren slopes of Sun Mountain or the surrounding bleak mountains,
bereft of life.

So I bundled the children, telling them we wouldn't go far—just a
few hours distant—to a place of love and healing. I told Mrs. Trenoweth
I'd return in a few days and to make sure my daughter lacked nothing.
We boarded a Virginia & Truckee coach and soon arrived in Carson.
There I hired a livery hack and drove the three hours to Genoa, a sleepy
hamlet I knew and loved. It lay hard by the eastern slope of the Sierras,
in a land of grassy meadows, rushing clear creeks, stately pines, and
peaceful farms. It had once been Mormon Station, back in Utah Territorial days, when the Saints catered to travelers on the main branch of
the California Trail. I possessed some hay land there.

I knew of a country inn just off the main street, next to the old
Kinnard home, and there we headed to heal ourselves in the midst of
grass and trees, calves and chickens, crops that grew lustily only to be
scythed down. I assured Caroline and Peter that we would be only a
few hours from home and could return if they wished. But they were
too grief-bound to respond, and I soon realized that they were consumed
by their own helplessness. They were utterly dependent on me, a relative
newcomer in their lives, and had no option but to accept my plans, my
verdicts, my way of life.

We settled there for a while, walked the creeks and irrigation ditches,
roamed through cottonwood groves turning golden, sat under stately
pines, smelled the autumnal air, and studied the corn stubble in the
fields. Winter was coming, like death, but someday spring would arrive,
and then these fields would come alive and the cottonwoods would veil
themselves in lime green and green shoots of new grass would climb
toward the sun.

Neither child cried, though I am sure the nights in particular troubled them. I talked, hoping not to sound like a schoolmaster, about eternal life, the rise and fall of all living things. We talked about winter and death. I told them that right there, in that hamlet, the *Territorial Enterprise* had been born and that it had later moved to Carson City and then up to the new mining camp a few miles away. I told them that all things would live and die and someday Virginia City would die and someday the United States would die and that great empires, like the ancient Roman one, had come and gone, in an eternal cycle of growth and decline.

I listened, too. Caroline insisted that her mother would return. Peter argued, saying she wouldn't. They wanted to know all about death and heaven and the journey of souls, and I couldn't help them much. But mostly they feared I would abandon them—that if I wasn't their real father, they had no hold on me. I replied as best I could, but no words seemed adequate, and I finally said, "Just watch me as the days go by and you'll know that I am as much your father as your real one."

There were bleak periods when the children moped and lingered in the inn, times when they wouldn't eat, but I had expected that. Gradually their spirits lifted. The little farming town with its grasses and trees and creeks was working its spell on them in ways that the arid slopes of Mount Davidson never could.

So the sojourn passed, and I was eager to return to work and to get on with living. We drove back, I settled with the Carson liveryman, and we caught the next train to the Comstock, tugged up the steep grade by Engine 20, the "Tahoe," one of Yerington's new Baldwins.

We returned to a clean, trim house and settled down. I would restore the children to their classrooms the next day. But the temporary housekeeper gave notice and I faced the task of putting some sort of life together for my children. Later, after I saw them to their rooms, I ducked out to visit Mrs. Trenoweth and found my beloved little Catherine asleep, her tiny hands slowly clenching and releasing, her body noticeably larger and smoother, and well. I held the quiet infant for a long and tender while and then surrendered her. It would be months before I could bring her to her own home, but I had blessings to count. Mrs. Trenoweth was a commodious and loving mother, with ample quantities of all that an infant would ever need, including love. Clearly, she loved the little stranger as much as her own.

I paid her a month's wage and returned home, wanting to deal with the pressing problem of finding a permanent housekeeper.

. . . .

CHAPTER 59

I advertised for a housekeeper, knowing that finding one would be difficult in a town in which there were two males for every female. I had but one goal: a woman who could nurture and comfort my children. If she couldn't cook or kept a messy house, I might forgive that, but if she lacked the innate kindness and loving nature I required, it wouldn't matter whether she was a blue ribbon chef; I would not have her.

Various matrons and one old maid responded, and I interviewed them all. The matrons were either widows or women supporting a husband for one reason or another, most frequently injury in the mines. I preferred someone who might live in and be available to sooth a child in the night, and that posed a dilemma.

The maiden lady, a thin and starched woman of fifty or so, with pince-nez and graying wavy hair ferociously disciplined into a bun, caught my eye. She had an unnerving stare that suggested that she was ascertaining whether or not I lived up to her standards. At first blush she scarcely seemed the fountain of maternal love I sought, but my initial impressions began to fade as we visited. Her name was Consuela Wellington.

"I'm closely related to the Duke of Wellington, you know," she said.

I knew that Arthur Wellesley, the Iron Duke and most prominent of the Wellesleys, would have been surprised to discover it, but I held my peace. We are entitled to our small foibles. Had I not started wearing a toupee to conceal my bald head? If I wished to pretend I had a mop of hair, then she could imagine herself to be a relative of a duke whose real name had eluded her.

She had come to Virginia City because she felt like it, and that suggested a daring, wilful nature in an unattached woman. So I introduced her to Peter and Caroline and watched closely.

"Well, my dears, your father is considering me for the position. I couldn't be your mother, but if you give me a chance, I'll be a good substitute for one. That is, if your father employs me. Now the first thing we shall do is stop wallowing. We'll just go along and do grand things, and I'll be here when you need me. I won't ever nag you or ask whether you've done your lessons or made your beds, but if you should incur my displeasure you will know it from my look. If there is a frosty look in my eyes and a compression of my lips, you will know. I am famous for it. Miss Wellington's Look is what it's called. But it never lasts long, and if you smile, you'll make me smile right back."

Something about her pleased the children.

I hired Miss Wellington. I told her about my infant and promised to take her there for an inspection. She, in turn, felt obliged to make her circumstances clear:

"I am a maiden lady by preference, Mr. Stoddard. I've had eleven proposals since arriving in this distinctly undomestic city and turned them all down. I have no taste for what might be called carnality and wish to live on the loftiest and most spiritual plane of existence."

I understood perfectly. Later it dawned on me that I had not even asked her for references. That's the sort she was.

She asked for a large bedroom and said she would be unhappy in a "maid's closet," so I gave her my own room. Catherine's and my room. Actually, that was a relief. Too many sweet and ultimately painful memories in that chamber. So I took the smallest room, quite content.

I planned to watch matters closely, and if the children seemed gloomy or melancholic I would have some private talks with them about Miss Wellington. But I believed I had at last put my life back in order.

Thus I fought my way back to a normal life.

At the beginning of eighteen and seventy-eight Virginia City exuded an aura of permanence and solidity. Mining men and financiers entertained at the rebuilt Washoe Club, the most elegant private accommodations in the West. Prosperous businesses lined the streets. Solid houses, built to last a century, filled the residential neighborhoods. The Virginia & Truckee kept to clockwork schedules, bringing in tourists and supplies and cordwood and hauling ore down to the mills on the river. Adolph Sutro's endless tunnel was almost completed, with head crews boring toward each other and only a quarter of a mile apart. Within a few months the mines would be able to drain themselves—at least down to the 1,600-foot level—out the tunnel, saving vast sums and making low-grade reserves more profitable.

I shared the widespread belief that the city would enjoy another decade of robust life and that it would remain the most exciting place on earth until the turn of the century. So I returned to work for Mr. Mackay buoyed by optimism and a belief in eternal progress. I refused to sell my Consolidated Virginia and California stocks—not yet, not when each of my multiplied shares was paying a solid two-dollar dividend each and every month.

But my employer greeted me with doleful news.

"Henry, for the first time a lawsuit threatens our existence. There are always lawsuits—blackmail, we call them—that go with the territory. Strike a bonanza and sharpers will find a way to pick your pockets in court. We refuse to settle any such suits because settlement is a sign of weakness and invites others to play that vicious game.

"But this new one has us worried."

The suit that concerned him had been filed by Squire P. Dewey, in San Francisco. I remembered that in 1875 Dewey, who had made money in San Francisco real estate, had asked Flood privately whether Consolidated Virginia would pay a dividend after the fire, and Flood had replied that the board would decide that at its next meeting and referred him to the company secretary, who reported to Dewey the amount of cash on hand. Dewey, suspecting that the company would not pay its dividend, sold his stock. But the dividend was paid, the stock rose, and Dewey claimed that Flood was responsible for his losses because the secretary had failed to mention the value of the bullion on hand.

The suit was laughable but for the fact that the de Young brothers, owners of the *San Francisco Chronicle,* got into the act. They, too, had lost in speculating on Comstock shares and had concluded that the Bonanza Firm was at fault. Their editorials grew even more abusive and heated, if that was possible. The paper was going to milk the bonanza partners if it could, allying with Dewey, and launched a vitriolic new assault in March:

"The Bonanza Kings." "Their Splendor Ruined Thousands." "California and Nevada Impoverished to Enrich Four Men." "Plain History of Swindling Perpetrated on a Gigantic Scale." "Colossal Money Power That Menaces Pacific Coast Prosperity."

Those were the headlines to a five-column diatribe that stirred public sentiment. Dewey had waited until the heat was up and filed suit. Mr. Mackay and his partners found ways of deflecting the suit, so Dewey bought a hundred shares of Consolidated Virginia, turned the stock over to a front man named Burke who brought essentially the same suit but as a stockholder on behalf of stockholders, which gave him better standing in court.

It alleged that the bonanza partners had made an illicit four-million in unlawful lumber profits, $26 million in unlawful milling of ore, and ten and a half million out of a sale of a minor mine claim called the Kinney to the Consolidated Virginia during the initial reorganization. The plaintiffs invited other stockholders to join in the suit, but none did.

All of that landed on John Mackay soon after I returned to work, and for the first time I beheld a man heavily burdened and weary. The drumbeat of abuse continued through eighteen and seventy-eight. Dewey gathered the *Chronicle*'s vitriolic pieces into a pamphlet, conveniently dropping the source of such diatribes, and distributed it to all the corporation's stockholders.

Grimly the bonanza partners refused to bow to such blatant propaganda, public hysteria, and blackmail, and eventually the suits went to trial, the first of them in December of eighteen and seventy-nine, the last in eighteen and eighty.

John Mackay had generously seen me through crisis, aiding every way he could, and now I discovered that I could assist him; my years as a veteran newsman could help tip the scales. I began by analyzing Dewey's scurrilous pamphlets and drafting responses to their misrepresentations and evasions, something John Mackay gladly turned over to me because he was temperamentally unsuited for that sort of verbal contest.

As a result of my quiet prompting and calling upon old friends in the press, such papers as the *Alta* and *San Francisco Bulletin* began to contest the *Chronicle*'s hyperbole. The *Bulletin* editorialized that "blackmailing has long been a disgrace to our society" and "the firm of Flood & O'Brien, or any other prominent firm, will confer a lasting benefit on the community fighting it to the bitter end."

Thus did I rally my old colleagues on behalf of the Bonanza Firm. The *Territorial Enterprise* weighed in with a scathing denunciation of Charles de Young and his rabid paper.

I was quick to point out that the stockholders of the Consolidated Virginia had received a monthly dividend ever since May 1874 and that stockholders of the California had received a regular monthly dividend ever since May 1876 and that anyone choosing to hang onto his shares, rather than speculate in them, would have made a fortune.

Not until 1879, when both mines suspended dividends, did I have complete figures, but by then the Consolidated Virginia had paid out almost forty-three million to its shareholders out of a gross production of sixty-one million, while the California paid out over thirty-one million out of a gross of forty-four million, in the process making numerous men millionaires and greatly enriching many others who bought and held on.

What's more, when low-grade operations began a few years later the mines yielded another sixteen million and paid nearly four million more in dividends. Even as I write at the turn of the century the bonanza mines continue to produce in a feeble fashion, and reworking their tailings has yielded another fourteen million. The two mines grossed nearly

one hundred thirty-six million dollars up to 1897, and the bonanza partners generously paid seventy-eight million to shareholders, the amount
available after operating costs.

I was able to make a substantial case, which I turned over to John
Mackay. But I don't doubt that Mackay, Fair, Flood, and O'Brien heart-
ily wished they had paid Squire Dewey the $52,000 he claimed he had
lost rather than endure the ordeal that was to come.

CHAPTER 60

nce again, Virginia City was changing before my eyes,
as sunsets change from dazzling orange and red to pur-
ples and finally murky blues. With Catherine in her
grave, things had inexorably altered. I sometimes hiked
the long distance to Pioneers Cemetery to be with her, trying hard to
remember our briefest of unions, the way she smiled, the touch of the
hand that told me of her love.

Often I hired a hack to take me there and drop me off and then I
walked back to the city, feeling lost. She was always on my mind. I
loved her in death, even as I had loved her in life. I always winced at
the harshness of her grave, the tan clay, naked earth, an arid patch of
sloping land without grace or greenery. That place made death all too
real and all too present and did nothing to heal my loss. I laid some
pine boughs upon it, but they browned and dropped their needles, reminding me that little lived in that arid land. I kept up my visits through
the seasons, hanging onto a tattered memory, fighting the Washoe zephyrs, ice and snow, and bitter weather.

Then, when I was sharing a glass of claret with Judge Goodwin, he
told me he was leaving the Comstock. He would be an editor in Salt
Lake City and looked forward to life in a town that had a future. I
grieved anew. One by one my closest friends and colleagues were abandoning the *Enterprise* and life on the Comstock. Where had they all
gone? Joe Goodman, Sam Clemens, Steve Gillis, Fremont Older, Bill
Davis, Denis McCarthy, Tom Fitch over at the *Union*.

Thank heaven a few remained, like Alf Doten and Wells Drury over
in Gold Hill, but these days I could walk into my old paper and not
recognize most of the men working there. Was this the same paper, the
same company, that Joe Goodman had built into a great enterprise? That

left only Rollin Daggett and Dan De Quille among my old comrades, and I feared they would soon leave, too, because something was eating at the heart of Virginia City at the apex of its life.

My home had changed, with Consuela Wellington ruling my roost rather than my beloved Catherine. Often, when my heart ached for my wife, I stopped at Mrs. Trenoweth's to see my infant, Catherine, a lusty little bundle who would enter my household when a wet nurse was no longer needed. I thought I saw more and more of her mother in her, but others laughed at me and told me the infant resembled me. I would peer at the blanket-swathed little girl and love her with a love so tender I cannot describe it, not even with all my training as a man of words.

Miss Wellington maintained a starchy regimen, but that was tempered by an affectionate nature, and my dear adopted children, Peter and Caroline, prospered. I could find no sign of anguish or even unhappiness, at least not the sort that lasted and wormed its way into the heart. I rejoiced in their progress and in their courage, living a life protected only by a strange middle-aged foster parent.

I could not fault my housekeeper and governess for anything more serious than a stiff nature that found little humor in the world. I often wondered why she had drifted to a wildly comic town, celebrated for its raucous humor, and could find no answer to that minor mystery. And so life proceeded, but in a city that was subtly decaying, sinking bit by bit into oblivion. I had come to it as a youth and shared its youthfulness. Now I felt its flesh shriveling along with my own, and sometimes I could not bear the thought of the death of a city that had rewarded me with a joyous life, a city that was surrendering to its fate, just as all living things do, sooner or later.

I was seeing less and less of John Mackay as well as the other bonanza partners that year. My employer had turned most of his business affairs over to Dick Dey in San Francisco, while retaining me in Virginia City to handle matters at the mines.

James Fair, also, had largely retreated to San Francisco but always hurried back whenever anything caught his fancy, such as leading important personages through the mines.

When Mackay was in town, he stayed in his suite on the top floor of the International and scorned the elevators so he could get his exercise. His passion for exercise has kept him alive to this day, long after the rest of his partners went to their reward. But more often than not, that suite was empty, and I sometimes used it as an office along with our cramped quarters at the Gould & Curry mine.

Mostly I dealt with visitors who flocked to the city to see the mines, and often to try to talk Mr. Mackay into investing in one harebrained scheme or another. Countless times I led them into the Consolidated Virginia, never enjoying having so much rock over my head. But I endured, and the works didn't fall on me, and somehow I led the visitors through various levels of the mine and encouraged them all to take assay samples with them.

So important had Virginia City become that visitors deluged us, and I remember those two years, seventy-eight and seventy-nine, as the time when I took party after party underground. I took Senator Logan of Illinois down the Consolidated Virginia shaft in a cage that dropped sickeningly and showed him the works. The former Civil War general wiped sweat from his brow and declared that the silver dollar was worth all of its hundred cents. I took Robert Ingersoll, the agnostic, down to the boiling bottom of the mines, and he later confessed that maybe there was a hell after all.

The visitors often arrived in posh private cars at the end of a V & T train, where I would meet them on behalf of Mr. Mackay and lead them to the changing rooms at the Consolidated Virginia hoist works. I would leave them in a carpeted room where they would don garb suitable for the boiling hot chambers below—cotton shirts and trousers, heavy shoes, felt hats, and a thick woolen coat to wear in the cages as they dropped from a cold climate into a roasting one. Women were taken to a separate room where they could dress in loose alpaca smocks, heavy shoes, and those shapeless felt hats that kept debris out of their hair. Then we would board a cage and plunge at an alarming rate, sailing past lit stations like an express train to hell.

I always had to assure them that the engineers were in perfect control and we would arrive safely at our destination. In fact, part of my duty was to show our guests the amazing machinery, the giant pumps, air blowers, triple-deck cages, ore cars, thundering stamp mills, and so on, that made our mines and mills efficient and safe.

So it happened that I accompanied Generals Sherman and Sheridan through the works, James G. Blaine, Presidents Rutherford B. Hayes and William Henry Harrison, and even that pious rogue Henry Ward Beecher. In most celebrity cases, Jim Fair would hasten to the Comstock from San Francisco and loudly play host and I would be relegated to errand boy. He had an eye for fame and liked to insert himself into the mining scene long after he had left it for more comfortable climes.

In some of those cases I was delegated to escort the women through the higher levels while he took his distinguished visitors down to the depths of hell. The C & C shaft, jointly operated by the bonanza mines, had pierced over twenty-five hundred feet, and the hundred-twenty-degree temperatures were more than visitors could bear for more than a few minutes. They all marveled at the endurance of our Comstock miners, who toiled ten minutes out of each hour in that furnace and then cooled themselves with ice.

Whenever a very important visitor arrived, he and his party were met at the railroad station with brass bands and escorted in a parade to the hotel, the marchers being drawn from our fraternal societies and firemen's companies. When Ulysses Grant arrived in our fair city, he observed that in all the time he had been a general of the armies he had never seen such splendiferous uniforms. After completing his tour, he announced to the world that the Virginia City mines were as close to hell as he cared to get. John Mackay himself took the former president to the bottom of the mines, while I escorted his wife, daughter, and Mrs. Fair through the higher levels.

Mackay rarely visited the Comstock in those days, preferring to stay at the Palace Hotel in San Francisco, so I saw less and less of him. He traveled to Paris each year to spend time with his wife and children and in-laws, who had set up residence there. Marie Hungerford Mackay had never cared for rough and barren Virginia City, and even before her husband struck the Big Bonanza, she had decamped to San Francisco. She and Mr. Mackay had produced two sons, John, whom they called Willie, and Clarence. And he had adopted a daughter from Marie's previous marriage as well. Marie Hungerford had first married a dissolute doctor named Bryant, cousin of the poet William Cullen Bryant, but he had eventually deserted her and she had divorced him, enduring harsh poverty until she met Mr. Mackay.

When she moved to Paris she was determined to live in style and win the acceptance of the reluctant and conservative Parisians. She bought a majestic house on rue Tilsit, hard by the Champs Élysées, and from that central locale made every effort to entertain in style and serve the most elegant of meals to the most elegant of guests.

John Mackay could barely tolerate most of his wife's new acquaintances and loved to regale them with largely invented stories about his uncouth childhood, when pigs and chickens supposedly shared the Dublin household. He had arranged with Dick Dey to send him a telegram requesting his immediate return to San Francisco whenever Mackay sent Dey a coded request for one, and with these he bowed out from polite society and hastened across the Atlantic and then the continent, to be with those he regarded as men and to escape the Parisian fops he loathed.

Marie spent lavishly, indulging all her whims, but I knew John Mackay didn't mind. A man earning a million dollars a month didn't feel much need to rein her in. And while Marie was extravagant, she was not a fool and did not squander funds on speculations or schemes or assorted indulgences of her children.

One of her Fourth of July parties, in which she redid the entire rue Tilsit mansion in red, white, and blue, astounded Paris but did not win her the acceptance she wanted. Marie Mackay's pining for social acceptance never ceased to needle her soul, and she was less than happy. My impression of Mackay in those years was one of great contentment. He was a typical Washoe widower, one of innumerable men on the Comstock whose wives lived down below, as San Francisco was called.

I suppose Mr. Mackay might scold me now for publicly wondering what sort of marriage it had become, with the mates separated by half a world except for the briefest of visits. She returned to the States only once, many years later, and even now lives in London, where she fled after a great contretemps about a portrait that she despised and burned, to the horror of nearly all of France. Actually, John and Marie Mackay have always loved and respected each other, even if she could not bear his simple and unpretentious way of living and he could not bear her effete life and friends. Money made possible a most amiable resolution to all of that, and the pair remain truly affectionate and close to each other and their children.

But on the Comstock, that source of such abundance, another fight was brewing.

CHAPTER 61

 dolph Sutro did it. On July 8, 1878, his tunnel company reached the Savage mine. For weeks the face crews, driving toward each other every hour of every day, could hear the sound of explosions from the opposing crews. Sutro's eloquent admonitions, delivered in his heavily accented English, had inspired them to prodigious feats of tunnel cutting. They worked in abysmal conditions, miles from fresh air, in choking dynamite fumes, frantically blasting ahead and shoveling the rubble into ore cars drawn by surly mules.

Sutro himself was present at the last blast, and as the debris settled and the opposing lanterns became visible and a rush of foul air greeted the miners on the Savage side the president of the tunnel company stepped through. A few weeks later the tunnel company completed and timbered its bore clear to the Savage Company shaft, and the Savage's giant pumps began discharging the water, most of it drawn from works far below the level of the tunnel, into Sutro's four-mile bore down to the Carson River.

Sutro and his company had achieved an engineering feat unparalleled in history. The tunnel ran 20,498 feet from the Carson River to the 1,650-foot-level of the Savage mine at the center of the Comstock. When its lengthy north and south laterals were completed, it drained the entire lode, carrying between 3,500,000 and 4,000,000 gallons of hot water out of the mines each day. It provided better air circulation and gave miners a new emergency exit in the event of cave-ins. It was to have been ventilated by four vertical shafts along its path, but numbers three and four were never completed because of flooding and unstable rock. The tunnel was seven or more feet high inside the timbering, eight feet wide across the top, and nine feet or more wide at the bottom.

It cost, in all, about three and a half million and took seven years to build. Its crews had encountered brutal obstacles, such as boiling water, acrid fumes, crumbling and unstable rock, and unbearable heat, but had never faltered. It was a monument to one man's faith, courage, audacity, and vision, but even more a monument to every brave and energetic man who had toiled through the bowels of the earth, day after day, miles from daylight.

The heady celebration of the monumental project, yet another of the wonders of the Comstock Lode, soon gave way to vicious maneuvering. Sutro insisted that the mines connected to the tunnel immediately begin paying him the two dollars a ton for ore that had been agreed upon a dozen years earlier when most of the Comstock mines had contracted with the Tunnel Company to drain water and take ore down to the mills on the river.

The mines' managements, mostly under the thumb of the bonanza partners, fiercely resisted and said the old agreements had long since been abrogated by Sutro's failure to complete his tunnel in a timely manner. And in every case those deals had been worked out with prior managements and owners, none of which were now operating the mines.

I found myself caught in the middle. Sutro's tunnel had come too late to be of much use unless another bonanza was discovered. The mining now was being done far below the level of the tunnel, so the mines still had to pump water up to the tunnel to discharge it. And the managements thought that Sutro's two-dollar-a-ton price tag was much too high in a time of declining ore tenors.

The Savage, caught just then in a flooding emergency, started to drain its excess into the tunnel, but Sutro turned back the water and threatened to bulkhead the tunnel unless he was paid. Things had come to such a pass that it appeared the Comstock would derive no use from the tunnel.

I both admired Adolph Sutro and kept a certain distance from him. He had been, for a dozen and more years, a tireless promoter of the tunnel. Meanwhile, the great bonanzas came and went, and years rolled by. With the Big Bonanza, the mines began to probe depths far below the level at which the tunnel reached the Comstock, so all the financial calculations changed. When the Virginia & Truckee began operating the mines no longer needed the tunnel as much, although they would have welcomed the competition.

Sutro ran for the United States Senate in several elections and never won a vote in the legislature because he had become unpopular with his constant admonitions and promotions. He was a loquacious and even eloquent man, using public forums to keep his tunnel project alive. But the longer he wrestled with his gigantic project the less scrupulous were his claims.

He had turned to English capital and eventually obtained funding in the form of a stock subscription in 1871. Two hundred thousand shares of the Tunnel Company were handled by the London banking firm of McCalmont Brothers & Co., which kept three-quarters of the shares and sold the rest to European investors. That was followed with another large subscription by Continental bankers, and thus financed, Sutro pressed the tunnel work at breakneck speed, using the new Burleigh drills and dynamite.

But to achieve his dream—and this became an acute disappointment to me—he had begun to exaggerate the prospects. In a prospectus designed to sell bonds, called "The Sutro Tunnel and the Railway," he made some wild claims, all of which proved false. He claimed that the Comstock possessed $500 million of low-grade ore—which was a hundred million more than the entire district produced in its life. He insisted that amazing, rich veins still awaited discovery. And he projected the tunnel revenues at $22 million, which was the wildest claim of all. After the tunnel was completed revenues amounted to $44,000 a year, rising to $100,000 a year during the decade when the voluminous low-grade ore was recovered.

Still, I felt the mine managers and owners had a moral obligation to the little man who had worked a miracle. And when my employer and his colleagues resisted, I went through another of those dark periods when I sensed the naked calculations that underlay the Comstock. Virginia City was showing me its mean side once again.

I considered resigning. I was actively promoting a viewpoint, on behalf of Mr. Mackay, to which I did not fully subscribe, and it troubled me almost as much as the prostitution of the *Territorial Enterprise* when William Sharon bought it and turned it into a mouthpiece for his political ambitions. But before I had made up my mind to leave the city I loved, the bonanza partners, mine managers, and Sutro began to talk.

Common sense prevailed. The Tunnel Company and the mines finally agreed to a fee of a dollar a ton on lower-grade ore, two dollars for rich ore, all for the privilege of draining the mines and transporting ore down the tunnel to the mills on the river. That seemed fair enough. The mines would still save enormous sums from reduced pumping and transportation costs. Running ore down the tunnel would be cheaper than paying the V & T to haul it.

Adolph Sutro's private calculations obviously improved upon his public ones, because he sold his interests in the Tunnel Company for a million dollars after he negotiated the deal with the mines and retired to San Francisco, there to pursue a life as a benefactor of the arts, a politician, and eventually a beloved and vital mayor of that great city.

The Comstock district returned to its usual ways; crews began cutting the laterals that would connect the tunnel to all the mines, and the city resumed its multiple tasks of mining ore, exploring new depths, supplying the gargantuan appetites of the mines and mills with cordwood, quicksilver, dynamite, cages, rails, ore cars, and all the rest. Life on the Comstock seemed to progress just as it always had.

During this whole period the bonanza partners were spending millions on exploration, driving shafts and winzes and drifts at incredible depths, from nearly every mine on the Comstock. But they never found ore, and people were saying the luck of the Irishmen had run out. These vast explorations, financed by assessments on stockholders, kept over two thousand skilled miners at work in addition to those employed by the two bonanza mines. So the man on the street scarcely was aware that the district was functioning at a dead loss and that the solid comforts of the mature brick-and-stone-built city were an illusion. But I knew, and so did anyone else who bothered to study the matter.

I had come early in the life of the city, and unless a new bonanza was uncovered soon I would see it fade away, watch its crowded streets, its jostling pedestrians, vanish until one day only silence reigned. I began to wonder what I would do, how I might support my ragtag family, where I might go. Mining towns were in my blood and bone. I loved the whistles of the mines, the endless thunder of the stamp mills, the soft jarring of explosions far beneath my feet, the camaraderie of the saloons, the fabulous performances, recitations, bands, and orchestras at Maguire's and Piper's opera houses, and, above all, the rowdy, joyous journalism that celebrated life on the Comstock and trumpeted our virtues and vices to all the world. Yes, I would miss that so much the very thought of leaving broke my heart.

CHAPTER   62

 he Bonanza firm, whose receipts and expenditures exceeded those of most of the states in the Union, was an inviting target, and not a few schemers and confidence men tried to pry loose some of that wealth. With disgust and loathing, I watched it all unfold.

Eighteen and seventy-eight and seventy-nine were bad years for Mackay, Fair, Flood, and O'Brien when it came to lawsuits and assorted species of blackmail, but the firm's determination not to be blackmailed proved to be a largely successful strategy.

I found myself dealing with these suits more and more on Mackay's behalf. One of them was brought by a San Francisco resident named William Smallman, who alleged that John Mackay had stolen the affections of his wife, Amelia. The suit was so improbable that I never believed a word of it. John Mackay was not that sort of man. Unlike many rich men who buy off blackmail regardless of the merit of the suit, Mackay fought it openly and publicly and refused to give an inch.

The news, of course, caused a minor sensation on the Comstock, and my erstwhile colleagues busily printed the allegations. I remember John Mackay pacing the floor of his Gould & Curry office worrying about that one and raging at the infamy.

"Let the press print what it will!" he said one day. "I know the truth, and that's good enough for me. I'll fight this round by round."

The very day the story broke in the Comstock papers Jim Fair pulled one of his mean pranks, for which he was famous. A young woman had caught Fair outside the Consolidated Virginia office and sought succor from him, saying her family was in need and her brother wanted a job. Enjoying the moment, he informed her that John Mackay was the man to see about that and steered her toward the Gould & Curry.

"Tell him your name is Amelia," he added. "I'm sure he'll give your brother a job if you do exactly as I say. He's queer, and you have to approach him properly. One of his peculiarities is that he can't refuse anything to any girl named Amelia."

Fortunately, I intercepted her before she reached Mr. Mackay, got her story, and foiled Fair's mean joke, sparing both my employer and her a bad moment.

That suit ended well for my employer. The Smallmans ended up in jail on criminal conspiracy charges. I don't doubt that the result discouraged a raft of other petty crooks and scoundrels from considering John Mackay as prey.

But the suits that continued to grind on the bonanza partners had more substance. These were the ones filed by Squire Dewey and his associate John Burke, with the connivance of the *San Francisco Chronicle*, alleging that the bonanza partners had made unlawful profits at the expense of stockholders.

California corporation law forbade directors to deal with a corporation for their own benefit no matter how fair the arrangements. The bonanza partners, through their own companies, had exclusive right to mill the mines' ore and to keep the slimes and tailings resulting from the initial milling. Their companies also had exclusive right to supply wood to the mines as well as water. The suits were intended to compel the trustees to disgorge to all stockholders an alleged $4 million profit from lumber sales, an alleged $26 million in milling profits, and $10 million in alleged profits from the sale of the Kinney mine claim to the Consolidated Virginia.

I didn't know how that one would come out, but I did know, from access to the books, that actual profits from the sale of timber and firewood to the mines came to $645,000 and actual profits from milling the mines' ore came to about $9 million.

The Bonanza firm, which ran the big California Pan mill and other mills, had charged the mines the standard $13 per ton for custom milling. The firm had built the mill for $800,000, and it proved to be a lucrative investment. Ownership of the tailings proved to be lucrative, too. The first run of ore through a mill extracted about 65 percent of the assayed value of the ore, and reworking the tailings extracted another 15 to 20 percent, so the firm was profiting from every ton of tailings it reworked.

There were other clauses in the contracts that had excited the fury of some of the stockholders, including one that allowed the mill operators to deduct 10 percent as the result of evaporation and wastage—which increased the firm's profits at the expense of mine shareholders. The result of all these generous arrangements that the firm had awarded itself was that it got back its $800,000 investment every ninety days.

There was more that stirred the wrath of their critics. Even though John Mackay and James Fair professed to be merely miners and not interested in manipulating the markets, the record speaks otherwise. James Flood was busy. Primarily through his market manipulations, the Bonanza Firm was milking the San Francisco stock markets every way it could, touting its discoveries or making public note of the mines' shortcomings, whatever the case may be, according to whether the partners wished to raise share prices or depress them.

Flood wasn't entirely successful, because the mines were run so openly that no secrets ever remained locked in the pits or in company offices. And, too, virtually every broker and speculator in San Francisco had his paid spies in the mines, ready to report the slightest news. When it became apparent in eighteen and seventy-seven that the Big Bonanza was swiftly being worked out, the firm began selling its holdings, using momentary rallies to get the best possible price.

Still, these very mines were each paying over a million dollars every month to shareholders, and the trustees had been uncommonly open about their business. Significantly, not one other shareholder joined the suit, and when the case was finally decided early in 1881, with the plaintiffs winning a small victory on the Kinney matter but no other, only one stockholder took advantage of the modest cash settlement to which all Consolidated Virginia stockholders were entitled. And the court ruled that the Kinney transaction had not been "actually or wilfully fraudulent."

After that, the partners settled with the stockholders for a small sum and that was the end of it. In truth, the Bonanza firm's ways of dealing with the public and investors were so superior to anyone else's that the company largely escaped the penalties and litigation that had mired so many other Comstock enterprises, including William Sharon's.

I stoutly defended my employer and the partners through this period, and the reader may well wonder whether Henry Stoddard's ethics had gone rubbery. Was this the same man who had departed from the *Territorial Enterprise* when its editorial policy was put at the service of William Sharon? The truth of it is that I did probably relax my standards. I so admired John Mackay for his simple life, his unaffected conduct, his generosity, and his gracious ways that I cast a blind eye toward the rapacity of the company.

I had many rationalizations, not least of which was the simple proposition that these four Irishmen, far more than any other of those who

feasted on the Comstock, had been the fairest, most open, most generous, most honest. Because of them, many hundreds of ordinary people
had made small fortunes and not a few Californians had ended up millionaires. Because of John Mackay, the destitute were cared for, the injured were hospitalized, entrepreneurs found capital, churches were
funded, and hardship was alleviated.

Perhaps you will accuse me of ethical laxity because I stoutly supported and defended Mr. Mackay during the very period when the practices of the partnership had come under closest scrutiny and were
exciting the greatest controversy. Even now, after decades of pondering
it, I would insist that the firm's virtues far outweighed its failings.

Now, as I write from the turn of the century, I have little remorse
about my allegiance to Mr. Mackay during that period and I see no
relationship between my hefty paycheck and my belief that he and his
partners deserve esteem and honor. Because of these men and their
mining genius, San Francisco now stands as the Colossus of the West,
its every park and boulevard and business gilded by Comstock wealth.
Let the critics carp.

I say all that with certain reservations about James Fair, whose ruthless and cunning conduct I could never stomach. He was a man without
conscience who was so satisfied with his viewpoints that it never occurred to him he might be wrong about anything. He so distrusted the
competence of others that he exhausted himself on all the details best
left to twenty-dollar-a-week clerks, and the self-imposed burdens he carried so wore him down that in the late eighteen-seventies his doctors
pressed him to rest himself—which he did, after a fashion, by spending
more time in San Francisco and less with his wife, Theresa, and his
children.

By eighteen and seventy-nine he had everything a man could want:
a major fortune and fame as the most gifted and competent mining man
in the West, if not in the world. But there was still something lacking in
the life of a man who was never, in his own estimate, wrong: public
office. So he announced that year that he would run as a Democrat for
the United States Senate against Republican William Sharon. That, of
course, had been the standard prize for many of the Comstock's great
men, including Stewart, Jones, and his old archrival, Sharon. I had little
doubt that Fair would buy the office and that he would make an atro-
cious senator, and my predictions proved to be accurate.

The standard means by which a wealthy Nevada man bought his
way into the Senate was first to elect the legislators who would, in turn,
elect him to high office. Fair soon learned that Sharon intended to spend
$100,000 to elect the legislators who would return him to Washington,

so Fair determined to spend $110,000. Never did the citizenry of Nevada profit so much from an election. If it took a jug to win a citizen's vote, he got a jug, and maybe two jugs and a quart.

Fair abandoned his fancy carriage, bought a one-horse rig, and toured the state's mining camps in workmen's attire, flannel shirt and slouch hat and affected a common-man pose laced with blarney and soon had the edge over the cold, distant, and aristocratic Sharon. Fair visited virtually every saloon, toured the bowels of every handy mine, and let it be known that he was no conniving politician. To be sure, Sharon spent almost as liberally as Fair but did not have bottomless silver mines to tap or a common-man persona and thus was disadvantaged.

So, in the end, Fair got his slate in the legislature, putting in sixty-one Democrats against Sharon's nine Republicans. Fair was duly elected Nevada's senator and in eighteen and eighty headed for the United States Senate, where he had the good sense to remain silent, and so spent six lackluster years largely achieving nothing. He had spent, in all, about $350,000 for his seat.

CHAPTER 63

hat accidental millionaire William S. O'Brien died in May of 1878 at the age of fifty-two. I had barely known him because he had scarcely set foot in Virginia City. He had been the least of the bonanza partners, had largely sloughed off the responsibilities assigned to him by the others, and had spent his time amiably entertaining and playing small-stakes poker.

He had been a hospitable and gregarious man, but the former barkeep lacked the wisdom or energy to make anything of himself and his fortune. Death had come early to a bachelor who lacked the imagination to do anything with his life or his riches other than make small-scale loans to his pals. His fortune, running perhaps a dozen million dollars, went to assorted sisters, nieces, nephews, and in-laws, who made much of it. He had seen the end coming and commissioned a bizarre family vault, which was being constructed when he died, so his remains had to wait until all the grotesqueries were complete.

And so they were three.

I sent my condolences.

James Fair, in Washington, finally discovered a place where he was out of his depth and sat silently in the Senate for six months before he tired of the whole business. He simply retreated to his Senate office, pulled out the brandy, and entertained other delinquents. He liked being addressed as Senator and enjoyed the emoluments of office, but he contributed only one thing, the rather dismaying Chinese Exclusion Act of 1881, as a fulfillment of his campaign promise to white mine workers to keep Orientals out.

He left the rest to Nevada's senior senator, John Jones, including the crucially important silver issues, and began spending more and more time in San Francisco, holding court at Lick House on Montgomery Street, where he maintained a modest suite for himself one block from a cluttered office from which he ran his far-flung business empire. Eventually he purchased that hotel and much of the business district of San Francisco, and the rents became his principal income even as he let the structures deteriorate to the point of ruin.

He had largely abandoned his wife, Theresa, and his children, Charley, Jimmy, Theresa, and Virginia, choosing to live in Washington alone. The family remained at the B Street home in Virginia City—and suffered his neglect. At one point John Mackay had to lend Theresa Fair some cash for household expenses. There had been tensions in that marriage, but most supposed it was because James Fair was Protestant while Theresa Rooney Fair was Catholic and the religion of the children had been a source of contention. But that proved to be inconsequential compared to what soon was revealed while Fair was in the Senate.

In 1883, Theresa filed for divorce, and the grounds were habitual adultery, which was something I had long known about. The news electrified the City on the Hill as well as San Francisco, and no one had a kind word for the blustering, self-infatuated braggart. The uproar preoccupied the Senate, which considered expelling the blackguard in accord with the precepts of Victorian propriety but ultimately did nothing.

The divorce hearing occurred that May, in Virginia City, and Theresa did not lack evidence or witnesses. She was asking for half their communal property, which Fair attempted to reduce, though he didn't contest the divorce. He ended up with custody of his two sons and she their two daughters and nearly five million of the Fair fortune, plus his payment of two hundred thousand in attorney fees, an amount that maddened the senator though he could do nothing about it. The drubbing he took in Virginia City did settle one thing in his mind: he would never return to that godforsaken mining town again, no matter that he was a Nevada senator and the city was his legal address.

I thought that these were the man's just desserts; indeed, I wished

Mrs. Fair had gotten custody of the sons as well because I feared that the boys would suffer neglect, indulgence, and ruin at the hands of their self-aggrandizing father, and my fears were soon validated. The Fair boys came to no good.

John Mackay had stayed close to Mrs. Fair and quietly helped her through the whole ordeal, thereby winning, at last, Fair's open hostility. So had James Flood. Between them, they supplied the advice that enabled Theresa to win so great a settlement from her wandering husband. They might yet be partners in business, but Senator Fair would never again be close to Mackay and always reserved his most withering barrages of vitriol for my quiet, decent, and levelheaded employer. After the divorce, his public pronouncements against his colleagues grew tart and mean.

When Flood began building a mansion at Menlo Park, Fair publicly proclaimed that "Flood should be popular at Menlo. There's not a bartender on the Coast who can make a better julep than Jim."

It had been Theresa Fair who had introduced John Mackay to the young Marie Hungerford Bryant and quietly encouraged Mackay's suit. They would remain friends evermore. That was a friendship I approved of, and I sometimes found myself wishing that John Mackay had married Theresa Rooney and James Fair had married Marie Hungerford Bryant.

Theresa raised her daughters well, seeing to their education and religious belief, looking after their deportment and social graces. Birdie and Tessie, as they were called, soon graced San Francisco and then Newport society with beauty and vivacity. Tessie, the elder daughter, eventually married Herman Oelrichs, from one of New York's most prominent families, while the younger and more vivacious Birdie only recently wed William K. Vanderbilt, grandson of old Cornelius and the nation's most eligible bachelor. For a while Virginia City and San Francisco glowed with proprietary pleasure. There we were, the roughest and most raucous city in the country, and there was Birdie, marrying a Vanderbilt in the most lavish wedding ceremony the country had ever seen.

But I am getting ahead of myself again. A man writing after so many years keeps forgetting that a story should be told in a chronological order. My life centered more and more upon my family. When the time came to restore my little Catherine to my hearth, we all suffered: Mrs. Trenoweth, whose maternal love and milk had nurtured my wee girl; Consuela Wellington, who, for once, seemed fearful that her new responsibilities were beyond her; my children, who stared at the bundled little newcomer with curiosity and perhaps dark suspicion that this true daughter of their stepfather might usurp his love. And they were right to suspect it.

And I. Suddenly I was aware of all the mouths I had to feed and bodies to shelter and the small, fragile selves there were to nurture, and I wondered whether I would be up to it. Miss Wellington handled the infant as if she were fragile china, something that would shatter at the slightest excuse, but I had no such dread and so I rocked the baby or spoon-fed gruel or lifted a cup to her lips and counted it a coup for an old bachelor.

But now, acutely aware of the transitory nature of wealth as well as life, I began to fret about my investments and ended up selling down most of my shares in the bonanza mines even though the California continued to pay handsome dividends. I had waited much too long. They weren't worth much. Real estate seemed the safest refuge, and I bought a small apartment building in Oakland and began to draw income from rents, using them to pay the mortgage. I took no flyers in Comstock mines though I had an opportunity to buy dozens, from the mighty ones like the Ophir to obscure ones that never would send a ton of ore to a mill. But I no longer had much faith in the town's future and preferred to ship my modest funds to California.

Several times each day I lifted my little Catherine from her crib and beheld my flesh and blood and remembered her mother just as vividly as ever. Catherine Iliff Stoddard would not ever vanish from my life. As for Peter and Caroline, they seemed to prosper, and I detected little sign of melancholia in them, though Peter was a serious and somewhat timid child. They were usually a match for their rough peers in school and somehow had absorbed the city's own cavalier attitude toward misfortune: tomorrow might offer a new bonanza, and in any case, loss wasn't worth worrying about. Little did I realize that the city's jaunty attitude was strengthening both of Catherine's older children and equipping them to deal with a hard world.

Each day, during those months of declining ore production, I found myself wondering what to do, where to go, how to proceed with my life. The changes were still not visible, and outwardly the city exuded prosperity. The miners still spent their four dollars a day prodigally. Solid stores fronted C Street. And yet, like a person who has lost blood and looks pale, the city seemed unwell. With each new mining bonanza in the West we lost some of our population. They would rush off to Aurora or Butte or Bodie or Bannock or—more recently—Tombstone, another silver camp down in southern Arizona Territory. And one would scarcely notice their departure.

But the ranks of men lining the bar rails thinned. FOR RENT signs appeared in boardinghouse windows. Dry-goods merchants held sales to get rid of unwanted bolts of cloth and other items. The ads in the *Territorial Enterprise* thinned, making the news hole larger at a time when there was less news to fill the hole. The Comstock papers all cheerfully assured their readers that more bonanzas lurked below, just a little deeper, and soon enough the town would spring back. But as the relentless exploration honeycombed the old mines at deeper levels than ever, finding only barren rock, the doubts that crabbed people began to appear openly, often in the form of specific acts such as selling shares of Comstock mines or quietly packing up one's trunks and boarding the Virginia & Truckee for a new life.

That time was coming. I felt it in my bones. The very house I lived in might drop so far in value, some bleak day, that I could not get my money out of it–and might not even be able to sell it at all.

The day was coming when John Mackay would not need me in Virginia City to oversee his mining business. He had a manager in San Francisco, Dick Dey, who oversaw Mackay's many enterprises, ranging from real estate to banking to an explosives company. When Virginia City died, so would my job and salary.

Like quiet fog, a certain melancholia began to pervade my life in the dying city. Where had the laughter gone? The buoyant devil-may-care life? The great hoaxes and jokes in the papers? The frenzy of speculators? What struck me most was the quiet. That was a paradox. We still lived amid the roar of the stamp mills, the shrill whistles of the mines, and the clatter of machinery–and yet my recollection of the last years of the Comstock's heyday is one of deepening silence.

CHAPTER 64

hen President Rutherford B. Hayes arrived on the Comstock on September 7, 1880, the weary old city painted itself up, gauded itself with bunting, and pretended to be young again. But it was to be the last hurrah.

The president's party included Gen. William Tecumseh Sherman, Maj. Gen. Alexander M. McCook, and Secretary of War Alexander Ramsey. The city's scattered magnates hurried over from San Francisco to welcome the president, and Governor Kinkead and Lieutenant Governor Adams danced in attendance. The reception committee included everyone from John Mackay to William Sharon, and we all pretended that the president's party was about to see a robust mining town in its prime. We met the president at Gold Hill with bands blaring, flags fluttering, and every mine whistle on the Comstock shrilling a welcome. The party was then escorted to the International, still a first-class hotel and now awash in bunting, for a bout of speeches and a banquet.

It was a fine charade. The president and his party stayed but one day, and as fast as he departed on the Virginia & Truckee so did the magnates of the Comstock. I played a small role, as usual, but at least my children and Miss Wellington got to meet a president of the United States, who shook their hands with reserve and dignity, for Hayes was no baby kisser and glad-hander.

After that, the great old silver town slipped into a torpor. The bonanza mines paid their last small dividends in 1879 and 1880 and devoted themselves to money-losing mining of low-grade ore. The rest of the mines levied brutal assessments on their stockholders, sucking in cash to continue their bootless explorations. The entire ore production of the Comstock fell to an appalling million dollars. The market value of the mines, once worth two hundred ninety-three million, fell to seven.

Later there would be a ghostly revival through a decade of low-grade mining and the great old mines would even pay some dividends again as they stripped away the ore that had been scorned in palmier days. But the grand old town would never be the same, and during that last period Virginia was a bucolic village full of destitute men with fantasies.

The city lived on hope. Wander into any saloon and engage the man next to you at the rail, and he would say that there was still plenty of ore, millions of tons of high-grade ore, lying down there, deeper, ever deeper, than the shafts had gone and someday some syndicate—boring at those levels was too costly for any one company—would strike silver and then old Virginia would leap to life; the saloons would ring; troupes would flock to John Piper's opera house, the brokerage houses would bustle, the mining exchanges would trade fortunes, the railroad would haul timber in and ore out, and the slumbering city on the slope of Mount Davidson would become the Lazarus of the West.

We all "knew" there was ore down there. Hadn't Virginia been through some tough times before? Hadn't the first boom, built on the Ophir and Savage and a dozen others, died away, only to be followed by the second, when the Crown Point and Hale & Norcross belched out tons of rich ore? And hadn't the bad times after that ended with the discovery of the Big Bonanza in the Consolidated Virginia and California? It all made sense. Plenty of ore, and someday some shrewd entrepreneurs like Mackay and Fair would find it.

Indeed, there had been one last bubble called the Sierra Nevada deal, and it was unmatched for madness. In eighteen and seventy-eight a small body of low-grade ore was discovered on the 2,000-foot level of the Sierra Nevada mine, which lay at the extreme north end of the Comstock Lode, and for a moment it seemed as if a new bonanza would rescue the town. The mine's 100,000 shares rocketed from $2.80 apiece in June to $280 in late September, and the Union, next door, rose from $3 a share to $182, purely on speculation.

But it was a bonanza built on dreams. The *Enterprise* and other Comstock papers touted the new discovery as if a new era were in sight, with reports of "crosscuts going forward to rich ore." The mine had never produced good ore though it had been prospected for years. It was under the control of a wily manipulator named Johnny Skae, who had quietly bought the outstanding stock before inviting the world into his mine for a look. There, indeed, visitors saw in a crosscut some high-grade ore that improved in value along the way. Some of it assayed at a heady $900 a ton.

That did it. Dan De Quille predicted another bonanza. The *San Francisco Chronicle* announced "a splendid prospect." Both Flood and Fair began investing heavily in the new bonanza. Fair bought 5,000 shares of the Union for a million dollars. Finally even John Mackay, returning from Paris, came for a visit. But unlike his bonanza partners, he was appalled by what he saw in the mine and telegraphed Flood, saying: "Fair is crazy." In October the bubble burst, and in November Sierra Nevada was back down to sixty-five dollars. Only the clever Skae profited heavily. The bubble broke the Comstock, ruined more investors, and shattered those last, desperate dreams. I had bought only ten shares of Sierra Nevada and lost most of what I had invested. That loss wasn't large, but it broke my heart.

And so we whistled our way past the gallows frames and lived on the fumes of old bonfires. In 1880 the town shrank visibly. The bawdy district down on D Street contracted suddenly when the ladies discovered they could mint more cash elsewhere. Buildings were boarded up. San Francisco brokerages shut their branch offices. Sometimes one could walk across C Street and see not a living soul.

And still John Mackay kept me on, though my own duties had diminished and some of my labor now involved selling off mine assets. Still, the giant Cornish pumps lifted hot water from the depths, and shifts of miners rocketed down the shafts to continue exploration, and the mine whistles blew on a clockwork schedule.

I loved the town and resolved to stay as long as I could. Some old pals remained: Dan De Quille, for one, and Alf Doten and Wells Drury. I saw more of them, rather than less, and we often gathered for lamentations in the Old Magnolia, the editorial annex where Rollin Daggett had once downed carafes of Steamboat gin and young Sam Clemens had hoisted more than a few glasses of claret.

De Quille called the town home, but Wells Drury talked of leaving Gold Hill and I sensed that someday soon he would. I talked of leaving but confessed I didn't know what to do. Alf Doten just drank and talked little. Youth and fun and comedy had fled our lives. We were becoming old men.

De Quille's output for the *Territorial Enterprise* dropped to virtually nothing. As late as 1878, he had published two dozen or so sketches, comic pieces, and anecdotal humor. In 1880 he published just two in that paper. But he had not been forgotten and in later years, at the prompting of Goodwin, published prodigious numbers of sketches and stories for the Salt Lake *Tribune,* our Virginia City master storyteller reborn on the other side of the Great Salt Lake. The *Enterprise* was becoming a ghost and made most of its cash by publishing legal notices from mines departing this earthly vale.

Sometimes I hiked the streets of old Virginia, remembering the nights at Barnum's with Artemus Ward, passing the glittering old Washoe Club, where millionaires had gathered to drink, play billiards or poker, and do business; passing the forlorn boarding houses where the best-paid miners on earth slept; passing the old bawdy district, half-shuttered and gloomy and redolent of shame but nonetheless a place where lonely miners in a male town found female companionship; passing the enormous heaps of tailings and country rock piled near each headframe, all of it gouged and shoveled from the deep caverns below by the muscle of mortals, especially the Irish and Cornish.

Sometimes I stared into the placid gloom of Marye's brokerage and remembered the wild days when crowds gathered on the streets, when the latest prices for Comstock shares were posted at the gallows frames of the mines so that even miners on shift could keep track, buy, and sell while they toiled.

I passed old saloons and remembered how crowded they had been, and I remembered the tragedies in some of them: broke speculators who shot themselves, brawls that turned deadly. I remembered Julia Bulette, our town's beloved dark saint, murdered in her bed, and I remembered the day the town had watched her killer swing his way to eternity. I remembered the happy day fresh, sweet Sierra water arrived just when we were parched and reduced to drinking vile and poisonous residues from countless wells poked into surly Mount Davidson.

I remembered the time we had tricked poor Sam Clemens into thinking he had been robbed on the Divide, and how he took it badly when we restored his watch and cash to him. I remembered the story De Quille wrote, in sober, scientific prose, about the solar armor that froze a man in Death Valley in the middle of summer, and I remembered how the London *Times* had reprinted it and made much of it, to our amusement.

Oh, there was so much to remember.

And I didn't know what to do.

By 1881, more than 150 million board feet of lumber had been packed into the caverns under Virginia City to prop up the rock, and one of the wonders of those last years was that it didn't burn. Much of that was because Mackay and Fair had rigorously enforced safety measures. But then, on May 3, 1881, just when the bonanza ore was gone, fire did break out and the chance of stopping it was nil. The remaining miners did seal as many stopes and drifts as they could, but three years later it was still burning. Mining stopped. Virginia City stopped with it. The great heart no longer beat.

But when the fire was finally snuffed by injecting carbonic acid gas the upper reaches of the mines were reopened and low-grade mining began, and it continued profitably into 1895 and even continues as I write. But Virginia City is a pale ghost.

When it became clear to Mr. Mackay that the fire would snuff the life of the Comstock, he asked me to sell off as much mining equipment as I could and then plan on other employment. All during those final months I placed ads in the *Territorial Enterprise* and the *Gold Hill News,* as well as the San Francisco papers and various mining publications. I got very little for old equipment, mostly pennies on the dollar, and turned over the proceeds as crews loaded stamps, amalgamating pans, cable, pumps, and other heavy equipment on the flatcars of the V & T—a railroad itself in distress and running fewer and fewer trains, although its line from Reno to Carson City continued to bear traffic. Like the better mines on the Comstock, the railroad had earned its California bank crowd millions of dollars in its heyday, and it had become renowned for its elegant coaches, handsome rolling stock, and the great personages who had traveled its twisting route.

I faced decisions that I kept putting off. My children attended schools with empty classrooms and small classes, in a town steeped with gloom. Miss Wellington was growing restless. I had discerned that that proper lady thrived in tumultuous mining towns and needed a booming camp to bring out the best in her. That was her paradox, the mannered, starchy, proper maiden lady who required the flinty soil of a wild mining camp to bloom, and I never had any explanation for it.

July Fourth turned out to be my Independence Day. Mackay came up from San Francisco to review my sales and closures, and we spent a few hours at the old Gould & Curry suite where I had kept his office for him.

"What are you going to do next, Henry?" he asked.

I shrugged. "Maybe newspapering again. I need to do something. My investments won't carry me."

"Why not superintend mines?" he asked.

"Me? I'm not qualified."

Mackay's direct gaze intimidated me. "Who knows the business better? From the time you set foot on the Comstock you covered mining news. You know every product that goes into mining and every piece of equipment that mines employ. You know miners and their needs and expectations. You know minerals, assays, costs. You know every economy of management. You know everything that happens in a mill, from the stamping of ore to refining the tailings."

"But I'm unproven."

"John Jones stepped into the mines with no experience to guide him and became one of the best superintendents on the Comstock. I tell you what, Henry. I'll put you in touch with a few men. There's plenty of mining in Arizona, Montana, and even California."

And that was how my own future was settled. And as usual, I owe it all to that prince of men, John Mackay.

CHAPTER 65

nd so we left the City on the Hill. Our destination was a rough mining camp called Warren in southern Arizona Territory, many miles from a railroad. Brooding there was the fabulous Copper Queen mine, producer of vast amounts of copper laced with silver, gold, lead, and zinc.

That very year, Dr. James Douglas, one of mining's great geniuses, had persuaded the Phelps Dodge mining company to purchase 51 percent of the mine and other properties in the district, which was newly named Bisbee. He would manage the enterprise himself and needed an assistant. John Mackay supplied my name, describing me in more flattering terms than a middling sort of man deserved.

That was the beginning of a new life for my odd family and me. Over the years we removed to Globe, Tombstone, Douglas, Butte, and half a dozen other wild towns where optimism was the currency of the soul. None of us ever regretted it. We thrived on rough surroundings, the challenges of a remote life, the cavalier's attitude toward fortune and misfortune. And for all this we could thank our cradle and mentor, the Comstock. We have mining in the blood. My son, Peter, is a mining engineer, now in Chile, and my daughter Caroline married a mining chemist and lives in Ely, Nevada. My dear Catherine lives in Nome, Alaska, now, the wife of a mining man she married after winning a degree from Mills College.

I will always remember those last days on the Comstock. I spent a lot of time with Dan De Quille, asking him over and over why he was staying on.

His answer was always the same: "It's home," he said. But years later, when his home had been reduced to a village, he did return to his home and grown-up family in Iowa, where he spent his last years with his elderly wife, she to whom he had regularly sent checks for decades.

The Comstock was home for me, too, but the young Henry Stoddard's home. It shaped and nurtured me, taught a middling youth the art of living in a rough and comic world. By eighteen and eighty-one my children itched to move. For too long had they been attending haunted schools. Even Miss Wellington talked brightly about new places and new friends. I did not have to persuade my family of gypsies. They knew they were living in a mausoleum. She stayed with me until all my children left my nest, and only when my dear Catherine headed for college did Miss Wellington tender her resignation, with many sighs and apologies. She wished to see Mexico, Australia, New Zealand, Brazil, Peru, Chile, Bolivia, and South Africa before infirmity overtook her. She had squirreled away a tidy sum and invested wisely in mines and could do whatever her sailing soul yearned to do, a bird of passage that would soar oceans, pause on the spar of a passing frigate, and then flap her wings and be off again.

When we left the Comstock, I put my house up for sale but found no takers. There were boarded-up houses all over town. Eventually I decided not to sell it for pennies on the dollar but just to keep it, let it decay in the harsh arid air. I don't know why. Maybe it was because my roots went down through the floor of that house into the fabulous rock below it. Maybe I was entertaining fantasies about living there some distant day. It was a wise decision.

My city had turned hollow and quiet. Not that it was dying. Each day, miners headed for the cages that would lower them to the abundant low-grade ore. Mills ran. The big stamp batteries still boomed and clattered. The mine whistles still blew. But I preferred the younger Virginia, crazy with fun, mad with drink, lunatic with optimism, cavalier about suffering and hardship.

This memoir is about Virginia City, so I will not dwell upon those engaging camps such as Bisbee, where we lived in a house perched on stilts. No, this is about the world's most enchanted city and how it lived and died and what it bestowed, from its flinty womb, upon the world. I was a part of it, and it is in my blood, even now as the past whispers.

And what of all my friends? Sam Clemens you know about, and I wish him well. Joseph Goodman became a noted archaeologist and lived in San Francisco. Judge Goodwin edited the Salt Lake City *Tribune*. Wells Drury married Ella Bishop in 1888, late in life, and moved to San Francisco, where he was a reporter for the *Examiner,* managing editor of the *Call,* and eventually news editor of the Sacramento *Union*. He became a friend of Ambrose Bierce and Jack London, among others. Rollin Daggett served one term in Congress and then got himself appointed minister to Hawaii, where his signal achievement was to teach King Kalakaua how to play poker.

My employer, friend, and mentor John Mackay lives in New York, within sight of the neighborhood where he spent his youth. He is busy with his plans to lay the first trans-Pacific cable, with its terminus at Manila. He is the president of the Commercial Cable Company as well as the Postal Telegraph Company and the Pacific Commercial Cable Company. He is vice president of a Yonkers sugar refinery, whose president is his friend Gus Spreckels. Mackay is a director of the Canadian Pacific Railroad and the Nevada Bank of San Francisco, a part-owner of an elevator company, and has numerous mining, land, and real estate interests.

His wife, Marie, continues to be one of London's great hostesses. Even though they have lived separate lives for a quarter of a century, they see each other frequently and have boundless affection for each other. They lost their older son, Willie, in a steeplechase riding accident in 1895, but the younger son, Clarence, is being groomed to take his father's place when the time comes. Mackay's stepdaughter, Eva, married Ferdinand Julian Colonna, Prince of Galarto, in 1885, in a glittering ceremony, but it was not a happy marriage and it ended in divorce. The price of that divorce was an enormous sum of American dollars, which John Mackay grimly paid.

Although his wife and sons and daughter have lived the glittering life of international socialites John Mackay remains unaffected by wealth, living simply in New York. He was never comfortable with his wife's aristocratic friends and took pride in his humble origins, often dwelling on them in the company of those he quietly scorned.

In 1886, an old man bitter about the losses he had endured speculating in mining stock followed Mackay into an alley behind Lick House and fired at his back from a distance of ten feet. Mackay was seriously, but not fatally, injured. That was the only occasion on which Marie Hungerford Mackay ventured back to her native land, in what the press depicted as a race with death. But by the time she had crossed the Atlantic and endured a week's ride on transcontinental trains, her husband was out of danger.

In 1887, Mackay and Flood had to rescue their firm's Nevada Bank from the wheat speculations of its cashier, George Brander. The young Scot had tried to corner the 1887 crop, only to sink the bank. No one knows how much the bank lost, but Flood and Mackay, its principal stockholders, rescued it at enormous cost, estimated at ten to twelve millions, and the strain contributed to Flood's death two years later. Fair, no longer associated with the bank, supplied funds to relieve "those kindergarten bankers" and took over its presidency, driving out Flood. Mackay and Flood had curtly dismissed Brander, who soon was in hot water again and fled to Edinburgh.

John Mackay continues to list Virginia City as his legal residence though he has no property there and has long since disposed of all his Comstock mining shares. He is admired as one of the most generous and charitable men alive, a sober and shrewd businessman, and a man who never let one of the world's great fortunes affect his conduct or belief. He is building an elaborate family mausoleum at Greenwood Cemetery in New York, where the Mackays will find their eternal rest.

I owe him much and honor John Mackay as one of America's greatest and finest men.

The Fairs have not been so fortunate. After the senator served out his lackluster term, mostly bored with politics, he retreated to Lick House in San Francisco and continued to build his financial empire with great acumen, if not business genius. At the time he died at the end of 1894, he was worth about forty-five million dollars, a remarkable improvement over the fifteen million he was worth at the time of his divorce. Mrs. Fair died in 1891, leaving most of her fortune to her well-married daughters but also establishing a million-dollar trust fund for each of her sons, Jimmy and Charley. Each was to receive a thousand dollars a month from it until the age of thirty, at which point he would receive the principal. But Jimmy died of drink only five months later, and the will provided that the remainder would go to the survivor.

Charley favored fast racehorses and fast women and was deep in debt, so he filed suit to break the will—which utterly alienated his sisters. His brother's death from boozing momentarily slowed Charley's voracious appetites, but not for long. He formed a liaison with a gorgeous blonde, Maude Nelson, whose actual name was Caroline Decker Smith, the proprietor of what the papers delicately called a questionable resort at 404 Stockton Street. In 1893 he suddenly married her, further alienating his socialite sisters and launching a newspaper rampage, with reporters tracking the notorious couple across the country as they headed for Europe, where they hid from the press for a year.

In late December 1894, James G. Fair died. Charley, back from Europe and reconciled with his father, was present. Fair had even, at the end, more or less reconciled himself to Maude. The will placed the fortune in the hands of trustees, with a third of the income from the trust to go to each surviving child. But if any tried to break the will, that child's share was to go to the two others. And Fair disinherited any of Charley and Maude's children by providing that on Charley's death his share of the trust would go to the surviving sisters.

Soon thereafter the will vanished, never to be seen again, which caused a delightful uproar. And so began a legal struggle that is not yet over. Then, in February, Mrs. Nettie Craven, a respectable school principal, announced that she possessed a second Fair will, written in pencil, and it was dated three days after the missing will. It provided that the estate pass directly to the children, which is what they wanted. Mrs. Carven wasn't mentioned in the will she said she possessed, so her motives seemed to be of the highest sort. But soon thereafter Mrs. Craven produced two penciled deeds to property she said Fair had conveyed to her, one of them a five-story office building. The value of the two deeds came to one and a half million dollars and yielded four or five thousand a month in rentals, which considerably cooled the ardor of Fair's children for Mrs. Craven's will.

The San Francisco papers had a grand time with all of this, but it was only prelude. The Fair children, who had supported the pencil will, sued to have the trust clauses of the first will declared invalid, and in February 1896 the court agreed. Whereupon the children's lawyers, with the trust clause declared invalid, reversed direction and sought to have the pencil will declared a forgery. Whereupon Mrs. Craven produced a marriage contract between herself and James G. Fair. The executors sued to have all the Craven documents declared invalid, and Charley swore out a warrant against the notary who allegedly witnessed the signing of the documents, while doughty Mrs. Craven produced a witness to the event, or so her side claimed. She had acquired the services of George M. Curtis, known as the Smasher because of his reputation for breaking wills.

The Fair will occupied San Franciscans for months as the combatants argued the case clear to the California Supreme Court. Eventually the estate bought Mrs. Craven off. But by now there was a parade of ladies claiming to be affianced to Fair, or his daughters-in-law, or sweethearts. One of these was a Los Angeles girl named Sarah Gamble, better known as Sally the Flower Girl, who said she got to know Fair by selling him boutonnieres. She was followed by half a dozen others and then one James Fair Stephens, who claimed to be born in Virginia City, the result of a romance between his mother and Fair. James was followed by a young woman who claimed to be a widow of Fair's son Jimmy. She came equipped with a child. In 1895 yet another fiancée, Miss Phoebe Couzins, world-famed women's rights advocate, proclaimed that she was entitled to some of the fortune. She had met Fair when he was a senator, she explained, and they had shared political ideals, and the friendship had ripened into a long-standing betrothal.

In April 1899, Fair's youngest daughter, Birdie, married William K. Vanderbilt, at a ceremony in which only the upper two hundred of New York's four hundred were invited. And the litigation goes on and on. I hear tell that Mrs. Oelrichs and Mrs. Vanderbilt plan to build a great hotel on the summit of Nob Hill, occupying the very the block that their father purchased long ago, and that they will call it the Fairmount. Who knows how it will all end?

As for me, I've had a marvelous life. Judge Stoddard's middling son did better than he ever imagined. I thrived in the rough camps, made friends in the rough saloons, organized mining companies, bought and sold claims, speculated, managed mines, celebrated discoveries, invested in water and lumber and freighting outfits, watched wild men and wilder women flood into a camp and eddy away when the pickings grew slim.

We all thrived on it, my peculiar family. These rough places answered something in Miss Wellington's soul, and my children prospered, growing up with lusty enthusiasm for life lived as an adventure. Each is strong and shrewd enough to keep out of trouble, tender and loving enough to possess friends and mates and colleagues. I hear from them frequently, for we managed to forge bonds in our years together that will never break.

I did all right, put aside a tidy sum and even managed to keep it, mostly by investing in solid California real estate instead of heady dreams inspired by the fumes of the mining camps. I've been in Arizona and New Mexico Territories, Idaho, Montana, South Dakota, and Sonora, as well as Nevada.

A year ago I returned to Virginia City, mostly out of curiosity. Mining continues even now, and in the three or four surviving saloons one hears the ancient and seductive chorus: the ore's down there, another big bonanza awaits, and someday, someday, some lucky cuss'll find it and the decrepit old city will explode once again. But the men who say that have gray hair and creased faces. I remember when there was scarcely an old man in Virginia City and we were all young, with young dreams, young ambitions, and young visions of the unrolling future.

The *Territorial Enterprise* was still functioning, after a fashion. It had ceased regular publication on January 15, 1893, but soon thereafter was leased to a series of operators, mostly compositors, who kept it running in some spastic manner. The first of these was John McKinnon, whose suicidal bent led him to editorialize against the congressional candidacy of William Sharon's son-in-law Francis G. Newlands. Sharon's old hatchet man, Henry Yerington, rushed up from Carson City and fired him on the spot. The paper sputters along, with perhaps a hundred subscribers and nothing new to write about.

My own future is considerably shorter now, and it occurred to me during that visit a year or so ago that I might well spend my days in the very place where I won so much happiness. I climbed Taylor Street until I reached B and found my old house, weathered and weary but intact except for some broken windows. It had never sold, and I had paid the property taxes on it all those years without quite knowing why.

But as I peered at that old house, kept in decent condition by the arid climate, I knew suddenly why I had not simply abandoned the place to the tax man. I pushed the creaking door open, wandered through the gritty and forlorn rooms, remembering the life we had lived there. I walked up the creaking stairs to my bedroom—Catherine's and my bedroom—and remembered. I sat quietly on the floor, in sunlight, amid a profound hush, my heart filled with gratitude and love and joy. And then I wept.

Virginia no longer had any hacks, so I hiked the long distance out to Pioneers Cemetery, walking slowly because I have no wind and some arthritis and a few other maladies, and beheld Catherine's grave, which was nothing but windswept clay that supported no life save for a weed or two. Gray clay and desert weeds, but such places had always been home for Catherine and me. I was glad to be with her. Someday I will lie beside her. I stayed there awhile, not sadly, but simply remembering her and our moments together in that briefest and sweetest of marriages. I knew I would come again because I liked being there and remembering her in the pale sun. I wanted to encase her grave in an iron fence, bring silk flowers, set the tilted stone upright, and come every few days.

I limped back to town, feeling my age, and hunted for a contractor who would refurbish and paint my house, put the plumbing in shape, get me a stove and icebox and furniture, and make it livable again. There was only one in town, a carpenter who dreamed of big bonanzas, but he was eager for work and set about his task at once.

I stayed at the decaying and silent International Hotel for fifty cents a night. Its great elevators had ceased to function, and the venerable Chinese proprietor's rates depended on how many steps the customer had to climb. The lace drapes in my room had rotted to shreds, and the carpet was threadbare. I remembered how grand it had been and all the important personages who had stayed there, and that took my mind off its shabby condition, worn decor, and weary silence.

Now I am in my old home, in the ruins of a great and noble city. Often I walk along C Street, remembering everything that happened in the saloons. I pass the old *Territorial Enterprise* building and marvel at its silence. Sometimes when my legs don't hurt so much I walk down to the mines and stare pensively at the hoist works and boilers and headframes, where mighty things happened and Yankee genius and sweat wrested amazing fortunes from the silent rock. I visit Catherine's grave frequently, and am content.

Author's Notes

· ·

oday Virginia City is a honky-tonk catering to hundreds of thousands of tourists each year. It shills kitsch and candy and ersatz history. It promotes slot machine museums and copper jewelry. Its denizens wear cowboy garb, attire that was utterly unknown to those handsomely dressed men and women who lived there in its heyday. It is only a shadow of its former self, and even less remains of Gold Hill. Most of the Comstock has burned away, decayed to dust, or fallen apart.

But the well-informed visitor, armed with history, can still go there and listen to the whispers in a quiet dawn, see in the bones the vague outlines of what was once a splendid American city, sense the penumbrae of great events that changed the nation.

The new technology employed on the Comstock Lode became one of the foundations of the industrial revolution. Metals became cheap and abundant because of the genius of those entrepreneurs and tinkerers. That is, no doubt, Virginia City's most important contribution, though it is little understood, because mechanics and engineering lack glamour and don't excite our attention. Some of the technology first employed there, such as square-set timbering, persists to this day. Much of what followed in labor relations and corporate organization began in Virginia City. But I love to remember the town for something else: its insouciant optimism and devil-may-care fun.

There are numerous sources extant, and I have employed many of them. But I trust very few and often found myself picking and choosing among wildly conflicting accounts. Even so, I made every effort to follow history as closely as possible. Except for my narrator, Henry Stoddard, and his family and a few invented minor characters, I have depicted historical people and historical events. I think I have come close to the mark, though some of the novel rests on shaky and contradictory authority.

Certainly Dan De Quille's *The Big Bonanza* is a fine source, as is Eliot Lord's *Comstock Mining and Miners*, originally published by the United States Geological Survey. Lord's pro-management biases are blatant, and he swallowed everything that James Fair told him. Another good source is *The History of the Comstock Lode, 1850–1920*, by Grant Smith, published by the Nevada Bureau of Mines and Geology, Mackay School of Mines. Smith's ethnic biases mar an otherwise splendid work.

For material about the *Enterprise* I relied heavily on Lucius Beebe's *Comstock Commotion* and also Mark Twain's *Roughing It* and several other sources. Beebe's book, published by Stanford University Press, lacks notes and a bibliography, and I was unable to ascertain where some of his material came from. I distrust it and urge caution upon any reader who is inclined to think I have told the story just as it happened. Indeed, Twain also colored his account of his newspaper days, adding to the confusion. Some of the events are well supported by *Print in a Wild Land*, by John Myers Myers.

Oscar Lewis's soberly written and superbly researched *Silver Kings* is unusually valuable and an entirely reliable source. *Early Engineering Works Contributory to the Comstock*, by John Debo Galloway, Mackay School of Mines, is particularly valuable in the realm of technology.

Other fine source material includes Richard A. Dwyer and Richard E. Lingenfelter's *Dan De Quille, the Washoe Giant*, Wells Drury's *An Editor on the Comstock Lode*, Marion S. Goldman's *Gold Diggers and Silver Miners: Prostitution and Social Life on the Comstock Lode*, and Mary McNair Mathews's *Ten Years in Nevada*.

Others worth mention are *Gold Miners & Guttersnipes: Tales of California by Mark Twain*, selected and introduced by Ken Chowder, *Comstock Women: The Making of a Mining Community*, edited by Ronald M. James and C. Elizabeth Raymond, and *The Legend of Julia Bulette and the Red Light Ladies of Nevada*, by Douglas McDonald. There are many more.

Excellent descriptions of frontier mining, including that done on the Comstock, can be found in Otis E. Young's superb *Western Mining* and *Black Powder and Hand Steel*, as well as his other books in that field.

There was no city on earth like Virginia. I hope my readers have enjoyed its magic.